Charlotte Illes is not a Detective

Charlotte Illes is not a Detective

Katie Siegel

KENSINGTON PUBLISHING CORP.

www.kensingtonbooks.com

KENSINGTON BOOKS are published by
Kensington Publishing Corp.
119 West 40th Street
New York, NY 10018

All Kensington titles, imprints, and distributed lines are available at special quantity discounts for bulk purchases for sales promotion, premiums, fund-raising, educational, or institutional use.

Special book excerpts or customized printings can also be created to fit specific needs. For details, write or phone the office of the Kensington Sales Manager: Kensington Publishing Corp., 119 West 40th Street, New York, NY 10018. Attn. Sales Department. Phone: 1-800-221-2647.

ISBN: 978-1-4967-4099-1 (ebook)

ISBN: 978-1-4967-4098-4

First Kensington Trade Paperback Printing: July 2023

10 9 8 7 6 5 4 3 2 1

Printed in the United States of America

For all the former child detectives

(You're never gonna be as good at escape rooms as you think you are)

Contents

Content Warnings

guns, non-brutal mugging, offscreen kidnapping, offscreen murder

Chapter 1

The Bowling Alley Is Closing (Also There Was a Murder)

"So . . . I Googled you."

They hadn't even ordered their food yet. The last time this happened, she was at least able to hide her involuntary grimace behind a curtain of spaghetti. The time before that, a fistful of fries.

Charlotte Illes quickly raised the giant diner menu, but not fast enough to conceal the wince.

The woman sitting across from her—Amy—smiled sheepishly. "Sorry," she said. "I do it before every date."

God, I hate that word, Charlotte thought as she slowly lowered the menu. *Googled.* Just thinking it felt gross.

"Oh!" she said, her voice several steps above its usual pitch. She cleared her throat, forcing her tone back down to normal. "Hope you didn't find my middle school–era fanfic. That'd be embarrassing." *But a relief,* Charlotte thought. She hoped that was all Amy found.

She cracked a smile, hoping her date would take the out, laugh at the joke, and change the subject to something more palatable. Like tax returns. Or lawn care.

"No, it wasn't that," Amy said, leaning forward eagerly. She had that look in her eye—the look of someone completely oblivious to the fact that the thing they were about to say was way more exciting to them than it would be to their audience. "I didn't know you were, like, famous!"

Like, famous. Charlotte heard that modifier a lot. Not super famous, or currently famous. But she had, at one point, been sort of, kind of, *like,* famous.

Charlotte shifted in her seat. "I wasn't really famous," she said, beginning what was now a well-rehearsed speech. "I just—"

"You were!" Amy said, as if she were gifting Charlotte a great compliment.

Oh, okay. She wasn't even going to listen to the speech. Charlotte sat back.

"I mean, there were so many articles about the mysteries you solved," Amy continued, her eyes bright. "You were, like, a mini Sherlock Holmes."

Yup, just a ten-year-old solving mysteries and doing cocaine. Charlotte had made that joke the first time she got the Sherlock Holmes comparison on a date. It didn't land. She never made it again.

"You helped so many people." Amy took a quick gulp of water, looking at Charlotte over the rim of her glass. She swallowed. "Did you really help the British Museum find a stolen artifact?"

Charlotte paused for a moment, going very still. Maybe if she stayed frozen and silent, the other woman would just keep talking, and Charlotte would never have to comment on her well-documented childhood.

But Amy was gazing at her expectantly, so she cleared her throat and said, "Yes. Yeah, I . . . yeah."

As Amy continued to gaze, Charlotte realized she was waiting for more than that. "Oh. Um, I was in London on a family trip when the museum got robbed. I looked around, talked to a few people, and saw that a screw on an air vent was a little loose . . . it was pretty quick work after that."

She paused for a moment, then added with a half-smile, "Of course, the statue had already been stolen way before then."

Amy's eyes widened with excitement. "This wasn't the first time it was stolen?"

"You know, because . . . the British Museum. Most of the artifacts were stolen from other countries." Charlotte hesitated as the eagerness in Amy's eyes began to dim. "A lot of artifacts in Western museums are . . . stolen."

"Oh." Amy took another drink from her glass, much longer than her last one.

Charlotte felt indignant as the mood suddenly shifted. Why did she always have to tell stories from her childhood to keep the date going well? Why couldn't she talk about looted cultural property instead?

She seized the opportunity to catch the eye of Maggie, the diner's manager (and host, on slow nights like this one). Charlotte flashed her a distressed look.

"*Already?*" Maggie mouthed back, stepping out from behind the host stand.

Charlotte gave a subtle nod, then looked back as Amy put down her glass. Behind her date's head, she saw Maggie flag down a server and send her towards their booth.

"Sooooo . . ." Charlotte said, drawing out the word for as long as she could as she watched the server—Jordan—approach the table. Right as Jordan was about to reach them, someone in the adjacent booth called out. To Charlotte's dismay, Jordan stopped to respond.

Charlotte's jaw tightened. She really didn't want to give Amy the opportunity to reopen her line of questioning, and she was clearly already gearing up for round two.

As Amy opened her mouth to speak, Charlotte blurted out, "So, did you just get out of a long-term relationship?"

The diner's retro jukebox, while usually one of Charlotte's favorite things about the place, chose that inopportune moment to end the song that had been playing, making the silence that followed even louder than it would've been otherwise.

Amy blinked. "Um . . . yeah, actually."

Charlotte glanced back at Jordan, who was still talking to the people in the other booth. "That must've been rough."

Amy shrugged noncommittally, looking vaguely confused. "It was a long time coming, honestly. I'm taking it better than I thought I would."

Charlotte bobbed her head way too enthusiastically. "Cool. Very cool. Good for you."

Amy stared at her. "How—"

Charlotte silently thanked the diner gods for their mercy as Jordan finally arrived at their booth, a wide smile on her face. "Hey there," she said, pulling out a pad and pen. "Ready to order?"

"So, what do you do?" Charlotte asked as soon as Jordan walked away with their menus. It was a question she normally hated receiving on dates, but one she found useful when trying to get the other person to talk about themselves for an extended amount of time.

Looking like she'd rather continue delving into Charlotte's childhood, Amy reluctantly began talking about her work. Charlotte tried to concentrate on what her date was saying, but her brain was already working in overdrive to figure out how to keep the conversation off of her sleuthing days.

Their food arrived, and Charlotte managed to squeeze in one mundane story about having to jump-start her car before Amy said, "I'm sorry, I just have to go back to the whole child detective thing."

Charlotte paused chewing for a moment, then continued, swallowing a mouthful of cheese and tomato. "Sure," she finally said, putting down her sandwich. "I mean, I promise you, it really wasn't as wild as a lot of the articles made it sound, but . . ." She put a tight smile on her face. "What do you want to know?"

Amy put her spoon down. "It's just . . . nuts, right?" she said. "How you kept solving mysteries that adults couldn't." Her brow furrowed as she suddenly looked concerned. "Was it a lot of pressure?"

Here we go.

Charlotte pursed her lips. In her experience, there were two types of people who wanted to hear about Charlotte's experience as a kid detective. In fact, she was convinced that she could write an entire dissertation on the topic:

The Two Types of People Who Want to Hear About Charlotte's Experience as a Kid Detective
by Charlotte Illes

As a former kid detective (FKD), it is only a matter of time after meeting a new person that the FKD's amateur sleuthing days become the main topic of conversation. After years of experiencing these conversations, it is clear that almost all people can be divided into two categories, determined by the kind of questions they ask about this time in the FKD's life. These two types of people will henceforth be referred to as the Audience Member and the Psychologist.

The first type of person—and the most common of the two—is the Audience Member. This person wants to hear as many stories as they can about the FKD, despite the former detective's semi-blatant distaste for the subject. The Audience Member wants to know about every celebrity the FKD met (the Hilary Duff story is a crowd favorite), every close call she had (getting stuck in the back of an 18-wheeler heading for the Canadian border always takes the cake), and every reward she'd received (her mom made her turn down most gifts, and any reward money went straight into her college fund). Essentially, the Audience Member wishes to be entertained.

The second type of person is the Psychologist—rarer in quantity, but arguably more stressful to deal with than the Audience Member. This person wants to get into the head of the FKD. The Psychologist wants to know how her childhood affected her, mentally and emotionally, and if she still experiences those effects as an adult. They ask about her scariest moment (train boxcar full of snakes), if her parents took advantage of her fame (no), and if her parents forced her to keep doing detective work (again, no—everyone always wants a story about her parents being horrible to her, and they're almost always disappointed with the truth). Essentially, this person wants to be the one to help the poor FKD work through any trauma she may have experienced.

It has become clear, over the years, that despite their differences, the Audience Member and the Psychologist have one big similarity: despite their intentions (most of these people only have good intentions), both make her feel like a bug under a microscope. Which is pretty FKD.

Amy was staring at Charlotte, waiting for a response, her spoon still lying in her rapidly cooling matzo ball soup.

Charlotte gave a small smile. "Sure," she said. "There was some pressure." She shrugged. "But, you know, who doesn't experience pressure as a kid?"

Of course, there was much more to it than that, but that was a conversation for a therapy session (of which she'd had many), not a first date.

Out of the corner of her eye, Charlotte saw Maggie watching them as she led a family to their table. Maggie Lewis was in her mid-fifties, White, with curly blond hair perpetually pulled up into a messy bun. She had known Charlotte as early as her pre-detective days, back when Charlotte's mom would bring her and Landon to the diner for milkshakes. Charlotte would sit at the counter, legs kicking against the vinyl cushion of the chair, solving the maze on the children's menu in under a minute.

But Maggie, unlike most other adults in Charlotte's life, wouldn't gush over how observant or clever Charlotte was. She would just disappear into the back and emerge a few minutes later with two milkshakes and a new maze drawn on a napkin for Charlotte to solve, always more difficult than the one on the menu.

Nowadays, Maggie and Charlotte's relationship was less mazes and milkshakes, and more of Maggie helping Charlotte escape out the back door of the diner during especially rough dates. Maggie particularly enjoyed making up excuses for why Charlotte had to run out, to the point where Charlotte had to tell her to ease up on the tall tales. ("In what world would NASA ask *me* to go to space?")

This date wasn't bad enough to warrant an emergency exit, although Charlotte definitely wasn't planning on there being a second one. She didn't blame Amy—no one, especially the Psychologists, ever considered how often Charlotte had been asked the same questions over and over again.

Charlotte just couldn't help but feel like she was sitting in a ten-year-old's shadow every time they looked at her.

The rest of the date went by quickly after that. Charlotte steered the conversation back to Amy, who talked about a TV show she was watching before pivoting to Charlotte's astrological chart.

"You have to find out what time you were born," Amy explained as their plates were cleared. "It's the only way to know exactly who you are. Astrologically, I mean."

Jordan brought over the check, and Charlotte managed to win the "no, let me pay" debate, despite not currently having an income.

"As long as you let me pay next time," Amy joked. Charlotte let out a *ha ha* and hoped it didn't sound too forced. The two walked out of the diner into the warm July evening.

"My car's over there," Amy said, pointing across the parking lot.

"Oh, I'm that way." Charlotte jerked her head in the opposite direction. "Um, it was nice meeting you!"

"Same!" Amy started to lift her arms, as if to go in for a hug, then seemed to rethink the move. She scratched the back of her neck instead. "I'll text you?"

"Sounds good."

Amy gave a little wave and said goodbye, then turned and walked to her car.

Charlotte stood under the diner's neon sign, bathed in its pink and blue light, and watched Amy cross the parking lot before walking over to her own car. She stopped, pretending to inspect the pressure of one of her back tires, listening for the sound of an engine turning on.

Giving the tire a little kick (she didn't actually know how to check tire pressure), Charlotte looked up to wave as Amy drove past. As soon as the car's taillights disappeared around the corner, she straightened, turned on her heel, and headed back into the diner.

"That didn't look too bad," Maggie commented as Charlotte pulled herself up onto a seat at the counter. "I'm a little disappointed. I had a really good excuse this time."

Charlotte rested her arms on the counter and dropped her chin on top of them. "Did it involve me going into space?" she asked wearily.

Maggie pulled a giant bag of mints out from under the counter and got to work refilling the little glass bowl next to the cash register. "No. I had you rushing to the hospital to donate your stomach to a woman in critical condition."

Charlotte grabbed a mint and popped it into her mouth. "Yuh con't donate yer shtomach wall yer stull alahve," she said, her words garbled by the mint.

"I know that," Maggie said, closing up the bag and bending over to put it away.

Tucking the mint into her cheek, Charlotte leaned over the counter, looking down. "You were gonna *kill me off*?"

Maggie straightened, tucking a loose blond curl back beneath her headband. "You would've died a hero!" she said. "Plus, it would've been a surefire way to make sure she didn't text you again."

"I *guess*," Charlotte said grumpily, sucking on the mint.

Maggie crossed her arms. "Hey, missy," she said. "You know, one of these days, you'll have to go on a second date."

"Wanna bet?"

Maggie rolled her eyes, then gently tapped twice on the laminate countertop with her fingertips, remembering something. "What was the name of the town your brother moved to?"

"Highview." Maggie began to walk away as Charlotte spoke, remaining in earshot. "It's up in North Jersey, close to the city. Commuter town."

Maggie returned with a newspaper in her hand. She dropped it onto the counter.

Charlotte looked down at it. "'Bowling Alley Chain Closes After Declaring Bankruptcy.' Burrito Bowl closed? Sad." She looked up. "That's where everyone used to have their birthday parties. And get food poisoning."

Maggie picked up the paper and used it to bop the top of Charlotte's head. "Not that, smarty pants." She put the paper down again and pointed a French-manicured finger at a different headline.

Smoothing down her hair, Charlotte returned to the paper and read:

Highview resident found dead in park

Charlotte's stomach dropped. She kept reading:

A man was found dead Monday night in Highview, with a gunshot wound in his chest, a New Jersey State Police spokesperson said.

The man has been identified as 27-year-old Bernard Hughes. The body was found in Carolina Park. Police are still looking for the shooter, according to Sgt. Abigail Rossi, of the State Police.

Highview resident Louise Finch was walking her dog when she saw Hughes lying in the grass.

"When I looked closer, I saw a big bloodstain on the front of his shirt," said Finch. She called 911, and Hughes was declared dead on the scene.

Residents in the area were unsure if they heard the gunshot due to fireworks being shot off nearby.

Hughes was a delivery driver for the online delivery company Scoop, but was not working at the time of his death, according to Sgt. Rossi.

Charlotte looked back up. "Okay, next time you ask me about Landon and then show me a news article about a *murder*, could you preface it with something like, 'This article is not about your brother,' or something like that?"

Maggie put her hands up defensively. "Sorry. But tell him to be careful."

Charlotte gave her an amused look. "Landon's one of the most careful people I know."

"I'm just saying. I worry about him, out there in the big city."

"Commuter town," Charlotte corrected.

Maggie narrowed her eyes. "I should've killed you off with the stomach donation story." She grabbed the paper out of Charlotte's hands and gave her one final bop on the head. "Alright, get out of here. You're scaring off the customers."

"But I'm your favorite customer!"

"Out." Maggie turned to walk away.

"Hey, Maggie?" Charlotte said quickly.

The older woman turned back, an eyebrow raised.

"I know we joke about the excuses you make up for me, but . . ." She flashed a tight smile that faded just as fast. "Thanks for never telling them I had to leave to solve a mystery or something."

Maggie pursed her lips, giving Charlotte the same look she would give when Charlotte was seven and finished another maze without touching her milkshake. Then she walked over to the case of baked goods by the cash register, grabbed a couple of big black-and-white cookies with a piece of wax paper, and dropped them into a paper bag. She slid the bag towards Charlotte.

"One of those is for your mom," she said warningly. "And I don't mean the two vanilla halves. I mean one full cookie."

Charlotte smiled. "Thanks."

Maggie gave her one last Look, then headed into the kitchen.

Charlotte pushed herself off of the chair, holding the bag of cookies in one hand, and walked out of the diner for the second time that night. She knew Maggie was probably right. Maybe she didn't give people a fair chance to really get to know her beyond whatever they had read on the first page of Google's search results. But as she walked past the spot where she had said goodbye to Amy, her farewell rang in Charlotte's head.

"Bye, Lottie."

Chapter 2

A Phone Rings, Which Is Weirder with Context

June 10th, 2009

Child Detective Lottie Illes Recovers
Money Stolen from Cancer Fundraiser

Ten-year-old Lottie Illes recovered $500,000 for the cancer research nonprofit Hands for Heartfelt Hope (HFHH) on Monday.

The charity had been robbed of the amount at their charity fundraiser gala last Friday. Officials say the money was discovered by the young Frencham resident at the house of Winston Parker, President of HFHH, who had reported the money as stolen after the gala.

The Star reached out to Illes for comment, but was told it was past her bedtime.

The gas light blinked on just as Charlotte pulled up in front of her house. Her dad called it the "idiot light," but the moniker never deterred Charlotte from almost always waiting for it to turn on before getting gas. She'd do it tomorrow.

The slam of her car door echoed down the quiet suburban street as she hopped up onto the curb and crossed the front lawn. The porch light illuminated the front walk with a warm yellow glow. Her mom always turned it on if she was out after dark.

"Hi," Charlotte called out once inside, closing the door and switching off the porch light. "I have cookies."

"Hi," her mother called back from the kitchen. "I have a digital pile of ungraded papers and didn't eat dinner."

Charlotte made her way to the kitchen, dropping the paper bag of black-and-white cookies onto the table next to her mom's laptop. "You should probably eat some real food first."

Her mom closed the computer and dipped her hand into the bag. "Probably." She pulled out a cookie and took a bite. "How was the date?"

"It was fine." Charlotte sat down across the table from her mom. Evelyn Hartman was in her early fifties, White, Jewish, with gray streaking the dark brown, almost black hair she shared with her two children. Her brown eyes were also passed down to her daughter, while Landon defied the Punnett square by inheriting his blue eyes from their father.

Charlotte had never believed anyone who said she looked like her mom. Until she chopped her hair to her shoulders right before her freshman year of college. Then she saw it.

Evelyn popped up, turning on the electric teakettle as Charlotte pulled the cookie bag across the table towards her.

"Not bad, nothing special," Charlotte continued, reaching for her cookie. "Probably won't see her again." She took a bite, bracing herself for her mother's response.

The silence that followed was even more painful than if her mom had pointed out that Charlotte hadn't been on a second date in years.

Just say something like, "Maybe next time, kiddo," or, "No one's good enough for my little girl." I'll even take, "There are plenty of fish in the sea." Just not this.

Evelyn stayed quiet as the teakettle's wheezing grew in volume.

Unable to take it any longer, Charlotte put down the cookie. "What?"

"I didn't say anything."

"Your silence spoke volumes." Charlotte crossed her arms. "Maggie already called me out. I'm aware of my dating habits."

Evelyn shrugged. "I didn't say anything," she repeated. She crossed the kitchen and opened a cabinet door, searching for a mug.

"It's just, like, I think I'm pretty good at figuring people out. And every time we reach the end of the date, I feel like I know the person well enough to decide if I want to see them again. It's not my fault that I haven't wanted to see anyone for a second date." She paused, the cookie halfway to her mouth. "Right?"

Evelyn had found a mug and returned to the kettle as it began to whistle. "I think," she said slowly, pouring hot water into her mug, "that you might go on these dates prepared to be disappointed, and don't give yourself a chance to not be. And you can get a little defensive if they bring up your childhood."

"I'm not defensive," Charlotte said defensively.

Her mother gave her a pointed look.

Charlotte sighed. "I'm just . . . tired of it."

"Why do you keep going, then?" Evelyn asked, dropping a tea bag into her mug. "If it just tires you?"

"Um . . ." Charlotte split her cookie in half with her hands. "There are some fun parts."

"Well, that's good!" Evelyn looked over at her, smiling. "Like what?"

Charlotte's expression turned sheepish. "I . . . like to deduce things about them from their dating profiles and social media and then find out if I was right."

"Charlotte Yetta."

Charlotte winced.

Her mother was looking at her with an eyebrow raised. "You're not seriously going on dates with these people solely to guess things about them?"

"No! That'd be weird. And terrible. I know that." Charlotte popped another piece of cookie into her mouth, feeling strangely lighter after getting that off her chest. "It's just a way to get to know more about them beyond all the boring first-date stuff."

Evelyn sighed heavily and sat down with her tea as Charlotte continued.

"Tonight's date, Amy? I looked at her Instagram before the date, and she seemed to be a pretty regular poster up until two and a half years ago, when her posting got a lot more infrequent. Then, recently, it got frequent again. I realized maybe her posting wasn't infrequent—maybe she just deleted a bunch of photos of an ex. Then on the date, I noticed she kept touching her ring finger on her left hand, like she wanted to twist a ring that wasn't there."

Charlotte mimicked twisting an invisible ring on her finger. "Probably a promise ring, or even an engagement ring."

"So did you ask her?"

"Yup, she confirmed it."

"Mhm." Evelyn took a sip of her tea. "And you see how you're doing the thing to her that you hate other people doing to you?"

"No, uh-huh," Charlotte said, pointing at her mom. "I looked her up on social media. That's totally different from Googling. On social media, *you* control what you post about yourself. If she looked me up on Instagram, she only found a few super old photos from high school and one picture of me, Lucy, and Gabe at Six Flags."

"So did she Google you?"

Charlotte looked down at the remaining two bites of cookie in her hand—one chocolate, one vanilla. "Yeah," she said quietly.

Evelyn took another slow sip of her tea, then put it back down onto the table. Charlotte avoided her eyes, not wanting to see whatever look she had on her face. She imagined it was some combination of concern, pity, and sadness.

Charlotte didn't like worrying her mother. She was just naturally incredible at it.

"Oh," Evelyn said suddenly, remembering something, "change of subject: you got a letter in the mail."

"From who?"

Her mom tutted. "Reading someone else's mail is illegal."

"It's not illegal to read a return address."

Evelyn waved a hand in the direction of the front door. "I left it by the door, on top of all the other mail you never go through."

"It's all junk mail."

"Also, did you email back that woman from the magazine?"

Charlotte looked up at the ceiling and groaned. The woman had emailed her a week and a half ago, calling herself "a big Lottie Illes admirer" and expressing interest in writing a *Where Is She Now?* piece about her. Charlotte had been tempted to reply, "Great question. Let me know when you find out."

Her mother stared at her, waiting.

After a beat, Charlotte dropped her chin and sighed. "I still don't know."

"You don't have to do it, bub."

"I know I don't; I'm just gonna give it a few more days."

"Well, what did Helena tell you to do?" Evelyn asked.

Shit. Charlotte still needed to schedule her next session with her therapist.

"It's not Helena's job to *tell* me what to do," Charlotte said, shaking her head. This was not the first time she'd had to explain therapy to her mother. "She helps me talk through my thoughts and feelings so I can determine what I feel is best for me."

"Okay, so what did you determine?"

"That I'm gonna give it a few more days."

"*Charlotte.*"

"*What?*"

"If you don't want to do it, you should email back and tell her. You're leaving that poor woman hanging."

"I *don't* want to do it," Charlotte said, popping the last bite of cookie into her mouth. "But Gabe said I should."

"Well, Gabe is a lot more concerned about your online presence than you are," Evelyn pointed out. "And I'm sure he wouldn't push you to do it if he knew you'd made up your mind."

"I haven't made up my mind. I'm giving it a few more days."

Evelyn grabbed the empty paper bag and wadded it up in her hand. "Suit yourself." She twisted in her seat and tossed it at the wastebasket across the kitchen. The two watched the ball of paper sail through the air and land in the sink.

Evelyn turned back around. "I'll get that when I get up."

Charlotte picked at crumbs on the tablecloth. "Someone was murdered in Highview," she said conversationally.

Her mother covered her face. "You can't *tell me* stuff like that," she groaned.

"Why not?"

Evelyn pinched the bridge of her nose, her brow furrowed with concern. "Because I worry enough already about Landon being out there on his own."

"He's not on his own, he's got Olivia."

"And I worry about both of them, alone in that city. And Lucy, in Manhattan."

"Commuter town," Charlotte corrected. "And Lucy's not alone, either. She's got dumb Jake."

"I'm sure you understand why your nickname for him doesn't reassure me at all." Evelyn pushed her chair back and took her now-empty mug to the sink. "Speaking of your brother," she said over her shoulder, "he told me you've still been ignoring his calls."

"He's been calling me?" Charlotte asked innocently. "They must still be going to spam."

"That's what I told him you said last time, and he told me that phones don't have spam boxes." She gave Charlotte a sharp look. "I don't appreciate you taking advantage of my technological ignorance."

Charlotte grimaced. She had known that weak excuse wouldn't last long.

"He said you haven't replied to him in months."

"He's *lying*," Charlotte objected. "I replied to his happy-birthday text."

Evelyn gave her A Look. "You thumbs-upped the message and didn't say anything else."

"Does that not count as a reply?"

"Talk to him, please. He wants to know how you're doing."

"Can't you tell him?" Charlotte whined.

"He wants to hear it from *you*."

Charlotte scowled. As much as she loved her brother, she really wasn't in the mood for a catch-up conversation with him. Especially the part where she'd have to talk about herself. Apparently, she'd been in that mood for a while.

"Do you remember what time I was born?"

Her mom blinked at the sudden change of subject. "What?"

Charlotte powered ahead, hoping that the faster she talked, the faster they'd get away from the previous topic of conversation. "This is the third date I've gone on where the person asked what time I was born. It has to do with my astrological chart or something. Do you remember?"

Evelyn shook her head, grimacing. "I was pretty busy at the time, so I don't remember exactly. But it should be on your birth certificate."

Charlotte pushed her chair back. "Where's that, the attic?"

"Garage. There's a file box on a shelf close to the door." Evelyn looked like she wanted to return to their earlier conversation, but stopped herself.

"Thanks." Charlotte breezed past her and headed downstairs to the garage.

"Thanks for the cookie!" her mom called after her. Charlotte heard the scrape of the kitchen chair as Evelyn returned to grading papers. Her mother had agreed to start teaching this summer course in addition to her usual fall and spring semester courses when Landon moved to Highview the year before. Charlotte knew she did it to distract herself from worrying about him too much, and remembering that, she felt a twinge of guilt for mentioning the murder to her.

Daughter of the year, she thought sarcastically, pulling open the garage door.

Flicking on the light switch against the inside wall, Charlotte breathed in the familiar smell of the garage. There was always a mild whiff of gasoline in the air, despite no one parking a vehicle in there since before she was born.

Charlotte stepped inside and turned to inspect the shelves her mother had mentioned.

"Ma!" she called through the open door.

"Yeah?"

"The box isn't here."

"Look around; I might've moved it when I was organizing."

Charlotte turned and surveyed the garage. Once upon a time, the boxes had been pushed to the back of the garage to make room for a small table. On one side, two folding chairs were set up with their backs to the garage door. On the other side sat an old desk chair, next to which Charlotte's pet rabbit, Rusty, would sit in his cage on the floor, either napping or nibbling on broccoli. A blue landline phone would rest on the table, its curly cord dangling off the side.

A paper sign taped to the table read: LOTTIE ILLES DETECTIVE SERVICE. The sign was written neatly in block letters with a black marker, flapping in the breeze every time someone sat down in one of the visitors' chairs.

Lottie's "office" was long gone, replaced by boxes and piles of old toys, file boxes, high school memorabilia, and so much more clutter that Charlotte couldn't imagine what her mother's "organizing" actually achieved.

Charlotte didn't give herself the time to reminisce—she was on a mission. Granted, it was a mission primarily fueled by wanting to move the conversation away from how she hadn't talked to her brother in months, but it was a mission nonetheless. She moved a box of photo albums to the floor, and, grunting with exertion, set a box of dumbbells down next to it.

The file box sat on top of a skateboard, where it had been hidden from sight by the two other boxes. Charlotte had no idea whom the skateboard belonged to. It was most likely a well-meaning (but misguided) Christmas gift from her father for either her or Landon, neither of whom ever demonstrated any type of athleticism that would warrant such a gift.

Charlotte popped the file box open and scanned the tags, pulling out a folder labeled BIRTH CERTIFICATES. She quickly found her own and made a mental note of the time (3:15 p.m.) for the next person who wasn't satisfied with, "I'm a Cancer? I think?" as a response to, "What's your Big Three?"

Charlotte returned the certificate to its folder, and as she restacked the boxes, something caught her eye. A flash of blue, half-hidden by an old sled leaning up against the wall.

She picked her way across the garage and moved the sled to the floor, revealing the powder blue landline phone—*her* phone—resting on top of a clear plastic box of gardening tools.

Charlotte lifted the phone from the box. It was a quintessential 1990s landline, though it had seen the most action from the late 2000s through the mid-2010s. She hadn't used it since she was fifteen, and although Charlotte had hit her final height of five-foot-four right before high school, the phone now seemed much smaller than she remembered. Its curly cord snaked off the side of the box and disappeared behind the lawn mower.

Still holding the phone, she carefully stepped over the sled, following the cord around the lawn mower to find its other end still plugged into the wall.

Okay, weird. Charlotte knew her mom was bad at getting rid of stuff, but she always thought the phone was packed away in a box somewhere, not plugged into the wall like it was still functional. Of course, it wasn't still functional.

Right?

Charlotte lifted the receiver from its base, and before she could even bring it to her ear, she heard the familiar drone of the dial tone.

"Mommm!"

She hopped back over the sled, put the phone down on top of the box, and bounded back upstairs to the kitchen, skidding to a stop at the kitchen table. "Did you know my old phone is still working? Are you paying the bill for that?"

Charlotte's phone had been a gift from her mother—although, looking back, Charlotte realized it was probably also a gift for Evelyn. Having your daughter run a detective business out of your garage is very cute, but less cute when your home phone is always ringing with calls from neighborhood kids (and the occasional adult) requesting your daughter's sleuthing skills.

The blue phone had its own number, allowing Evelyn some quiet inside the house while her daughter took calls in the garage. Charlotte always assumed her mom had stopped paying for the phone once she stopped taking cases.

Evelyn looked up at her, mild embarrassment crossing her face. "Yes. I'm still paying for it."

Charlotte made an incredulous face. "Why?"

Her mother shifted in her seat. "I . . . just thought . . . well, a lot of people have that number, and I thought *maybe*, one day, someone might have a case for you and call."

Charlotte frowned. "And you thought I'd answer the phone and just jump back into detective work for the first time in years?"

"Only if you wanted to."

Charlotte resisted the urge to roll her eyes. As frustrated as she could get at her mother's not-so-subtle hints that she might want to try taking on cases again, just like with the questions people asked her on dates, she knew there was nothing but good intentions there.

"Stop paying for the phone," was all she said, turning to leave the kitchen. "Seriously. It's a waste of money."

"It's my money, I can do what I want with it," her mom replied, returning to her grading. "I will take your suggestion into account."

Charlotte sighed and retreated to her room.

Later that night, Charlotte was sprawled on her bed, stomach down, scrolling on her laptop through her fifth job board of the night. She had been laid off the month before, which was a bittersweet experience. Data entry, she had realized early on, was not Charlotte's passion, but without any more enticing options on the horizon, she had stuck with the job.

She had experienced a small wave of relief when she was told about the layoffs, followed by a larger wave of guilt for feeling relieved, followed by the sickening realization that she now had to return to her least-favorite corner of the Internet: the job boards.

Taking a break from scrolling, she shot off a text to Amy. Charlotte used to think it was better to not contact people once she decided she didn't want a second date ("Why bother them with a text?"), but ever since Lucy gave her a thirty-minute lecture on the rudeness of ghosting people, she always made sure to send an "It was nice to meet you, but I won't be able to go out again" message. That off her shoulders, she returned to the boards.

She was skimming the description of yet another "entry-level" position requiring three to five years of prior experience when she heard the sound of her mother's voice, muffled by the two walls between their bedrooms. Charlotte glanced at the clock, knowing that the only person who'd call this late was her brother.

Shutting her laptop, she sat up and reached over to switch off the lamp on her bedside table. She crawled under the covers, cradling the laptop in her arms. A minute later, she heard her mom's bedroom door open, followed by a light tapping at Charlotte's door. A few moments passed before Charlotte heard a whispered, "I think she's asleep," followed by the sound of Evelyn's door shutting again.

Charlotte sat up and deposited her laptop onto her night table, then groaned inwardly, realizing she hadn't brushed her teeth yet. It was too late to leave the room now. Not unless she wanted her mom's phone shoved into her hand with Landon on the other end.

She'd call him soon. But not tonight.

The low drone of a lawn mower broke through the peaceful silence of the morning, slowly rousing Charlotte from her sleep. She drowsily pulled a pillow over her head. After a few minutes passed, she threw the pillow off and groaned, begrudgingly coming to terms with being awake.

The clock read 8:16 a.m. Charlotte did the math in her head. It had been around 2 a.m. when she had finally shut her laptop and gone to sleep. Six hours of sleep—not too bad. Since Charlotte was wont to stay up late into the night, and summer lawn work in the suburbs made it difficult to sleep past 9 a.m. most mornings, six hours was, frankly, an accomplishment.

Charlotte grabbed her phone from the bedside table, flipping onto her back as she unlocked it. She swiped away the reply from Amy she had seen last night ("Aw, okay, no problem, nice meeting you too! Let me know if you ever need someone to talk to"). Below it, there was an unwanted notification from

Instagram recommending people she should follow, a news alert from a publication she kept forgetting to turn off notifications for, and three missed video calls from Gabe, all from around 2:20 a.m.

He must've called right after I went to sleep, she thought. Knowing there was no way he'd be awake at this hour, she opened Instagram and searched for @thepinoylegend ("I picked the name when I was fourteen, and I have an emotional attachment to it," Gabe would always say defensively).

Pulling up his profile, she glanced at his follower count, which she knew was nearing 80k followers, due to him regularly texting her and Lucy every time he hit a new milestone. His bio read, "your friendly neighborhood menace" followed by the Philippine flag emoji, the transgender flag emoji, and the pride flag emoji.

Charlotte clicked on his story. Gabe had invited her to go out with him and some of his old college friends the night before, as he did every time he went out, despite Charlotte always turning him down.

"It's trivia night at the Blob!" he'd said, using their nickname for the local bar. "You love trivia!"

"I don't *love* trivia. Why do you always say I love trivia?"

"I dunno. It fits your brand."

Gabe was very into people having "brands." He was the social media manager for a mattress company, but also had his own influencer status on multiple social media platforms. He was always offering to help Charlotte capitalize on her former fame to "build a following." She always declined.

"Blob bar trivia is almost exclusively sports and music," Charlotte had said. "Let me know when they have a 'Weird Animal Facts' trivia night. Then I'm there."

"You joke, but I *will* put in a request when I get there."

Charlotte had hung up that call feeling the usual mix of relief and guilt: relief from not having to spend an evening of sports trivia and soggy mozzarella sticks with Gabe's extremely extroverted college friends, and guilt from always saying no to hanging out with one of her best friends.

Tapping through Gabe's story, she saw the usual—Gabe singing along to the bar's music, him celebrating over getting a trivia question right before getting yelled at for having his phone out during trivia, and a mirror selfie in the bathroom. Halfway through the story, he shared an infographic from an LGBTQ+ advocacy organization. Then it was back to a video of him complaining about the mozzarella sticks.

The setting then changed from Blob to a club in the next town over, with music so loud she couldn't hear what Gabe was laughing about in the video.

His story ended there, and Charlotte checked his location. Seeing that he had made it home, she continued scrolling through Instagram, not yet having enough energy to climb out of bed.

She stopped scrolling when she saw a picture of Landon. Her brother didn't have an Instagram account, and a glance at the username confirmed that it had been posted by his girlfriend, Olivia.

Charlotte had never met Olivia in person, despite her and Landon having been together for about six months. She'd waved hello over her mom's shoulder during the occasional video call, but that was about it. It wasn't that she didn't want to get to know her brother's girlfriend. She just didn't have a very good track record when it came to connecting with new people.

Case in point: when she and Gabe had become friends, freshman year of high school, it had very little to do with any effort on Charlotte's part. It was mainly due to the sweet, kindhearted Lucy inviting the new kid, who was openly bisexual, trans, and looking for friends, to sit with them at lunch. Then Gabe's unbridled charisma pulled Charlotte out of her shell before she even realized what was happening.

Second case in point: literally every date Charlotte had ever been on.

She double-tapped the photo to like it, then continued scrolling. For ten more minutes, she continued to procrastinate getting out of bed, before finally putting her phone down and untangling herself from the sheets. She changed out of her pajamas (sweatpants and a T-shirt) into regular clothes (a different pair of sweatpants and a different T-shirt), ducked into the bathroom to brush her teeth, and then headed downstairs.

The house felt empty, and a glance out the window at the deserted driveway confirmed that her mom had left for work. Evelyn taught class on campus twice a week, and split the rest of her working hours (and some extra weekend hours) between her office and home, depending on whether or not she was in the mood for students knocking on her office door to beg for an extension on their *Hamlet* papers.

Charlotte dropped two pieces of bread into the toaster and went to the fridge to grab the apple juice.

When the ringing started, she thought it was the toaster going off prematurely. But as she popped her head out of the fridge, the muffled ringing continued.

She knew that sound.

Returning the apple juice to its shelf, she shut the refrigerator door and went downstairs, pulling open the door to the garage and staring at the powder blue phone, which was still sitting on the box where she had left it last night.

Ringing.

Mom, was her immediate thought. It was too much of a coincidence that anyone else would call that number the morning after she discovered the phone was still operational.

Charlotte picked up the phone. "Hello?" she said drily, pressing the receiver to her ear. The plastic of the phone was familiar against the side of her face, and she waited for her mom's response.

"I'm calling from inside your house."

Charlotte froze with surprise upon hearing a deep voice that didn't belong to her mother. The shock was quickly replaced with annoyance.

"*Landon.*"

Her brother's laugh rang out from the phone's speaker, tinny and bright. "How'd you know it was me?"

Charlotte's heart was still pounding from the initial shock, and she realized she was holding the receiver way too tight. She loosened her grip slightly and responded, "That's the same creepy voice you'd use whenever we played Mafia." She cleared her throat, her voice still raspy with sleep. "*Before* my lifetime ban from playing Mafia."

"Damn. I gotta get some new voices. So, what's up?"

Charlotte pulled the phone away from her face to look at it with confusion, then returned it to her ear. "What's *up*?"

"I mean, Mom tells me some stuff, but since you've been dodging my calls and ignoring my texts, I figured it was a fair enough question to ask."

"Yeah, I heard you were *slandering* me. I replied to your birthday text."

"You reacted to my birthday text. Doesn't count."

Charlotte rubbed the back of her free hand across her eyes. It was too early for this.

"I haven't been dodging your calls," she said. "I've just been busy."

"What about last night, when I was talking to Mom?"

"I must've been asleep."

"Lottie."

"*What?*"

"That's bullshit. When was the last time you went to sleep before midnight?"

He had her there.

"Fine. Maybe I haven't been answering your calls because I have nothing to talk about. Nothing's happening. Nothing to report. All quiet on the home front."

Landon was silent for a moment. "Okay," he finally said. "Fair enough."

Charlotte heard the toaster ding in the kitchen. "My toast is waiting for me," she said.

"See? That's news!"

"Why're you calling on this phone?" Charlotte asked, done with the small talk. "How did you even know I'd be awake to hear it ringing?"

"To answer your second question first, Olivia told me you just liked her photo."

"Hi, Charlotte!" came Olivia's voice, quiet compared to Landon's volume, like she was across the room from him. That was one thing Charlotte knew she liked about Olivia—Landon's girlfriend had very quickly picked up on the fact that "Lottie" was a nickname reserved for very few people nowadays.

"Hi, Olivia," Charlotte called back. She debated whether she should add something more conversational, like, "Nice photo!" Thankfully, Landon continued talking before the pause got awkwardly long.

"And to answer your first question: why else would someone call the Lottie Illes Detective Hotline?" He paused, then said, "I have a case for you."

Charlotte hung up the phone.

Chapter 3

Charlotte Illes Is a Poker

"You're being dramatic. And that's saying something, coming from me."

Charlotte hit the speaker button and put her phone down on the kitchen table. "I think I had a very reasonable reaction."

She picked up her toast and took a bite, then grimaced. It had been left out for too long, and was crunchier than she liked it to be. "Howmiy bein' damatic?" she asked, her words garbled.

"Um. You *hung up on him.*" There was a muffled rustling of sheets on the other end of the phone. Charlotte had known she'd be waking Gabe up when she called, but she couldn't wait. She needed to talk about this.

"Okay, but then I answered when he called back!"

After Charlotte had dropped the phone receiver back into its resting spot, she stood, frozen, in the middle of her garage. The lawn mower still droned faintly in the distance. Dust danced in the diffused morning light that shone through the garage door windows.

It *was* a bit of a dramatic reaction, though she'd never admit it to Gabe. But Landon had been equally dramatic! If not more!

"I have a case for you." Come *on.*

Charlotte had stared at the phone for a moment, then grabbed the cord that was plugged into the receiver and yanked it out, letting it fall to the floor, before leaving the garage.

She hadn't told Gabe that part. He'd *really* double down on the whole "dramatic" accusation if he knew about the cord-yanking.

She had been about to start spreading peanut butter onto her toast when her phone lit up. It was mildly surprising that it took Landon five whole minutes to call back—although some of that time might have involved him calling back the garage phone and getting a rejection message.

"Hello?"

"I'm guessing we didn't get accidentally disconnected."

"No, I hung up on you."

"So you don't want to hear about this case?"

Charlotte turned the speaker on and put down her phone, picking up the jar of peanut butter and a butter knife. "What gave it away?"

"Can I just tell you about it? Then you can decide if you wanna take it or not."

Charlotte dipped the knife into the jar. "You can talk. But I'm not going to take it." She started spreading peanut butter onto her toast.

"Okay, so here's what's happening." Landon started talking faster, as if afraid he'd get hung up on again before he could get everything out (a valid concern). "It's not actually my case; it's more for Olivia."

Charlotte paused, feeling a little guilty. She was okay with being a jerk to her brother, but it was different if Olivia was the one who needed help. And Landon definitely knew Charlotte would have a harder time declining if that were the case.

"She—hang on, she should just tell you herself. Olly?"

That scheming—

Charlotte put the knife down and turned to look at the refrigerator, finding a picture of Landon from his college graduation. She flipped it off.

There were some muffled sounds from the other end before Olivia's voice came through. "Hi, Charlotte. Sorry, I told him not to bother you with this."

Charlotte lowered her hand and turned back to the phone, taking a deep breath. "Hey, no, it's okay. What's going on?"

"It's probably nothing."

If Charlotte had a nickel for every time someone pitched a case to her by starting with the phrase, "It's probably nothing," then . . . well, she'd have a lot of nickels. Probably enough to use one of those machines that converts small coins into an actually useful form of currency.

"Honestly, I think Landon's more concerned about it than I am," Olivia continued, "but I've been getting these anonymous notes stuck to his door."

"Notes addressed to you? At Landon's apartment?" Charlotte tried to keep her tone neutral, in case Landon was listening in. She didn't want to sound too intrigued.

"Yeah. No messages at my place. Sometimes they even come in when I'm not here."

"What do these messages say?"

There was a pause on the other end of the line, then a rustling of paper.

"'Olivia, you are so beautiful. I think we should be together. I love you,'" Olivia read aloud.

"Just those three notes?"

"Oh, no, that was all one note. I've got, like, eight here."

Charlotte sat down at the table. "What do the messages look like? The paper, the writing utensil?"

"They're just plain yellow sticky notes. And the person used a purple pen."

"That's strange," Charlotte said, her brow furrowing.

"Yup."

"And you're sure it's not just Landon trying to do a weird, romantic gesture?"

Olivia laughed. "He says it's not him. It's not you, right?"

Landon's voice was distant in the background. "It's not me! I don't even own a purple pen."

"Yeah, that's just what a purple-pen-using freak would say," Charlotte said drily.

Olivia laughed again.

"Do you have any bitter exes?" Charlotte continued, still trying to keep her tone conversational. "Any weirdos at work?"

"I only have one ex, who lives kind of nearby," Olivia said slowly, "but I don't think she'd do something like this. And work . . . no, I can't think of anyone who'd send these."

Charlotte noted a shift in Olivia's tone when she mentioned work, but didn't push the subject. That was something someone trying to solve a mystery would do. Charlotte was not trying to solve a mystery.

"Oh, Landon's asking for the phone again. 'Bye, Charlotte!"

"B—"

"So what do you think?" Landon asked, jumping back onto the call before Charlotte could finish saying goodbye. "It's weird, right?"

Charlotte narrowed her eyes. "You sound way too excited for someone whose girlfriend is being *stalked*."

"I'm not worried about her. Olivia would kick their ass if anyone tried anything." Charlotte pictured her brother turning away from his girlfriend as his voice lowered. "But of course, I'm worried. That's why I want you to come figure out who's behind this."

"I don't know if this is—wait, *come*?"

"Yeah! You can crash in Dale's room. He's always at his girlfriend's, anyway. That way you can check out the messages in person, scope out the area—you know, your usual stuff."

"I don't have *usual* stuff; I haven't done detective work in years. This isn't *usual*." Charlotte closed her eyes, her mind racing. *It could be the ex. Or someone from the building. And what's up with Olivia's work?* Against her best efforts, her interest was piqued. But she couldn't let Landon know that.

"Okay," she finally said, eyes opening. "I will come *visit*. Just for a couple of days. And during that time, I will *poke around*. I'm not officially taking this on as a case."

"Works for me!"

Charlotte resisted rolling her eyes, picturing her brother grinning at Olivia. He was probably giving her a thumbs-up, too.

"Put down your thumb," she said.

Olivia let out a loud laugh from the background, confirming Charlotte's guess.

"I hate when you do that," Landon grumbled. "It's creepy."

"Well, stop being so predictable."

They hung up soon after, Landon telling her to let him know when she'd be coming. As soon as the call disconnected, Charlotte called Gabe.

"I was very mature about it all," she said.

"Any child can answer a phone," Gabe rebutted. "Answering when he called back isn't necessarily *mature*."

"I thought it was really brave of me." Charlotte suddenly remembered the three missed video calls. "How was trivia? Did you guys win?"

"Nooo," Gabe groaned. "There was a whole category on *hockey*, and that's a weak spot for Parker, our token dudebro. We lost to a team called Risky Quizness."

"What was your team's name?"

"'Give Us Free Mozzarella Sticks, Cowards.' My idea."

"It's kind of long. Did you get free mozzarella sticks, at least?"

"NO!"

"Sounds like a rough night." Charlotte took another crunchy bite of toast.

"What is that? Are you eating *cement*?"

"*Oberdun post.*" Charlotte swallowed. "Overdone toast. Why'd you call me at two a.m.?"

"I called you at two a.m.?" There was a pause as Gabe checked his phone. "Oh. I called you at two a.m. Gotta admit, I was *very* inebriated by the end of the night. I was probably calling to tell you how much I love you."

"Gross."

"Oh, no, I remember. Keith's moving out."

Charlotte paused. "Keith . . ."

"Keith, my roommate?"

"Ohhhh, *Keith.*"

In truth, Charlotte had trouble keeping track of Gabe's roommates. It wasn't his fault—he once told Charlotte and Lucy he thought he had an ancestor who was a terrible roommate, which caused his family to be cursed to never have the same roommate for more than six months. Lucy had gently suggested he try using something other than Craigslist to find people to live with.

"He came out with us last night and waited until I was good and drunk to break the news. I think he thought I'd take it better that way."

"Did you?"

"Yeah. I gave him a hug and wished him well."

Charlotte snorted. "But you told him he had to find his own replacement, right?"

The line was silent.

"Right?" she repeated.

"Shh, I'm trying to remember."

"*Gabriel.*"

"It's fine, I'll find someone. Probably. But back to the important matter at hand—you're a detective again!"

"I'm not—" Charlotte paused, composing herself. "I'm not a detective again. I'm just doing some poking around."

"Yeah, you keep saying that. I'm pretty sure that's just a synonym for 'detecting.' "

Charlotte rolled her eyes.

"Anyway," Gabe continued, "I think it'll be good for you. You're unemployed. Your dating life sucks."

"*Thanks.*"

"Maybe taking on a mystery is what you need to get you out of this rut."

Charlotte scrunched up her nose. "What *rut?*"

"You know." Gabe paused. Then, realizing Charlotte *didn't* know, he continued. "You've just been, like, stuck. In high school, you were always keeping busy. Same with college. And then . . . nothing."

"I haven't been doing *nothing,*" Charlotte argued. "I've been trying to find myself."

"Well, you're not gonna find yourself when you're moping around your mom's house, surfing job boards, and watching *Taskmaster* clips on YouTube."

Charlotte glanced out the window, half-expecting to see Gabe peeking in at her over the window box of zinnias. He really knew her too well.

"I already told Landon I'm going," she grumbled. "You don't have to talk me into it."

"I'm not trying to talk you into it," Gabe said seriously. "I'm trying to talk you into *enjoying* it."

"Ow. Mom."

Evelyn held Charlotte in an embrace, patiently waiting until Charlotte felt like every bone in her body was about to snap, before finally letting go.

"I'm going to miss you," she said tearfully, holding her daughter at arm's length.

"You know, I think this is healthy for both of us," Charlotte said, squirming out of her mom's grip. "You should find someone other than me and Landon to talk to."

Evelyn pouted. "I have friends."

"Your TAs don't count."

"Alright, get out of here," Evelyn said, stepping back. Then her eyes lit up as she remembered something. "Did you open that letter you got in the mail?"

Charlotte winced. "I forgot. You can open it; it's probably junk mail."

"I won't—"

"I'm giving you permission!" Charlotte readjusted her backpack on her shoulders. "You can open it!"

"I'll add it to the pile for when you get back."

Charlotte gently rolled her eyes with a smile, then stepped in to give her mother one more quick hug. She dodged out of the way before she could get pulled into a longer embrace, and began walking across the parking lot toward the Frencham train station.

"Love you!" she called over her shoulder.

"Love you, too," her mom called back.

As she reached the stairs to the train platform, Charlotte glanced over her shoulder to see her mom pulling out of the parking lot.

No turning back now, she thought. Granted, she could've called Gabe to pick her up. Or ordered a car. Or made the forty-five-minute walk back home. But it was easier to just tell herself that there was no turning back now.

Not that Evelyn would've let her turn back if Charlotte tried to bail on visiting her brother. However, the siblings had agreed not to tell their mom about the true purpose of Charlotte's trip. As supportive as Evelyn had always been about Charlotte's proclivity for solving mysteries, her mother was never a fan of the more dangerous aspects of certain cases. Charlotte and Landon agreed that it'd probably be best to not tell her about the potential stalker situation.

About an hour into the train ride, an automated voice announced, "This station stop is: Highview. When leaving the train, please watch the gap."

The train hadn't been very crowded, since it was well past Monday's rush hour, but as most of the passengers were heading into Manhattan, Charlotte was one of the few to get off at Highview. She quickly caught sight of Landon standing at the other end of the platform, grinning and holding up a piece of paper that she couldn't read from where she disembarked. As she got closer, she saw it read LOTTIE ILLES in big black letters.

"Funny," Charlotte said as she approached him. "You can put that down now." A couple of people walked past, glancing at the sign. Embarrassed, she grabbed at the piece of paper, but he held it over his head.

Landon was three years older and a good seven inches taller than her. He'd been taller their whole lives, but the gap really widened when he hit his growth spurt the summer after seventh grade. Needless to say, she wasn't able to reach the sign.

"What is UP?" Landon pulled her into a hug with his available arm, the other one still held aloft. He had gotten his affinity for hugs from Evelyn, while Charlotte had inherited their father's preference for firm nods and, on occasion, a friendly handshake.

"How was the train?" he asked, releasing her and tugging at her backpack strap.

"Fine," Charlotte said, shrugging off her backpack and letting her brother sling it over his shoulder. "Spent most of the time listening to two guys argue loudly about football."

"That's what we call the 'Classic NJ Transit Experience.'" Landon started walking towards the stairs leading off the platform, and Charlotte trailed after him.

"Why aren't you working?" she asked.

"Lunch break. My apartment's just a couple blocks away, so I took a late lunch to walk over and pick you up."

Landon worked as a developer for a midsize video game company, often working from home but occasionally commuting into the city to the company office. He'd joke about missing out on his coworkers' random Nerf gun fights, but Charlotte knew her brother worked best when it was quiet. That was something the siblings had in common: preferring environments where they could hear their own thoughts and take their time with them.

Not that Landon didn't like to talk. Charlotte walked in silence for the two-block walk while Landon chattered away, occasionally throwing in an *Oh* or a *Right* to show that she was listening.

"Here we are," he said, pulling his keys out of his pocket and holding a fob up to the panel by the front door. The panel beeped, and the lock clicked. Landon pushed the door open for Charlotte to walk in. "Stairs are over there. Second floor, first door on the right."

The apartment was brighter than she expected. When Landon still lived at home, the curtains in his room were permanently shut, his computer monitor perpetually the brightest light in the room. Charlotte was ready for his apartment to be a larger version of what Evelyn called "a hegdesch" and what Charlotte called "The Troll Hole," but as they walked inside, she was surprised.

As she emerged from the short hallway that served as the apartment's entrance, the first thing she noticed was a large window looking down onto the street, the curtains pulled open to let the mid-afternoon sunlight spill onto a dining table. There was a ceramic vase of flowers on said table, and both the counter and kitchen peninsula were clean, the sink devoid of dirty dishes.

Charlotte started to back out of the apartment, pushing Landon behind her. "I think we walked into the wrong place," she whispered loudly. "There's no way you live here."

Landon slipped the backpack off of his shoulder and swung it at her, pulling an "Oof!" out of Charlotte as it slammed into her stomach.

"Hilarious." He kicked off his shoes and walked past her into the kitchen, depositing the LOTTIE ILLES sign into a recycling bin as he passed. "Water?"

"Sure." Charlotte dropped the backpack and continued to look around as the door shut behind her. "I thought this was going to be Troll Hole two-point-oh."

"You haven't seen my room." He pulled a water filter out of the fridge, then grabbed a glass from a drying rack that was sitting next to the sink. "I share this space with Dale, so we both keep it clean."

"Is Olivia at work?" Charlotte asked, kicking off her shoes and following him into the apartment.

"Yeah. She usually gets off around five or six, sometimes later." Landon filled the glass with water and handed it to Charlotte. "Things have gotten even more intense with . . ." He looked over his shoulder at her as he returned the filter back to the fridge and shut the door. "Did you hear about the murder that happened here last week?"

Charlotte nodded over the rim of the glass as she took a gulp. "Maggie told me about it. She said to tell you to be careful."

Landon's face lit up. "How *is* Maggie? I miss her. And the diner."

"She's good. The diner's good."

Charlotte waited for a moment as Landon continued to stare at her, expecting her to say more. "The murder?" she prompted.

"Right." Landon leaned back against the kitchen counter. "The guy who was murdered was one of the delivery people for Olivia's company."

Charlotte raised her eyebrows. "Olivia works for a delivery company?"

"Oh, sorry. I didn't know how much Mom tells you about stuff I tell her. I thought you knew about Olivia's job."

Charlotte shook her head. "She doesn't tell me much. I think she wanted me to . . ."

She stopped before finishing her sentence with, ". . . *just call you myself."* Charlotte didn't want to remind him of how she had been ducking his calls for so long, because then she'd have to explain *why* she'd been ducking his calls for so long. And she wasn't sure she had a good explanation for that.

Landon continued, ignoring Charlotte's unfinished sentence. "Olivia's a software developer for this delivery app called Scoop."

"Catchy."

"They're still pretty small," Landon continued, "but they have a ton of workers in the area who can pick up and deliver people's takeout orders, groceries, clothes—basically anything that has pickup, they have people who'll go get it for you."

"So this guy was one of their workers." Charlotte took another sip of water.

"Yeah."

"Why's the company taking it hard? I mean, if they already have so many delivery people?"

Landon raised an eyebrow as Charlotte winced.

"That came out wrong. I meant, why is this making things at work 'intense'?"

He scratched the back of his head. "That's where things get a little confusing for me, actually. Olivia hasn't talked a lot about it, since she tries not to bring work stress home with her." He crossed his arms. "From what I understand, some of the delivery people have been getting together recently to try to start a union to bargain for better pay and benefits."

Charlotte nodded.

"But," Landon continued, "as is usually the case with these kinds of things, the higher-ups at the company aren't super pumped about it. Their back-and-forths started to get some news coverage, and I think there were rumors about the workers possibly going on strike."

Charlotte was starting to catch up. "Was the guy who was murdered a part of the union talks?"

Landon nodded.

"So there's suspicion aimed at the company for his murder."

He nodded again, unfazed by his sister quickly piecing together the situation. "The police are calling it a mugging, even though he still had his wallet on him. Things have been extra tense ever since."

"I'll bet." *That must've been why Olivia's tone changed when she mentioned her work over the phone.*

Charlotte let this information roll around in her head before she stopped, reminding herself that this had nothing to do with why she was there. *Unless* . . .

"Let's get you set up in Dale's room." Landon crossed the kitchen and grabbed Charlotte's bag from the floor. There were three doors along one wall, presumably leading to the bedrooms and bathroom. He headed for the farthest one.

"When did Olivia start receiving the notes?" Charlotte asked, following behind him.

Landon opened the door and walked in. "You can ask her all about it when she gets home," he said, dropping her backpack onto Dale's bed. "She'll remember more than I will."

Charlotte sat on the bed next to her bag. "I was just wondering if they were somehow connected to what's going on at her work."

Landon laughed. "Oh, no, I don't think so."

Charlotte cocked her head. "Is that funny to imagine?"

"No, I mean, it just doesn't seem like they're related." He shrugged, heading for the door. "And Olivia already said she doesn't think anyone she works with would write them."

"Okay, well, you also said you didn't think Henry Clarke would steal your Spider-Man action figure, and *where* did I end up finding your Spider-Man action figure?" Charlotte held a hand behind her ear, waiting for an answer.

Landon paused in the doorway, turning. "In Henry Clarke's backpack," he mumbled.

Charlotte spread out her hands. "I'm just saying. When multiple weird things are happening, they tend to be related."

"Hey, you're the detective, not me. I won't tell you how to do your job."

"I'm not a detective anymore. I'm just poki— checking it out."

"Sure. Anyway, I still have to do some work, but make yourself at home. We'll eat when Olivia gets here, unless she has to stay late." He paused, then added, "Don't get too distracted by the murder stuff, okay?"

"I thought you weren't gonna tell me how to do my job," Charlotte said flatly.

Landon cocked his head. "I thought you weren't a detective anymore."

He shut the door before Charlotte could come up with a retort.

Chapter 4

Dale's Room (Derogatory)

Charlotte never really had much of an eye for interior design. Her room at home was pretty nondescript—a bed, two bookshelves, a messy desk. On one wall was a map of the world she had hung up when she was thirteen, and on another wall hung a photo collage Lucy had given to her before their high school graduation. A framed certificate from the Mayor of Frencham hung over her desk, thanking her for recovering the rare coin that had gone missing from his office (rolled into a grate). That was the only piece of girl-detective history she kept on display—the rest of the certificates, thank-you notes, and one key to the city were stored safely in a box under her bed.

Overall, she never cared much about aesthetics. That being said, she hated Dale's room.

Giant band and movie posters covered three of the four walls, all secured with multicolored pushpins. Dozens of eyes stared down at her—musicians, superheroes, middle-aged men who could definitely benefit from therapy (or some combination of the three). A battalion of Funko Pop figures stood on his dresser, with even more stacked in boxes on the floor underneath the window that let out onto a fire escape.

The fourth wall was blanketed by a large black-and-white tapestry with a pattern that made Charlotte dizzy if she looked at it for too long. Fortunately, the tapestry was hung behind the bed, so she wasn't subject to its hypnotizing design from where she lay propped up on the pillows. *Un*fortunately, facing that direction put her in the direct eyeline of Dale's *Joker* poster.

Charlotte rolled over onto her side to avoid Joaquin Phoenix's unblinking gaze and grabbed her phone from the bedside table. After Landon returned to his work, she had snooped around the room for a bit, finding a mostly empty dresser drawer of plain T-shirts and a tube of spackle in a plastic bag in the closet. Failing to find anything more interesting than the spackle, she quickly looked something up on her phone, then decided to take a quick thirty-minute power nap, which she woke up from about three hours later.

Still feeling groggy, she unlocked her phone. There was a text from Landon from an hour earlier, asking what she wanted for dinner, along with a link to a restaurant menu.

There were also new texts from her group chat with Gabe and Lucy (a chat currently titled *foot canal*, due to an accidental mistype from Lucy that was followed by a solid week of merciless teasing):

Lucy: Charlotte. Are you at Landon's right now?
Gabe: what's landon's place like
Gabe: is it a troll hole
Gabe: is his roommate cute
Gabe: wait nvm you said he wouldn't be there
Gabe: are there pics of his roommate is he cute
Lucy: So she is there??
Gabe: yah
Lucy: Since when??
Gabe: she went today

Gabe: should I not be telling you this
Gabe: I feel like I'm in trouble
Lucy: @Charlotte ???

A pained expression crossed Charlotte's face. She hadn't told Lucy she was visiting Landon, putting her just a short train ride away from where Lucy lived in the city. It wasn't like Charlotte didn't want to see her. On the contrary, there wasn't a day that went by when she didn't miss her best friend. It was just . . .

Charlotte: I'm sorry!! It was very last minute
Charlotte: Landon's roommate isn't here and I haven't seen any pictures but I'll report back if I find any
Lucy: How long are you going to be there?
Charlotte: not sure yet
Charlotte: I'm helping Landon with something
Lucy: Very specific.

Charlotte heard the front door open and muffled voices greeting each other.

Charlotte: Olivia's here gotta go
Lucy: CHARLOTTE

Feeling the eyes on the walls following her, Charlotte tossed her phone onto the bed and left Dale's room.

"—might be napping—" Landon stopped mid-sentence as Charlotte emerged. "Never mind, there she is."

Her brother was standing in the kitchen with Olivia, who turned around and flashed Charlotte a huge smile. Olivia Kimura: twenty-seven years old, Japanese American, dark brown eyes, thick, wavy black hair pulled back with a large clip. Stylish. She was wearing a white ribbed top with high-waisted blue-and-white-striped pants. Medium-sized gold hoops peeked out through her hair as she threw her arms up excitedly.

"Yes!" Olivia cheered, grinning. "Finally!" She dropped her arms as Charlotte crossed the apartment. "I've been so excited to meet you in person."

"It's true," Landon said. He was pulling tape off of a cardboard box to flatten it. "She couldn't even sleep last night."

Olivia scowled playfully at him. "How would you know? You were snoring before I even turned out the lights." She glanced over at Charlotte, nodding in Landon's direction. "He's been excited, too; he just won't admit it."

Landon looked dismayed. "I'll admit it *easily*! Two of my favorite people on the planet finally meeting? Of course I'm excited." He chucked the flattened box at the recycling bin and missed by a mile, almost knocking down the grocery list and the magnet holding it to the fridge. "Oops."

"He gets that from our mom," Charlotte said as Landon scrambled to retrieve the box.

"The unbridled enthusiasm or the terrible aim?"

"Both, actually."

Olivia laughed, and Charlotte grinned back. She liked Olivia—and not just because she didn't try to hug her as soon as they met.

"Didn't Dale ask you to save any cardboard boxes for him?" Olivia asked as Landon leaned over to pick it up.

Landon froze. "Shoot, you're right. I'll leave it in his room." He scooped up the box and crossed the apartment, disappearing into Dale's room.

Olivia turned back to Charlotte. "We figured Dale's bed would be more comfortable, but you're free to crash on the couch if you'd prefer." She made a sour face. "I know his room is . . . a lot."

Charlotte laughed. "It's fine, thanks. I did think I might have trouble sleeping in there, but then I ended up napping for three hours, so . . ."

"Hey, we've all been there." Olivia went to the fridge and pulled the door open. "I'm going to take, like, fifteen naps this weekend to make up for all the sleep I've been losing lately." She looked over her shoulder at Charlotte. "Do you want anything? Beer? Soda? Water?" She turned back and stuck her head farther into the fridge. "I think there might be some seltzers back here . . ."

"I'm good, thanks." Charlotte watched Olivia pull out a bottle of beer as Landon returned to the kitchen. "Yeah, Landon was telling me about everything going on. With the union, and the man found dead."

"Wait, how did Maggie hear about that, anyway?" Landon asked. He shook his head slightly as Olivia looked at him and pointed into the fridge, silently asking if he wanted anything.

"It was in the paper."

"Oof." Olivia straightened and shut the fridge door with her foot. "Candice isn't gonna be happy about that."

"Who?"

"Our CEO. Candice Watts." She pulled open a drawer and started rummaging around. "From what I've heard, she's been trying to tamp down any connections people are making between Bernard's death and all the stuff with the union, but the more the news spreads about his death, the more people will be talking about it. *There* it is." She pulled a bottle opener out of the drawer and cracked open her beer.

"The article did mention Scoop," Charlotte said, remembering.

Olivia took a sip, then pulled herself up to sit on the kitchen peninsula. "Yup. So then people start looking into Scoop, and start reading about the company fighting with the workers trying to unionize, and start theorizing that Candice or someone else at the company was involved in the murder . . . it's not a great look."

Charlotte walked into the kitchen and leaned against the fridge, watching Olivia deposit her bottle cap into a tall glass vase that was sitting on the counter. It landed on top of dozens of other caps that almost filled the container.

"I mean," Olivia continued, "the worst thing is that a man is dead. That's really getting lost in all of this. We had a moment of silence in the office the day after he was found, and then Jensen let us leave early—that's our manager." She sighed. "It's just a lot."

Landon crossed the kitchen and pulled himself up onto the counter to sit next to Olivia. She leaned into him slightly as she took another sip.

"Plus," Charlotte added, "I'm sure getting those anonymous notes isn't making things any easier."

Olivia's eyebrows jumped. "Right!" She handed her beer to Landon and hopped off the counter, running into the other bedroom.

"They started coming in about a month ago," she called from the other room. She came back out with a handful of sticky notes. "Maybe two or three times a week, one of us finds one stuck to the outside of the door to the apartment."

Charlotte took the notes from her and flipped through them as Olivia hopped back onto the counter and retrieved her drink from Landon. On each note was written a short compliment or declaration of love for Olivia.

" 'Let's run away together,' " Charlotte read out loud.

"And it's like, one: Okay, sure, but how am I going to run away with you if I don't know who you are?"

Landon looked over at Olivia. " '*Sure*'?"

"Let me finish. And two: Can my boyfriend come?"

Landon nodded, appeased.

"Okay, so we're looking for someone with access to your building who writes with a purple pen." Charlotte paused. "I guess anyone could get into the building if they just waited to slip in behind someone with access. I've done that before."

"Me too, and I live here," Landon chimed in. Charlotte narrowed her eyes at him questioningly, and he gave a sheepish grin. "I forget my key fob a lot."

Charlotte turned back to Olivia. "Do you think this could

have anything to do with what's going on at your job?" she asked. "I mentioned it to Landon, but he didn't think so."

"Um . . ." Olivia glanced at Landon, then back at Charlotte. "I don't know. I mean, no, I don't think so? I think I said this on the phone, but I can't think of anyone I work with who'd do this. A lot of my coworkers are remote, so it's a small office." She shrugged. "I'm not sure how these weird love notes would connect to a murder, anyway."

"Sure." Charlotte looked down at the notes again as she chewed on the inside of her cheek. "You mentioned an ex on the phone?"

"Annette? I don't think she'd do something like this. We broke up almost two years ago, and we don't talk. She lives in the East Village."

"Can I get her address?"

Olivia's face grew alarmed. "Are you going to talk to her?"

Charlotte handed Olivia her phone. "I'll try my best not to. Text yourself so you have my number, then send me the address."

Olivia glanced at Landon, who nodded. "She usually knows what she's doing," he said.

"Alright." Olivia sent herself a text from Charlotte's phone, then slid off the counter to grab her own phone and send the address. Charlotte ducked back into Dale's room and grabbed her purse. She re-emerged and headed for the front door.

"Wait, you're going now?" Landon asked. He swung his legs over the peninsula so he was facing Charlotte, narrowly avoiding kicking over the vase of bottle caps. "I already ordered dinner."

"Stick it in the fridge for me; I'll eat when I get back." She pulled out her phone as Olivia's text with Annette's address came in. "Hey," she said, looking up at her brother, "maybe I'll find the purple pen right away and take the late train back. Then Dale would have his room back."

"You can stay as long as you want," Landon said, looking a little hurt. "Dale's never here, anyway."

"Oh, I know," Charlotte said, slipping her phone back into her pocket. "He's moving out soon, right?"

"What?" Landon laughed. "I mean, yeah, he's not here a lot, but he's not moving out."

"I think he's hardly ever here." Charlotte crossed her arms. "I noticed the bottle caps."

"The bottle caps?" Olivia asked, emerging from Landon's room.

Landon sighed as Olivia pulled herself back onto the counter. "You're about to do a whole thing, aren't you?"

Charlotte ignored him and pointed at the glass vase holding the bottle caps. "The vase is pretty full," she said, looking at Olivia. "Most of the caps that make up the bottom half are from the same brand, plus a couple from the brand you're drinking now. Landon doesn't like beer, so I'm assuming Dale drinks the other brand."

Her finger rose to point at the upper half of the vase. "But then there's a layer of caps that's just your brand, none of Dale's. And I don't think you drink beer very often, at least not here, since it took you so long to find the bottle opener. So that implies a long amount of time has gone by when you were the only one in the apartment drinking beer."

"Maybe Dale quit drinking," Landon challenged. This was a game they often played—they both knew Charlotte was right, but Landon loved to play devil's advocate.

"Sure, maybe." Charlotte pulled her purse strap over her head. "But then there's the shirts."

Landon groaned. Olivia grinned, fully intrigued now. "What shirts?"

Charlotte bit back a smile. "Well, only knowing Dale from his room decor, I'd assume this is a guy who has a lot of pop culture T-shirts." She looked at Landon, raising her eyebrows. "True?"

"Yes," Landon replied flatly. Charlotte could tell he was only pretending to be annoyed.

"I might've snooped a little," she admitted, "and didn't find any. Just some plain T-shirts and a couple of dress shirts in the closet. Which implies that he's keeping the majority of his clothes at his girlfriend's place."

"That still doesn't prove that he's moving," Landon said.

Olivia's eyes went wide. "The boxes!" she exclaimed.

Charlotte broke into a grin and pointed at Olivia.

Landon looked helplessly between the two of them. "What boxes?"

Charlotte gestured to Olivia, giving her the floor.

"Dale asked you to save cardboard boxes for him," Olivia explained. "Boxes that one might want if they're planning on *moving*!" She punched the air victoriously.

Landon covered his face with his hands and groaned again.

Olivia reached over and rubbed his back. "Oh, sweetie, it's okay. I'm just a better detective than you." She laughed as Landon playfully pushed her off the counter, then righted herself, leaning against the counter and looking at Charlotte. "Was that everything?"

"Almost. There's a tube of spackle in his closet, probably to cover up all the holes his posters made in the wall." She unlocked her phone and started typing, walking back towards them. "Also, I checked Facebook Marketplace on a whim and found this."

Olivia and Landon squinted to look at her screen as Charlotte held out her phone.

"Is that Dale's weird tapestry?" Landon asked, fully defeated.

"Yeah." Charlotte looked at her phone again. "Priced way too high, if you ask me. I'm guessing his girlfriend is pushing him to get rid of it, so he's listing it at a high price to make sure no one actually buys it."

Olivia turned to Landon. "Not that I ever didn't believe you about the whole 'my sister's an incredible detective' thing, but I absolutely believe you now."

Landon held his hands out towards his sister. "Lottie Illes, everyone."

"I'll be back later," Charlotte said, turning and heading for the door. "'Bye!"

She stuffed her feet into her shoes and let herself out of the apartment. Landon laughed at something Olivia said as the door shut behind Charlotte, who smiled. As much as she tried to put the detective stuff behind her, she had almost forgotten this feeling. The confidence that she was right about something. The validation of having someone be super impressed by her deductions. And that ridiculous look Landon got on his face as he tried to follow her line of thinking.

Chapter 5

The Official Breaking-and-Entering Checklist

Charlotte pushed open the door to the stairwell and headed downstairs, pulling out her phone to look up the train schedule. As she exited the building, she looked up from her phone just in time to avoid crashing into the man standing on the other side of the door.

"Oops, sorry!" Charlotte said, skidding to a stop. She quickly clocked the red insulated bag he was carrying as he looked up from his phone. "Trying to get in?"

The man: early thirties, White, light blond hair, and some scruff under his chin. He smiled. "Yeah, I was just checking the order. Forgot which apartment to buzz." He nodded to the panel of buzzers as he took the door from Charlotte. "Thanks."

"No problem." Charlotte paused, thinking. "Not much of a security system, right?"

"Sorry?"

Charlotte pointed at the open door. "Anyone could just walk in if they waited long enough for someone to come out," she said lightly. "Then that person could go inside and do . . . gosh, whatever they wanted to, I guess." She stared at the man. "Do you deliver to this building a lot?"

"Yeah." The man suddenly did a double take. "W—I'm sorry, this is such a weird thing to ask. Are you Charlotte Illes?"

Charlotte's eyebrows shot up. *Did not see that coming.*

"Yes . . . ?" she said hesitantly.

The man let out a little laugh. "Sorry, I just . . . I'm delivering this to a *Landon* Illes, and I was thinking, 'Wasn't that the last name of that girl detective from back then?' And then I saw you, and was thinking you looked familiar, and then it all clicked." He shook his head in disbelief. "This is so wild."

Charlotte smiled weakly, unsure how to respond. "So, so wild."

Getting recognized in public happened a lot more when she was younger. Her mother had stopped bringing her along to the grocery store because people would always stop to say hi or to applaud her on a recently solved case.

Evelyn said errands always went a lot faster when they weren't being stopped every two minutes, but looking back, Charlotte realized her mother was also likely concerned about her daughter getting a big head from all the attention.

She was recognized a lot less as an adult—either because she cut off several inches of her hair when she was eighteen, or simply because most people eventually forgot about Lottie Illes. But even so, sometimes . . .

"Sorry if this is weird, but could I get your autograph?" the man asked.

Charlotte could see the Reddit post in her mind:

AITA for asking a former kid detective for her autograph?

I (33M) ran into former kid detective Lottie Illes (25F), and asked for her autograph. She said no, even though I asked very nicely and it would've only taken a second. I was really disappointed, especially because I had already been having a pretty bad day. First, my dog died—

"Sure," she said, watching him scramble to grab a napkin from the bag on his arm. He started patting his pockets.

"Shoot," he said, "I don't have my pen on me."

"Oh . . . no . . ." Charlotte said with unconvincing disappointment.

The man looked at her. "Do you . . . have a pen?" He thought for a moment. "Or we could just take a photo—"

"You know, I think I do have a pen," Charlotte said quickly, grabbing her purse. She fished it out and accepted the napkin from the man, using the pizza boxes he was holding as a surface to write on.

"Oh, sorry," she said, lifting the napkin from the box as she finished and noticing the indents her writing had made on the soft cardboard.

"Not a problem," the man said, taking the napkin back from her. "I assume this is going to your . . . ?"

"My brother, yeah. Actually, could I just . . . ?"

"Oh, uh, sure," the man said as Charlotte opened the bag. She pulled out the box of pizza and quickly retrieved a slice before returning the box.

"I'll text him," she said, seeing the concerned look on the man's face. She took a bite of pizza, turned on her heel, and threw a garbled "Thank you!" over her shoulder.

"You're welcome! I mean, thank *you*! 'Bye!"

Charlotte shot off a quick text to Landon as she retraced their earlier steps back to the train station:

Charlotte: I solved the mystery of the missing pizza slice

Landon: wut

She arrived at the train station and bought a ticket, pulling up a subway map on her phone while she waited on the platform. It wasn't until she was settled on the train that Landon's second message came in:

Landon: oh
Landon: ha ha

Several minutes later, her view out the window cut to black as the train hurtled into a tunnel. Soon after, the automated voice announced: "New York Penn Station. New York Penn Station. Final stop. All passengers must exit the train."

Charlotte climbed out of her seat and walked to the front of the train car, stepping into the crush of her fellow passengers as the doors released them onto the platform. She let the flow of traffic sweep her up a broken escalator and into the main floor of Penn Station.

She was hit with a waft of warm summer evening air as she walked outside, pulling out her phone to check Annette's address. Charlotte dodged a family of four rolling their luggage towards the station as she read the texts that had just come in:

Lucy: Hello??
Lucy: Are you in the city rn??

Before Charlotte could begin formulating a response in her head, Lucy called her.

"Hi."

"Okay, what is happening? Did you get kidnapped? Are you being held against your will?"

Charlotte paused at the curb, waiting for the light to turn. "Yeah, but my kidnappers were nice enough to let me take this call. Hang on." She pulled the phone away from her face. "No, she can't pay my ransom. Yeah, I'm sure. She's a middle school teacher." She brought the phone back to her face. "The nice men with weapons say that I have to hang up now, but they're very sorry you aren't paid more for educating our youth."

A middle-aged woman with arms draped with shopping bags looked over her shoulder at Charlotte, a bemused look on her face. Charlotte gave her a wry smile in return.

"Hysterical," Lucy said. "I could afford your twenty-dollar ransom."

"Ooh, zinger. Why are you looking at my location, anyway?" The light turned, and she crossed the street. "Kind of creepy, Ortega."

"I'm working on lesson plans, and any time I'm working on something and want to take a break, I check your location. If you're home, I get to go on Instagram for five minutes."

Charlotte carefully sidestepped a suspicious-looking puddle in the middle of the sidewalk. "But I'm always home."

"Exactly. I get to go on Instagram a lot."

A truck blared its horn, drowning out Lucy's next few words.

"—at Landon's, so I wanted to see what you were up to. Since you were explaining *so much* in your texts."

"Someone's been sending creepy notes to Olivia. Landon asked me to check it out."

"YOU'RE ON A *CASE*?"

Charlotte pulled the phone away from her ear. "Ow. No. I'm just looking into it a little."

"So what're you doing here? More importantly, where am I meeting you?"

The walk sign flashed as Charlotte reached the next curb. She slipped past a couple who hadn't noticed the light change and crossed the street. "I don't think you'll want to join me for this."

"There are very few things I'd choose lesson planning over right now. Try me."

"You've never approved of breaking and entering before."

"Charlotte Illes, you are *not* breaking into someone's apartment right now."

"Not right now, no." Her pace slowed briefly as she passed a McDonald's, her stomach growling. That one slice of pizza hadn't lasted very long. "I'm just gonna check out Olivia's ex-girlfriend's apartment. If I find a way to poke around inside, well . . ."

She heard Lucy sigh and mutter something to herself. "Okay, this kind of thing was cute when you were ten. You're twenty-five. Meaning, if you get caught, you will be *charged as an adult.*"

"Maybe you *should* come, then," Charlotte heard herself say as she rounded the corner. "Keep watch for me."

There was silence on the other end. Then:

"Fine. Send me the address."

"Really?" Charlotte had started regretting the invitation as soon as it left her mouth. *Lucy doesn't want to do this. She shouldn't be doing this. She has lesson plans to write. She has—*

"If the only way I get to hang out with my best friend for the first time in months is by making sure she doesn't get caught committing a crime, sure, I'll come."

"We literally hung out at Gabe's birthday, like, two months ago."

"I mean a hangout without a bunch of drunk people I barely know doing loud karaoke."

"I don't know what Olivia's ex is into, so no promises." Charlotte grinned despite herself. "I'll text you the address."

"This is so stupid," Lucy groaned, then hung up.

When Charlotte turned onto the street of the address Olivia gave her, Lucy was already outside of Annette's apartment building, wearing a light blue sundress and white sneakers. Argentinian on her mom's side and Puerto Rican on her dad's, she had long, straight brown hair that was pulled up into a baseball cap, and was wearing large sunglasses that covered half of her face.

do it." Charlotte stepped into Lucy's cupped hands and put a hand on her shoulder, bracing herself.

"Ready? Okay!" she chirped.

"Don't say that." Lucy shuffled her feet to get a sturdier stance. "Okay. One, two, down—"

Charlotte jumped and went flying, stumbling to keep her balance as she hit the sidewalk.

Lucy threw her hands into the air. "What was *that*?!"

"I think I did it wrong."

"You think? Come back and *listen* to me this time."

Charlotte trudged back over to Lucy, humbled. "Okay, I'm listening."

After slightly longer instructions from Lucy (and only one interruption from Charlotte), the two were ready to try again.

"One, two, down, *up*—"

This time, Charlotte was launched straight up into the air, and managed to grab onto the bottom rung of the ladder, which didn't budge when she pulled on it. If she was being honest with herself, she hadn't been sure whether the ladder would stay in place, or if her weight would send it (and her) hurtling to the ground, but she figured either result had its pros and cons.

Lucy adjusted her grip, pushing up on Charlotte's shoe. "You good?"

"*Yup*," came the strangled reply of someone who rarely exerted herself physically. Charlotte grabbed onto the next rung and pulled herself higher. Lucy stepped back as Charlotte managed to get one leg up, then another leg, and finally climbed up and over the railing and onto the first level of the fire escape.

She threw her hands up in celebration, looking down at Lucy, who shook her head as she dusted off her hands.

"Who am I keeping a lookout for?" Lucy asked, trying to make her voice carry while still keeping it at a low volume.

"Um, um um um . . ." Charlotte quickly pulled out her phone and found the text Olivia had sent her with Annette's description. "'Curly brown hair, five-foot-five, poor listening and communication skills.'" She paused, looking back down at Lucy. "At least two of those things should be helpful."

"Sure. I'm very familiar with poor listeners."

"Sorry, did you say something?"

"Ha. Go."

Charlotte began climbing the stairs of the fire escape, stopping when she reached the third floor of the building. Sidestepping a dead potted plant, she peeked into the window that, if her counting was correct, belonged to Apartment 3B. It was a nice-sized apartment, as far as Manhattan apartments went. More importantly, it was dark, and seemingly empty of people.

Thankfully, the window was very slightly cracked open. Charlotte managed to dig her fingers under the sill and pull it up. She dropped her purse on the floor inside, then maneuvered herself through the opening, careful not to knock over the succulents that sat on the inside sill.

Once inside, she paused to get her bearings. She had two thoughts, almost simultaneously:

1. There were countless places in this apartment where someone could keep a purple pen, not to mention the fact that even if this *was* Annette's apartment and she *was* the person writing the notes and therefore the owner of the purple pen, she might currently have the pen with her, leaving no proof in the apartment that would tie her back to the notes.
2. There was definitely a cat in this apartment.

Charlotte's phone lit up, and she quickly answered. "What is it? Is she here? Is she coming?"

"No," Lucy's voice came through the phone. "I just figured it'd save time to already have you on the phone in case she does show up. Also, I was bored. What're you doing?"

Charlotte began looking around the desk that sat by the window. She immediately clocked a couple of small framed photos that featured a woman matching Olivia's description (minus the communication problems—even Charlotte couldn't identify those from only a photo).

"Just looking for a purple pen. All the notes to Olivia were written in purple, so I figured that'd be the best place to start." Charlotte picked up a cup full of pens and pencils that sat on the desk and began looking through them. "It's kind of weird. Do you remember Daisy Tremaine?"

"Yeah."

"'The Case of the Missing Bathroom Pass'?"

"Ohhh . . . right."

"She used a purple pen. Gave herself away almost immediately. Definitely one of my quicker solves." Not finding a purple pen, Charlotte put the cup down. "It's just so specific. If they had used a black pen, it wouldn't be a clue at all."

"You know today was the first time you answered a call from me in months?"

Charlotte winced as she crossed the room to investigate the coffee table. "Has it been that long?"

"Mhm. And the only reason I'd call you is because you've also been terrible at replying to texts."

Charlotte started reading the spines of the books that sat on the coffee table. She didn't know what she was looking for, exactly. *Winning Your Ex Back for Dummies*? A pen catalog with a purple pen listing that was circled a bunch of times? This was ridiculous. Why did she think she could do this?

"Char?"

"Sorry, sorry, I was reading something." On a whim, she glanced under the couch, and was greeted by two green feline eyes peering out from the shadows. *There's the cat.* "I know I've been MIA recently," she continued. "I've just—"

"No, not that. You said Annette has curly blond hair, right?"

Charlotte straightened. "No, brown."

"Oh, shoot. Get out. She's coming up."

"'Bye, cat!" Charlotte whispered, stuffing her phone into her pocket and running to the window. "I was never here."

She practically hurtled over the sill, then lowered the window back down, leaving it open a crack. As she started back down the fire escape steps, she went through her mental breaking-and-entering checklist:

The Official Breaking-and-Entering Checklist

By Charlotte "Lottie" Illes, circa 2008

- Leave everything as you found it, unless you discover a stolen item, in which case steal it back and return it to its rightful owner.
- If you see shoes by the door, be respectful and take off your shoes, too.
- Don't read any diaries unless it's *crucial* to the investigation.
- Do NOT eat any cookies left out on plates. You can't risk the crumbs.
- DON'T LEAVE ANYTHING BEHIND!!!

Check, check, check, check . . . wait.

Charlotte froze. Her purse.

"Charlotte? Charlotte!" Lucy's small, tinny voice coming from the phone in her pocket echoed Lucy's actual voice that floated up from the sidewalk below. "Did you get out?"

"Hang on," Charlotte said, quickly heading back up the stairs. She approached Annette's window again, careful to keep to the side and out of sight from the inside. Crouching, she peeked into the window just in time to see the apartment door open and Annette walk inside, talking on the phone.

"Yeah, that's what I told her." Her voice squeezed out through the crack between the window and the sill. "No, I didn't, because she should've known that going into the party!"

Charlotte watched her drop her bag by the door and make

her way to the couch, thankfully not noticing the strange purse sitting on the floor by her window. Yet.

Crouch-walking to the stairs, Charlotte made her way back down the fire escape. She leaned over the railing to look down at Lucy. "I left my purse inside."

"You're joking." Lucy looked around like someone was about to jump out from behind a car and arrest them both. "What happened to the checklist?"

Charlotte tapped her fingers on the railing, trying to think. "In my defense, I'm not used to having a purse with me when I do stuff like this."

"'*Don't leave anything behind*!!!' " Lucy hissed.

"I know, I know, you don't have to quote my own checklist to me. I messed up!" Charlotte pulled out her phone and hung up on the call with Lucy. She shot off a text to Olivia:

Charlotte: hi urgent what's Annette's phine number
Charlotte: phone nunber
Charlotte: PHONE NUMBER

"What's happening?" Lucy whispered. Her voice had gotten significantly quieter as the risk of capture got significantly higher.

"I'm working on it," Charlotte said, leaning against the railing on her forearms and watching her phone. Thirty seconds later, three dots appeared as Olivia began to type.

Olivia: at what point am I allowed to put my foot down?
Charlotte: preferably not at this point. please??

There was a pause. Then:

Olivia: 555-503-7991

Charlotte quickly copied the number. "Incoming," she said, texting it to Lucy.

Lucy looked up quickly, as if Charlotte was about to drop something on her head. Then, seeing Charlotte hold up her phone, she looked down at her own.

"Call Annette, and be a delivery person or something," Charlotte said, turning to go back up the fire escape. "Just get her out of the apartment."

"*Be* a delivery person?"

"You got this!" Charlotte whispered loudly. Lucy's grumbling faded as she ascended the stairs, crouching again outside of Annette's window.

"Hi, baby!" Charlotte froze, then realized she most likely wasn't the one being addressed (which was a relief, not only because it meant she hadn't been discovered, but also because she disliked infantilizing terms of endearment). She slowly peeked through the window to see Annette scooping up the fluffy gray cat from under the couch and cradling it in her arms.

"How was your day?" Annette cooed. "Did you have a good day? I bet you napped a lot. Mommy wishes she could nap as much as you do. Yes she does!"

A ringtone interrupted the cat coddling, and Charlotte watched Annette release the cat onto the couch and pick up her phone. "Hello?"

Charlotte could hear the murmur of Lucy's voice from the sidewalk below but couldn't make out the words.

"I didn't order any food," Annette said, dropping down onto the couch next to the cat.

Another murmur from Lucy.

"Yeah, that's my name, but I didn't order anything."

More murmuring from Lucy. Charlotte was able to make out the words *underpaid* and *cobb salad.*

She couldn't imagine how Lucy managed to make cobb salad sound threatening, but Annette hopped back onto her feet.

"Okay, okay, I'm coming down," she said, heading for the door.

Charlotte waited a beat after the apartment door shut, then pulled the window open again, sending the cat scurrying back under the couch.

"Sorry, me again, forgot my purse." Charlotte leaned in through the open window and grabbed her purse strap, almost knocking over a succulent as she pulled it up and over the sill. "Remember," she said in the direction of the couch, "I was never here." She closed the window and made her way back down the fire escape for what she hoped would be the last time.

Stopping at the bottom level, she peeked over the railing. Lucy had vanished, and the street was quiet. A minute later, Charlotte shrunk back as Annette appeared on the sidewalk, looking around.

"What the hell . . ." Annette glanced at her phone, looked around one more time, then turned and went back into the building.

Charlotte counted to sixty, then climbed over the railing and down the ladder. Realizing too late that she could have just released the ladder and lowered it to the ground as it was intended, she dangled from the bottom, then dropped to the sidewalk.

She bent her knees as she landed, but still felt a pinch in her ankles upon impact. Cursing under her breath, she rolled her ankles one at a time to relieve the pain.

"You're a maniac," Lucy said, appearing from behind a parked car. "Did you hurt yourself?"

"Nah," Charlotte said, giving her legs one last shake. "I'm super strong and in shape." She kicked up her right leg to prove her point and immediately regretted the decision as she felt her muscles cramp. She dropped her leg, bending over. "AGH, I'm okay."

"My god." Lucy sighed. "So, what now?"

Charlotte straightened, thinking for a moment. "Now . . . I think I need to eat." As if on cue, her stomach rumbled. "Dinner?"

Lucy cracked a smile. "Yeah, I think that's a good idea."

"But I need you to carry me," Charlotte said, reaching out her arms. "I think I pulled a muscle."

"Absolutely not." Lucy started down the street. "There's a good falafel place a couple blocks over."

Charlotte jogged to catch up with her. "My leg! It's cured!"

"A miracle."

Chapter 6

My Friend and I Saw You from Across the Bar and We Really Think You're a Suspect

September, 2003

Lottie Illes was five when she solved her first mystery.

That wasn't entirely true. For the previous year or so, Lottie had proved herself very handy when it came to locating missing items around the house, such as her mom's reading glasses (between the cushions of the couch), or her brother's comic books (under his pillow), or, on one occasion, her pet rabbit (also under Landon's pillow, strangely enough).

But these instances of missing items were always the result of something being misplaced (or just a loose rabbit). After three of her kindergarten classmates' boxes of crayons had gone missing within one week, Lottie knew that this wasn't the same as when Landon would fall asleep reading *Superman*.

Her kindergarten teacher, Mrs. DeNardo, was a very kind but often frazzled woman, and had enough on her plate without concerning herself over a few missing Crayola boxes. The complaining victims were given boxes of crayons from the classroom's supply to use during coloring time, and that seemed to be the end of it.

But not for Lottie. It was almost two weeks into the school year, and she still hadn't managed to make any friends. Not that she had been trying very hard—she preferred to spend recess inside the classroom, working her way through Mrs. DeNardo's collection of 120-piece puzzles, while her classmates were more inclined to spend their free time on the playground.

Of course, if anyone wanted to work on the puzzle with her, they would have been more than welcome. Alternatively, if anyone were to invite her to join them on the playground, she might have also taken them up on their offer. But no one did, and no one had, so Lottie saw the missing crayons as an opportunity to endear herself to her fellow classmates.

All three crayon boxes had been discovered missing after recess. Lottie knew that the boxes couldn't have been taken during recess, since she was always in the classroom during that time, while Mrs. DeNardo sat in the doorway to watch over both the playground and the classroom. This would have typically made Lottie the prime suspect, if Lottie hadn't been sure of the fact that she did not take the crayons. Thankfully, no one else in the class appeared to be conducting their own investigation, so she was free from suspicion.

The only time the classroom was completely empty during the school day was lunchtime. Which meant that Lottie had to be in the classroom at lunchtime in order to catch the culprit. Not that Lottie actually knew the word "culprit" at the time. In her head, she was calling them the "crayon-taker."

It shouldn't have been as easy as it was for Lottie to slip into the closet right before the class lined up for lunch, but Mrs. DeNardo had bigger troublemakers to keep an eye on, and had no reason to double-check to make sure that quiet Lottie Illes was in her spot in line. The door shut firmly, and the classroom fell silent.

Lottie pushed the closet door open a crack so she could keep watch on the classroom. She leaned forward to peek through the crack. An eye peeked back.

"Ah!" Lottie fell backwards into the closet, knocking over a few backpacks on her way down.

The closet door was pushed open, and a girl stood in the doorway.

The girl: Five, Latine, long brown hair and dark brown eyes, stern look on her face. She was gripping a frog-patterned lunchbox in one hand, as if prepared to use it as a weapon.

"You're not supposed to be in here," the girl said, looking down at Lottie and narrowing her eyes.

Lottie scrambled to her feet. "You're not, either." She started returning backpacks to hooks. "Why're you here?" She froze, backpack in hand, and slowly turned. "Are you the crayon-taker?"

The girl scrunched up her nose, loosening her grip on the lunchbox. "No! I thought you were. Why are you in the closet?"

(Years later, this girl would ask a similar question after Lottie shyly admitted to her crush on Natalie Forest.)

"I'm going to catch the crayon-taker." Lottie was trying to remember this girl's name. She was wearing a gold nameplate necklace, but it was in cursive, and Lottie was still working on reading print letters. Instead, she asked, "You know about the crayon-taker?"

"Yeah. Someone took Jayden's crayons, and Taylor's crayons, and Jackie's crayons." The girl glanced nervously over at the classroom door, then looked back at Lottie. "Mrs. DeNardo said they were just lost, but Jackie was really sad, and when I asked her why she was sad, she said that she would never lose her crayons, because her aunt just got them for her and she knew she left them out on her desk, just like Jayden and Taylor."

She took a deep gulp of air, then continued. "Except that she kept Razzmatazz in her pocket because she really likes the color. Also Bailey and Kiyana are missing glue sticks. And Faith can't find her purple eraser. The one that looks like a star."

Lottie blinked. She hadn't known all that stuff about Jackie. She also hadn't known that the crayons had gone missing from desks. She didn't even know who half these people were, much less that even more stuff was missing than she had initially thought.

"How did you know all that?" she asked, curious.

The girl shrugged. "Just talked to them."

Oh. Lottie hadn't been doing much of that with her classmates.

"So what *are* you doing here?" the girl asked.

Lottie threw her shoulders back. "I'm gonna catch the crayon-taker"—she paused—"and glue-taker, and eraser-taker—when they come to take my brother's crayons."

The girl gave her a strange look. *"What?"*

During coloring time earlier that morning, Lottie had made an uncharacteristically grand display of showing off her new erasable crayons, which actually belonged to Landon and were loaned to her in exchange for Lottie's movie-picking privileges the following Saturday. She then left the crayons on her desk for the rest of the morning, where she would have a clear view of them from her hiding spot in the closet. Then, when the crayon-taker showed up, she would leap out of the closet, and . . .

Actually, she realized at that moment she hadn't thought that far ahead. But it was too late to back out now, because footsteps were approaching the door to the classroom.

"Come on!" Lottie hissed, reaching out and yanking the girl into the closet. They began sliding the door closed, and Lottie stuck her sneaker out at the last second to keep it from closing all the way, leaving them a crack to peek through.

Mrs. DeNardo walked into the classroom, and Lottie deflated. She had been sure she was going to catch someone from her class coming to take the crayons. Maybe even a big kid who liked to take kindergarteners' school supplies. But with the teacher there, the supplies-taker (which is what Lottie had re-dubbed them) wouldn't dare come into the room now.

Lottie looked over at the other girl, who had backed away from the door, eyes wide with fear.

"What's wrong?" Lottie whispered.

The girl clutched her lunchbox to her chest. "I don't wanna get in trouble," she whispered back.

"You won't. Don't worry." Lottie turned back and watched Mrs. DeNardo as she hurried around the room, picking up blocks from the play area and returning books to the bookshelf. She breathed a sigh of relief as her teacher left the near-finished dolphin puzzle alone in its spot on the back table. She had plans to finish it during recess later that afternoon.

Mrs. DeNardo went to the front of the room and picked up a plastic container from behind her desk, which Lottie recognized as the classroom's supply bin. She watched her teacher make her way around the desks, collecting leftover paper and glue sticks from their morning craft and returning them to the bin.

Reaching Lottie's desk, she paused, hand hovering over Landon's pack of erasable crayons, before moving on to the next group of desks. Once she had finished her rounds, she turned and began walking towards the closet.

Lottie glanced over at the girl, who was giving her a wide-eyed look of fear. Thinking fast (meaning she didn't really think at all), she pushed the closet door open a little more and slipped out.

Mrs. DeNardo jumped, almost dropping the bin. "Lottie! What are you doing here?" She put down the bin. "You're supposed to be at lunch."

"I know." Lottie clasped her hands in front of her and brought her shoulders up, suddenly feeling shy. She looked down at the bin of supplies. "I was trying to catch the person who took the crayons."

Her teacher sighed. "Sweetie, no one took the crayons. It's nice of you to want to help your friends—"

"But I know what happened." Lottie suddenly dropped her hands. Her mind was racing, her body almost vibrating with adrenaline. She felt like she did last Halloween, when she ate half of her candy in one sitting. Minus the throwing up.

She looked up at her teacher. "I know what happened. I think you took them."

Mrs. DeNardo raised an eyebrow. "Excuse me?"

Lottie reddened. She wasn't used to getting in trouble (not yet, at least), and she felt like she was on the precipice of being in very big trouble. She had to start talking as fast as her brain was moving.

"I don't think you meant to," she said. "But Jayden and Taylor and Jackie left their crayons out on their desks, and I think that maybe you put them in the bin when we went to lunch."

She knelt down and began going through the bin before her teacher could respond. "I think maybe you didn't take the crayons on my desk, because you know the classroom bin doesn't have crayons like that." As she spoke, she pulled out a box of crayons, quickly looked through it, then returned it to the bin and pulled out another one. "I think maybe you took the other ones because you didn't know they belonged to kids." She studied the second box of crayons, then held it up triumphantly, looking at her teacher. "This one's missing Razzmatazz. Jackie keeps Razzmatazz in her pocket because she really likes the color."

Mrs. DeNardo wordlessly took the box from her as Lottie continued rummaging through the bin. "This is Faith's," she said, pulling out a purple star-shaped eraser. She dropped the eraser back into the bin, then stood up, dusting off her knees. "I don't think you meant to," she repeated. "But that's what I think happened."

Five minutes later, Lottie was in the cafeteria, sitting by herself at the end of a lunch table. Mrs. DeNardo had scolded her for hiding in the classroom, then thanked her for helping recover her classmates' "misplaced supplies."

Lottie poked at her potatoes, feeling too excited to eat. Despite being scolded, she really liked this feeling. She really, *really* liked this feeling.

The girl from the closet suddenly appeared, sliding onto the bench across from Lottie, whose eyes widened.

"You!" Lottie put down her fork. "I wanted to tell Mrs. DeNardo you helped, but I . . ." She didn't want to admit that she didn't know the girl's name. ". . . didn't want to get you in trouble."

"It's okay." The girl put her lunchbox down on the table between them. "I'm glad you found the crayons. And the other stuff. That was cool."

Lottie mirrored her shrug. "You told me about Razzmatazz. And the eraser. I didn't know about any of that."

The girl nodded. "Cool."

"Cool," Lottie repeated.

The girl began unzipping her lunchbox, and Lottie momentarily returned to her potatoes before looking up again.

"What does your necklace say?" she asked casually, trying to not make it sound like she was asking for the girl's name.

The girl glanced down at her necklace. "It's my name. Lucia." She looked back up. "But everyone calls me Lucy."

Lottie nodded, and both girls returned to their lunches.

A minute later, Lottie looked up again. "Do you like puzzles?"

Lucy blinked at her. Then she smiled.

Present Day

Charlotte and Lucy sat at a table tucked into a corner of the warmly lit falafel place, digging into their food.

"This is so good," Charlotte groaned. "I haven't eaten anything since breakfast." She paused, remembering the delivery guy outside of Landon's apartment. "Except for the slice of pizza I kind of stole."

"What?"

Charlotte shook her head. "Don't worry about it. So how've things been?"

Lucy wiped her mouth with a paper napkin and dropped it onto her tray. "They've been good," she said, nodding.

Charlotte narrowed her eyes. "What is it?"

Lucy leaned her head back and sighed loudly. "I tried to say that as normally as possible."

"Your voice went too high on 'good.' " Charlotte took another bite of her sandwich. "Also, you had too much eye contact. Felt forced."

Lucy picked the napkin back up, folding it neatly in half. "I don't know. This school year was just a lot." She folded the napkin again. "The administration at my school kind of sucks. The other teachers don't really talk to me, and all the students are spoiled rich kids." She hesitated, folding the napkin a third time, then quietly added, "I think Jake might be cheating on me."

Charlotte's jaw dropped, her sandwich frozen halfway to her mouth. "No *way*."

Lucy gave her A Look.

"What?"

"You don't have to pretend; I know you hate him."

Charlotte put down her sandwich and sat back in her seat. "Okay, one: I don't *hate* him," she lied. "I just think you could do a lot better. And two: even if I'm not his biggest fan, I still didn't think Dumb Jake would be dumb enough to *cheat on you*." Her expression softened. "Are you sure?"

Lucy shook her head. "No," she admitted. "It's just a feeling. We haven't felt very close lately, and he goes out a lot with 'the boys.' " She made air quotes with her fingers.

"I wouldn't worry too much about it then." Charlotte raised

her eyebrows, then added tentatively, "Do you want me to look into it?"

Lucy's eyes wandered up to the artwork on the wall over Charlotte's head. "I don't know," she said. She fiddled with her necklace. "I feel like asking you to look into it makes it real."

Charlotte made a thoughtful face. "Well . . . I guess you don't have to *ask* me to look into it," she said. "Just tell me that if I looked into it, you wouldn't get mad at me."

Lucy gave her a small smile. "Yeah, okay. If you *happened* to look into it, I wouldn't get mad."

"Good." Charlotte sat forward and picked up her sandwich. "Then I may or may not look into it."

Lucy returned the folded-up napkin to the table. "But tell me if you do."

"'Course."

They continued eating, Charlotte giving Lucy a quick overview of what Olivia had told her about the anonymous notes. She also told her what Landon and Olivia had said about the murder in Highview, and the man's connection to Olivia's company.

"That poor guy," Lucy said, her brows furrowing. "Do you think it was actually a mugging?"

Charlotte shrugged as she finished her water, a gurgling sound rising from the bottom of the cup as the last of it went up the straw. "Haven't really thought about it," she said, putting her cup down. "It's not like I'm trying to solve the case."

Lucy raised an eyebrow. "You have a hunch," she said.

"Okay, only because his wallet wasn't stolen. And it was late, he was in a park, and he wasn't doing deliveries that night. Weird time to go on a stroll."

"I don't know," Lucy said drily. "Men can do that sort of thing. Take walks at midnight. Not as risky for them as it is for us."

"Yeah." Charlotte began chewing on the plastic straw. "The union stuff does give motive to some people, though. I guess I'd have to find out how involved he was with all that. It'd definitely be more suspicious if he was a part of the leadership—" She paused as she saw Lucy suppressing a smile. "What."

"Nothing." Lucy shrugged. "Just nice to see you getting back into it."

Charlotte scowled. "I'm not."

"You said, 'I'd have to find out . . .' "

"*Hypothetically*." Charlotte pushed her chair back and picked up her tray, walking it over to the garbage bin by the door.

Lucy followed her lead. "You are so *frustrating*," she said, waiting for Charlotte to dump her trash before dumping her own. "I don't get why you're so dead set on never solving a mystery again."

"Because I don't do that anymore!" Charlotte retorted, taking Lucy's tray and adding both trays to the pile on top of the bin. "I've moved on! I don't know why you and everyone else are so 'dead set' on me getting back into it." She turned and pushed the door open, letting herself out.

"Have a good night, thank you!" Lucy waved at the people behind the counter before following Charlotte out onto the sidewalk. "It's only because we've seen how happy you are when you're solving mysteries, and we don't understand why you wouldn't want to do that again."

Charlotte leaned against the glass window of the falafel place and crossed her arms, looking at Lucy. "I get it. I do. I just—" She shook her head, gesturing as she tried to find the words. "I was a detective for years, right? It was all I did. So how was I supposed to know if there's anything else out there for me if I just kept doing that one thing?"

Lucy nodded. "Okay. So you've been trying different things."

"Yeah."

"And how's that been working out for you?"

Charlotte opened her mouth to respond, her gaze flicking over Lucy's shoulder for a moment. She stopped, eyes widening. "Annette!"

"What?" Lucy started to turn around.

"Don't turn around!"

Lucy froze mid-turn.

"Okay, either turn around or turn back to me; whatever it is you're doing now looks really weird."

Lucy glanced over her shoulder just in time to see Annette walk into a bar across the street. She turned back to Charlotte. "Should we . . . go? Do a stakeout?"

Charlotte sighed. "She is our prime suspect, currently. I guess it couldn't hurt." She started across the street. "Also, I could use a drink right now."

Lucy shook her head and followed Charlotte across the street.

The two entered the bar, greeted by dim lighting and Alanis Morissette's "You Oughta Know." Charlotte showed her ID to the bouncer, then looked around as Lucy pulled her wallet out of her purse. She quickly spotted Annette sitting at the far end of the bar, ordering from the bartender.

Annette Ruiz: late 20s, White, Latine, brown curly hair, wearing black shorts and a yellow spaghetti-strap top. As the bartender walked away, she leaned her forearms on the bar and stared at her phone.

After Lucy showed her ID, Charlotte led them to a two-person table as far from Annette as they could get.

"What d'you want? Pinot grigio?" Charlotte asked as Lucy slid into her chair. Knowing she was right, she made a beeline for the bar without waiting for an answer.

The bartender glanced over her shoulder as Charlotte approached. She had a green buzz cut and a septum piercing, and was reaching for a copper mug from a row of them that sat on a shelf behind the bar. "I'll be right there," she said.

"Actually," Charlotte said, depending on Alanis to keep her voice from carrying to Annette, "I'd like to pay for her drink." She nodded at Annette. "And order two more, when you're ready."

"Oh, alright. Shoot."

Charlotte ordered the wine for Lucy and a gin and tonic for

herself, then checked her phone as she waited for the drinks to be made. There was a text from her mom asking how things were going, and she sent a vague but positive reply. There was also a text that had just popped up in the *foot canal* group chat, from Gabe:

Gabe: I just made the mistake of looking at your locations and I'm sad

Gabe: drink something with tequila in it for me

Gabe: keep my memory alive

Charlotte smiled, then glanced over her shoulder at Lucy, who had also just checked her phone. She looked up at Charlotte and shook her head, also smiling. Charlotte turned back to the bartender, who was making her gin and tonic. "Could we also get two tequila shots?"

Soon after, Charlotte returned to their table with a tray of drinks.

"Noooo," Lucy groaned, spotting the shot glasses.

"We must," Charlotte said, putting the tray down. She picked up one of the tequila shots and put it in front of Lucy, then sat down and picked up the other one.

Out of the corner of her eye, she saw the bartender deliver Annette's drink and say something, nodding in Charlotte's direction. Charlotte quickly looked away before Annette could turn around, focusing on Lucy again.

"Wait, I need to send a video to him." Lucy picked up her phone and started filming Charlotte. "Okay, go."

"To Gabe," Charlotte said, raising her glass. "Wish you were here to convince us to make even worse decisions than this. Cheers."

"Cheers!" Lucy echoed. They both tapped the bottoms of their glasses to the table, then brought the glasses together, then tapped them on the table once more before throwing back the shots.

Lucy stopped the recording as she picked up a slice of lime, sucking on it. "Oh, I'm gonna regret that," she said, her voice raspy.

Charlotte laughed into her own lime. She could feel Annette still looking at them, waiting for Charlotte to look back.

Gabe: I'm crying
Gabe: deeply honored thank u

"Okay, don't look," Charlotte said, "but Annette keeps looking at us."

Lucy froze. "What? Why? Oh my god." She sank down in her seat, as if that would hide her from view.

"Probably because I paid for her drink."

Lucy's look of fear was quickly replaced with disbelief. "Why did you do that?" she hissed, sitting up again. "I thought we were doing a stakeout!"

"I never said stakeout. *You* said stakeout."

"I thought it was a mutually agreed-upon stakeout!"

Charlotte took another sip of her gin and tonic. "We're not going to get any information from just watching her drink alone at the bar."

Lucy thought for a moment. "Unless she signed her credit card receipt with a purple pen. Which we'll never know now, because *you paid for her drink*."

Charlotte's eyebrows shot up. "I . . . actually did not consider that. That's good thinking."

Mollified by the compliment, Lucy suppressed a proud smile. "Well, what *was* the plan then?"

"I figured the best way to get any info is to talk to her. But it'd be weird to just go up to her, so I paid for her drink. That way, I'll look like a Good Samaritan, and when she comes over to talk to us, it'll feel like *her* choice, and there won't be any suspicion on us."

Lucy narrowed her eyes. "'A Good Samaritan'?"

"Trust me." Charlotte noticed movement from across the room, and saw Annette pick up her purse, then get off the barstool and make her way towards them. "Oop, showtime."

Annette approached their table. "Hey."

Like hitting a switch, Lucy's face went from panicked to pleasant as she looked up and smiled. "Hi!"

"Um," Annette started, pulling her purse strap over her shoulder, "thanks for paying for my drink."

"Oh, it's no problem," Charlotte said. "We just saw you drinking alone, so we wanted to pay it forward."

"Sort of a Good Samaritan thing," Lucy added. Charlotte tried to kick her under the table, but her foot made contact with the table column instead. She struggled to keep her face neutral as pain shot through her leg.

"Right," Annette said slowly. "Well, I'm flattered, but if you're looking for a third or something, I'm not interested."

Lucy made a choking sound as Charlotte quickly jumped in, saying, "Oh, no, it wasn't like that at all. Just . . . trying to do a nice thing."

Annette seemed relieved. "Oh, okay. Well, thanks again."

Charlotte glanced over at Lucy, who looked like she was using every muscle in her body to not start laughing at how quickly Charlotte's plan had started going downhill.

"Uh, wait," Charlotte said, scrambling to get things back on track. "Do you wanna join us for another drink? We were just talking about exes we're still hung up on."

Lucy's eyes started filling with tears of mirth. Thankfully, Annette wasn't looking at her.

"I'm good, thanks," Annette said awkwardly. "I did actually have a question, though, if you don't mind."

"Sure, what's up? Pull up a chair!" Charlotte was trying so hard.

"No, this'll be quick. I saw you two outside my apartment earlier. Are you following me or something?"

The smile Lucy had been struggling to rein in dropped off her face, panic returning to her eyes.

Charlotte's mind raced. Time for a new approach.

"Have you been sending messages to your ex-girlfriend?" she asked, shrugging off the pleasant demeanor and leaning back in her chair. She ignored Lucy's eyes boring into her from across the table, clearly not expecting the extreme strategy pivot.

It was Annette's turn to look surprised. "What . . . how did you know about that?"

Okay, that was easy. Charlotte raised her eyebrows. "So you *have* been sending messages."

"Who are you?" Annette demanded.

Charlotte extended a hand. "Charlotte Illes, former detective." Annette made no move to shake her hand, so she gestured to Lucy. "This is my friend, L—"

"Jennifer," Lucy cut in. ". . . Aniston." Charlotte saw a flicker of regret in Lucy's eyes as her brain caught up with what her mouth was saying.

Annette stared at her. "Like . . ."

"Why've you been sending messages to Olivia Kimura?" Charlotte asked quickly, moving past Lucy's confusing alias. Lucy, in turn, picked up her glass and took a long drink.

Immediately, Charlotte could tell that this was not what Annette was expecting to hear. Her eyebrows shot up. "Olivia? I haven't been sending messages to Olivia. I haven't talked to her in over a year."

Okay, not so easy. "Then what were *you* talking about?" Charlotte asked.

Annette looked around, annoyance crossing her face. "Not that it's any of your business, but since I guess I'm being *investigated* or whatever—"

"Just to clarify," Lucy cut in, "you're under no legal obligation to answer—"

"You were saying?" Charlotte interrupted, once again accidentally making a victim of the table column (and her own foot). Lucy sat back, shaking her head, blissfully unaware of how narrowly she'd avoided being kicked, twice.

Annette huffed. "I was drunk-texting an ex last night. Not Olivia. I thought you were talking about that." Her face softened by a couple of degrees. "I don't know anything about any messages being sent to Olivia."

"Okay," Charlotte said, nodding. "Thanks. Sorry for bothering you."

Annette took a step away from the table. "Yeah, well . . . thanks again for the drink." She turned and walked out of the bar.

"Do you believe her?" Lucy whispered, as if Annette could still hear them despite having fully made her exit.

"Jennifer Aniston?"

Lucy looked pained. "I didn't wanna give her my real name! I thought of Jennifer, and then 'Aniston' just kind of followed naturally."

"Naturally."

"Okay, you're not really in a position to make fun of *me* for not thinking fast on my feet." Lucy gestured at the door Annette had just left through. "That was a disaster."

"I wouldn't call it a disaster," Charlotte objected. "We got answers."

"So do you believe her?" Lucy repeated.

Charlotte picked up her gin and tonic. "I think so." She took a sip. "I mean, if she was going to lie, she would've said no to the initial question. Unless she was just caught off-guard and then recovered, I guess. But she seemed genuine."

"How do you feel?" Lucy asked suddenly.

"What?" Charlotte rolled her eyes, realizing what she meant. "Not again."

"Doesn't it feel good to be back at it?" Lucy asked, powering through Charlotte's glare. "Working the old brain muscles? Putting together the pieces?"

"I'm not gonna answer that."

"Fine." Lucy sighed.

The two continued to talk, slowly finishing their drinks. Neither of them brought up the mystery again.

Lucy led Charlotte to a nearby subway stop and pointed her in the direction of the train that would take her back uptown to Penn Station. She then made Charlotte swear to hang out with her at least one more time before going back home, and sent her off with one more hug.

After a quick subway ride and a mad dash to make the train, Charlotte fell into her seat, panting. This day had been a rude awakening to the fact that she was sorely out of shape, and she resolved to work out more often once she got home. She then came to terms with the knowledge that she would likely not stick to that resolution and, self-reflection complete, she sat back in her seat and let the train carry her weary flesh bag back to Highview.

The platform was nearly empty as Charlotte disembarked at the station, besides a couple of passengers who got off several cars back and headed for the other platform exit. She headed down the staircase closer to her, trying to remember the way back to Landon's now that it was dark out.

She was only a block away from the apartment when the figure appeared.

The footsteps behind Charlotte had been growing in volume, but she was so focused on retracing her steps to Landon's apartment that she didn't notice how close they had gotten until a gloved hand roughly grabbed her arm. She whirled around, trying to pull away, and came face-to-face (if you could call it that) with a figure wearing a black ski mask and sunglasses.

The ski mask was definitely the most distinguishable thing about the person. The rest of their outfit was composed of a dark green hoodie, dark jeans, and black sneakers. Their eyes were hidden behind the sunglasses, which were pointed down at her as another gloved hand reached out and gripped Charlotte's other arm, pinning them to her sides.

"Stay out of other people's business," the figure demanded. Their voice was deep and raspy, sounding like the person was disguising it. Then, as quickly as she had been grabbed, Charlotte was released. She stumbled backwards a few steps, regaining her balance.

"Go home. Or else." The figure turned and ran off, disappearing around the corner.

Adrenaline pumping, Charlotte's first thought was to pursue. She quickly reminded herself that she had *just* concluded that she was out of shape and therefore not physically equipped to chase after an assailant, much less equipped to do anything to the assailant in the unlikely instance that she actually managed to catch up to them.

Charlotte's second thought was: *Holy shit. WHAT? Holy shit.*

Chapter 7

She Knows

May 3rd, 2011

Lucy,

I couldn't wait until lunch to tell you what happened. So I snuck into Eddie Fontana's car to see if the stolen cash box from the library fundraiser was there. Landon told me he heard a rumor that Eddie took money from the senior prom proceeds to throw a party. If he wanted to cover his tracks, he'd have to get more money to replace it. MOTIVE!!

Then while I was in there I saw him walking over, so I climbed over the seats and hid in the trunk. And there was the cash box!!! Then he drove home, and I started FREAKING OUT. He lives in one of those big new houses with the woods behind them. The perfect place for him to make me DISAPPEAR FOR GOOD.

So he parked at his house and opened the trunk and saw me. I tried to tell him that I was looking for my rabbit, but I was holding the cash box so he didn't believe me. He got angry and tried to take the box, but I told him I knew he stole it and that he needed to return it.

I thought this was my end.

Then out of NOWHERE he started CRYING! He told me to just take the box and go tell on him. I felt bad so I told him if he promised not to steal anymore, I'd just tell the library I found it or something. He said thanks, and then he drove me back to the parking lot because my bike was still there.

I'll see you at lunch. Bye!

-Lottie

P.S. I was right about him stealing the money to pay back the prom fund

P.P.S. Can you help me with my Spanish homework at lunch? I'm stuck on sentences 3 through 20

Present Day

Charlotte woke up with a start, her heart racing. She tried to calm herself, but found little solace in her surroundings. Pulling the pillow over her face to avoid the dead black eyes of the Funko Pop figures, she focused on slowing her breathing as she gathered her thoughts.

After about a minute, this was what she'd gathered:

1. Upon returning to the apartment last night, all she told Landon and Olivia was that she had looked into Annette and hit a dead end.
2. She did *not* tell Landon and Olivia about the ski-masked person who grabbed her and:
    a. Warned her to: "Stay out of other people's business."
    b. Encouraged her to: "Go home."
    c. Ended with the very descriptive threat of: "Or else."
3. She wasn't really sure why she didn't tell them. On the one hand, telling them could mean Landon would deem the case too serious for her to keep working on,

and she could go home. On the other hand, the attack had made her stubbornly determined to continue working on the case—especially if leaving meant abandoning Olivia to deal with a secret admirer who wasn't above grabbing and threatening people.

4. This event had thrown a large-sized wrench into the hunch she had started developing on the train ride home.
5. Pancakes.

Her last thought, brought on by the distinct smell of pancakes that was hanging in the air, was enough to get her to climb out of bed, change out of her pajamas, and go investigate.

Landon was sitting at the dining table, looking at his phone, and using a fork to stuff half a pancake into his mouth.

"You eat like an animal," Charlotte said, passing him to grab a glass from the drying rack by the sink. "There's no way you do that in front of Olivia."

Landon swallowed. "I think she finds it endearing," he said defensively. He cut a slightly smaller piece of pancake and popped it into his mouth. "Good *morning*."

"Morning." Charlotte got the water filter out of the fridge and poured herself a glass before returning the filter and sitting across the table from her brother.

He passed her a plate and fork and gestured to the small stack of pancakes that sat between them. "Pancakes."

"I can see that," Charlotte said. "Did Olivia make them?"

"Nope, I did."

Charlotte looked at him with disbelief as she began serving herself. "Since when do you make pancakes? Or, just, *cook* in general?"

Landon shrugged, clearly trying to look humble but failing to disguise the smug look on his face. "I've got a few new tricks up my sleeve. I think I'm slowly becoming a Full Adult."

"Gross. Mazel, I guess." Charlotte took a bite. "Call me when you're finally able to do your taxes without calling Mom, and then we'll celebrate."

Landon pointed his fork across the table, looking indignant. "Those forms are designed to confuse people."

Charlotte snickered, taking another bite. "Did Olivia go to work?"

He nodded. "Her manager called her team in early today. Seems like they're working hard on releasing some new features." Landon rubbed his brow. "She thinks the company's trying to distract from any more theorizing that might be going on about Scoop being connected to the death."

Charlotte nodded. "Sounds like it."

"So how'd sleuthing go last night?" Landon asked, stuffing the rest of the pancake into his mouth and pushing his chair back. "You didn't say much when you got back." He stood and brought his plate to the sink.

"It was fine," Charlotte said, keeping her tone neutral. Landon didn't have her knack for reading friends and family, but he'd surprised her many times in the past by figuring out when something was amiss with her. Thankfully, he was occupied with cleaning his plate, and didn't seem to suspect she was withholding anything.

"It was great to hang out with Lucy," she continued. "But like I said last night, kind of hit a dead end with the ex. Not sure what else there is to do."

"I'm sure you'll figure it out," Landon said cheerfully, scrubbing his plate with a sponge. "You just have to do what you always do and look somewhere else."

"What I always *did*," Charlotte corrected.

"Sure. What'd I say?"

She rolled her eyes, cutting another piece of pancake and popping it into her mouth. Chewing thoughtfully for a moment, she said, "Are you sure there isn't anyone else in Olivia's past who might be doing this? Anyone . . . like, *dangerous*?"

Landon deposited his plate on the drying rack, grabbed a hand towel, and turned. "What do you mean by 'dangerous'?"

Slowly, Charlotte said, "You know, like . . . I'm just trying to gauge how serious this situation actually is."

Landon tossed the towel onto the counter and leaned against the sink. "Well," he said slowly, "Olivia doesn't seem *too* concerned about it. So *I'm* not too concerned about it. But it'd be nice to know who's behind it."

The siblings stared at each other for a moment. Charlotte suddenly got the feeling that she wasn't the only one treading carefully, though she wasn't fully sure why.

Landon straightened. "But I wouldn't worry about it being anyone dangerous," he said. "Anyway, I've gotta get started on work. You good to chill out?"

"Yeah," she said. "I might meet up with Lucy."

"Oh, nice." Landon headed for his room. "Invite her over for dinner. I'll order pizza."

"Again?"

He turned, looking embarrassed. "I got these coupons for this one place and then forgot to use them . . ."

"And they expire soon?"

"In three days. I have two left."

Charlotte gently rolled her eyes. "Pizza it is." She watched Landon disappear into his room, chewing on the inside of her cheek for a moment, then returned to Dale's room to text Lucy.

"Please understand that I am so happy you guys are spending time together," Gabe said, his face filling the screen of Lucy's phone. "It's great. I'm so glad you're having a nice day." His face got even closer to the camera as he lowered his voice and said, "But I need you to also understand that I'm insanely jealous and wish I was with you and not at work right now."

"Gabe." A tired-sounding voice came from offscreen. "If

you're going to take personal phone calls, can you take them in the other room?"

"I didn't take this call. I called them."

"*Please.*"

"You got it, Suze." Charlotte and Lucy watched Gabe pick up his phone and start walking, his camera jiggling with every step. "That's Susan. I've told you guys about Susan."

"How have you not driven that poor woman into early retirement yet?" Lucy asked. "Her tenacity is astounding."

"Solid SAT words. You see"—Gabe pushed open a door—"it's about having *just* the right amount of charm to balance out all the other stuff I do that drives her insane. Plus, our social media's been doing better than ever, thanks to me, so everyone here can't help but love me." He pushed open another door, and Charlotte caught a glimpse of the sky behind his head.

"Did you just *leave*?"

Gabe looked down at the phone. "Hell yeah, I left. I was going to clock out in thirty minutes anyway. Figured if I was leaving the room to talk on the phone, I might as well just go home."

"Gabe . . ." Lucy started.

"They're not gonna *fire* me, Luce. Did you hear what I just said about how good our social media's doing? If they fire me, they're just gonna go back to posting grainy screenshots on Instagram with unclickable links in the caption."

Charlotte looked up as Lucy took the phone to continue lecturing Gabe on the importance of professionalism in the workplace. They were sitting on two wooden loungers on the High Line, an old, elevated rail line that had been turned into a park that stretched over twenty blocks.

The city was having a mild week for July, and the walkway was bustling with people enjoying a break from the usual ninety-degree weather. Charlotte and Lucy had nearly plowed down a group of kids in matching camp shirts to grab the loungers as they became available.

A warm breeze washed over them, and Charlotte leaned back

and closed her eyes, listening to the sounds of people passing and the drone of traffic.

Lucy's voice faded back in over the other sounds of the High Line.

". . . should come up this weekend and we'll go."

Charlotte's eyes popped open. She turned her head. "What's happening?"

Lucy looked over at her. "I was saying that Gabe should come up this weekend so we can all hang out. He wants to go to that place that just opened where everyone wears headphones—"

"I don't know if I'll still be here this weekend," Charlotte cut in.

Lucy's face fell. "Oh." She glanced at the phone, then back at her. "Are you in a rush to get back?"

"I mean, I . . . I . . ." Charlotte stammered. "I don't want to overstay my welcome at Landon's. And—"

"No problem, you guys can stay with me and Jake," Lucy said. "You can take the couch and Gabe can use the air mattress. Or I can make Jake sleep in the living room with Gabe—"

"Fun, boys night," Gabe said flatly.

"We'll work it out!" Lucy finished. She put on an inflated pout. "Please?"

Charlotte hesitated. She wanted to stay. She wanted to hang out with her two best friends. She even wanted to spend more time with Landon, and with Olivia. They had decided to wait for a new anonymous message to come in, to see if Charlotte could learn anything from that. She knew that it wouldn't be a problem if she just stayed with them for the rest of the week (especially since Dale was *definitely* not living there anymore).

And yet . . .

"I can't," Charlotte said.

"CHARLOTTE," Gabe yelled. Lucy's fake pout dropped into a real frown.

"I'm sorry, I can't," Charlotte said. "I've got to keep job hunting, and my mom needs me to remind her to eat dinner—"

"These are all things you can do from New York," Gabe complained.

"—plus there's some mail I haven't opened yet, and—"

"Charlotte. It's fine." Lucy said.

"But—"

"It's *fine*," Lucy said, cutting off Gabe's protests. She looked at the phone. "You can still come visit! Or we'll plan another time for you both to come up." She turned back to Charlotte with a forced smile on her face, her eyes disappointed and . . . pitying? Was that pity? "It's all good."

They said goodbye to Gabe and headed for the train station to go to Landon's for dinner.

Charlotte felt awful.

"—so he told me to fix it, but he couldn't even fully explain to me what the problem was." Olivia shook her head. "He just said he couldn't explain everything to me—which is news to me, because he spends a *lot* of time explaining things to me that I already know about."

"I hate when people in charge don't even understand what you do," Lucy said, glancing over at Olivia.

"That's the thing, though—he used to have my job. He understands it well enough. So he wants to tell me exactly how I should be doing everything, until I actually ask him for help." Olivia rolled her eyes. "He'll also threaten to give my work to someone else if I can't get it done fast enough for his liking. He never does it, but he keeps saying he will."

"Her manager sucks," Landon chimed in. "She knows way more abou—Lottie, don't you dare use that on me."

"Okay," Charlotte said, pressing a button on her controller and sending a blue shell hurtling towards Landon. "Lucy, go!"

"When did I get to second place?" Lucy asked, veering around Landon as his character got caught in an explosion. Now in first place, her car sped across the finish line. "Oh, I won!"

Charlotte rolled her eyes with a smile. Lucy was effortlessly good at most games, but never failed to be genuinely humble about it.

"You had an accomplice," Landon grumbled, taking second place. Olivia's car crossed the finish line in third, and a bit more time passed before Charlotte finished in a respectable 8th place.

"I know my strengths," Charlotte said, dropping her controller and stretching her fingers. "I'm fine with being an accomplice."

There was a ringing sound by the front door, signaling that someone hit the buzzer for the apartment.

"That's the pizza," Landon said, tossing his controller onto the couch and scrambling to his feet. He crossed the apartment to hit the button for the front door of the building, unlocking it.

Lucy and Olivia also stood.

"I'm gonna use the bathroom," Lucy said.

"I'll get out the plates." Olivia headed for the kitchen.

Landon also made a beeline for the kitchen. "I'll help. Lot, can you get the door when the Scoop driver comes up?"

Charlotte suddenly found herself alone in the living room, still holding her video game controller. ". . . Okay?"

She stood and collected all the controllers, depositing them into a basket that sat underneath the television. A minute later, there was a knock at the door.

"Got it," Charlotte said, going to the door.

She realized, as she opened the door and saw the same delivery guy she had bumped into the day before, that she was not at all surprised to see him there. A cocktail of emotions began to mix inside of her as her thoughts clicked into place—some combination of satisfaction, annoyance, and confusion. But that didn't stop her from saying, in a surprised tone, "Oh, hi again!"

The man grinned as he pulled the pizza boxes from his insulated bag. "Hey, Charlotte!"

Charlotte took the boxes from him. "Sorry, I didn't get your name last time," she said as he pulled out a receipt for her to sign.

"It's Eric." He tucked the now-empty bag under his arm. "I actually deliver to this building pretty often."

"Yeah, I asked you that yesterday."

"Oh." He paused. "Uh, sign here?"

"Sure." Charlotte looked around for a place to put the boxes down in the narrow hallway. Seeing nothing but walls and floor, she opted for the spot where gravity would serve her best.

"Oh, and I know I forgot my pen last time," he said as she rose from the floor, "but I've got it today." He began digging around in his pockets.

Charlotte nodded solemnly. "Yeah, that makes sense." She held out her hand.

Once again, surprise was not a primary emotion when Eric dropped a purple pen into her outstretched hand.

"Mhmm." Charlotte blinked at the pen. Then she chuckled.

He gave her a strange look. "Is something wrong?"

"No, it's all good," Charlotte said, still laughing to herself. "Something very dumb is happening to me right now, that's all." She scribbled her name onto the receipt, then returned the pen to him. He hesitated before taking it, looking confused.

Charlotte knelt down to pick the pizzas up from the floor as Eric turned to leave. Then he turned back. He looked thoughtful, and hesitated before speaking again.

"Can I ask you something? As a detective? It's for a friend."

Charlotte paused, and Eric quickly continued. "Say someone offered to pay you to—"

"Hey, it's okay," Charlotte cut him off. "You don't have to explain. You did a good job." She gave him a smile. "Did you get tipped already?"

Eric blinked, then nodded. "Um, yeah. Yup, you're all set." He smiled and gave a little wave. "Have a good night."

"You too," Charlotte said. She shut the door and walked back into the apartment, where she was met by three sets of eyes that immediately looked away from her.

"Pizza's here," she said casually, walking over and depositing the boxes onto the kitchen counter.

"Did, uh . . ." Landon started, slowly opening one of the boxes, ". . . did the guy leave?"

"Yup. I signed the receipt, we're all good. Ooh, pepperoni." Charlotte grabbed a plate, then turned to see the three of them looking at one another. "Hey."

They all quickly looked at her. She pointed at the pizza. "May I?"

"Oh, yeah." Landon moved out of the way so Charlotte could remove a slice from the pie and drop it onto her plate.

"Hey, Char," Lucy said, "what, um . . . how's the case going?"

Charlotte took a bite of pizza. "You mean with the person writing notes to Olivia with a purple pen?"

Lucy let a long second pass. "Yes."

Cocking her head, Charlotte pretended to think for a moment. "You know, I'm kind of just . . . waiting for something to turn up." She shrugged, then took another bite.

The two of them stared at each other for another long moment. Lucy's eyes narrowed almost imperceptibly as Charlotte raised a brow as if to ask, "Something to share?"

Finally, Lucy sighed in defeat. "She knows."

"*Lucy*!" Landon yelped.

"What? She knows. She clearly knows." Lucy gestured at Charlotte, who was continuing to eat her pizza, an innocent look on her face. "She's just messing with us."

"Maybe he forgot to do it," Olivia said quietly to Landon.

"He didn't forget," Lucy said. "She saw the pen. She knows."

Landon threw his hands into the air. "You just blew the whole thing."

"No, I knew," Charlotte said.

Lucy gestured at her, looking pointedly at Landon.

Landon crossed his arms, determined not to give it up. "Okay then. Prove it. What exactly do you know?"

"That you guys made up a mystery for me to solve and were behind the whole thing."

Landon dropped his arms, looking dejected. "Okay, she knows."

"*How* did you know?" Olivia asked, looking baffled.

"Well, to be honest," Charlotte said, picking up a glob of cheese that had fallen onto her plate and dropping it into her mouth, "I was only, like, ninety-nine percent sure."

"So she *didn't* know!" Landon exclaimed, turning on Lucy.

"She *knew*."

"But *how*?" Olivia repeated, silencing the other two.

Charlotte grabbed a napkin as she put her plate down. "The purple pen was weird. It was also a main clue in a case I solved in middle school, which not a lot of people know about." She looked at Lucy. "Daisy Tremaine?"

"In my defense," Lucy said, ignoring Landon's accusatory gaze, "I . . . completely forgot about that. But I probably pulled it from my subconscious, yeah."

"The delivery guy was also weird," Charlotte said, continuing. "I was suspicious of him at first, but then he said he knew me from my detective days." She wiped her mouth with the napkin. "But he called me 'Charlotte.' Anyone who knew me from back then calls me Lottie. So that was . . . off."

She balled up the napkin and dropped it onto her plate. "I just started having an inkling that the mystery was made up. I realized it would make sense why Landon had Olivia tell me the details, because I can usually tell when he's lying. I almost dropped the theory last night, but when the same delivery guy showed up at the door, with the purple pen . . ." She looked around at the others. "I mean, come on. Did you really think that'd be a tough solve?"

Landon and Lucy looked at each other helplessly.

"It didn't really have to do with the difficulty—" Lucy started.

"We definitely *thought* it was a good enough mystery," Landon grumbled.

"They were just trying to help you," Olivia cut in. "And . . . they missed you."

Now Charlotte was confused. "What?"

Olivia turned to Landon, who sighed. "Well, first of all, you've been really bad at replying to texts lately."

"Maybe not the best way to start," Lucy said gently.

"Well—" Landon ran a hand through his hair, looking frustrated. He raised his shoulders almost to his ears. "You've been really bad at replying to texts—"

"Guess he's sticking with that," Charlotte murmured drily to Lucy.

"And Lucy and I were talking one day, and she mentioned how she hadn't really spoken with you in a while, and I joked that if we had a mystery for you to solve, maybe you'd come visit, and . . ." He dropped his shoulders as he trailed off.

"You could've just *asked* me to come visit," Charlotte said, trying to keep her tone light. "You know, like a normal person."

"Would you have come?" Lucy asked quietly.

Charlotte opened her mouth, then closed it. Then she opened it again. This time, words came out. "And you were trying to help me? How?"

Lucy bit her lip. "You've been . . . kind of . . ." She looked to Landon for assistance, who very helpfully pretended to be interested in the countertop tile.

"I've been what?" Charlotte asked, her tone getting sharper. She immediately felt bad as she saw her friend's face start to crumple. Lucy could easily face down an angry parent complaining that the material she was teaching wasn't appropriate for middle schoolers, but when it came to personal interactions, she was *not* good with confrontation.

"You've been lost," Landon finally said. "And you won't let any of us help you."

Charlotte narrowed her eyes. "I don't need help."

"You do. You think you can handle everything on your own, but you can't. You at least need support, but you won't talk to us, Mom says you won't talk to her about anything serious, you won't even consider trying detective work again—"

"I *knew it,*" Charlotte cut in. She laughed, shaking her head. "It always comes back to that with you guys. Why is it so hard to understand that *I don't do that anymore*—"

"Because it was the last time you were really happy!" Lucy yelled.

Charlotte stopped. "That's . . . dramatic. And not true at all."

"I-I mean," Lucy stammered, "obviously you've been happy since then. But not fully, not . . . consistently." She swallowed. "Ever since you started taking on fewer cases in high school, and then stopped altogether, you've just been different. And that'd be fine, except that we don't think you're happy." She took a shuddering breath as she tried to hold back tears. "But we can't figure out why, or how to help, because you won't talk to us. So . . . so we just . . ."

"So this was all, like, a weird intervention?" Charlotte asked, looking around at them. "You thought that I'd solve the mystery and suddenly feel good about myself, and realize that mystery solving was what I've been missing in my life, and everything would be good again?"

Lucy stayed quiet, knowing that Charlotte wasn't really expecting an answer to that.

"The delivery guy was my coworker Eric," Olivia offered, successfully breaking the silence and not-so-successfully breaking the tension. "We work together, but he also does Scoop deliveries. I asked him to play the part of the creepy secret admirer."

"We planned for you to run into him yesterday to plant the seed of suspicion," Landon added, looking contrite.

Charlotte nodded, staring at the floor. "Yeah, he started to explain himself to me once he realized I had figured it out." She looked at Landon. "Was the coupon thing also part of it, or . . . ?"

"No," Landon mumbled. "That was actually real. I still have one more."

"Please don't be mad!" Lucy burst out.

"I'm trying not to be, because it's a really silly thing to be mad about," Charlotte said. "But I just . . . this is . . ." As she looked around the room, she realized that the feeling that was overwhelming her wasn't anger. It was embarrassment. And shame.

Face reddening, she grabbed another piece of pizza and dropped it onto her plate next to her first unfinished slice. "I think I just . . . need a few minutes." Avoiding eye contact, she walked out of the kitchen and retreated to Dale's room. She shut the door, cutting off the loud whispers that had started up as soon as she was out of sight.

Finding the atmosphere of Dale's room as uncomforting as ever, Charlotte walked to the window. She pulled it open and climbed out onto the fire escape, almost losing her pizza to the sidewalk below when her foot caught on the sill.

As she recovered from the scare of almost losing her pizza and having to sit there, alone, without anything to eat, she heard a car honk down the street. Looking over, she could just make out the back of a car parked around the corner. She heard footsteps on the pavement and saw Eric, the Scoop delivery guy who worked with Olivia, jogging down the sidewalk towards the car. He walked past the trunk and disappeared around the corner.

She heard the pop of a car door as he opened it.

"Glad to—" she heard him say before he closed the door behind him, cutting off the rest of his sentence. A sputtering sound echoed off the buildings as the car slipped past the corner and out of sight.

A few minutes later, the door to Dale's room opened. She silently shifted to the side, giving Lucy room to climb out and sit next to her.

"Did you wait exactly five minutes before coming after me?" Charlotte asked.

"There's not really a universally agreed-upon number when it comes to the definition of 'a few,' " Lucy said, settling down and leaning her back against the brick behind them. "I thought that five was probably good. Also, Landon's being broody, and I had nowhere else to go."

Charlotte snorted.

"I'm sorry," Lucy said gently. "*We're* sorry. We got so caught up in our scheme that we didn't think about how it might make you feel. *Obviously* we knew you'd find out eventually. We just didn't think that far."

Charlotte nodded. "Thanks." She sighed. "I know I've been . . . distant. I can't . . . I can't really explain it."

"That's okay. I understand." Lucy paused. "I mean, I don't really understand, but I'm here for you."

Charlotte chuckled. "Thanks. All of this reminded me that I still need to schedule a session with Helena." She let out another breath, bigger than the last one. "I will say, you guys almost threw me off the scent with the attack. I was almost positive the mystery was made up, but that definitely made me reconsider whether you'd actually—"

"Wait, *what*?" Lucy asked.

"The guy you got to attack me."

Lucy went still. "When did this happen?"

Looking at the expression on her friend's face, Charlotte began to have a sneaking suspicion that Lucy had no idea what she was talking about. "Last night," she said slowly. "After I got off the train. I was walking to Landon's, and a guy in a ski mask grabbed me and told me to stay out of other people's business and . . . that guy wasn't with you."

Lucy shook her head slowly.

Charlotte leaned her head back. "Hmm."

"What do you mean, 'Hmm'?" Lucy asked, panic creeping into her voice. "We have to tell someone about this. We have to tell Landon—"

"No! No, Luce—" Lucy had started to stand to climb back into the apartment, and Charlotte grabbed her arm and pulled her back down. "We can't tell Landon."

"Why not?"

"'Cuz you know how he gets. He'll freak out and call the police or something. And what's that gonna do?" Charlotte was still holding onto Lucy's arm, as if to keep her from diving through the window. Which was a valid concern, considering how the panic in Lucy's eyes only continued to grow as Charlotte spoke.

"It was probably just a misunderstanding, or something," Charlotte said, trying to make it sound like she actually believed that. "Either way, it doesn't matter, because I *am* staying out of other people's business, and I *am* going home soon. So, I don't need to worry about the 'or else.'"

Lucy slowly untensed.

"Okay," she said, as Charlotte released her arm. "Alright. We'll leave it alone."

"We'll leave it alone," Charlotte echoed, watching Lucy cautiously. Then she narrowed her eyes. "You sure he wasn't with you?"

"I think I'd remember asking someone to *attack you*!" Lucy said, incredulous. Then she saw the look on Charlotte's face, which had shifted to a stifled grin. "Oh. You're messing with me."

"I'm messing with you." Charlotte bumped Lucy's shoulder with her own. "I know you were just trying to help me."

Lucy sighed. "Just, you know, talk to us more, when you can." She bumped Charlotte's shoulder back. "Love you."

"I know."

"Say it back."

"Ahluvu," Charlotte mumbled.

"Louder."

"I . . . am going inside," Charlotte said, getting to her feet. "It's getting crowded out here."

"Boooo." Lucy waited until Charlotte had one leg over the sill and her head ducked inside before giving her a push, sending her tumbling through, laughing.

She felt relieved that this was over, even if it was all made up.

Against her better judgment, Charlotte had felt herself starting to get invested in the mystery. It was all for the best that none of it was real. Tomorrow she'd head back to Frencham, and return to her life of . . .

Charlotte realized she couldn't finish that thought. But it didn't really matter, because the next day she found herself at the Highview police station.

Chapter 8

Bathroom Party

True to her word, Lucy didn't tell Landon what Charlotte had said about the attack. The siblings apologized to each other, and Charlotte waved off Olivia's apology, assuring her that she had nothing to be sorry for. Lucy decided to sleep over, and she and Charlotte stayed up half the night talking about Lucy's school horror stories and Charlotte's string of failed dates.

Charlotte woke up the next morning to someone shaking her shoulder.

"Whuuuuut," she mumbled into the pillow.

"It's Landon," Lucy said, sounding just as groggy. She collapsed back onto the bed as Charlotte sat up and rubbed her eyes, finally hearing the knocking on the door.

"Coming," Charlotte groaned. She climbed out of bed and trudged to the door, pulling it open. "What?" she said, squinting at her brother. "It's too early for a wake-up call."

"It's eleven-thirty."

"Okay? And?"

"Olivia just called from the office," he said, his face serious.

"Apparently, Eric missed a meeting last night. He isn't at work this morning, and he's not answering his phone."

Charlotte willed her brain to work faster as she processed this information. *Eric was the Scoop delivery driver who also worked with Olivia. Eric was at Landon's apartment last night.*

"It hasn't been that long," Charlotte said, rubbing her eyes again. "Seems a little early to panic."

"I thought the same thing. But after what happened to that other Scoop delivery guy, some people from the union committee want to go to the police."

A delivery person from Scoop was murdered recently. Eric missed a meeting last night, wasn't at work this morning, and isn't answering his phone. Eric got picked up by a car.

"Eric got picked up by a car," Charlotte said. "Last night. I was out on the fire escape, and I saw a car pick him up."

Landon's eyes widened.

Two hours later, Charlotte was walking out of the Highview police station.

"What'd you tell them?" Landon asked, standing up from the bench where he had been sitting with Olivia and Lucy.

"Not much more than you, probably," Charlotte said, walking over to them. "I didn't get a good look at the car he rode away in." She narrowed her eyes thoughtfully. "They kept offering me car brands, as if that would help. I said it might've been a Jeep. Honestly, I can't tell the difference between a Kia and a Kenmore."

"Well, one of those is a refrigerator brand," Lucy said, staring at her. "So . . ."

Olivia wrapped her arms around herself. "It didn't sound like they're too concerned right now. I guess since it hasn't been very long." Her brow had been furrowed since they picked her up at the train station. She had been at work, but Eric lived in Highview, so she took the train back to join the others in telling the police what little they knew.

"It's just not like Eric to not show up to work without saying anything," Olivia continued, shaking her head. "And it's even more strange that he wouldn't show up for the union committee meeting."

Charlotte cocked her head. "It was a union meeting?"

Olivia nodded. "Eric's our graphic designer, but he does Scoop deliveries on the side." Her expression briefly shifted from worry to annoyance. "He has to work two different jobs for the same company to make a decent wage. So yeah, he's very involved in working to unionize the Scoop deliverers."

"Now *that's* interesting," Charlotte mused.

"You think this is related to Bernard's murder," Olivia said, reading her face. "Right? That's what I said to the cop, but she just told me not to worry about it."

Charlotte hesitated. "I mean . . . maybe."

"Oh god." Olivia let out a long breath. Landon wrapped an arm around her shoulders as Charlotte quickly continued.

"I wouldn't jump to conclusions," she said. "Even if it is connected, that could still mean anything. Maybe he got threatened and left town for a bit."

"Or maybe it's not related at all, and he just thought today was Saturday," Landon added. "What?" he asked, reacting to a sideways look from Charlotte. "I've done that."

"And he turned off his phone for the weekend?" Charlotte asked.

"Some people like to unplug!"

"His roommate said he's not home."

Landon paused at that. "Maybe he . . . went on a weekend retreat." He looked at Olivia, who had fallen deep into thought. "Hey. We've done everything we can. Best we can do now is wait."

"Or you can look into it." Olivia suddenly turned to Charlotte. "You could find him."

Charlotte hesitated. "We don't even know for sure that he's really missing," she finally said, as gently as she could.

"But you think he is. You think this is connected to Bernard's murder."

Again, Charlotte paused, looking over at Lucy for backup.

Lucy raised an eyebrow. "You do, right?"

Charlotte let out a long breath. "If Eric really is missing, having these things happen to two Scoop delivery people so close to each other is—"

"Probably not a coincidence," Lucy finished for her. Charlotte nodded.

"So will you do it?" Olivia asked. "Look into it?"

Charlotte gave Landon a helpless look. "Mom said no murders."

Growing up, Charlotte and Landon's mother had always been supportive of her children's endeavors, doing things like driving Landon to the mall to pick up a new video game, or driving Charlotte to the same mall to interview the jewelry store clerk about a recent diamond theft.

Her main rule for both: no murders. Which was mainly targeted at Charlotte, but also heavily limited the kinds of video games Landon was allowed to play. For Charlotte, at least, it meant steering clear of almost any mystery involving a dead body.

Olivia looked at Landon, who, to his credit, did a good job at not looking like someone stuck between a rock and a hard place. He thought for a moment.

"Well," he said slowly, ". . . as far as we know, Eric's case has nothing to do with a murder. And if it eventually turns out to be connected to Bernard . . ." He trailed off.

"You're twenty-five," Lucy said flatly.

"Yes," Landon said quickly, pointing at Lucy. "That. You're an adult, and Mom knows that." He cleared his throat. "But also don't tell her I said that, or that I was even present for this conversation."

"Please?" Olivia asked Charlotte, pleading.

There was that feeling again. She wanted to take the case. She wanted to help. But more than anything, she wanted to be confident that she could do it. And as Charlotte considered this, she realized that she wasn't. She just wasn't.

"I'm sorry," she finally said. "I really wish I could help. I just don't think there's anything I can do, and I don't want to get your hopes up."

"You wouldn't be," Olivia said quickly. "If you can't find anything, it's fine. Really."

Charlotte shook her head. "I just . . . don't think it's a good idea."

Olivia nodded, deflating a bit. "Okay. I understand."

Charlotte chewed on the inside of her cheek as they began walking back to Landon's car. She stopped when she realized Lucy wasn't following, and turned to see her giving Charlotte an admonishing stare.

Knowing what was coming and feeling indignant about it, Charlotte steeled herself as she raised her eyebrows. "What?"

Lucy crossed her arms.

"What?"

Lucy shook her head.

"This question might come as a surprise to you, but: *What*?"

Lucy let out a long, heavy sigh, and looked away.

"Okay, if you're not gonna say anything, I'm going back to the car." Charlotte turned and began walking again.

"You're being ridiculous," Lucy said, trailing after her.

"*I'm* being ridiculous?" Charlotte threw over her shoulder as she continued walking away from the station. "I'm not the one talking in crossed arms and dramatic sighs."

"You need to take that case." Lucy sped up to walk next to her.

"Why?"

"Olivia's asking you for help, and you know you can help her."

"I *don't* know that."

"Well, *I* know you can."

"No, you don't!" Charlotte stopped walking, and Lucy swung around to face her.

"If Olivia called you with a flat tire," Lucy said, "you would go help her change it."

"No, I'd tell her to call Triple-A. You think I know how to change a tire?"

Lucy paused. "Okay, bad example." She huffed with frustration. "My point is, in any situation, any way you could help, you would. And we both know that even if you can't solve this mystery—even if there isn't a mystery to solve—just agreeing to help would be help in itself. And you're not the kind of person to turn down helping someone."

Lucy raised her eyebrows; Charlotte narrowed her eyes. Lucy cocked her head; Charlotte let out a long stream of air through her nose. And with that, Lucy knew she had won.

"Are you guys good?" Landon called.

Charlotte and Lucy began walking the rest of the way to the car.

"We're good," Lucy said when they arrived, opening the door to the back seat. "Charlotte's going to take the case."

"Really?" Olivia asked from the passenger seat, her eyes lighting up.

Landon raised his eyebrows as Lucy climbed into the car. "Are you actually?"

Charlotte threw her head back and let out a loud groan. She stood like that for a moment, then dropped her chin back down. "Yeah."

Landon's face broke out into a grin. "That's awesome." His smile dimmed briefly. "Maybe, um . . . maybe we don't tell Mom about it right away?"

"Yeah, that's a good call," Charlotte said, walking past him and around the car.

"Or maybe never," Landon proposed, settling into the driver's seat. He started the car as Charlotte climbed in. "Maybe . . . maybe we never tell her."

Charlotte and Landon dropped Olivia and Lucy off at the train station. Olivia was returning to work for a few more hours, and Lucy said she had to go home to see how many dishes Jake managed to pile into the sink while she was gone for one night.

First, though, she made Charlotte swear on her dead pet rabbit that she would keep Lucy updated on the case. Charlotte argued that there was no reason to bring Rusty's soul into this, but Lucy refused to leave the back seat of Landon's car until Charlotte relented, swearing on the deceased rabbit that she would keep her updated.

The short car ride back to the apartment was silent. It wasn't until Landon parked the car that he said, "You don't have to do this, you know."

"Pfft. Doesn't really feel like I have a choice."

"No, I mean . . ." Landon tapped his fingers on the steering wheel, staring straight ahead. "I know we've all been pressuring you back into this. But only because we think it . . . it could be good for you."

"I know," Charlotte said, unbuckling her seat belt. "It's fine. I'll probably just poke around for a day, and then Eric will show up tomorrow from his accidental phoneless weekend retreat that he didn't tell his roommate about."

"Right," Landon said, not sounding convinced by his own theory.

The siblings went back up to the apartment. Landon disappeared into his room to do some work, and Charlotte poured herself a glass of water before heading for the living room.

Settling onto the couch, she pulled out her phone. Upon request, Olivia had sent her Eric's roommate's number, which Eric had given to her "in case of emergency." Figuring this qualified as an emergency, she called it.

Voice mail.

"Hi, my name's Charlotte. I'm friends with Olivia Kimura. We're just trying to figure out where Eric might be and wanted to know if you could answer a couple questions. Call me back when you get the chance, thanks."

A minute later, she got a call.

"Hello?"

"Hey, this is Ajay."

"Hi, thanks for calling back."

"This is about Eric, right? I didn't listen to the full message."

"Right." Charlotte pulled her feet up onto the couch to sit cross-legged. "Olivia said you hadn't seen him this morning?"

"Yeah, but that's not weird. He usually leaves for work before I get up."

"When was the last time you saw him?"

"Hmm." There was a pause on the line. "Yesterday morning, I think? I heard him come in last night, but I didn't see him. He sounded like he was in a bad mood, so I just left him alone."

"What time was that?"

"Mmm . . . a little before eleven, I think."

"And you didn't hear him leave at any point?"

"No."

Charlotte paused for a second, feeling dizzy from how quickly the questions were coming out of her. Like riding a bike. "What made you think he was in a bad mood?"

"I said 'hey' from my room when I heard him come in, and he kind of just grunted at me. We're not super close, but he's a friendly guy. Usually says 'hey' back, at least."

"Do you know why he might've been in a bad mood?"

"No idea."

"So you don't know if he had any vacation plans or anything?"

"No, but he probably would've told me if he did. He asks me to water his plants when he's gonna be gone for more than a couple days."

Charlotte thought for a moment. "Any family in the area?"

"Nah, not that I know of."

"Was he seeing anyone?"

There was a pause. "Yeah . . . I think so. He sometimes stays at their place, but he's not usually gone for more than two nights in a row."

"Okay. Um . . ." Charlotte drew out the *um* as long as she

could to give herself time to think of anything else to ask. Coming up empty (and rapidly running out of breath), she said, "Thanks for your time. Can you let me know if you think of something else that might help us figure out where he is? Or if you hear from him?"

"Sure, you got it."

Saying goodbye, Charlotte hung up. What next, what next . . . ?

The metaphorical bike she had so deftly climbed back onto began to wobble. What was she thinking, letting Lucy talk her into this? She had no idea what she was doing. She was an idiot for previously showing Olivia her little observation trick, making her think she was still . . . that she was anything like . . .

Charlotte groaned, letting herself flop sideways onto the couch. She eyed her phone, which she had set down on the coffee table. One text and this would all be over. *Hey Olivia, so sorry, my mom needs me home, I have to leave.* Wait. Two texts. *Hey Lucy, so sorry, my mom needs me home, I have to leave.* Three texts. *Hey Mom, if anyone asks, tell them you said you needed me home so I had to leave.* Three texts, and this would be all over.

She sat back up and picked up her phone, unlocking it. *Hey Olivia . . .* she began.

Then she stopped. *Might as well do a little research into Scoop first. Just in case the company had something to do with Eric's disappearance.* Not that she was necessarily going to stay on the case, but maybe she could give Olivia some information to work with before she went home.

A little while later, Landon's door opened. "Hey," he said, sticking his head into the living room. "Olivia said her coworker suggested the development team go out for drinks after work. To 'boost morale.' "

Charlotte looked up from her phone. "A good excuse as any to get drunk, I guess."

"She said we're invited." He shrugged. "Could be a good chance for you to talk to some people, gather some intel."

"Ew. Don't say 'intel.' " Charlotte thought for a moment. *Might as well go get a drink. Talk with whoever's there.* If she did learn anything, she could just let Olivia know before leaving.

Charlotte twisted in her seat to look over the back of the couch. "Sure, I'm in."

"It's at this place in the city. We can leave around five."

Might as well hang out with Lucy one more time before leaving. "I'll tell Lucy."

"You better," Landon said, heading for his room. "You promised to keep her in the loop about the case. Rusty's soul is on the line."

He didn't know Charlotte wasn't on the case anymore. She decided not to tell him yet.

The train into the city was packed with people going in to see shows, have dinner, or investigate a missing person. Maybe the last one was only specific to Charlotte (or not, since she wasn't on the case anymore). Regardless, she and Landon had to stand, leaning against the walls for balance, as the train made its way to Penn Station.

Olivia was already there when they arrived, sitting at the end of a long table with a couple of other people. Above their heads, across the entire ceiling, dangled dozens of bare lightbulbs, casting a yellow glow on the large room. The tables were made of dark wood, and the chairs and booths were all padded with dark, faux leather. The bar sat along one side of the room, made of the same dark wood as the tables, with shelves of expensive-looking alcohol behind it.

Charlotte glanced over at her brother, who was tugging at the collar of the short-sleeved blue button-down he'd changed into before they left. She knew that, as outgoing as Landon could be, he could get a little shy in unfamiliar group settings. But this seemed different.

"Are you *nervous?*" she asked.

"No. What? No."

"You're acting nervous."

He hesitated for a moment, then said, "I've never met Olivia's coworkers before."

"Oh." Charlotte thought for a moment. "So?"

Landon spread his hands, indicating that he felt his reasoning for being nervous was obvious enough. "*So* . . . I want to make a good impression."

Charlotte's brow furrowed. "Why? You're not trying to get a job there."

Landon rolled his eyes. "Come on." He shoved his hands into his pockets and headed towards Olivia and her coworkers. Charlotte followed.

"Hey!" Olivia looked up and smiled as they reached the table. She was sitting with two other people, whom Charlotte quickly surveyed.

The woman: early thirties; White; straight, long, dark-blond hair. The man: early forties, White, light brown hair, stubbly beard with traces of gray.

The woman smiled at Landon as he sat down next to Olivia. "So *this* is the famous Landon," she said.

Charlotte bit back a grin as she took the chair next to Landon. Between the two of them, her brother was definitely less accustomed to being referred to as "famous," and it showed by the blush that crept up his neck.

Olivia quickly clocked Landon's shyness and jumped in. "Landon, this is Arielle and Jensen. And this is Landon's sister, Charlotte."

Charlotte put up a hand in an awkward greeting as Arielle shifted her gaze from one Illes sibling to the other.

"You're the detective, right?" Arielle asked, her tone intrigued. Charlotte saw Landon's shoulders relax once the attention moved off of him.

"Used to be," Charlotte said lightly, smiling. "When I was a kid. I don't really do that anymore."

"Still, that's very cool," Arielle said. "A little child detective—so cute."

"Why'd you stop?" Jensen, whom Charlotte remembered Olivia saying was her manager, took a sip of his drink. He had a sort of arrogance about him that made Charlotte have to actively keep herself from scowling when he spoke.

"Just wanted to try other things," Charlotte said, shrugging. She leaned her forearms against the table. "Are you currently in the career you thought you'd be in when you grew up?"

Jensen laughed. "Absolutely not. I thought I was going to be a firefighter."

"I wanted to be a marine biologist," Arielle chimed in. "I just really liked dolphins."

"What about you, Kimura?" Jensen asked Olivia. Charlotte looked over and could tell that Olivia had a similar issue with controlling her expression when Jensen spoke to her.

"I don't really remember," Olivia said. "I've always been into computers. Maybe I thought I'd build them."

"Landon, you're in video game development, right?" Arielle asked. "Did you always want to do that?"

Charlotte tuned out as Landon started talking for the first time since they sat down, and took the opportunity to check her phone to see if Lucy was on the way. There was a text from her from five minutes before:

Lucy: Apologies in advance
Charlotte: why

A couple of minutes later, Charlotte glanced up in time to see Lucy walking through the open door of the bar. And behind her was . . . Jake.

Ugh.

Jake Pierson: late twenties, White, tall, and broad-shouldered, dark brown hair parted to one side, hazel eyes that scanned the bar like he was appraising it. Apparently finding it suitable enough for his tastes, he followed Lucy inside.

"*Sorry*," Lucy mouthed to Charlotte as she and Jake approached the table.

Landon was still answering a seemingly unending string of questions from Arielle, but looked relieved when he caught sight of Lucy and Jake (a feeling Charlotte had often experienced with seeing Lucy, never with Jake).

"Hey!" he said as the couple walked up to the table.

Charlotte gestured to Lucy, addressing Arielle and Jensen. "This is my friend, Jennifer Aniston."

"Lucy," Lucy corrected, giving the group a wave.

Charlotte pointed at Jake. "That's Jake."

Arielle and Jensen introduced themselves, then Jake clapped his hands and rubbed them together. "Alright, alright," he said, looking at Lucy, "what're we drinking?"

"I'm good for now," Lucy said, sliding into the seat next to Charlotte.

"Okay, no prob." He pointed at Charlotte. "Lottie? What're you feeling?"

"A lot of emotions, *Jakey*," Charlotte said drily. "Oh, to drink. Gin and tonic."

Jake chuckled. He was either oblivious to Charlotte's contempt, or so used to it by that point that he just assumed it was an ongoing joke they shared. "You got it."

He took Landon's drink order, then headed for the bar.

"He's *cute*," Arielle said to Lucy.

Lucy let out the polite laugh of someone who heard that a lot and still never really knew how to respond. "Thanks."

Getting nothing else, Arielle turned her attention back to Landon as Charlotte leaned over.

"*Why*?"

"I'm *sorry*," Lucy said quietly, glancing over at the bar where Jake was standing. "I told him I was meeting you and some other people for drinks, but I didn't think he'd ask to come. I just assumed he'd be going out with his friends again."

"Well, actually," Charlotte said, pulling out her phone, "as much as I hate to defend the guy, he might be telling the truth about 'his boys.'" She pulled up her Instagram messages, tapped one open, and handed her phone to Lucy.

Lucy looked at the screen. "What am I looking at?"

Charlotte rested her cheek on her fist and leaned an elbow against the table, keeping her voice low. "I asked this woman who catches people cheating on their partners if she'd do a loyalty test on Jake."

"You *what*?" Lucy hissed.

"You asked me to look into it!"

"Actually, the agreement was that I wouldn't get mad at you if you happened to look into it."

"Okay, so . . . stop being mad!"

Lucy let out a breath. "I'm not mad. I—"

"Before you say, 'I'm just disappointed,'" Charlotte cut in, "would you just look at the screenshot she sent me?"

"I thought you'd, I don't know, do the kind of detective stuff you used to do," Lucy finished. "I just didn't expect this."

Charlotte dropped her arm and sat back in her chair. "Yeah, well, if I had the resources I have available to me now when I was ten, I would've done a lot of things differently back then. At the very least, I wouldn't have had to use so many pay phones. Can you look at the screenshot before your boyfriend comes back, please?"

Lucy quietly read the screenshot of the exchange between the woman and Jake. She had opened with a flirtatious message, and he quickly and politely shut her down, telling her that he had a girlfriend. She tried to continue the conversation, but he declined again, then stopped replying.

Charlotte studied Lucy's expression as she was handed back her phone. "If you're worried about her posting this or something, she said that it wouldn't be 'good content,' so—"

"No, I'm not worried. And I'm not mad." She gave Charlotte a weak smile. "Thanks for looking into it."

"I can keep digging, if you want," Charlotte offered, her tone gentle. "I mean, not that I necessarily think I'll find anything, but . . ."

As much as Charlotte disliked Jake, she didn't actually believe he was dumb enough to cheat on Lucy. Cocky? Sure. Self-absorbed? Absolutely. Mildly misogynistic at times? You bet. But would he actually cheat on the woman who spent the majority of her junior year of college helping him study for the LSAT, and then managed to organize his entire fraternity to throw him a huge party when he passed? It'd be a new low for him.

But Lucy nodded. "Yes, please," she said quietly.

Charlotte stared at her for another moment, but before she could say anything else, Jake returned with a tray of drinks.

"Okay, rum and Coke for my dude," Jake said, depositing the glass in front of Landon.

"*My dude*," Charlotte mouthed at Landon, smirking. She stopped to gape at the drink Jake placed in front of her.

"French 75 for Lottie," Jake said. "Thought you'd like that better than a gin and tonic. It's got gin and champagne, and—"

"I know what a French 75 is," Charlotte said flatly.

"Alright!" he said, once again painfully oblivious to her tone. "And, Luce, I got you a martini."

"Oh," Lucy said as he put the martini down in front of her. "I said I didn't want anything."

"Yeah, but I figured you'd change your mind." Jake sat down and took a sip from his glass. "You like martinis, right?"

"Sure," Lucy said, unconvincingly to most but not to Jake, who grinned and turned to Jensen. "How's it going?" he asked, extending a hand. "Jake."

As the two men shook hands, Charlotte quietly switched her and Lucy's drinks, and took a big gulp of the martini.

Ten minutes later, Charlotte grabbed her empty glass and followed Jensen to the bar as he went for a refill.

"Hey," she said, walking up to stand next to him, "it's really great how you take the time to support your coworkers like this."

Jensen looked sideways at her. "Well, I'm their manager. Gotta keep morale up, and all that."

"Absolutely." Charlotte leaned a forearm against the bar. "Olivia told me a little about what's been going on. It must be tough being in a leadership position with everything that's happening."

Jensen shrugged. "Not really. Just have to keep everyone on track. When rumors start flying and different stories are going around, it's important to make sure everyone stays focused on their work."

Charlotte nodded as the bartender brought his drink over. "For sure, for sure." She returned her empty glass and ordered a gin and tonic, then quickly started talking again before he could take his drink back to the table.

"You don't think there's any truth in any of the rumors, do you? About Bernard?" she asked.

Jensen raised an eyebrow. "You mean the ones implicating the company in his death?" he asked, a subtle laugh in his voice. "No, believe it or not, I don't think there's any truth to that."

"Why not?"

He took a sip of his drink. "Because it's an absurd idea. You know what I think?"

"What?"

He leaned in conspiratorially, lowering his voice. Charlotte tensed every muscle she could to keep herself from leaning away from him. "I think the rumors were started by the union folks. To put pressure on Scoop to give in to their demands. In fact, if Bernard's death really was a murder, it was probably one of the union people trying to pin it on the company."

Charlotte's eyebrows shot up. "That's a bold claim."

Jensen scoffed. "No bolder than the claims they're making about Candice—Ms. Watts," he corrected himself.

"That's your CEO, right?"

"Yup. It's a shame to see what she's having to deal with. All this union bullshit." He took another sip of his drink as the bartender brought over Charlotte's gin and tonic.

"So you're not a fan of the delivery people unionizing," Charlotte said as she paid for her drink.

Jensen shook his head. "It's counterproductive," he said. "I understand that maybe they'd like for things to be a little different, but a union's only going to drive a wedge between them and the company. It won't fix anything."

"Does everyone else in the office agree with you?"

"Well, Eric doesn't, of course. He's one of the main organizers, apparently. And Kimura's been pretty vocal about her support for them." He thought for a moment. "Not sure where Martin stands, but that guy doesn't talk much about anything."

Charlotte's brow furrowed. "Martin?"

"Another member of the team. He didn't want to come for drinks; said he had to go to the mechanic or the dentist or something."

Charlotte realized Jensen might've been drunker than she thought if he couldn't differentiate between a mechanic and a dentist. Either that, or he was just a really bad listener. Or both.

"He's not really one for socializing, anyway," Jensen added, before taking another sip.

Tucking away that info for later, Charlotte glanced across the bar at their table. Jake's voice, always a few decibels too loud, carried across the room as he told a story that was making Lucy's face twist with embarrassment.

"What about Arielle?" Charlotte asked, her gaze landing on the woman sitting next to Olivia. She was laughing, fully engaged in Jake's story. "How does she feel about the union?"

"Hmm," Jensen said. "Not sure. I'd assume she's against it, just because she's good friends with Candice."

"Really?"

"Yup."

Realizing he wasn't going to elaborate on that statement, Charlotte shifted gears. "Do you know Eric well?"

Jensen shrugged modestly. "Pretty well. As a manager, I like to be a friendly ear to everyone in the office."

"Did he have any enemies?"

Jensen laughed so loud that Lucy looked over at them from the table. Charlotte was impressed that any external sound could manage to break through Jake's booming monologue.

"I thought you said you weren't a detective anymore," Jensen said, still chuckling. "Am I being interrogated now?"

"No, I just—"

"How'd you even interrogate people as a kid? Did you threaten them with your imaginary pet unicorn if they didn't tell you what you wanted to know?" He laughed again at the mental image he had painted for himself.

"No, no unicorn. I was pretty good at getting what I needed without threatening people." Charlotte picked up her glass and took a sip.

Jensen's eye twitched. Then he snorted. "I'm sure the puppy-dog eyes got you far."

Charlotte resisted the urge to roll her distinctly un-puppylike eyes. "Did he have any issues with anyone?" she pressed. "Someone he might've complained about?"

Yet another chuckle from Jensen, with an expression on his face that clearly read, *Okay, I'll humor you.* "Nah. Eric's friendly with everyone in the office." He held up a finger, like he just remembered something. "I did hear him complaining to Kimura about someone who's a part of the union business." He snapped his fingers. "Finn."

"What was he saying about Finn?" Charlotte asked.

Jensen shook his head. "Don't remember. Kimura would know."

Charlotte remembered Eric's roommate mentioning a possible romantic partner. "Do you know if Eric's dating anyone?"

Jensen nodded. "He's vaguely mentioned her a few times.

Pretty private about it." He snickered. "I've always just assumed she's not very blessed in the looks department, if you know what I mean."

Charlotte made her face go blank. *Did he really just say that?* "What d'you mean?"

"You know . . . not really the kind of girl he's eager to show off." He looked at Charlotte, waiting for what he was saying to sink in.

Okay, he's really saying that.

Determined to keep him waiting, she tilted her head questioningly. "What?"

His laughter was a little more uneasy this time. "I'm saying, I think the reason why he doesn't talk about her much is because she's . . . well, ugly."

"Ohhh." Charlotte nodded. "You're saying that you think the most likely reason a person wouldn't be comfortable opening up with *you* about their romantic partner is because they might be concerned that you'd judge them for their looks."

Jensen paused as he tried to process what she just said, clearly not expecting such an outpouring of words.

"But you'd never do something like that," Charlotte added, a touch of sarcasm creeping in.

". . . Right," Jensen said, still struggling to catch up.

She took his floundering as an opportunity to throw another question at him. "Where were you last night?"

Jensen took a long sip from his drink. "Home," he finally said, putting the glass back down on the bar. "And yes, Your Honor, I have witnesses."

Charlotte picked up her glass. "Well, thanks for chatting with me," she said. She turned away from Jensen and returned to the table.

Olivia's other coworker proved more difficult to get alone. Charlotte was about to throw in the towel when Arielle pushed back her chair and said, "Be right back—gotta use the ladies' room."

"I'll come with," Charlotte said, maybe a little too quickly and a little too excitedly, as she pushed her chair back and stood. Arielle didn't seem put off by Charlotte's extreme enthusiasm (or maybe she felt it was just the right amount of enthusiasm to have about going to the bathroom with someone). The two started towards the back.

"I love this bar," Arielle said, her voice slurring a bit. She only had about one and a half drinks since Charlotte had arrived, but it seemed like she might've started earlier than that.

Charlotte pulled the bathroom door open for her, relieved to see that there were stalls. She hadn't been excited about the idea of conducting an interview through the closed door of a single-person restroom.

She was about to follow Arielle inside when Lucy appeared from behind. "Realized I have to pee," she said, passing Charlotte and walking into the bathroom. "I also didn't wanna miss the *party*!"

"Woooo!" Arielle cheered. "Bathroom party!" She disappeared into a stall, and Lucy turned to look at Charlotte, who was still standing in the doorway.

"*Bathroom party!*" Lucy mouthed, making her hands into fists and shaking them with excitement. She went into her own stall, and Charlotte crossed the bathroom to wash her hands.

She found herself hesitating as she stopped by the sink. It was one thing to talk to Jensen without anyone else listening. Having Lucy there made it feel more like she was conducting an actual investigation. Which she wasn't.

We're already here; might as well say something.

"So, Arielle." She waved her hand by the sink's sensor to activate the motion detector. "How do you like working at Scoop?"

Charlotte frowned as no water came out of the sink, and waved her hand again as Arielle responded.

"It's so great," she called from her stall. "I love the work, and the people I work with. I feel like we're growing something really special."

"That's awesome," Charlotte called back, tapping on the sink's sensor as it continued to refuse her water. "It's great to like the people you work with. Lucy's been having a rough time with people at her work."

"Yeah," Lucy chimed in from her stall. "I'm jealous; I don't have any friends at my job. Just a bunch of rich seventh graders who'd hunt me for sport if given the opportunity."

"Oh no!" Arielle whined sympathetically. "That sucks."

Charlotte moved over to the second sink and waved her hand in front of its sensor. Nothing. "Jensen actually told me you're friends with Candice. Must be nice, being friends with the boss."

Arielle was quiet for a moment, and Charlotte wondered if she'd heard her.

"Yeah, Candice and I are friends," Arielle finally said, her voice a few degrees cooler than before. "I try to keep work and my personal life separate, though. I don't get special treatment or anything."

"Oh, of course," Charlotte said quickly. "I wasn't implying that you did. I just meant, it's cool to have such a successful friend. You must be proud of her."

"Absolutely," Arielle replied, her voice brightening again. "Lucy? Could you pass me some toilet paper? I don't have any."

"Sure, here." Lucy passed Arielle a wad of toilet paper from under their dividing wall as Charlotte tried tapping the sensor on the second sink again. Still nothing.

Two toilets flushed, almost in unison, and Arielle and Lucy emerged from their stalls and headed for the sinks.

"I don't think the sinks are wo—" Charlotte started, then stopped as the other two women stuck their hands under the sinks and were immediately rewarded with streams of water.

". . . Huh."

"What's up?" Lucy asked, looking at her.

"Nothing. Arielle, what do you think about the delivery people trying to unionize? I was just talking to Jensen about it."

"Oh, I don't wanna talk about that silly stuff," Arielle said, getting a pump of soap from the automatic dispenser that Charlotte knew for sure wouldn't have worked for her if she had attempted to use it.

"So you think it's silly," Charlotte pressed.

"'Course. I mean, I don't really understand it all, but Candice explained it to me. It's just going to complicate things." She finished scrubbing her hands with soap and held them under the sink. Charlotte felt a pang of indignation as the sink turned on again. "They'll be making their lives harder by doing it, did you know that?"

"How so?"

Arielle paused. "Well, just . . . oh, I don't know, but it made sense when Candice explained it, even with Jaya arguing with her."

"Jaya?" Lucy asked, waving her hand under the automatic paper towel dispenser. Charlotte scowled at the machine as it obediently spit out a sheet of paper, which Lucy ripped off and handed to Arielle.

Arielle accepted the paper towel and began drying her hands. "Jaya was the head of our team before Jensen. We all went to college together, and Candice hired Jaya and me when she started the company. But when the delivery workers started talking about unionizing, Jaya supported them, and she and Candice kept fighting about it." Arielle threw her paper towel at the garbage can—at least, that's what Charlotte assumed she was trying to do, as she watched the ball of paper land a good four feet away from the receptacle.

"Then Jaya left," Arielle continued, not noticing Lucy going to pick up her rogue paper towel ball. "Not sure if it was because of the union stuff; it all happened really fast, and she didn't say much to me before she left. I think she was mad at me for siding with Candice." She shrugged. "I haven't talked to her since. Candice doesn't like to talk about it, either."

"When was this?" Lucy asked, opting for an easy dunk as she dropped the paper towel into the can.

Arielle thought for a moment. "Five months ago? Four months ago. God, I'm drunk." She laughed. "Four months ago, I think."

"Hey," Charlotte said quickly, sensing that Arielle was about to suggest they leave the bathroom. "Where were you last night?"

Arielle squinted at her. "Why?"

"Just something I'm asking everyone."

"I was out with my friends. It was Tequila Tuesday." Arielle suddenly seemed defensive. "I don't know what happened to Eric. I know you're just, like, doing your job, but if I knew anything I'd tell you."

"She's just trying to gather information," Lucy said soothingly. "You're not being accused of anything."

"Do you know anything about his girlfriend?" Charlotte asked, changing the subject.

Arielle's eyes went wide, the defensiveness melting away. "No, do *you*?" She turned to Lucy. "He's so private about his love life; I don't know anything about it."

"No, Jensen just mentioned a girlfriend. Thought you might know more."

Arielle shook her head. "Nope. Let me know if you find out anything, though; I'm curious." Her expression sobered. "And, would you let me know if you find out anything more about Eric in general? I'm . . . I'm worried about him."

Her eyes started welling up, and she looked away from them, blinking rapidly. "Sorry," she said, her voice cracking slightly.

Lucy put an arm around her shoulder. "Hey, hey, don't worry about it. I'm sure he's fine. Charlotte's going to find him."

"Luce," Charlotte said, her voice cutting through Lucy's gentle words.

Lucy gave her a *What?* look as Arielle fanned her face.

"I'm fine, I'm fine," she said. "Woo. I think I need some water."

The three of them left the bathroom, Charlotte shooting one last glare at the automatic sinks as they exited. Then, as Arielle continued back to their table, she grabbed Lucy's arm.

"You can't just tell people everything's going to be fine," Charlotte said in a low voice. "Especially when you're putting the responsibility on *me* to make things fine."

"I was just trying to comfort her," Lucy said defensively.

Charlotte released Lucy's arm. "It's not helpful to give her false hope. I'm not trying to be pessimistic here, but if Eric's disappearance is connected to Bernard's murder, things aren't looking good for Eric."

"Well, I don't think there's any harm in a little bit of hope," Lucy said, continuing back to their table.

"God, what Disney movie did you fall out of?" Charlotte grumbled before following.

Drinks wrapped up soon after, much to the relief of both Charlotte and her growling stomach. Arielle was the first to leave, with Jensen bidding the group farewell soon after. The remaining five made their way out of the bar.

Jake pulled out his phone to order a car, and Charlotte held up a finger to Landon and Olivia as she pulled Lucy out of earshot down the sidewalk. Landon narrowed his eyes at them as they walked away, but didn't follow.

"What's up?" Lucy asked.

Charlotte quickly filled her in on her conversation with Jensen.

"Sounds like there's a bunch of people who aren't happy with the idea of the union," Lucy said when she finished. "Jensen's clearly against it, and Arielle seemed like she was on Candice's side, although she didn't sound like she really knew what she was talking about." She shook her head. "But is that motive enough for *murder*? And whatever might've happened to Eric?"

"Only if they had enough to lose," Charlotte said. "Which could be any number of people. I'm sure a bunch of people have a stake in this company. If any of them believed a union could somehow lose them money . . ."

"But how will you track all those people down?" Lucy asked.

Charlotte shrugged. "I can't. I'm just gonna focus on Eric right now, see what comes from that."

Lucy nodded. "So what's next?"

Charlotte looked over Lucy's shoulder to see Jake walk back over to Landon and Olivia, looking curiously over at them as he did so.

"Jensen said Eric would complain to Olivia about someone named Finn, who was also a part of the union," Charlotte said. "I'm going to see what Olivia knows about Finn. And I want to talk to anyone else in the office who might know something about Eric."

"What about the girlfriend?" Lucy asked.

"I'll see if Olivia knows anything about her, but it seems like he was pretty private about that. I'm not sure Olivia will know any more than the others." Charlotte hesitated, debating whether to share this last piece of information. This was the real reason why she had pulled Lucy away from Landon and Olivia. "There's one more thing."

"Luce!" Jake called as their car pulled up to the curb.

"Coming!" Lucy called over her shoulder. She turned back to Charlotte. "Text me, okay?"

"Okay." She followed Lucy back to the others, where farewells were exchanged before Lucy and Jake climbed into the car and left.

It wasn't until they had begun walking to the train station that Charlotte remembered she had decided she wasn't on the case anymore. *Damn.*

Chapter 9

Take Your Boyfriend's Adult Sister to Work Day

Landon really was a disgusting eater.

Charlotte gawked at her brother with mild disgust as he continued to shove half a meatball parm into his mouth. Olivia sat next to him, unwrapping her sandwich, seemingly unfazed by the speed at which Landon's sandwich was disappearing down his throat (or the noises that accompanied the phenomenon).

Agreeing that they were all tired of pizza, the three of them had gotten takeout from a sandwich shop, then landed a coveted four-seater on the train back to Highview.

Charlotte's sandwich sat in her lap, the growling in her stomach quickly quieting at the sight of her brother devouring half of his sandwich in thirty seconds. Instead, she looked over at Olivia.

"How many of your coworkers knew I was in town before today?" she asked, trying to make her tone as conversational as possible. "And that I'm . . . that I used to be a detective?"

Olivia thought for a moment, continuing to unwrap her sandwich. "Just Eric," she said. "Arielle might've heard us talking about it. It's a pretty small space, so anyone could've overheard."

"Including Jensen?"

"Maybe. Why?"

"Just curious." Charlotte quickly moved on. "Do you know someone named Finn?"

Olivia blinked, then laughed. "You really did some sleuthing in there. Damn." She shook her head in disbelief, then pivoted to nodding. "Yeah, they're on the organizing committee with Eric."

"Has Eric complained about Finn at all?"

"Oh, a bunch of times." Olivia peeled back the wrapper on her sandwich, picking up a runaway piece of lettuce as it dropped onto her lap. "Finn and Eric would butt heads about what exactly the union should be asking for from Scoop. Eric felt like Finn wanted them to ask for too much, and Finn would tell Eric that he wasn't demanding enough." She suddenly froze. "But . . . but Finn wouldn't have *done* anything to Eric. They would just bicker a lot."

"Sure, sure, just gathering information," Charlotte assured her. Mollified, Olivia took a bite of her sandwich.

The gears of Charlotte's brain turned as the conductor came by to check their tickets. She had originally thought that the masked person who told her to mind her own business was referring to the anonymous notes. *What if they were talking about Bernard and Scoop, thinking that Olivia brought her in to investigate?*

"What else did you find out?" Landon asked as the conductor walked away.

"Not much else." Charlotte looked back at Olivia. "How well do you know Eric?"

"Not super well, but I'd say we're friends. Like, if regular coworkers are here"—she held up her hand, palm flat, to indicate levels—"we're, like, *here.*" She raised her hand an inch higher. "We actually met through mutual friends last year. He was the one who told me about the job opening at Scoop."

"Some people think Eric might be dating someone," Charlotte said. "Know anything about that?"

Olivia gave her a mouth shrug. "A little, not much. He was—"

"Pretty private about it?"

"Yeah. Oh!" Olivia paused. "He actually did just mention them the other day, though. Sort of."

"Sort of, how?"

"Well . . ."—Olivia rolled her eyes good-naturedly—"he presented me with a hypothetical that made it very obvious he was talking about himself. He does that a lot."

"What was the hypothetical?"

Olivia's brow furrowed as she worked to remember. "He asked . . . 'What would you do if Landon was being really stubborn about something that you knew would be good for him?' " She winced. "I probably butchered it, but it was something like that."

Charlotte could see Landon try to keep his face neutral as he balled up his sandwich wrapper. "Huh. What, uh . . . what'd you tell him?"

Olivia glanced over at him, a smile tugging at her lips. "Oh, I just said something about having a mature, adult conversation about it, and ultimately respecting your feelings despite our difference in opinion."

Landon made a pleased sound in his throat as he stuffed his sandwich wrapper into his pocket. Olivia looked at Charlotte and shook her head, mouthing, *Not what I said.*

Charlotte snorted as Landon glanced at her suspiciously.

"What?" he asked.

"Nothing." She turned back to Olivia. "So you don't really know about the person he's with?"

"Nope," Olivia said. "Just that I think they've been together since before I started working there."

"Which was?"

"March."

Charlotte's eyebrows shot up. "So you've only been there for a few months." She hadn't realized she'd been operating under the assumption that Olivia had been working at Scoop for longer than that. *Sloppy.*

Olivia nodded, taking another bite of her sandwich.

Returning to her conversation with Arielle in the bathroom (and repressing the memory of her mortal enemy, the automatic sink), Charlotte asked, "Were you there when Jensen was made manager?"

"He was promoted before I started. I was hired to fill his position on the team."

"What do you know about it?"

Olivia shrugged. "Not much. Eric's mentioned the old manager in passing. I think she was supportive of the union and would fight with Candice about it. Not sure if she was fired or quit. Then Jensen was promoted."

Charlotte thought for a moment. "Why wasn't Arielle made manager?" she asked, more to herself than to Olivia.

Olivia pursed her lips, considering this. "Not sure. I know she's worked there longer than Jensen has, so she's definitely qualified. She's never said anything about it to me."

"What were you talking to Lucy about?" Landon asked suddenly.

Charlotte paused as the Highview station announcement came through over the speaker, giving her the opportunity to pause and think before replying to her brother.

"I was just filling her in on some of the stuff I learned," she said. "I wanted to keep her updated without Dumb Jake overhearing." This wasn't untrue, but a more truthful answer would've been that she didn't want Landon overhearing, either. Even though Dumb Jake had interrupted before Charlotte got to the part she didn't want Landon to hear.

"Jake seems . . . nice," Olivia offered cautiously.

"Sure. I guess. In *theory*."

"Lottie's hated Jake since he and Lucy started dating in college," Landon explained.

"No, *no*," Charlotte said, quickly jumping in, "not true. When they started dating, he just gave me bad vibes." She crossed her arms. "I started officially hating him after he planned a ski trip on her birthday for the second year in a row."

Olivia looked confused. "Does Lucy . . . not like skiing?"

Charlotte shrugged. "She's never been. Because he *didn't invite her.*"

Olivia winced. "Oh."

"Yes. Exactly. Thank you." Charlotte rolled her eyes. "He's *fine.* He just, y'know, also sucks."

She thought back to Lucy asking her to keep digging into the possibility of Jake cheating on her. Charlotte hated Jake, but still couldn't see any signs that he might be cheating on Lucy. What was Lucy seeing that she wasn't?

Putting that to the side for the time being, she returned to an earlier thought. "Do you think you could get me Finn's number?"

Olivia thought for a moment, then nodded. "Yeah, I could probably get that. Just so you know, if you talk to Finn, they use they/them pronouns."

"Got it. Thanks." Charlotte had another thought. Actually, she had two thoughts. Actually, she had a lot of thoughts crashing around in her brain, but only these two involved her asking questions of Olivia.

"Do you think I could get an interview with Candice Watts?" she asked.

Olivia's nose scrunched. "I doubt it. It's definitely not something *I* could make happen. She was already lying low when the union news started spreading, and she's definitely lying even lower now."

Charlotte mentally marked talking to Candice as a soft "maybe" and moved on to her second thought. "Could I come with you to the office tomorrow? To talk to some more people?"

"Sure. It's a small office, though—most people work remotely." Olivia started counting on her fingers. "There's me, Jensen, Arielle, Martín—he's also on the development team; he wasn't there tonight."

Charlotte remembered Jensen mentioning someone named Martin. Olivia pronounced this name with an accent over the "i". Based on what little Charlotte had learned about Jensen that evening, she assumed they were referring to the same person.

"Vincent, Alison, and Ellie do customer service," Olivia continued, uncurling three more fingers, "and Jane is our HR manager, but she's only in the office a couple days a week." She paused, thinking. "Oh! And Sasha, our intern. She's also only in the office a few days a week. That's everyone."

"Great. I'd love to talk to them all." Charlotte actually would've preferred to not talk to any of them, but an unfortunate requirement of detecting was talking to people, which was a truth she had come to terms with many years ago.

The beginning part of a mystery had always been her least favorite. It was like if, instead of being able to pour all the puzzle pieces out of a box and get to work, you had to go around and retrieve pieces from a bunch of different people. It got tiring, especially when people were giving you pieces you already had.

Charlotte liked it when she had more pieces. Not necessarily all of them, but just enough to be able to start putting some of them together, and maybe look at what she had and say, "Okay, there's definitely a river in this picture." That was when she could really put her brain to work.

But for now, it was all about collecting pieces. Which was why, when they got back to Landon's, she texted a person she knew enjoyed collecting pieces from people more than she did:

Charlotte: I'm going to Olivia's office tomorrow morning to talk to people

Charlotte: wanna come

Charlotte: you can be super nice to people and I'll stand behind you and see if they say anything useful

Lucy replied about fifteen minutes later:

Lucy: Sorry. Jake and I were fighting

Charlotte knew what Lucy meant when she said she was "fighting" with Jake. It meant that Lucy expressed unhappiness about something, and Jake shrugged it off as not a big deal. Then Lucy calmly emphasized that it mattered to her, and Jake unconvincingly said he'd try better next time. Then Lucy left to "take a shower" but really just hid in the bathroom so they wouldn't have to talk about it anymore.

Lucy: I wish I could. I have a kickboxing class tomorrow morning.

Lucy: But keep me updated!!!

Charlotte: is everything okay

Lucy: Yeah! It's just a fun way to exercise

Charlotte: I mean with Jake

Lucy: Oh

Lucy: It's not a big deal. I just told him some of the stuff he was talking about at drinks wasn't appropriate to talk about in front of people we'd just met

Lucy: He said he didn't think it was that serious but he'd keep it in mind for next time

Yup.

Lucy: But I can come hang out later tomorrow! Jake's going out with his friends in the evening

Interesting.

Charlotte: do you think this would be a good opportunity to see if he really is hanging out with ~the boys~

Lucy: You mean follow him?

Charlotte: yeah

Lucy started typing, then stopped. Then started, then stopped. Charlotte waited.

Lucy: I don't know.

That was not worth the wait. Time for some linguistic finagling.

Charlotte: what if we go out and happen to stumble across wherever Jake's gonna be tomorrow
Charlotte: it's not "following" it's "stumbling"
Lucy: Okay

That was easy. Charlotte had thought that would be a harder sell. She hadn't even played the ace yet (or, as he'd probably prefer to be called: the king).

Charlotte: is it okay if I invite Gabe? And tell him what's going on
Charlotte: or would you rather tell him
Lucy: You can tell him. And yes!! I'd love that
Lucy: ALSO what were you going to tell me before I left??

Charlotte debated making something up. She was probably wrong, and she didn't want to worry Lucy for nothing. But she was going to explode if she didn't tell *someone.*

Charlotte: I don't know this for sure
Charlotte: but I think there's a CHANCE that Jensen was the one who grabbed me the other night
Lucy: WHAT???
Lucy: OH MY GOD
Charlotte: I'm not positive it's just a hunch!!!
Lucy: OH MY GOD!!!!!
Lucy: Your hunches are always right
Lucy: How do you know?
Charlotte: like I said, I DON'T

Charlotte: but there was a point when I was talking to him that he lowered his voice, and it got deeper, and it just really sounded like the person who spoke to me

Charlotte: then later I mentioned something about threatening people, and he got a weird look on his face

Lucy: SO HE KNOWS YOU KNOW??

Charlotte: he doesn't know I know

Charlotte: and I don't KNOW

Charlotte: you know?

Lucy: No

Charlotte: oh no

Lucy: Stop that

Charlotte: no I just remembered he's also gonna be at the office tomorrow

Charlotte: he was already giving me a hard time about acting like a detective tonight

Lucy: Just tell him you're not a detective. That's been working out well for you so far

Charlotte: ha

Charlotte: ha ha

Charlotte: enjoy your shower

Lucy: How did you know I'm about to take a shower??

Charlotte paused, her first instinct being to reply (albeit tongue-in-cheek), "Because I'm a detective."

Charlotte: night

Lucy: Goodniiiight

Charlotte sent a long text to Gabe, telling him about Eric, and the Jake situation, and telling him he should come up the next evening. Despite her previous inclination to avoid making any plans that would keep her there longer than she had planned, she was resigned to the fact that she was going to be looking into Eric's disappearance for the next day or so. So, she figured she might as well try to get Lucy some peace of mind while she was at it. And if things got emotional, Gabe was much better at dealing with emotional than she was.

She took a shower while she waited for Gabe to reply. Then she put on sweats and a T-shirt while she waited for Gabe to reply. Then she climbed into bed, still waiting for Gabe to reply. She decided to close her eyes to avoid a staring contest with Dale's army of Funko Pops (still waiting for Gabe to reply). And then it was morning.

Charlotte awoke to a gentle knock on the door.

"Charlotte?" Olivia's muffled voice came through the door. "I'm leaving for work in ten, if you're still coming."

"Yes, yeah, I'm coming," Charlotte called back, pushing back the covers and scooting off the bed.

Charlotte quickly got dressed and headed for the kitchen, commandeering Landon's bowl of cereal he had just poured for himself.

"Thank you," she said, grabbing his spoon from the counter and dodging out of the way as he lunged for the bowl. She quickly scooped some into her mouth as she walked over to the dining table.

"You *suck*," Landon grumbled, grabbing another bowl from the cabinet. "What's the plan for going to the office with Olivia?"

Satisfied that her claim to the bowl of cereal was no longer being threatened, Charlotte settled into a chair.

"Just gonna talk to some people," she said, scooping another spoonful of cereal into her mouth. "See if I can get any new information about Eric, or anything related."

"I wanted to ask," Landon said, putting his new bowl down on the counter and reaching for the cereal box. "Why did you ask Olivia if her coworkers knew you used to be a detective?"

Charlotte hesitated.

Because someone attacked me the other night, and I think it might've been Jensen, but I don't have any proof and I don't want you to freak out, especially because you have so much faith in me as a detective that you'll just assume that I'm right, even though I'm probably wrong.

Charlotte pretended to take a long time chewing and swallowing her cereal before speaking. Which was probably not very convincing, since she had just been talking with cereal in her mouth. Finally, she swallowed, and by then had developed an airtight response.

"Did I?"

"Yeah."

Never mind, then.

"I guess I was just curious, since Jensen and Arielle already seemed to know about me," Charlotte said, shrugging. "Not that serious. I don't even remember asking it."

Landon stared at her as she continued to eat, clearly unconvinced. Charlotte pretended not to notice. Landon realized Charlotte was pretending not to notice him staring at her and stared harder. Thankfully, by then, she had finished eating, and got up to put her bowl in the sink.

The toilet flushed in the bathroom. With movements clearly molded by habit, Landon abandoned his cereal to grab a green reusable water bottle from a kitchen cabinet and start filling it with water.

Olivia emerged from the bathroom. "Ready?" she asked Charlotte.

"Yup, coming." Charlotte ran into Dale's room and grabbed her wallet from her purse, pulling out the essential cards and some cash and slipping them into the front pocket of her shorts. After the debacle at Annette's, she didn't want the added responsibility of keeping track of her purse.

She left Dale's room in time to see Olivia sling her purse over her shoulder, then turn to accept the water bottle Landon had brought to her.

"Thank you," she said sweetly, kissing him.

He kissed her back, then lowered his voice conspiratorially. "Text me if she starts misbehaving."

"Where's *my* water?" Charlotte asked petulantly, crossing the apartment.

"You know where the fridge is." Landon turned and headed back to his bowl of cereal. "Be good. Don't piss anyone off."

Charlotte followed a laughing Olivia out the door. "No promises!"

The Scoop office was located off of Times Square on 43rd Street. Charlotte almost missed Olivia turning a corner as she navigated the crush of people that already populated the sidewalks.

Speed up, merge, dodge to the right, avoid the pigeon. Charlotte didn't like being in situations where she had to focus all of her brainpower on not getting stampeded. Not that she was planning on focusing much of her brainpower on solving this mystery, but there were certainly other things she would've preferred to focus her brainpower on instead. Like . . . window shopping. Or reading the ads on taxis.

She wavered as she passed a roasted nuts vendor, the stolen cereal feeling like a faint memory, before quickening her pace and catching up to Olivia.

Inside the building, Olivia showed her ID to the person behind the front desk.

"They always order breakfast for anyone who comes into work early," Olivia said as she signed Charlotte in as a guest. "But you couldn't pay me to come in earlier than I have to."

She finished signing and dropped the pen, shooting Charlotte a wry smile. "And they don't! All set, let's go."

They went up an escalator and walked over to a hallway of elevators, each door sandwiched by mirrors. As they waited for an elevator to arrive, Charlotte examined her reflection in the mirror, realizing that maybe she should have been more mindful about what she was wearing.

Her shorts were high-waisted light denim, with slight fraying on the cuff of the right leg—the result of Charlotte absentmindedly picking at a loose thread one too many times. Tucked into the shorts was a slightly wrinkled white T-shirt with a small cartoon rainbow printed on a pocket over the left chest.

Charlotte squinted at her image, trying to determine if she could see her bra through the shirt. Satisfied that she couldn't, she glanced over at Olivia's reflection, which was clothed in a much nicer black sleeveless turtleneck and light brown pleated pants.

A few other well-dressed people had joined them by the time the elevator arrived, and as the group piled inside, Charlotte hoped no one would suggest playing, "Which One of Us Doesn't Work Here?" as they waited to arrive at their floors.

"This is us," Olivia said as the elevator stopped on the twelfth floor. A couple of people stepped out of the way to let them exit the elevator into a short hallway.

To their left was a glass door that appeared to lead out to a balcony overlooking the city, furnished with a couple of chairs and a small table. Ahead of them was a door with SCOOP emblazoned on it in bright red letters.

"Welcome to Scoop," Olivia said, holding the door open for Charlotte.

Like Olivia had said, it was a small office. There was a kitchen to their right as they walked in, with a counter half-covered with baskets and containers brimming with chips and candy. The other half of the counter was home to a very nice-looking microwave, a sleek electric kettle, a coffee maker that looked like it belonged on a spaceship, and a device that was either a smoothie blender or a very advanced pencil sharpener. The refrigerator, which was much more identifiable than some of the other gadgets in the room, hummed softly against the far wall.

They rounded a corner and were met with a room of three

long tables serving as workstations. Each table had two computers, one on each side, with wires running across the floor covered with cable protectors to prevent people from tripping. Small file cabinets sat under the tables at each workstation. There were two doors on one side of the room and one on the other, all seemingly leading to smaller offices. There was a large window on the far wall with a view of rooftops and clear blue sky, next to which sat a printer on a small table.

Arielle was sitting at the middle table with her back to them. She took off her headphones as they walked into her periphery.

"Good morning!" she chirped. "Hi, Charlotte!"

Charlotte waved. "Hey."

"I wanted to show Charlotte the office," Olivia said as they walked over to where Arielle sat. "And," she added in a lower voice, "we thought she could talk to a few more people about Eric."

They had agreed on the train to try not to publicize the fact that Charlotte was investigating Eric's disappearance. However, Charlotte knew that anyone in the office who had previously heard about her and her history as a detective would probably be able to figure it out on their own. Unless they were somehow able to convince everyone it was "Take Your Boyfriend's Adult Sister to Work Day."

Arielle nodded solemnly, then put her headphones back on and returned to her computer as Olivia walked around the table and hung her bag on the back of a chair. "You can bring that chair over if you want," she said to Charlotte, pointing at an empty chair at the table they had just walked past. "Our intern sits there, but she won't be in the office today."

As Charlotte moved to carry the chair over to Olivia's table, she snuck a peek at the fourth person in the room. He was sitting at the farthest table, his face hidden behind a large computer monitor.

Charlotte picked up the chair and walked it around the table, managing to catch a glimpse of who she assumed was

Martín: mid-thirties, Latine, dark brown skin, curly black hair, dark eyes that were focused on his screen. He had wireless earbuds in and didn't look away from the monitor, even when Charlotte's foot caught on one of the cable protectors, causing her to stumble.

"Oop, you okay?" Arielle asked, looking up. "I trip over those all the time."

Charlotte mumbled something about being fine, her face reddening. She finished her walk of shame, placing her chair down at the end of the table next to Olivia's seat, which was diagonally across the table from Arielle.

"Who works there?" Charlotte asked, nodding her head at the empty workstation at the other end of the farthest table.

Olivia glanced over. "That's Eric's spot," she said. "But usually he's on his laptop, so sometimes he'll work over here." She gestured at a spot directly across from Arielle.

"It seems like he might appreciate having the space to himself," Charlotte said softly, her eyes darting over to the man at the other table.

"That's Martín," Olivia whispered back. "He's quiet, but nice enough. Usually keeps to himself." She looked over at him. "He does seem to open up a bit more when Eric sits over there, but Eric has that effect on everyone."

"And the offices?" Charlotte asked.

"That's Jensen's," Olivia said, pointing to one of the two along one wall. "He's probably not in yet; he tends to come in later. And that's the customer service office." She nodded at the other door. "They take a lot of calls, so usually they're sealed off in there. Apparently at Scoop's old office, they used to all be in one room, which sounded like a nightmare."

She turned to point at the third door on the other side of the room. "And that's Jane's office. HR. She mostly works from home, but comes in on Mondays and Fridays." She winced. "Sorry, I didn't really think this through. You'd definitely have more people to talk to if you came in tomorrow."

Charlotte shook her head, indicating that Olivia shouldn't worry about it. "Where does Candice work?"

"She's in her own office a few floors up." Olivia pushed her chair back and stood. "Let me introduce you to the customer service team so you can talk with them while I start working."

Olivia led Charlotte into the other room, where she quickly introduced Charlotte as a friend of Eric's to the three people sitting inside, before leaving her to fend for herself with the extremely busy customer service team.

After about forty minutes of pausing mid-sentence for someone to take a call or answer a message, Charlotte realized that she wasn't going to get much information from the people who were essentially cut off from the rest of the office for most of the day.

"Thanks for your help," she finally said, edging towards the door. "If you think of anything else that might be helpful, you can let Olivia know, and she'll pass it on to me."

Realizing that they were all fully engaged with answering messages on their computers and likely didn't hear a thing she said, Charlotte sighed and left the room. She walked over to Eric's workstation, hoping to redeem herself after that massive waste of time.

Martín glanced over at her from the other end of the table, and she gestured at Eric's station. "Just thought I'd see if he left any . . ." Martín was already looking back at his screen.

"Okay, you're not listening to me, cool." She knelt down by Eric's filing cabinet as Martín continued his work, showing no sign of hearing her.

The contents of Eric's file cabinet turned out to be no more helpful than the Scoop customer service team. The top drawer contained a couple of pens, an ice pack, some sticky notes, and a box of tea. The bottom two drawers were . . . empty.

You're hot on the trail, Illes, Charlotte thought, closing the bottom drawer. She stood and walked over to Olivia, plopping down into the seat next to her. "Hey."

Olivia took out her earbuds. "Hey. Any luck?"

"Not really." She glanced at Jensen's office door, noticing a small sliver of light coming out of the bottom where there had been darkness before. "Is Jensen in?"

Olivia nodded. "I didn't get the chance to tell him you were here. He just went straight into his office and shut the door. Which is normal, unless he has an announcement from Candice about something."

Charlotte thought about that for a moment. "You call the CEO Candice. Do most people call her by her first name?"

"Yeah, pretty much." Olivia scrunched up her nose. "They want the company to feel like a family, or whatever. Except Jensen calls her Ms. Watts when he's talking to us. He sees it as a respect thing, I guess."

"And him calling you by your last name? That doesn't feel as respectful."

"Yeah, no." Olivia rolled her eyes. "He does it to Sasha, too. Sometimes he just calls her 'Intern.' I think it's because we're the only people who were hired under his reign. It separates us from the rest."

"God. That sucks."

"Yeah. Well." Olivia shrugged. "Microaggression in the workplace is nothing new to me, and nothing I can't handle." She sighed. "I just feel bad for Sasha. She's a smart kid. She deserves a better boss than Jensen."

Charlotte glanced over at the door to the empty office across the room. "Have you brought it up to HR?"

Olivia made a choking sound, stifling a laugh. "Sorry. That wasn't funny. Um, no. Jane's nice enough, but Candice puts so much on her plate that if she was given anything else to deal with, I genuinely think she would combust."

Charlotte nodded, then pushed her chair back. "I'll stop distracting you now."

"No, you're fine." Olivia reached her arms over her head and stretched, lowering her voice. "I needed a break from imagining how it would feel to punch Jensen in the face."

"*Ha.*"

"He just sent me the dumbest notes on something I've been working on." She dropped her arms and leaned in. "The bright side is that the work takes me a lot less time than he thinks it will, which gives me time to work on my own app."

"You're making your own app?"

Olivia nodded. "It's still in the early stages—I've only told Eric about it." She glanced over at Arielle, lowering her voice even more. "Arielle's great, but she's best friends with my boss. I'm not going to risk her finding out I'm working on personal projects on company time."

Charlotte was about to ask Olivia more about the app when Jensen's office door opened. Olivia ducked back behind her monitor and pretended to look busy.

Jensen stopped as he caught sight of Charlotte. She waved.

He pointed at her. "You don't work here."

"I'm shadowing Olivia," Charlotte said, nodding to Olivia, who was still pretending to be deeply focused on her screen. "I have an interest in software development."

"Do you?" Jensen didn't look convinced. "Well, while you're here, you might as well make yourself useful. Intern's out today. Why don't—"

"Sasha," Olivia said suddenly, looking up from her monitor at Jensen.

Jensen looked back. "Yeah."

"I'm just saying, that's her name."

"Ooookay." Jensen turned back to Charlotte, giving her an amused look that she did not return. "*Sasha* is out today, if that wasn't clear from what I originally said."

Olivia flipped him off behind her screen.

"Why don't you go fill up the water filter in the kitchen?" he finished.

Charlotte started to laugh, which she quickly turned into a fake cough, which quickly turned into a real cough. Olivia slid her water bottle across the table, but Charlotte waved it off.

"Uh, yeah," she rasped, clearing her throat. "Sure, yeah, I'm on it." She got to her feet, shooting double finger-guns at Jensen. "You're the boss."

"Yeah, I am," Jensen said. "Which is why next time I'd like to be told when we're going to have guests in the office." He looked over at Olivia, who sunk lower behind her monitor.

"Jensen," Arielle said suddenly. "Can I show you that glitch I found? You said you'd take a look."

"Sure." Jensen raised his eyebrows at Charlotte and nodded towards the kitchen before turning and joining Arielle at her workstation.

"Thank you, Arielle," Olivia muttered. She looked up at Charlotte. "You don't have to—"

"Don't worry about me," Charlotte said, waving her off and heading for the kitchen.

With all the fancy gadgets she had noticed when first entering the office, Charlotte was relieved to see a normal sink with a handle. She retrieved the water filter from the refrigerator (which, she quickly noticed, was more than halfway full already), and filled it up.

She returned the filter to the fridge and was about to stuff a granola bar into her pocket when Martín walked in, holding a mug. He paused when he saw her, then continued to the coffee machine.

"Just organizing the snacks," Charlotte said, guiltily dropping the granola bar back into the basket.

Not making any sign of having heard her, he switched on the electric kettle, then quickly switched it off, as if he'd just remembered he was getting coffee. Realizing that she was maybe making him nervous, Charlotte doubled down on her small talk strategy.

"I like this kind a lot," she continued, pointing at the granola bars in the basket. "The crumbly kind make too much of a mess, I think. Which I guess is fine if you're out on a hike or something, you know, outdoors, but I'm sure they wouldn't be as easy to eat in an office setting."

Feeling like she had just run a mile, she looked to Martín, hoping that something she had just said would lure him into a conversation. Either unaware or uncaring of her extreme effort to socialize, he continued to silently make his coffee.

Maybe granola bars weren't the best conversation starter.

"Do you like working here?" she asked, shifting tactics. "Not because of the granola bars, but, in general?"

Finally, *finally*, Martín glanced at her. "Mhm."

Cool. She could work with *mhm*.

"Seems like there are some great people here," she continued, leaning against the counter. "Olivia, Arielle . . . of course, everyone's worried about Eric." She tilted her head. "Were you close with him?"

"Not really," Martín said, bringing his total word count up to three. (Or two, depending on whether or not you count "mhm" as a word, which Charlotte did.)

"Gotcha," Charlotte said, nodding. "You're more of a 'clock in and clock out' kinda guy. I respect that." She decided to give up on smooth transitions. "How do you feel about all this union stuff going on?"

Martín shrugged. (Which even Charlotte had to admit didn't count as a word.)

"For sure," she said, powering forward. She hadn't stopped nodding for the past fifteen seconds and could not see herself stopping anytime soon. "It's all pretty confusing. So you're just kind of indifferent to it?"

"Kind of," Martín said. The word count was up to four or five, depending.

Charlotte's neck had started to ache from nodding so much.

She wondered if she had tripped over one of those cord protectors on her way to the kitchen and cracked her skull open, sending her straight to hell, and this was her eternal punishment.

Just then, Jensen walked into the kitchen, which didn't help to disprove the hell theory.

"Sent you an email about those fixes I was talking about," Jensen said to Martín. Then he glanced at Charlotte, who was leaning against the counter in a way that neither looked nor felt casual. "Is our substitute intern bothering you?"

"It's fine," Martín said, picking up his fresh mug of coffee. "I'll go look at that email."

Eight words?? Jensen got *eight whole words*?

Martín left the kitchen, and Jensen turned to Charlotte. "Doing your little girl detective thing again?"

"Just saying hi."

"Sure." He didn't sound convinced. "You're not going to have much luck figuring out if something happened to Eric by bothering Martín. Eric has some secrets, but if he was sharing them with anyone, it wouldn't be him."

Charlotte narrowed her eyes. "What 'secrets'?"

"Isn't that your job to find out?"

"But why would you even say he has 'secrets'?"

Jensen rolled his eyes. "I don't know. He was just a really private guy. Seemed like he had some stuff going on, but he'd never talk about it. Might be worth looking into."

"But not here," Charlotte said flatly.

He shrugged.

Charlotte took a deep breath to temper her frustration, then forced herself to smile. "Unrelated to that," she said, turning to straighten a snack basket to seem more intern-y, "do you think I could chat with the CEO at some point? As the substitute intern, I thought I should learn about every facet of the company."

"Nice try. Absolutely not."

"What if I deliver her mail?"

"If Ms. Watts gets any mail," Jensen said, "I'm going to give it to the *real* intern to bring up, not a snoop who'll ask her a bunch of invasive questions."

Charlotte paused. "But what if she gets some important mail *today*?"

"Then I'll send Kimura to bring it up. Serves her right for bringing you in here with no warning."

"Can I ask you something?" Charlotte said, trying to move the topic away from Olivia. She was fine getting herself into trouble, but didn't want to drag Olivia down with her.

"No."

She already knew Jensen wasn't going to answer her question (his "No" being a strong indicator), but she wanted to see his expression when she asked.

"What's your relationship with Candice Watts?"

Charlotte Illes was by no means an expert at reading faces. In fact, she had discovered a long time ago that there were no real, all-encompassing indicators when it came to reading someone's body language, and anyone who claimed to be exceptionally good at it was full of shit. She was above average at reading the voices and expressions of people she was close to (hence her lifetime ban from playing Mafia), but less so for those she didn't know as well.

But Jensen did not like that question. Anyone could tell that. His primary emotion was confusion, probably from him wondering why this question was being asked in the first place.

There was also some annoyance, and . . . curiosity? Maybe not; she might have made that one up. She wished he would just tell her how he was feeling instead of her having to do all this observational crap that wasn't reliable anyway.

"How're you feeling right now?" Charlotte asked.

Now Jensen looked even more confused. "What?"

Charlotte nodded slowly, deciding that she didn't want to let him know how unhelpful this interaction was. "Thank you. I really appreciate you taking the time to talk with me, seeing as how I'm just an unpaid intern. I assume you don't pay your interns."

"Listen," Jensen said, putting a hand on the counter and looking down at Charlotte, "I was fine tolerating you at the bar, and I was even fine seeing you here today, because I figured if they all"—he gestured to the office—"felt like someone was working to find Eric, they'd be able to stay focused on their work." He leaned in closer. "But if you start pointing fingers at the wrong people, or spreading stories about things you know nothing about, I'll make sure you never step foot in this office again."

Charlotte blinked. "So . . . that's a no to paying your interns?"

"Stay out of other people's business," he said, straightening.

Charlotte narrowed her eyes. "Interesting choice of words," she said slowly.

Jensen's expression didn't change. He either didn't realize he had used the exact same phrase the masked attacker did, or he didn't care.

Technically there was a third option: she was wrong, and Jensen hadn't been the one to attack her.

Come on. What're the chances they'd say the same exact thing?

Charlotte thought about that for a moment.

Okay, the chances aren't that wild. It's not the most uncommon phrase.

Another pause. Jensen was still staring at her, as if challenging her to argue.

It was him. She was 99.9 percent sure. 99.8 percent sure. She was at least 97.2 percent sure it was him.

"Jensen?" Arielle was standing in the doorway. She glanced at Charlotte, looking concerned.

He gave Charlotte one last look, then turned around. "What?"

"Your phone's ringing in your office."

Without saying another word, Jensen brushed past Arielle. "Martin! Meet me in my office in five."

Charlotte looked at Arielle. "He's *fun.*"

"Was he giving you a hard time?" Arielle frowned. "I'm really sorry about him. We've all been under a lot of stress lately, and he's taking it especially hard."

"Him?" Charlotte asked, pointing past Arielle. "That's the chillest guy I've ever met."

Arielle shook her head, giving her a small smile. "He's just protective of the company, and with everything that's been going on, he's been getting more and more defensive."

"Protective of the company, or protective of Candice?"

Arielle stared at her for a moment, looking thoughtful, then sighed. "Both, probably."

Now things were getting interesting. Charlotte lowered her voice. "Are they together?"

"Oh, no," Arielle said, shaking her head quickly. "God, no." She hesitated, then said, "He definitely has feelings for her. But I can tell you for a fact that they are *not* reciprocated."

"Gotcha." Not as interesting as she had hoped. But still kind of interesting. "Hey, Jensen said I couldn't talk to Candice. Do you think you could help me with that?"

"Um . . ." Arielle paused, then let out a breath. "Look, I really want to help you in any way I can. I . . . I *really* appreciate you looking into this. But Candice has been having a rough time these past few months, and if she thinks she's being investigated or something . . . I don't think she'd take it very well."

"Sure," Charlotte said, trying to cover her annoyance with a layer of sympathy.

"If it helps," Arielle said, "I've been friends with her for a long time. If Eric's . . ." She took a deep breath. "If something bad has happened, Candice wouldn't be involved."

Charlotte nodded, mentally sprinkling a grain of salt onto that information before tucking it away for future review. If Arielle and Candice were really such close friends, Charlotte wasn't going to give much weight to Arielle's opinion of the CEO's character. "Can I ask you a question?" *Stop opening with that. Just ask the question.*

"Sure."

"Why is Jensen the manager, and not you?" Charlotte asked. "You said last night that you and Jaya were hired at the same time. Even if you weren't made manager then, why didn't you get it when Jaya left?"

Arielle's eyebrows raised slightly, and Charlotte quickly added, "If you don't mind me asking. I hope it's not a sore subject."

"No, no, not at all," Arielle said quickly. "It's a valid question. I *was* actually offered the promotion, but I turned it down."

"Why?"

She smiled, almost sheepishly. "I tend to work a lot better when I'm not in the spotlight. I think that's why Candice made Jaya manager in the first place. She was always more of the leader type than me." Her smile faded. "But sometimes I worry it was too much responsibility for Jaya. If maybe that contributed to her leaving."

Charlotte thought about that for a moment. "You seemed to think that she left because she disagreed with Candice about her stance on the union."

"Right. Well, as a manager, I think she felt like she had a responsibility to stand up to Candice. And she had to do that alone."

Arielle hesitated, looked over her shoulder, then turned back, satisfied that no one was standing directly behind her in plain sight. Charlotte would've checked around the corner as well, but apparently, Arielle wasn't as paranoid as she was.

"I know last night I was calling the union talks silly," she said softly, "but Eric's explained it to me, and I do support them. I don't like to be vocal about it, because Candice is my friend, and I don't want her to find out." She smiled sadly. "Eric even asked me a few days ago if I'd help with some stuff for the union, and I said yes."

"What kind of stuff?"

"Something to do with getting out messages to more of the

workers. I'm not sure exactly." Her face fell. "I never got to talk with him about it."

Charlotte could see tears appearing in Arielle's eyes again, which was her cue to exit. "Thanks for talking with me," she said. "I really appreciate it."

Arielle cleared her throat, blinking back the tears. "Could you . . . if you don't mind," she said, "could you keep me updated about Eric? I'm really worried about him, and if he's . . ." She stopped as more tears sprung into her eyes.

Charlotte stepped forward and reached out a hand, patting her awkwardly on the shoulder. "I'll keep you updated," she said.

Arielle nodded. "Thanks." She sniffed. "And if you need any help with anything . . . I mean, I know you have Olivia, but . . ." She gave her a small smile. "Feel free to reach out."

Charlotte nodded. Then, making her escape from the kitchen, she headed back to Olivia's workstation.

"Are you okay?" Olivia asked as she sat down. She lowered her voice. "I'm so sorry about Jensen; he's a dick."

"Yeah, definitely don't think I'm gonna get hired here anytime soon," Charlotte said.

Olivia chuckled. "Oh!" she said, stopping mid-laugh. "I've got something for you." She picked up her phone and started typing. "I got Finn's number."

Charlotte had to think for a second, trying to remember if Olivia had said she was going to try to set her up with someone named Finn. Then she remembered. "Oh! From the organizing committee. Perfect, thank you."

She pulled out her phone as Olivia's text popped up on her screen. She was about to shoot off a text of her own when movement caught her eye.

Martín got up from his chair and crossed the room, disappearing into Jensen's office and closing the door. Arielle was still in the kitchen. Olivia, who had returned to her work, was the only other person in the room with her.

Charlotte just had to give her deniability.

"Hey, don't look at me, okay?" Charlotte said.

Olivia immediately turned to look at her, confused.

"Okay, so, what you just did? Don't do that."

Olivia looked even more confused. "What?"

Charlotte stood, knowing she didn't have much time. "I'm giving you deniability. Just do your work and don't look at what I'm doing."

Olivia's expression shifted from confused to apprehensive. "Okay," she said slowly, turning back to her screen.

Backing out of Olivia's peripheral vision, Charlotte quickly moved towards the door to the third office belonging to the HR manager, Jane. She pulled open the door, light spilling into the office, and slipped inside. As she closed the door behind her, she caught a glimpse of Olivia peeking over her shoulder, eyes wide, before whipping her head back around again.

So much for deniability.

The room was dim. There was a window along one wall, but the blinds were pulled down and shut tight, with only the smallest amount of sunlight squeezing through the sides. Charlotte turned on her phone's flashlight, not wanting to risk someone seeing the overhead light from underneath the door.

The office was very small, with few personal touches. It seemed that, since she spent the majority of her week working from home, Jane didn't care much to decorate this office. A wooden desk took up a large portion of the floor, with two chairs set up on one side, and a desk chair for Jane on the other.

Charlotte made her way to the desk, which was home to a computer monitor, a keyboard, a desk planner, and a mug full of pens. A voice in her head told her to check for a purple pen. *Wrong case*, she replied.

Trying the desk drawers, she found them all locked. She tapped the keyboard to wake up the computer, which was also locked. (Charlotte quickly tried "password" and "password1," both of which failed.)

Fortunately, Jane hadn't deemed it necessary to lock up her desk planner. Charlotte held her phone over the calendar, squinting to decipher the scribbled writing.

It was a spiral-bound monthly planner, showing the full month of July. Based on the columns of writing on Mondays and Fridays and the empty boxes for the rest of the weekdays, it seemed like Jane only used the planner for her in-office days. Most of the entries were for meetings, often with Candice or Jensen, but Charlotte's gaze was immediately drawn to an entry for the following day, which had been crossed out with a single line:

~~*Meeting w/ Eric and Martin (10:30)*~~

Not a great look for HR to misspell an employee's name, Charlotte thought. Reminding herself that she didn't have much time, she held her phone high over the planner and took a photo, wincing as the light from the flash filled the room.

She was about to head out, then paused. Placing her phone down on the desk, she flipped the planner back to March, picking up her phone again to examine the new month.

Once again, her gaze was immediately drawn to a specific day—not because it was crossed out, but because it was a rare Tuesday entry, the first one Charlotte had seen:

Jaya exit interview (9:00am)

Charlotte took another photo before setting her phone down and flipping the planner back to July. She wanted to examine the other entries surrounding that one, but she knew it was well past time to leave—partially because she had a pretty good sense of time, but mainly because of the muffled footsteps that were approaching the office door.

Chapter 10

Headless Elmo and Other Surprises

Charlotte dropped to the floor.

She debated trying to crawl under the desk, but that would involve moving the chair out of the way, and the doorknob was already turning. Too late, Charlotte realized she had left her phone on the desk (flashlight side down, thankfully), and silently vowed to stop putting down her belongings while sneaking into places.

As the door swung open, she thought about how ironic it would be if now was the moment Gabe finally texted her back, lighting up her phone for whomever was now in the doorway to see.

"Jane's not in today!" Charlotte heard Olivia call from her desk, panic tingeing her tone.

"I know," said the person in the doorway. Now up to a total word count of fifteen, Martín started to close the door. "Thought I saw a light on inside."

Charlotte took a deep breath and let it out slowly as the office was once again plunged into semi-darkness. She heard Martín's footsteps fade as he returned to his desk. Then she regretted her premature sigh of relief, realizing that if Martín was back at his desk, there was no way she was getting out of there without being seen.

She stood up to snatch her phone from off the desk, then dropped back down to the floor, just in case. Then she texted Olivia:

Charlotte: okay screw deniability
Charlotte: HELP
Olivia: THAT WAS SO SCARY
Olivia: HOW DID HE NOT SEE YOU???
Olivia: he's back at his desk and Arielle's back too
Olivia: I don't know what to do??

Charlotte tried to think of what Olivia could possibly do to get both Arielle and Martín to leave the room that didn't involve fire or personal injury. She was about to reconsider her exclusion of fire-related ideas when Olivia texted her again:

Olivia: I've got it. Hang on

A couple of minutes later, there was a quick knock at the door. Charlotte froze, then realized that no one else had any reason to knock on the door of a presumably empty office other than Olivia, who knew that the office actually contained one slightly unnerved Charlotte Illes.

Before she could move, the door opened.

"Quick," Olivia hissed, standing in the doorway. "They won't be gone long."

Charlotte scrambled to her feet and out of the room. Closing the door behind her, she looked around. Martín's and Arielle's workspaces were vacant. "How'd you do that?"

Olivia quickly walked back to her computer, and Charlotte

followed. "Our internal messaging system is super broken," she said in a low voice. "I think some friends of Candice from college built it for a class project, but it's really terrible. It glitches all the time, doing stuff like resending old messages or getting a sender's name wrong. I tried looking into it once, and realized it was *way* too easy to do some stuff I shouldn't be able to."

She gave her keyboard one last tap. Charlotte peeked at the screen, realized she had no idea what she was looking at, then looked back at Olivia for explanation.

Olivia looked proud of herself. "I sent Arielle and Martín a message and made it look like it was sent by Candice, asking them to go up to her office." She gestured to her screen, as if the lines of code displayed there could show for themselves what she had just accomplished (which, granted, they probably could, just not to Charlotte).

"And now . . ."—she moved her mouse to delete a few lines—"I've made the messages disappear. Which is another thing that happens a lot, especially if a message was a glitch in the first place."

Charlotte wasn't sure how foolproof this plan was, but Olivia seemed confident. She allowed that to assuage her doubt, but not completely eradicate it. Charlotte didn't know how to live her life without harboring some doubt about something at all times.

She looked around the empty office, then back at Olivia. "How much time do I have?"

Olivia glanced at the entrance to the office. "Um . . . three to five minutes? Depends on the elevators, and how much time they spend up there."

"Great." Charlotte headed for Arielle's workstation.

"Oh, god." Olivia nervously checked the office entrance again as Charlotte knelt down and opened the top drawer of Arielle's file cabinet.

"This is what you signed up for when you asked me to help,"

Charlotte said. She kept her voice low, not wanting to give Jensen a reason to come out of his office.

The top drawer of Arielle's file cabinet held her purse, which Charlotte quickly poked through. Finding nothing of interest, she moved on. The second drawer was equally interesting—pencils, sticky notes, paper clips. A card, an empty pack of gum, and a bracelet with a broken clasp. The third drawer took the prize for Least Interesting, being completely empty.

Charlotte shut the bottom drawer, stood, and jogged across the room.

"You left everything like you found it, right?" Olivia asked, watching her approach Martín's workstation.

"Of course. I'm a professional." Charlotte gave her pocket a quick pat to make sure she still had her phone on her before crouching down again.

She pulled on the handle of the top drawer. There was some resistance, and she had to jiggle it a bit before it finally slid open. It was mostly empty, holding only some loose-leaf paper.

"These cabinets really don't get much use, do they?" Charlotte asked, starting to close the drawer. She stopped as something caught her eye.

"I mostly use mine for my purse," Olivia said, shrugging. "And snacks." She opened her top drawer and peered inside. "I've got osenbei—rice crackers—and sour gummies, if you want some."

"And an envelope full of cash?"

Olivia looked over at her curiously. ". . . No?"

"Well, if you ever need one . . ." Charlotte held up a royal-blue envelope of cash that had been tucked into the side of the drawer.

Olivia let out a low whistle, getting up from her chair and joining Charlotte at Martín's workstation. "How much is in there?"

"Looks like several thousand," Charlotte said, leafing through the stack of hundreds. "Seven, maybe eight."

"What's that?" Olivia asked, pointing into the envelope.

There was writing on the inside of it, written in black pen. Charlotte pushed the money back to read it:

Thanks

"Recognize the handwriting?" she asked, looking up at Olivia.

Olivia shook her head. "No. But I don't really know a lot of people's handwriting, especially around here. We mostly just message and email each other."

"It looks pretty sloppy, anyway," Charlotte observed. "Like someone trying to disguise their handwriting." She studied it for another moment, then pulled out her phone to take a photo of the message.

Olivia also continued to stare at it. "But I think I've seen that envelope."

Charlotte took the photo, then looked up at her again. "Where?"

"Hang on." Olivia headed back to her workstation. After returning the envelope and quickly checking the second and third drawers (which contained a couple of empty manila folders and nothing, respectively), Charlotte joined Olivia, who was holding an identical royal-blue envelope.

"It wasn't filled with hundred-dollar bills when it was given to me," she said drily, handing it to Charlotte. "It's a congratulations card that everyone got for a successful Q1 and Q2."

"From who?" Charlotte asked, opening it.

"Candice, technically. But they were written and handed out by Sasha, our intern."

"Interesting."

If Candice had given Sasha the cards and envelopes to fill out, then it was possible she had more envelopes left over. *But why would the CEO give Martín all that cash? What could she be thanking him for?*

She didn't notice the elevator dinging in the distance until Olivia grabbed the envelope and card from her hand and dropped it back into the bottom drawer, kicking it shut.

Charlotte watched Martín return to his workstation as Arielle complained to Olivia about the glitch that had sent them an old message from Candice. For a moment, she almost expected him to check and see if the money was still there. Unsurprisingly, he didn't, instead returning to his computer as silent as he had been before, like someone who didn't have eight thousand dollars in cash tucked away in a drawer.

She turned back to Olivia. "I think I'm gonna head out."

"I'll walk you to the elevator."

They stood. Charlotte paused, remembering her hunger and her failed attempt at stealing a granola bar. "Um . . . could I get one of those rice crackers?"

Olivia smiled, then pulled open her top drawer and reached inside. "You can have *two*," she said, handing Charlotte two large crackers in a plastic package.

"Thank you," Charlotte said gratefully, tucking them into her pocket. She waved at Arielle as they walked out. "'Bye, Arielle."

"Oh, 'bye!" Arielle looked up from her computer and waved. "Nice seeing you again!"

Charlotte didn't bother trying to get a goodbye from Martín, who had returned his earbuds to his ears (and probably wouldn't have said anything even if he could hear her).

"Thanks for rescuing me, by the way," Charlotte said in a low voice once they exited the office into the hallway.

Olivia waved a hand. "No problem. It was incredibly stressful and probably took a couple years off of my life, but other than that, no problem."

"Could I come back tomorrow?" Charlotte asked as she pushed the button for the elevator. "I'd like to see if I can talk to Jane."

"Sure." Olivia rolled her eyes. "Don't worry about Jensen. Sasha will be in all day tomorrow, so he'll have someone else to boss around."

Charlotte glanced down the hall at the door of the Scoop office. "Hey, um . . . be careful around him, okay?"

Olivia's face grew serious. "What do you mean?"

Charlotte tried to look for the right words, not wanting to scare Olivia too much, but also wanting to make sure she didn't get herself into a bad situation with a man who was possibly capable of attacking people on dark sidewalks.

"Did you find out something?" Olivia asked, seeing Charlotte hesitate.

Charlotte quickly shook her head. "No, no, it's fine," she said. "Just . . . can you have Landon pick you up from the train station after work?"

"Okay." Worry crossed Olivia's face, and Charlotte's shoulders slumped. She wished she could be more like Lucy, who could easily throw out assurances that everything was going to be okay. Or Gabe, who could put anyone at ease with a smile or a joke to break the tension. The best Charlotte could do was give a vague, ominous warning, leaving her victim confused and unsettled.

"I'll see you later," Charlotte said, stepping into the elevator as the doors opened.

"Alright."

Charlotte pressed the button for the lobby, then gave Olivia a thin-lipped smile as the doors closed shut.

A few minutes later, she was out of the building and back to navigating the Times Square sidewalk crush, which was considerably thicker now that it was later in the day. Once she fell into the flow of traffic, she shot off a text to Finn:

Charlotte: Hi Finn, my name's Charlotte. I'm a friend of Olivia Kimura from Scoop, who's friends with Eric Walsh. I'm trying to help figure out what might've happened to Eric. Would you be free to meet up sometime?

She paused, then sent a second text:

Charlotte: I'm not a reporter

She paused again.

Charlotte: also not a cop. also I don't work for Scoop

Disclaimers out of the way, she then checked to make sure she hadn't missed a response from Gabe. Still nothing.

He definitely should have replied by now, Charlotte thought, putting her phone back into her pocket as people started crossing the street. She began cycling through all the reasons why Gabe wouldn't text her back:

1. Dead
2. Kidnapped
3. In the hospital
4. Phone broke
5. He suddenly realized he hated Charlotte
6. Alien abduction

Charlotte realized that alien abduction could probably be categorized under *Kidnapped*. She restarted the list:

1. Dead
2. Kidnapped
    a. By humans
    b. By aliens
3. In the hospital
4. Phone broke
5. He suddenly realized he hated Charlotte

She was so absorbed with her mental list-making that she almost ran into someone wearing an Elmo costume with the head tucked under their arm, looking at their phone.

"Ah!" She dodged out of the way. "Sorry."

Headless Elmo didn't respond, which was probably for the best.

Unable to think of any more reasons why Gabe hadn't texted her back, she decided to call Lucy.

"Good morning!" Lucy sang.

"You sound cheerful."

"I am, thank you for noticing! Kickboxing was great; I needed that. What's up?"

Charlotte smiled at the thought of conflict-averse Lucy taking out her frustrations on a punching bag. "Wanna get lunch?"

"Yes! I'm just heading to school to sign a purchase order for supplies, but I'll be free in, like, forty-five minutes."

Charlotte groaned, but then remembered the rice crackers in her pocket. "Okay. I'll try to survive until then."

"We're still on for tonight, right? Is Gabe coming?"

"That is an excellent question." Charlotte veered to the left, giving some pigeons a wide berth. "He hasn't replied to me. Do you think he hates me?"

"OH, HOW THE TABLES HAVE TURNED," Lucy hooted. "Doesn't feel great when your friend doesn't reply to your texts, does it?"

"Yeah, okay, I get it," Charlotte grumbled. "But really, does he hate me?"

"He doesn't hate you, silly," Lucy said. "He's probably just busy at work."

"Since when does Gabe ever let work keep him from replying to a text? Or a call? Or from literally anything else he wants to do?"

"I'm sure he'll reply soon. Did you learn anything at the office?"

Charlotte quickly filled Lucy in on everything that had happened.

"Jensen sucks," was Lucy's first assessment.

"Astute observation."

"Can't really get a read on Martín based on what you said," she continued. "He might just be shy."

"I guess," Charlotte said. "He said more to Jensen than he did to me."

"Well, Jensen's his boss."

"But I'm a *joy* to talk to!"

Lucy laughed.

Charlotte spotted a group of chairs and tables that were set out in the middle of a blocked-off street for people to sit and enjoy the . . . flashing lights of advertisements and six-foot-tall Sesame Street characters. Not wanting to walk any farther until they decided where they were going for lunch, she slid into an empty chair.

"I don't trust Arielle," she continued.

"What? Why not?"

"She's just . . . I can't pin her down. First, she's against the union; then she's helping the union. She's super passionate about the company, but she doesn't want to be a manager. She's loyal to Candice; she's not loyal to Candice." Charlotte shook her head. "It's just weird."

"Definitely seems like she's struggling with a lot right now," Lucy said.

"I wonder why Eric asked her to help with the union stuff," Charlotte mused. "I'd assume Olivia could do whatever he was going to ask Arielle to do. I got the impression that Eric and Olivia were closer than Eric and Arielle."

"Arielle's worked there longer. Maybe she *can* do more than Olivia."

"I guess." Charlotte watched a young woman directing her boyfriend to take a photo of her in front of the Disney Store, oblivious to the giant obstacle she had become in the flow of pedestrian traffic. "I don't know. She's just so *nice.* I feel like she's hiding something."

"I'm sorry, are we just ignoring the fact that Jensen *attacked you?*" Lucy said.

"No, trust me, I am very aware of that fact." Charlotte thought for a moment. "I don't know if he'd personally have enough motive to do something to Eric, but if what Arielle says is true, it's possible he did something on Candice's behalf, whether or not she knows it. But I need proof."

"Are you going to try to talk to Candice?"

"Not sure how. No one will let me near her."

"That never used to stop you before."

"Yeah, well, I'm a little too big now for crawling through vents. I'd have to figure out another way to get info from her."

"I'm sure you will. Okay, I'm going into the subway. I'll text you the address of this restaurant and meet you there in fortyish."

"Sounds good."

"'Byeee."

Charlotte hung up and tucked her phone back into her pocket. The Disney Store woman had finished her photoshoot and was going through the pictures her boyfriend had taken. She didn't look happy with the results.

A thought started creeping its way to the front of Charlotte's mind as she mulled over the new puzzle pieces she had collected. It left a weight in her chest that made her start taking deep breaths to try to make the feeling go away. (Unfortunately, the air quality of Times Square prevented deep breaths from being as relaxing as they should have been.)

What if I can't do this?

The thought began to repeat. The more she tried not to think it, the louder it got. As it echoed in her brain, a posse of additional thoughts joined the chorus:

What if Eric's disappearance has nothing to do with the union?

Why did I say yes?

What if I'm talking to the wrong people?

Seriously, why did I let Lucy talk me into this?

What if this case isn't solvable?

What do I tell Olivia if I can't do this?

What if I can't do this?

What if I can't do this?

What if—

"Excuse me, are you interested in seeing a comedy show tonight?"

"No, thank you," Charlotte murmured, not looking away from the flashing billboard in the distance she had locked her gaze onto as she continued to spiral.

"You sure? It's gonna be really funny."

"No thanks."

"You're reaaaally in the zone right now, huh?" Gabe said drily.

Charlotte snapped out of her spiral and looked up, her jaw dropping as Gabe grinned down at her. "Shut *up.*"

"For real though, do you wanna go see this comedy show?" He waved a flier he was holding in one hand, looking at it. "Some guy just offered this to me, and unlike you, I felt bad saying no."

"What're you doing here?" Charlotte asked, still in shock, as Gabe slid into the seat across from her.

"You told me to come," he said, slipping his backpack off his shoulder and dropping it on the ground.

"I wasn't sure you even got my text, since you *never replied.*"

"I wanted to surprise you!" Gabe spread his arms. "Surprise!"

Charlotte shook her head in disbelief, staring at her other best friend (and feeling relieved that he hadn't been abducted by aliens or realized he hated her).

Gabe Reyes was Filipino-American, with dark brown hair that flopped over his forehead as he grinned, his eyes hidden behind a pair of round-rimmed sunglasses. He was wearing a black, short-sleeved collared shirt with white squiggles all over it, a white T-shirt underneath, and black shorts. His backpack, which sat at his feet, displayed a colorful array of buttons, ranging from Protect Trans Kids to If you're reading this, YOU'RE TOO CLOSE.

"I thought you'd come up after work." Charlotte narrowed her eyes. "Shouldn't you be at work right now?"

Gabe leaned back in his chair, the front two legs rising off the ground. "I decided to take a three-day weekend."

"Today's Thursday."

"Ah. Four-day weekend."

"*Gabe.*"

"It's fine!" He dropped the front two legs of his chair back down onto the pavement and leaned forward, pulling out his phone. "I roasted Wendy's new burger from my company's Twitter account, and Wendy's replied, and we got, like, two hundred new followers. And counting."

He held out his phone to show Charlotte a tweet that read, "*tbh would rather eat one of our mattresses than the new @Wendys salmon burger.*" Below it was a short response from the Wendy's account: "*ratio.*"

"Wow," Charlotte said, pumping enthusiasm into her voice despite understanding very little about how Gabe's job worked.

Gabe returned his phone to his pocket. "So basically everyone's in love with me right now." He put his hands behind his head and leaned back in his chair again. "They practically begged me to take a long weekend."

Charlotte stared at him until he threw his hands up, almost toppling over from the sudden movement.

"Okay, I told them I'm working from home. It's *fine,*" he repeated.

"Alright, alright," Charlotte finally relented, smiling despite herself. "I'm glad you're here. Lucy's gonna lose her mind. We're getting lunch with her in a half hour."

"Oh, hell yes. I'm starving."

The pair soon left their table, passing Headless Elmo, who was in the process of reattaching their head, rendering that title a misnomer, and headed uptown to meet Lucy. Who did, as Charlotte predicted, lose her mind.

"Sorry, I'm so sorry," she apologized to the couple passing her on the sidewalk, who truly hadn't given her a second glance when she practically screamed in their faces upon seeing Gabe.

Still, her face was red with embarrassment as she continued down the sidewalk towards her friends and threw her arms around both of them.

"I am . . . so happy right now," she said, squeezing them both. Gabe quickly reciprocated the hug, and Charlotte stood very still with her arms pinned to her sides, which the other two knew was her way of reciprocating.

"I just need, like, ten more minutes of this, and then we can go in." Despite her threat (which is how Charlotte interpreted that chilling statement), she leaned back a bit to narrow her eyes at Gabe. "Wait. Why aren't you at work?"

"I'm working from home. Charlotte already yelled at me. Let's eat!" Gabe wriggled out of the group hug and bounded into the restaurant before Lucy could say anything else.

Lucy looked at Charlotte, who shrugged. "I think he's got it under control."

"So," Gabe said after they were brought to their table and settled in their chairs, "I want you to tell me everything."

Charlotte opened her mouth to speak.

"But first," he continued, "I need to tell you guys that I've interviewed *five* people to be my new roommate, and each one got progressively more terrible."

"New roommate?" Lucy's brow furrowed as Gabe reached for the bread that had just been placed in the middle of the table, slapping Charlotte's hand away as she tried to snatch the roll he had been aiming for. "What happened to Colby?"

"Keith," Charlotte said, grabbing another roll. "Colby was two roommates ago."

"Colby was *three* roommates ago," Gabe corrected. "Unless you count my cousin Lou, but he just crashed on my couch for three days when my tita found weed in his room and temporarily kicked him out of the house. But I didn't ask him for rent."

"Did you ask him for weed?" Charlotte asked, raising an eyebrow.

Gabe sighed, nodding. "His mom took it all."

Lucy held her hands up, silently pleading with them to slow down. Charlotte always talked pretty fast, but Gabe spoke even faster, words falling out of his mouth like quarters from a winning slot machine. Their conversations were often observed by Lucy like she was watching a professional tennis match. Or an amateur game of ping-pong. Or, for that matter, a professional game of ping-pong. "So it was Colby, then Lou, then Keith."

Gabe used his roll to point at her. "Wrong." He took a bite, his mouth filling with bread as he continued to speak. "Cloby, Blu, Parlie, *den* Keed."

"Did you just say you had a roommate named *Barley?*" Lucy looked over at Charlotte. "I think I would've remembered *Barley.*"

"I think he said 'Charlie,' " Charlotte translated.

"Ah."

Gabe swallowed. "Charlie. Yes. Best roommate I ever had."

"Wait," Lucy said, "wasn't Charlie the one who kept live cockroaches in his sock drawer as pets? Leading to a cockroach infestation in your laundry room?"

"So you understand how low my bar is." Gabe put down the bread and folded his hands, his face serious. "Which is why I have waited for this council meeting to propose this . . . proposal." He turned to Charlotte, who gave him a confused look, then shook her head.

"Forty," she said. "We said if neither of us are married by *forty*—"

"No, not that." Gabe laid his hands palms-up on the table. "Move in with me. Be my new roommate."

"Ohhh," Charlotte said, nodding. "No."

"Why *not?*"

"We *just* established that your laundry room has cockroaches."

"*Lucy,*" Gabe whined, looking to her for support.

"I mean," Lucy started, watching a waiter make his way to their table, "Charlotte doesn't have an income right now."

"*Exactly.* Plus—" Charlotte stopped as their waiter reached the table and took their drink orders. Then she picked up a menu, partially to decide what to eat, partially to block her view of Gabe's pleading face.

"Plus," she continued behind her menu shield, "I have no reason to move out. I'm saving money on rent, and my mom makes me dinner on weekends."

"*No reason?*" Even without seeing his face, Charlotte knew Gabe was putting on an exaggerated wounded expression. "What about the reason of wanting to live with one of your best friends and save him from interviewing any more weird roommate candidates?"

"Why don't you ask one of your social media friends?" Lucy suggested. "Your mutuals, or, whatever."

Gabe slumped back in his chair. "Almost everyone lives in LA or New York. No one's trying to move to *New Jersey*."

"Why not? We have so many gardens," Charlotte deadpanned, lowering her menu.

"Not the biggest selling point for social media influencers, believe it or not." He crossed his arms, sulking. "I guess I'll figure something else out."

"Sure you will," Lucy said, looking over at Charlotte. "We'll help you vet candidates!"

Charlotte gave her a sideways look. "We will?"

"You're telling me you don't want to dig into people's lives and find out if they have any skeletons in their closet?"

"Cockroaches in their sock drawer," Charlotte corrected. "You're right, I'm in."

At that point, their waiter returned, and none of them wanted to admit that they still hadn't looked at the menus, so they all quickly picked the first thing that sounded appealing and gave him their orders.

"Do I like arugula?" Gabe asked as their waiter departed with the menus.

"Yes" and "How should I know?" replied Lucy and Charlotte, respectively.

Gabe nodded, satisfied, then sat back in his chair. "Okay, now we can move on to you telling me everything."

Charlotte gave Gabe the rundown of everything that had happened in the past three-and-a-half days, with Lucy jumping in with occasional commentary ("She almost kicked me in the face trying to get up to the fire escape"; "The sinks worked fine for me. Is this really relevant to the story?").

"It's the manager," Gabe said when she finished. "The manager guy, Jensen. Jensen, in the park, with the gun. He killed that guy Bernard."

"Gabe," Lucy reprimanded, "you can't just go around accusing people of murder without proof."

"I'm not *going around*, I'm just telling you guys. And it sounds like there's plenty of proof." Gabe began counting with his fingers. "Charlotte's sure he's the one who grabbed her—"

"Ninety-five-point-four percent sure," Charlotte clarified. "The percentage is constantly changing."

"—he's obsessed with the CEO and would probably kill someone for her, *and*, he has a gun."

Charlotte narrowed her eyes questioningly. "Who said he has a gun?"

Gabe shrugged, dropping his hand. "Just the way you've been describing him gives me 'owns a gun' energy. Either way, he's a dick."

"Just because he's a dick doesn't mean he's a murderer," Lucy said.

"Right," Charlotte agreed. "All murderers are dicks, but not all dicks are murderers."

Gabe nodded sagely. "A real 'squares and rectangles' situation."

Lucy turned to Charlotte. "You said you took photos of the planner? Have you looked at them?"

Charlotte shook her head. "Didn't get the chance." She pulled her phone out of her pocket and pulled up the photo of the July page, putting her phone on the table in front of her (she figured it was safe enough to put it down, since she wasn't sneaking into the restaurant). Lucy scooted her chair over to get a better look, and Gabe got up and rounded the table to look over their shoulders.

"This was the date I found the most interesting," Charlotte said, zooming in slightly to center the crossed-out meeting with Eric and Martín on the following day.

"'Send out workplace policy updates' didn't pique your interest?" Gabe asked, pointing to an entry a week prior.

"Funny."

"What's interesting about a canceled meeting?" Lucy asked, looking over at Charlotte. "You don't even know what it was about."

"I'm more interested in *why* it was canceled," Charlotte said. "And *when*. There's no sign of it being rescheduled to later this month. So either it was canceled because the topic of the meeting went away, or because one of the people who was supposed to be in attendance did. Go away, I mean." She paused, furrowing her brow. "I *am* still interested in the topic of the meeting. I don't know why I said that like it wasn't interesting."

"Hang on, okay," Gabe said, returning to his seat. "So you think that this meeting was canceled because Eric went missing?"

"Wouldn't that imply that whoever canceled it didn't think Eric would be back by tomorrow?" Lucy asked.

"It's even deeper than that," Charlotte said, zooming out on the photo again. The other two leaned in to look as she ran her finger over the Monday and Friday columns of the planner. "Jane's only in the office on Mondays and Fridays. That's when she's in to update her planner." She looked up. "Eric went missing yesterday. Or Tuesday night, at the earliest. Which means . . ."

"The meeting had to have been canceled before Eric went missing," Lucy finished.

Charlotte nodded. "So if the meeting was canceled by someone who knew Eric wasn't going to be around on Friday, that person had to have known that *before* Eric went missing."

"And by 'someone,'" Gabe said, "you mean either Jane or Martín."

"Or Eric," Lucy said.

"True." Charlotte chewed on the inside of her cheek. "It's still possible he disappeared on his own, for whatever reason."

"Why would he just leave without telling anyone?" Gabe asked.

"I don't know." Charlotte felt her train of thought start to veer off in that direction. *Why would Eric want to disappear?*

"What about the other option?" Lucy asked. "That the meeting was canceled because the topic of the meeting went away?"

Charlotte blinked, resetting her thoughts. She forgot how much it helped to talk through a case out loud—especially to Lucy, who was good at pointing out pieces Charlotte had mentioned that she had already lost track of in the jumble.

"It's a weird duo to have a meeting, right?" Gabe asked. To his credit, Gabe was also helpful to talk things through with. He often made statements that seemed so obvious they weren't worth examining, when more often than not they were actually worth the examination. "Martín and Eric? They're not even on the same team." He suddenly gasped, slamming his hands down on the table, making the silverware rattle and the other two jump. "Or maybe they *are*."

Charlotte and Lucy stared at him blankly.

"Why do people have meetings with HR?" Gabe asked.

"Because multiple people you work with complained about

your excessive sarcasm during the *super* important and *super* necessary hour-long daily meetings?" Charlotte asked.

Gabe blinked. "No. I mean, yes, I assume, since that sounded like it came from a very personal place, but not where I was going with that."

"Because they're getting fired?" Lucy ventured.

"Also yes, but no." He looked at them both expectantly. "Because they're declaring a relationship!"

Charlotte cocked her head. "It's a thought . . . but, no, Jensen said Eric has a girlfriend."

"I thought you said no one knows anything about Eric's partner?"

"They don't, other than Jensen saying he has a girlfriend."

"Well . . . maybe he's polyamorous!"

Lucy held up a hand. "It's a theory," she said, looking at Charlotte. "Do you have a different one?"

Charlotte's mouth shrugged. "Sort of. It's just that Arielle said that Eric recently asked her for some tech help for the union organizing committee. She said it had something to do with messaging more of the workers. The union organizing committee's been around for a bit. I'm wondering why he's just now reaching out to Arielle for help."

"Maybe they're just now trying to widen their reach," Lucy suggested.

"Or maybe he was already getting help. From Martín. But then that help stopped, for some reason, which is why Eric asked Arielle for help."

"Maybe Eric and Martín had some kind of fight," Lucy suggested. "That could explain the HR meeting."

"Love and hate are very similar emotions," Gabe added. "So you're basically suggesting the same thing I did."

Charlotte tapped her fingers on the tabletop as she thought about that. If Martín had a reason to be upset with Eric, that could be a motive. A motive for what, she didn't know yet.

Her mind wandered back to the envelope of cash in Martín's drawer. *"Thanks." Thanks for what?*

"You took a photo of another month?" Lucy asked, pulling Charlotte out of her thoughts.

Just then, their waiter appeared with the food, and they all began the usual routine of clearing space on the table for him to relieve himself of the plates. Once the waiter departed, Charlotte returned her phone to the table and swiped to the next photo, which was the one she'd taken of the March page of Jane's planner.

"That's weird," Gabe said through a mouthful of pasta, pointing at the one Tuesday entry that read, *Jaya exit interview (9:00am)*. "That's weird, right?"

"Right. Jane's usually only in the office on Mondays and Fridays. And everything on this calendar is just for stuff she does when she's in the office. Which means that for some reason, she had to come in on a Tuesday to do Jaya's exit interview."

"Jaya was the manager before Jensen, right?" Gabe asked.

Charlotte nodded. "Arielle said Jaya and Candice were fighting about the union. But no one knows whether she quit or was fired, or if it was even because of that."

"Whatever it was," Gabe said, twirling his fork in his pasta, "it happened fast."

Charlotte finally turned away from the phone and picked up her own fork, stabbing it into her salad. "Because Jane had to come in on a Tuesday? I agree."

"But also the time." Gabe gestured with his fork, a strand of pasta flopping back onto his plate. "I've seen a couple people at my job have exit interviews, and both times, they took place at the end of their last day. I don't know if that's normal, but . . ."

Lucy pulled Charlotte's phone towards her to look at it again. "'Nine a.m.,'" she read out loud. "First thing in the morning." She looked up. "Seems early."

"It's looking more and more like Jaya didn't leave on the best terms," Charlotte said. "Also . . ." She pointed at the following Monday:

Onboarding with new hire (10am)

"That's Olivia," she said. "She got hired to replace Jensen after he got promoted to manager. I'd assume they would have had her start sooner than a full week after Jaya left if they knew in advance that Jaya was leaving." She thought for a moment. "I should ask Olivia about that. Someone remind me to ask Olivia about that."

Gabe raised his hand.

"Not *now*."

"No, it's something else."

"What."

He dropped his hand. "As fascinated as I am about the drama with this Jaya person, what does this have to do with Eric?"

Charlotte tilted her head, thinking. "It might not have anything to do with him. But it's kind of weird, right?" She picked up her fork. "And I've solved enough mysteries to know when something weird pops up in the vicinity of the thing you're investigating, and *keeps* popping up, more often than not, it's somehow related." She speared a tomato and popped it into her mouth. "It's worth looking into, at least."

"You're the detective," Gabe said, shrugging.

"Don't start." Charlotte pulled her phone back towards her as she swallowed the tomato. The Friday before Jaya's exit interview had a note about a meeting with Jaya and Eric.

"Another weird duo," Charlotte said, pointing.

Gabe spun the phone around so he could read the writing. "So maybe *they* were lovers."

"I'm going to strangle you."

"Or," Lucy said, "going with Char's theory, maybe Jaya had been helping Eric with union stuff."

Charlotte nodded. "It'd make sense, if she was so supportive of the union that she'd fight with Candice about it." She sighed. "We have both a lot and also very little information."

"Well, it all means *something*," Lucy said. "The questions are, one, Can you get any more information? And two, Will that information even be worthwhile?"

"I think anything having to do with Eric is worth pursuing." Charlotte tapped on the date with Jaya and Eric's meeting. "And I'm going back to the office tomorrow. I'll see if I can get any information out of Jane then."

Gabe was polishing off the last of the table bread when Charlotte got a reply from Finn:

Finn: Sorry, I don't know anything that could help you

Charlotte: I just have a few questions, won't take more than 20 minutes. I'm in midtown right now, but I can come meet you wherever, whenever you're free

Charlotte reread her response, hoping she didn't sound too desperate. If she was being honest with herself, she didn't expect to be able to get much information out of Jane. If Finn didn't agree to meet up, she had no idea what to do next.

"You okay?" Lucy asked.

"Yeah." Charlotte tapped at her phone, as if that'd make Finn respond faster. "It's the person from the union committee, Finn. I'm trying to convince them to talk to me."

"This is the Finn who Eric didn't get along with, right?" Gabe asked.

"Olivia said they would 'butt heads,' yeah." Charlotte looked up in time to catch the gleam in Gabe's eye. "Don't."

"Don't what?" Gabe asked innocently.

"Don't say they were *lovers*."

"I wasn't going to!"

Charlotte's gaze moved back to her phone as Finn began typing. She glanced back up as Gabe leaned over to whisper something in Lucy's ear.

"What did he say?" she demanded as he pulled away.

"He thinks Finn and Eric are in an 'enemies-to-lovers arc,' " Lucy said plainly.

"Wow! Snitch!" Gabe said, looking betrayed.

"Okay, you"—Charlotte said, pointing at Gabe—"are officially banned from theorizing. They can't *all* be having sex with each other!"

"Can I take this for you?" their waiter asked, materializing at Charlotte's side and pointing at her empty bowl.

Charlotte reddened. "Yes, thank you," she mumbled as Gabe ducked his head, his shoulders shaking with laughter.

"So sorry about them," Lucy said as the waiter whisked the bowl away. "Thanks so much."

Charlotte turned back to Gabe, who smiled sweetly back at her.

"Banned," she repeated, looking back down at her phone as Finn's reply finally came in:

Finn: I'm actually in midtown too. If you're free right now, I have 30 minutes before I need to leave.

Oh, thank god.

"Where'd the waiter go?" Charlotte asked, whipping her head around to look over her shoulder. "We have a thirty-minute window to talk to Finn." She quickly sent a text back, confirming and asking where they wanted to meet, as Lucy craned her neck to look for the waiter. Gabe picked up a napkin and started waving it in the air.

"Stop that," Lucy said, reaching for the napkin. "He's going to think you're being rude."

"Or surrendering," Charlotte added, eyes glued to her phone. A text came in with the address of a bubble tea shop, and she jumped to her feet. "Got the meeting spot."

"One of us can stay here to pay the bill," Lucy said. "You should get going."

Gabe looked over at her. "Who's gonna stay—"

"Nose goes." Lucy's finger shot up to touch the tip of her nose.

Gabe threw the napkin down onto the table. "You *know* I have slow reflexes," he said, crossing his arms and slumping down in his chair.

"You're a hero," Charlotte said, pointing at him as Lucy got to her feet. "Really, you're saving the day right now."

"I know you're just saying that to make me feel better." Gabe sighed. "And it's working. Go."

"I'll text you the address!" Charlotte called over her shoulder as she and Lucy rushed out of the restaurant. "Meet us there!"

Chapter 11

I Spy

Quarterly Report Card
Student: Charlotte Illes
Grade Level: 7

Subject	Instructor	Final Grade	Comments
Language Arts	Li, C	A-	1
Advanced Math	Grant, R	A+	1
Social Studies	Singh, D	A-	1
Science	Day, P	B+	2
PE	Stuart, E	C	7
Health	Hammond, K	A	1
Computers	Coates, G	A+	1
Spanish	Flores, S	A	1

1: Student is doing excellent work
2: Student is progressing satisfactorily
7: Other (see below)

Stuart, E: Lottie continues treating gym class like a free period. While she keeps telling me she's off doing "more important work," she needs to be present for class.

According to Charlotte's phone, the bubble tea shop Finn had chosen was a fifteen-minute walk from the restaurant. She and Lucy got there in eight, high of spirits and short of breath.

"Hang on," Lucy said, resting her hands on her knees as they came to a stop outside. "We can't go in there like this."

"Remember when we used to ride our bikes everywhere?" Charlotte wheezed, massaging a cramp that had developed in her side. "I miss that. No one rides bikes anymore."

Lucy watched two bikers speed by as Charlotte continued to rub her side. "Sure."

"Okay, we gotta go in," Charlotte said. "We don't have much time. Plus, Finn can probably see us through this giant window."

Sure enough, as they entered the shop, Finn raised a hand to catch their attention. They were sitting facing the door, and had clearly just watched Charlotte and Lucy struggling to breathe for the past minute.

Finn: early thirties, Black, close-trimmed beard, dark brown hair falling across their forehead in tight coils. They were wearing an olive-green T-shirt tucked into black jeans, a small watch on their wrist, and wire-rimmed glasses. An empty bubble tea cup sat on the table in front of them.

"Sorry to make you rush," Finn said, a look on their face that was a mixture of puzzled and amused.

Charlotte waved a hand. "No big deal," she said, slipping into a seat across the table. She winced as the cramp in her side flared up. "I'm Charlotte. This is my friend Lucy."

Lucy waved. "Hi." She turned to Charlotte. "I'm getting a tea. Want something?"

"Yeah, whatever you're getting. Thanks." Charlotte turned back to Finn as Lucy headed for the counter. "I really appreciate you taking the time for this."

Finn shrugged. "Like I said in my text, I don't know how much help I'll be. I didn't really know Eric outside our meetings."

"You had a meeting Tuesday night, right?" Charlotte asked. "Eric didn't show up. Has he missed meetings before?"

Finn shook their head. "He's been a part of the committee from the beginning. Never missed one before."

"Where was the meeting?"

"My place."

"Here in the city?"

"Yup."

"What time?"

"Ten. A lot of us work late, so."

"I heard that you and Eric sometimes had differing opinions about the union." Charlotte winced again, this time internally, hoping that didn't come off as accusatory.

"We've had a few debates," Finn said, shifting in their seat. "Eric thought we should pull back on some of the demands so that we might have an easier time getting Scoop to voluntarily recognize the union."

"And what did you think about that?"

"Thought it was bullshit," Finn said calmly. "If we know what we're owed, we should demand all of it." They gave a small, wry smile. "Besides, Candice Watts probably wouldn't voluntarily recognize the union if we were just asking for new shoelaces. Heard she even hired a union avoidance consultant for a hot second. And folks have been talking about company-wide layoffs if the delivery people unionize."

Charlotte's eyebrows shot up. "Really?"

"It's just Scoop trying to scare people out of supporting the unionizing efforts. They're never going to work with us. So why bother holding back on the demands?" Finn shrugged. "But Eric thought we could compromise, or whatever."

"What did the rest of the committee think about that?"

"A couple people said they saw Eric's point," Finn said, shrugging a shoulder, "but most of them sided with me. Everyone's desperate for better working conditions—better pay, better health insurance. Workers' comp, especially." They looked at Charlotte. "A bunch of workers have gotten assaulted and robbed while on the job. And Scoop won't even acknowledge it, much less pay for medical bills."

"That's terrible," Charlotte said as Lucy returned, handing her a tea and a straw and sitting down with her own.

"Scoop does a lot of other shady stuff, too. Like hiding the tip amount from us until we accept the delivery, so we can't avoid orders with no tip. You know, tricking their workers instead of making sure we're earning a living wage." Finn shrugged. "So, yeah. People weren't psyched about pulling back on the demands."

"Whose side was Bernard on?" Charlotte asked, putting down the cup and straw.

"Bernard?" Finn thought for a moment. "Don't remember. He was pretty quiet during most meetings."

Charlotte's brow furrowed. "Why was he on the committee, then?"

"He told someone he had organizing experience. Sounded like he'd be an asset. He came to every meeting, but never really talked unless he was asked a question."

"Did anyone find that weird?" Charlotte asked.

"I guess. But no one felt comfortable kicking the guy out. He wasn't causing any trouble." The corners of their eyes wrinkled slightly. "Other than eating too many of the donuts people would bring to the meetings." The wrinkles disappeared. "I was sorry to hear about his passing."

There was a brief pause, which Charlotte took as an opportunity to collect her thoughts and come up with her next question. Lucy beat her to it.

"So are the delivery workers salaried?" Lucy asked.

Finn nodded. "That's one of the 'appeals' of Scoop," they said, making air quotes with their fingers. "It's not *great* pay—that's something we're fighting for—but it is steady."

"So to form the union," Lucy said, "you have to get workers to agree to an election, right?"

"Yeah. We need support from at least thirty percent of the workers to hold an election. If we get fifty percent, there's a possibility of not even having to hold one if Scoop voluntarily recognizes us as a union." Their mouth shrugged. "It's not likely Candice would recognize the union without being forced to, so we're not holding our breaths for that. Thirty percent is our main goal."

"And are you close to that?" Charlotte asked.

Finn nodded, looking proud. "Yeah. We're able to do it all digitally, thankfully. We've been having a rough enough time collecting signatures without having to get physical cards from everyone."

"Because people aren't interested?" Lucy asked, taking a sip of her tea.

Finn shook their head. "It's just hard to get in contact with the other workers. There's not any email list or anything we can go off of. But we've been making progress."

Charlotte straightened a bit. "How *have* you been contacting the other workers?"

Finn hesitated, and Charlotte could tell they were debating how much to share, and maybe starting to regret how much they had shared already.

"Eric would handle that," they finally said, their gaze dropping to the table. "I don't know much about it."

Charlotte deflated, then jumped as a chair was dropped down next to her with a loud *CLANG*.

"Sorry, 'scuse me," Gabe said. He dropped his backpack on the floor and plopped into the chair, holding a bubble tea.

"How long have you been here?" Lucy asked, looking over her shoulder as if to catch a glimpse of the magic portal Gabe had just stepped through.

"Two minutes? The waiter brought the check as soon as you

guys left, and I took a cab here." Gabe moved his tea into his other hand as he leaned forward to shake hands with Finn. "Hi, I'm Gabe."

"Finn." They looked even more anxious at the sudden company, Charlotte noticed, chewing on the inside of her cheek.

"Great choice of meeting place," Gabe said appreciatively, stabbing his straw through the top of his cup. "It's funny, I didn't really like the taste of bubble tea before I started taking testosterone, but now I love it. I got peach, which I don't even really like as a fruit, but I like it as a flavor, which is weird." He peered at Charlotte's tea, which was still sitting, full, on the table. "What flavor did you get?"

Lucy and Charlotte both gave him A Look.

"Zipping it." Gabe sat back in his chair and took a sip.

Charlotte turned back to Finn, who seemed a little more at ease from Gabe's usual upbeat chatter. She made a mental note to ask Gabe how he did that.

"Finn?" Lucy said gently, interrupting Charlotte's thoughts. "I know you're in a tough spot, and you don't know us. But Eric might be in real trouble. Anything you know could help us figure out what happened with him."

Finn looked back down at the table for a moment. "I really don't know much," they finally said, looking back up, "but I know Eric's had help from some people he works with in the office. There was that one woman for a while, um . . ." They tapped their fingers on the tabletop, trying to remember the name.

"Jaya?" Charlotte offered.

"Yeah." Finn's eyebrows shot up. "You know about her?"

"Not much. Do you?"

"Nope. Only that she was the first person to help Eric start contacting the other delivery workers. And then she left, or got fired, or something. I'm not sure if it was because of the union, but Eric got a lot more private about who was helping us after that. I figured it was to protect the job of whoever it was."

Charlotte lowered her chin. "Protect from who? Do you think someone on the committee told Scoop about Jaya helping you?"

"No. I mean, I dunno." Finn pushed their glasses up their nose. "I think he was just being cautious. And I don't even know if that's what happened with Jaya. I never really asked. As long as Eric was getting us contact info, we didn't care who was helping him." They paused. "He did mention something last week, about how he was going to start getting help from someone new."

"Did he say why?" Charlotte asked.

"No. He just mentioned it in passing and said not to worry about it." Finn suddenly looked up at Charlotte. "You said you know Olivia."

She nodded.

"He said something about her that day," Finn said, nodding as they remembered. "I heard him talking to someone else at the meeting. He said he asked her for help, but she said no. He seemed frustrated."

Charlotte made a questioning face. "That doesn't sound right. Olivia supports the union. Why wouldn't she help?"

"That's just what I heard."

"But he said he found someone else, right?" Gabe asked.

"He said he was working on it," Finn said, shrugging.

Charlotte nodded to herself. So she had been right; Eric did ask Olivia. But why would Olivia say no?

"Are you concerned about being able to get more signatures, with Eric . . . ?" Lucy trailed off.

"I've been trying not to stress about it," Finn said, sliding their empty cup across the table back and forth between their hands. "It hasn't even been two days. We'll figure something out if he . . ." They also trailed off. No one seemed to know how to finish that sentence.

Charlotte had sorted through enough of this information to form a new question. "You seemed confident that no one on the organizing committee would tell Scoop anything. Why do you think Eric was so private about who was helping him, then?"

Finn thought for a moment. "Just figured it was a precaution, I guess." Their brow unfurrowed as they remembered something. "There was one suspicious thing that happened. A couple weeks ago, we were talking about making pins for the workers to wear to show their support for the union. Then, last week, all the delivery workers got an email from Scoop, with an updated dress code that banned any stickers, pins, buttons, or patches from being worn while making deliveries."

"That can't be legal," Gabe said.

"We're looking into filing a charge," Finn said, nodding in agreement. "It could've just been a coincidence—it's not too wild to guess that we were planning on making pins. A lot of organizers do it. But it was weird."

"When you talked about the pins, was that before or after Bernard's death?" Charlotte asked.

"Um . . . after? No, before. It was around the same time, but definitely before." Finn glanced at their watch. "I should get going," they said, standing.

The three of them also stood.

"You've been super helpful," Lucy said. "Thanks so much."

"If you think of anything else that might be relevant," Charlotte said, "or even anything you think might be irrelevant, feel free to text me."

Finn nodded, picking up their empty cup and passing them to head for the door. Then they stopped, turning back around.

"You're thinking Eric's disappearance might be connected to Bernard's death, right?"

Charlotte hesitated, then gave a half-shrug. "Maybe."

Finn thought for a moment, then took a couple steps back towards them. "This might be irrelevant," they said, lowering their voice, "but in case it's not . . . Bernard had a gun."

"Yikes," Gabe muttered.

"How do you know?" Charlotte asked, her brain immediately starting to whir, trying to put this new piece into a spot that fit.

"Heard him talking about it with someone after a meeting.

We'd been discussing how a delivery worker was mugged the week before, and I heard him telling someone that he kept a gun on him whenever he was out, for protection."

"Do you know if he had a license for it?" Lucy asked.

"I wasn't getting that impression from the way he was talking." Finn shrugged. "Not my business, though. Just thought you might want to know."

Charlotte nodded. "Good luck with the union."

Finn cracked a smile. "Thanks." They turned again, raising a hand in farewell over their shoulder before exiting the shop.

The three fell back into their chairs, Gabe getting up to take Finn's seat. Charlotte unwrapped her straw and stabbed it through the top of her bubble tea.

"So," Lucy said.

"So," Charlotte repeated, taking a sip of her tea.

They both looked at Gabe, who was trying to suck up a stray tapioca ball from the bottom of his cup. Successful in his endeavor, he looked back up at them, chewing. He swallowed.

"Oh. So."

"Learned a lot more about Bernard," Charlotte said, taking another sip of her tea.

"Yeah, from the way you were talking, I thought that guy was, like, the head of the union committee," Gabe said. "Now it sounds like he was just in it for the free donuts."

"Well, I thought maybe someone was trying to take out the leaders to put a stop to the organizing," Charlotte admitted.

"So either whoever killed Bernard thought he was more involved than he was," Lucy said, "or . . ."

Charlotte looked at her. "Or?"

"I don't know, I just figured you had another idea."

"Oh. Well, there is one new theory. The whole pin situation makes it sound like the committee had a spy."

"Oooo," Gabe said.

"Thank you," Charlotte said, tilting her cup to point it at him. "Love an engaged audience. Plus, Finn knew about Jaya, but didn't know who started helping the committee after she left. Which makes it sound like something happened with Jaya to give Eric a reason to want to keep the committee from knowing who else was helping them. Maybe he also suspected there was a spy." Charlotte's eyes suddenly went wide. "Oh my god, I'm an idiot."

"We knew that, but why specifically?" Gabe asked.

Charlotte pressed her fingers to her temples. "People keep saying they don't know what happened with Jaya. But obviously we know what *didn't* happen with her."

"Obviously," Lucy agreed, nodding.

Gabe narrowed his eyes at her. "It's obvious to you?"

"Yeah. It isn't to you?"

"Shut up." Gabe chuckled. "You don't know any more than I do." He stopped laughing, the smile dropping off his face. "Right?"

Lucy shrugged, turning back to Charlotte. "Go on, tell Gabe the thing that's obvious to both of us."

"Jaya didn't get fired," Charlotte said, ignoring Gabe's "Pfffftttt" in response to Lucy. "Or, if she did, it wasn't because she was helping with the union. Because if Scoop is firing people for working with the union committee . . ." She trailed off, looking at them.

"They'd have already fired Eric!" Gabe blurted out. He smirked at Lucy. "I got it."

"Proud of you."

"So it's still unclear why Eric would want to keep whoever was helping him a secret," Charlotte said. "If their job wasn't at risk, I mean."

"Maybe the company still would've given them a hard time," Lucy suggested. "Even if they wouldn't get fired, they could still be punished in other ways."

"Yeah. Yeah, that makes sense."

"Question," Gabe said, raising his hand. "We keep saying

'whoever was helping Eric.' We know it's not Jaya, because she left. We know it's not Olivia, because she apparently said no."

"Which is weird, right?" Lucy asked. Charlotte nodded.

"And we know it's not Arielle, because she was about to start helping." Gabe spread out his hands. "So . . . process of elimination, right?"

"I guess," Charlotte said. "Especially considering that HR meeting on Jane's schedule. The weird thing is, Martín didn't seem to care much about the union."

"Well, yeah," Lucy said, raising an eyebrow. "Of course he wasn't going to tell *you*, a total stranger, that he supported the union. Not to mention the fact that you asked him in his workplace, with his dickish boss lurking around the corner."

"I thought I was being very charming!" Charlotte objected.

"Did you do that thing where you just ramble on and on because you think it puts people at ease?"

"It *does*! Usually."

"No, it freaks people out."

Charlotte gave Lucy an appalled look. "You've never told me that."

"I've told you that *multiple times*. A year. Since we were nine."

"Well, you've never told me in a way that'd I'd actually *retain it*."

Lucy narrowed her eyes. "Maybe—just as a rule of thumb—retain any and all advice I give you."

"Okay, noted."

Gabe looked at Lucy. "She's not going to retain that."

"Fine." Charlotte put her tea down and raised her hands in defeat. "Martín was helping Eric. And then stopped, for some reason. Um . . ." *Martín was helping Eric . . . Eric kept that a secret . . . Jaya wasn't fired . . . Eric wasn't fired . . . Eric asked Olivia for help . . .*

Charlotte closed her eyes, trying to focus. Her finger tapped on the tabletop like she was sending a gibberish telegram as she desperately attempted to get her thoughts in order. It would have been an easier task if she were feeling confident in her line of thinking, but she found it to be much more challenging as she continued to doubt every thought she had.

Seeming to notice that Charlotte was struggling to keep her thoughts in order, Lucy said, "We can put that on the back burner, for now. Back to Bernard?"

Charlotte opened her eyes and nodded, relieved. "Right. Thanks. Bernard." She stopped tapping. "So. Let's say Bernard was the spy."

"Wait, are we saying that?" Gabe asked. "I missed that."

"Skipped ahead, sorry. Let's say Bernard was the spy. He joined the committee claiming to have organizing knowledge, but barely participated, despite attending every meeting. The committee discussed the pins right before Bernard's death, which would have given him time to pass that information on to whoever he was reporting to before he got murdered."

"But why was he murdered then?" Lucy asked.

"Maybe someone in the union found out he was a spy?" Gabe suggested.

"Maybe." Charlotte pursed her lips. "Finn seems pretty tapped into the committee, though. And they didn't even seem to suspect there was a spy at all, much less to suspect Bernard."

"You said Eric might have known," Lucy pointed out.

"Right. Right, I did say that."

"Did *Eric* kill Bernard?" Gabe asked.

"That's . . . possible." *Did Martín discover something about Eric that made him want to stop helping him? Could Eric have had something to do with Bernard's death? And what was that envelope of cash for?*

Charlotte thought for another moment, then covered her face. "Auuug*hhhhh*."

"Hello?" Gabe asked, looking both amused and concerned. "Are you good?"

"There's too much information," Charlotte groaned through

her hands. "I don't know how I used to remember everything. My brain feels fried."

"You didn't remember everything," Lucy said. When Charlotte uncovered her face and looked at her questioningly, she continued. "You had that little notebook. The blue spiral one? You'd write all your notes in there."

Charlotte straightened. "Oh my god. Yes. Perfect." She glanced around. "Does anyone have a pen and paper?"

Lucy and Gabe stared at her.

"What." Charlotte blinked. "Oh. Right." She pulled her phone out of her pocket.

Three minutes later, she had typed out everything they had learned so far.

"Okay." She scrolled through what she had written, her brain feeling slightly less chaotic. Charlotte wasn't sure why she hadn't started typing this all out earlier. Maybe because it was harder to deny that she was being a detective when she had a phone full of clues.

"Finn said there's been talk of company-wide layoffs if the union succeeds," Charlotte said, stopping at that bullet point in her notes. "Whether or not that'd actually happen, it gives almost everyone at Scoop a motive for wanting to stop the unionizing efforts."

"Great, glad we've narrowed down the suspect list," Gabe deadpanned, dropping his head back to look up at the ceiling.

"So what's next?" Lucy asked.

Charlotte continued staring at her phone, the overwhelmed feeling creeping back into her brain. She needed to think about something else, or else the workers at the bubble tea shop were going to have the unique experience of seeing a former kid detective run screaming out the door.

Then again, it was New York. It probably wouldn't be the strangest thing they'd see that day.

Her chest tightening, she quickly locked her phone and put

it facedown on the table. "Next," she said, looking over at Lucy, "you're going to tell us what's really going on with Jake."

Gabe's head snapped back down, his eyes wide as he turned to Lucy, who scowled. "I don't want to talk about it."

"But—"

"No." She crossed her arms. "Kickboxing put me in a good mood. Don't ruin it for me." Lucy raised her eyebrows at Charlotte, daring her to continue pushing.

Instead, Gabe spoke up. "I was told we were following him tonight."

"*Stumbling*," Lucy quickly corrected. "Charlotte said we'd stumble across him tonight."

Gabe narrowed his eyes with amusement. "That just sounds like her 'poking around' bullshit." He dropped the face. "Seriously, though. If you're going to ask Charlotte to look into it, you should at least tell us why." He cocked his head. "Technically, you don't have to tell *me* why, but you should anyway, because I like knowing things."

"I already told her why!" Lucy said, uncrossing her arms. "I said we haven't been feeling close, and he's been going out a lot."

"Right, but then I did some poking around," Charlotte said, flipping Gabe off as he snorted, "and it came up empty."

Lucy frowned. "You DMed a woman on Instagram to do your work for you."

"It got results!"

"Was she his type?" Gabe asked. The other two looked at him, and he shrugged. "I know it was one of those loyalty tests, but was she even his type?"

Lucy gestured towards Gabe. "Exactly! It was a half-assed investigation."

"Well, *maybe* if you gave me a little more information than a 'feeling' . . ." Charlotte grumbled.

"Again, I told you that he goes out with his friends a lot! Which is why we're going to stumble across him tonight." Lucy sat back in her chair. "I found out what bar he's going to. Should be around seven. If he's there, then . . ."

Charlotte and Gabe stared at her, waiting.

"Then you'll be satisfied?" Charlotte finally asked, not convinced.

Lucy shrugged. "Sure."

Gabe didn't look convinced, either, but then he drummed the table with the palms of his hands in an attempt to break the tension.

"So. What're we going to do for the next"—he flipped over Charlotte's phone to check the time—"five hours?"

Charlotte silently chewed on the inside of her cheek as Lucy studied the tabletop.

Gabe looked back and forth between them. "Ooooookay, I'll go first. Find the nearest park and help me take some pics to post?"

They watched Lucy almost literally shake off whatever she had been feeling as she brightened, happy to have a distraction. "That sounds nice."

She turned to Charlotte, who nodded. "Sure, let's go."

"*You* won't be taking any photos," Gabe said to Charlotte as they got up to leave the shop. "You're a terrible photographer."

"What? I take great photos of you."

"Never," Gabe said, pushing the door open for them to walk out as Lucy waved goodbye to the person behind the counter. "Never in my *life* have you taken a single postable photo of me."

Charlotte scowled. "You don't understand my artistic vision."

"Your artistic vision needs an optometrist."

This continued for the entirety of the walk to Bryant Park, where they managed to snag an empty patch of grass with a good view of three people juggling brightly colored clubs.

"I could do that," Gabe said confidently as he dropped to the ground, shrugging off his backpack and nodding at the jugglers.

"Like, *immediately*?" Lucy asked, checking the grass carefully before also sitting down. "Absolutely no way."

Charlotte also sat down, soaking in the warm afternoon sun. The tightening she had felt in her chest had begun loosening as they walked, and was now almost entirely gone.

"I firmly believe I could figure out how to juggle in under five minutes if I really put my mind to it. I'll show you; give me something to juggle." Gabe looked around, then held his hand out to Charlotte. "Give me your phone."

"Absolutely not."

"Well, I guess we'll never know." He flopped onto his back, pulling his backpack over to use as a pillow. "This is nice."

"It is," Lucy agreed.

Charlotte watched as the jugglers began tossing clubs back and forth to each other. "Yeah."

Gabe started doing some work from his phone, while Lucy read an e-book and Charlotte people-watched. This was followed by a photoshoot that resulted in no fewer than eighty photos for Gabe to choose from to post.

"See this?" He held out his phone for Charlotte to look at. "*This* is a good photo."

Lucy bowed her head and waved her hand in humble thanks.

"I could take that photo." Charlotte grabbed the phone, standing up. "Do that pose again."

Gabe sat down and draped one arm over his knee, tilting his head to the side. Charlotte took the photo. "There, see how that looks."

"I can tell you already, it was terrible," Gabe said, retrieving the phone. He looked at the photo, then immediately looked back up. "Horrific."

"It is *not.*"

"Your angle sucks, you cut off my foot, and that man in the background is mid-nose pick." He deleted the photo. "You're fired." He made a show of deleting the photo from his Recently Deleted folder, to add insult to injury.

"Fine," Charlotte grumbled, kicking at the grass. "I didn't wanna do it anyway."

But she knew Gabe was probably right. He had an eye for that kind of thing—which played a large part in him gaining his steadily growing Instagram following. That, and his knack for community building, his sense of humor, and his thirst traps.

They moved to a more shaded table to avoid the sun as the afternoon wore on. Eventually the park started to get more crowded, so they left to walk around. After an hour of ducking into stores that resulted in Gabe buying a dark green bomber jacket and Lucy getting a pair of gold drop earrings, they all agreed that it was time to eat.

Charlotte was mopping up her pasta sauce with a piece of bread when she noticed Lucy fidgeting with her silverware.

"What?" Charlotte asked.

Lucy looked up at her, confused. "What?"

"You're fidgeting."

"No I'm not." Lucy dropped her hands into her lap.

"Now you're squeezing your hands together under the table."

"Stop that."

Gabe waved at their waitress, who walked over. "Could we get the check, when you get the chance?" he asked, smiling at her.

"Sure thing, be right back." She smiled back at him for a long beat before turning and walking away.

Charlotte gently rolled her eyes. "One day," she said as he turned back. "I'd love to go just one day without having to watch you flirt with someone."

Gabe waved a hand modestly. "I was just being polite. And she's just being nice, it's her job."

"Yeah, okay."

"I'm sorry," Lucy said, pointing at the spot their waitress had just occupied, "you thought *that* was flirting?"

"They both did the long, drawn-out smile thing!"

"That's *barely* flirting."

"Maybe that's why you haven't been on a second date," Gabe said innocently, leaning back in his chair. "You don't know how to flirt."

"I know how to flirt," Charlotte said flatly.

Gabe spread his hands as if to say, *Prove it.*

"The reason I haven't been on a second date," Charlotte said, folding her hands on the table, "is because *everyone* Googles their dates beforehand. And what do you think they find when they search for 'Charlotte Illes'?"

"That video of you falling into the fountain at Six Flags?"

"*What*? Who posted that?"

"Nothing. Not me. What *is* the first result for your name?" Gabe asked, pulling out his phone.

"It's her interview on *Good Morning America* from, like, twelve years ago," Lucy said. She shrugged as Charlotte turned to look at her, bemused. "I was curious one time."

"Okay, but I'm confused," Gabe said, putting his phone away. "Most people would kill for a conversation starter like that. And I know—*shut up*—" he said, as Charlotte opened her mouth to reply—"that you don't wanna be a detective anymore, but people think it's *cool*. They wanna talk about it."

"Yeah, but it's *all* they want to talk about," Charlotte said. "Half the time, they don't even want to talk about themselves, because they feel like they're boring in comparison. You know how hard it is to motivate yourself to go on a second date with a person you barely know anything about?"

Gabe paused, thinking. "How hot are they?"

"*Gabe.*"

"It was a valid question!"

"So why don't you try to talk about something else?" Lucy asked. "Just say, 'Hey, I don't really like to talk a lot about the detective stuff, can I tell you about *blank* instead?' "

Charlotte furrowed her brow. "And what's 'blank'?"

"Whatever else about yourself you want to talk about."

Their waitress returned then with the check, putting it down in front of Gabe and telling them to take all the time they needed, as Charlotte stared at the table and contemplated her entire existence.

What else *was* there to talk about? How she was recently unemployed? How she had no idea what she wanted to do with her life? How she invented a snack that involved coring an apple and stuffing peanut butter inside, but then stopped making it because the apple corer broke and she didn't feel like trying to replicate it with a knife? She had spent so much time lamenting that people only seemed to want to talk about her girl detective days, and never considered that maybe that was all there was *to* talk about.

Charlotte snapped out of it long enough to help pay the check, then zoned out again after the waitress left with their cards. A few minutes later, the waitress returned, placing the leather check holder with their cards in front of Gabe before telling them to have a good night and walking away.

Gabe opened the check holder as Lucy peered across the table, both of them unaware that their friend was in the middle of a crisis.

"Is that . . . ?" Lucy leaned forward and grabbed the check, beating Gabe to the punch. "Yup," she said, waving it in Charlotte's direction and grinning, "that's a phone number, folks."

Charlotte pushed her thoughts aside to smirk at Gabe. "Like I said."

Gabe snatched it back to a chorus of *oooOOOooo*s.

"Well," he said, looking straight-faced at the number scribbled on the bottom of the check before pocketing it, "that's very flattering."

His face broke into a grin as the other two started booing him.

"Fake modesty is *not* a good look for you," Lucy said, throwing her napkin at him.

"Hey!" Gabe winced as crumbs sprayed onto his shirt, then chucked the napkin back at her.

"Sorry," Lucy said, deftly grabbing the napkin out of the air. "Are you gonna text her?"

Gabe shrugged, brushing crumbs off of his shirt before sitting back in his chair. "Perhaps," he said noncommittally.

He pretended to look shocked as he was met with another round of boos. "I don't think it's any of your business!"

"You were just prying into *my* dating life," Charlotte protested. "The *least* you could do is tell us if you're gonna text her."

Gabe pushed back his chair and stood. "Let's bounce."

Rolling her eyes good-naturedly, Charlotte stood, too. Lucy stayed in her seat, suddenly very still.

Charlotte paused. "Luce?"

Lucy was holding the napkin in her lap, twisting it with both hands.

Charlotte and Gabe looked at each other. The following is a loose transcription of the conversation they had via facial expressions and small head movements:

> Gabe: Uhhhh . . .
> Charlotte: Uhhhh . . .
> Gabe: What do we do?
> Charlotte: I don't know. Talk to her.
> Gabe: *You* talk to her!
> Charlotte: You're better with this stuff than I am!
> Gabe: I don't even know what's happening!
> *[10 seconds of staring]*
> Gabe: FINE.

Gabe flopped back down, leaning in towards Lucy. "Hey, Luce? Luce Goose? Are you ready to go?"

Charlotte gingerly sat back down in her chair as Lucy mumbled, "Mmm . . . I dunno." She didn't look up from the napkin in her hands. "I'm nervous."

"There's nothing to be nervous about!" Gabe gently pulled the napkin out of her grasp and took her hands, resting them on the table. "We're just gonna go to a bar, see what we see, and odds are it'll all be okay, right?" Gabe looked over at Charlotte, eyes wide.

"Right," Charlotte answered quickly. "It's all totally chill and casual, nothing to be nervous about." She leaned forward and awkwardly added a hand on top of theirs. "Everything's fine."

Lucy nodded. "Okay." She extracted herself from the hand pile and stood, pulling her purse over her shoulder. "Let's go before I chicken out."

Despite the assurances of one former (definitely not current) detective, everything was *not* fine.

One would have thought that everything was fine as the trio arrived at the bar where Jake said he'd be with his friends, and saw through the front window that Jake was, in fact, there with his friends. Charlotte and Gabe allowed themselves twin sighs of relief, not realizing that relief was premature until they noticed Lucy staring blankly at Jake through the glass.

Then her face crumbled, and she began to cry.

Chapter 12

Bathroom Party (Reprise)

They quickly pulled Lucy away from the window before Jake noticed them. Gabe held Lucy as her shoulders began to shake with sobs, while Charlotte frantically did the first thing she could think of that could potentially deescalate the situation: looked up the nearest ice cream shop. There was one right around the corner, and Charlotte led them to it, walking ahead while shooting anxious glances over her shoulder every few seconds.

Gabe deposited Lucy onto a bright pink bench that sat in front of the ice cream shop, silently directing Charlotte to sit next to her. Then, like a man on a mission, he disappeared inside.

Lucy's sobs had quieted. She sat hunched over on the bench, elbows on her knees, her face hidden in her hands. Charlotte quietly rubbed her back, not knowing what else to do.

Her mind raced. Logically, seeing Jake at the bar *not* cheating on Lucy was a good thing, right? Her brain fought to argue the logic of this, considering Lucy's less-than-enthusiastic reaction. These were the facts:

- Lucy and Jake had been dating for almost four years
- Lucy was in love with Jake
- Jake was at the bar, which meant:
    - Jake was not cheating on Lucy
    - Jake and his friends had shitty taste in bars

Charlotte was about to give up on this particular mystery and just head back to the shitty bar to hit Jake with a chair for *whatever* it was that he did to make Lucy cry. Then Gabe burst out of the shop, holding an ice cream cone in one hand and stuffing change into his pocket with the other.

He glanced at Charlotte as he moved to sit on Lucy's other side, silently asking if Lucy had said anything yet. Charlotte shook her head.

"Hey, Luce," Gabe said gently, putting a hand on her shoulder. "Got your favorite: mint chocolate chip with rainbow sprinkles, for some reason."

Lucy uncovered her face, sniffing. She accepted the ice cream cone, but just stared at it. "The sprinkles make me happy," she said softly.

"Oh, I'll take it back then. You're honestly a little *too* happy right now, and it's freaking us out."

Lucy let out a small laugh, and Charlotte felt her shoulders untense a bit. She hadn't even realized they *were* tensed.

"Do you . . . you don't have to," Gabe quickly added, "but do you wanna talk about it? Or just eat ice cream?"

"I'm not really hungry," Lucy said, taking a large bite. She swallowed, then sighed. "I don't know. I didn't really realize . . . I mean, I knew I was nervous about finding out if he was cheating on me, but I didn't really let myself think about . . . about if I was nervous he was or nervous he wasn't." Her eyes started to well up again, and it finally clicked for Charlotte.

- ~~Lucy was in love with Jake~~

"I guess I was just looking for a 'good' reason to break up with him," Lucy said softly.

Charlotte silently took Lucy's free hand as she continued talking. "I've just been so . . . unhappy. I thought that moving here with Jake, starting my new job . . . I really felt like I was moving forward with my life. And my dad was so excited about me living in the city where he grew up . . ."

Lucy's face grew cloudy with anger. "But I *hate* our apartment, and I *hate* my school, and I *hate* those teachers who make me feel like shit all the time. My favorite bakery was featured in a YouTube video, so now it's always crowded, and I *hate* that. And I *hate*—" She stopped, squeezing Charlotte's hand. Her ice cream was melting down the cone, but she didn't notice. Gabe did, however, and silently pointed it out.

Lucy licked the ice cream before it could run onto her hand, then fell quiet for a bit. Finally, she said, "I don't hate Jake. I do care about him. But I thought this was gonna be a big step we were taking together, and he's, like, *thriving* here, and I've been . . . drowning."

"Have you told him how you've been feeling?" Gabe asked gently.

She scoffed. "He just keeps saying I need more time to adjust. But I know how I feel. About living here, about working at that school, and . . ." She sighed. "I guess, now, about him."

Charlotte swallowed hard. She felt her eyes filling with tears, and silently fought to keep them at bay. She must have been squeezing Lucy's hand a little too hard, because Lucy looked over at her, alarm suddenly crossing her face. "Why are *you* upset? You don't even like Jake."

"I just, I . . ." One traitorous tear escaped Charlotte's eye and rolled down her cheek. "You were going through all this, and I wasn't even . . . I didn't know, and-and you were . . ."

She trailed off, guilt and shame turning her tongue to lead. Of course she didn't know. Assuming her best friend was out living her best life, Charlotte had never given Lucy the chance to tell her otherwise. She thought she'd been doing what was best for Lucy, but . . .

Oh my god. I'm a terrible friend.

Before she knew what was happening, Lucy had her in a hug, holding the ice cream cone safely out to the side before Gabe retrieved it from her hand. "Hey," she said, wrapping her now-free right arm around Charlotte. "It's okay."

That only made Charlotte cry harder, though she tried to turn it off. She was supposed to be consoling Lucy, not the other way around.

Strangely enough, though, consoling Charlotte seemed to make Lucy feel better. They pulled apart as Charlotte rubbed her eyes, feeling embarrassed.

"You guys are such babies," Gabe said from Lucy's other side, quickly swiping a tear away with his free hand. He took a bite of Lucy's ice cream, then scrunched up his nose with disgust. "Salty."

The other two laughed weakly, still wiping away tears.

"Do you wanna talk more about it?" Charlotte asked after a moment.

Lucy's mouth shrugged. "I dunno. Not now." She let out a big sigh. "That felt good to say out loud, though. Not just to tell you guys, but . . . I think also to hear myself say it. That helped."

"Would it also help if I posted a mediocre review of your favorite bakery on YouTube?" Gabe offered, returning her ice cream cone to her. "Not bad enough to put them out of business, just enough to get rid of the tourists."

Lucy laughed again as Charlotte pulled out her phone, sniffing a bit. She had seen a text from Olivia come in as they got to the bar, before getting distracted by The Case of Why Is Lucy Crying All of a Sudden?

Olivia: are you still in the city?

Olivia: follow-up: do you still want to try to talk to Candice?

Charlotte's eyebrows shot up.

Charlotte: yes and yes
Charlotte: will she meet with me?
Olivia: no, but Arielle just posted a photo of them at a club in midtown
Olivia: it's called Roots
Charlotte: thank you!!
Olivia: please don't get me fired
Charlotte: I won't!!

Charlotte winced as she sent off that last text. She really hoped she wouldn't, at least.

"What's happening?" Lucy asked, nibbling at her cone.

Charlotte quickly filled them in. She had barely said the word *club* when Gabe whooped.

"Now the night is getting *interesting*," he said, rubbing his hands together. He dove into his backpack, digging out the jacket he had bought earlier.

"I was just *crying*," Lucy said. "Was that not interesting enough for you?"

"Yeah, no, you're interesting, you're interesting," Gabe assured her. "But this is the perfect opportunity to debut the bomber."

Lucy turned back to Charlotte as Gabe shrugged off his overshirt and wriggled into the jacket. "What's the plan, then?" she asked.

"Um." Charlotte blinked. "I thought I'd kind of just . . . wing it."

Lucy gave her A Look. "If Arielle tells Candice who you are, she's not gonna want to talk to you."

Charlotte nodded thoughtfully. "So . . . we make sure Arielle doesn't see me?"

Lucy sighed, standing. "It's definitely *a* plan."

"Are you guys going to wear that?" Gabe asked, eyeing the two of them as Charlotte stood. He tucked his chin in defensively against the withering looks he received in return. "I mean," he added quickly, "you both look *great.* Very fun outfits. They're just not . . . *club.*"

Charlotte and Lucy eyed each other. Charlotte was wearing the aforementioned wrinkled white tee and frayed shorts, and Lucy was wearing a burnt-orange blouse embroidered with flowers and light blue jeans.

"Where is this place?" Lucy sighed, crossing her arms.

Charlotte quickly pulled up a map and held out her phone. Lucy leaned in to examine it.

"My apartment's not too far out of the way," she said, straightening. "We can stop there and change."

"Do we *have* to?" Charlotte whined. "I don't need to look nice while trying to determine if someone's guilty of something. Really, I'd rather be dressed as comfortably as possible in that situation."

"Gabe's right," Lucy said. "If you're trying not to be noticed by Arielle, it'll be better to blend in."

"Yup," Gabe chimed in. "That's exactly what I was thinking."

"No it wasn't," Charlotte scoffed, looking around Lucy to scowl at him. "Don't give him credit for that."

"Plus," Lucy said, ignoring them both, "if Arielle *does* notice you, it's better to look like you were actually planning on going to a club tonight, not like you just found out that a suspect you've been trying to talk to is there." A smile crept onto her face. "Besides, I've had this jumpsuit for almost a year and still haven't worn it out."

Charlotte groaned, but knew that every moment she spent complaining was more time wasted. "Fine. Let's go."

After the scathing review of Lucy and Jake's apartment they had recently received from the former, neither Charlotte nor Gabe was particularly interested in getting a tour. Not that there was time for that, anyway. Lucy power-walked to the bedroom, the other two hurrying behind.

"Let's see if I have something that'll fit you," Lucy said, sliding open her closet door. "You're smaller than me."

"That's a nice way of saying your boobs are bigger than mine," Charlotte said, flopping down onto the bed, where Gabe had already taken up residence. "I don't want anything too low-cut."

"I know, I'm on it." Lucy began digging through her hangers.

Charlotte looked around the bedroom. It was pretty boring, especially compared to Lucy's childhood room. There were no fuzzy pillows, no brightly colored storage boxes bursting with crafts and art supplies. They had passed a small bookshelf on their way to the bedroom, but there was no way it held Lucy's entire collection of books.

The only sign that Lucy Ortega lived there (besides the closet full of clothes that she was currently buried in) was a small corkboard that sat on the night table on the left side of the bed, leaning against the wall. At least, Charlotte had to assume it was a corkboard, since its entire surface was plastered with photos stuck on with colorful tacks. A picture of Lucy with her parents and siblings at her college graduation. Lucy with her dad's family in Puerto Rico, and with her mom's family in Argentina. A couple of photos with some college friends. And multiple photos of Lucy with Charlotte and Gabe.

Charlotte smiled at a photo of eight-year-old Lottie and Lucy walking in their school's annual Halloween parade. Lucy was dressed as a cheerleader, and Lottie was dressed as Steve Martin in *The Pink Panther*, her fake mustache half falling off her face. Lucy was waving a pom-pom at the camera while Lottie gazed intently at a kid wearing a *Scream* mask (he had been a suspect in an investigation, though Charlotte couldn't remember exactly what the investigation was. Something about pumpkins).

She could only see one photo of Jake on the board, of him and Lucy at one of his frat formals in college. Before she could do a thorough search for any other Jake photos, Gabe's voice pulled her back to the matter at hand.

"I love that dress on you," he said to Lucy, pointing into the closet. "Wear that."

Lucy pulled out a jumpsuit and tossed it at him. "I'm wearing this."

It was dark red, with a deep V neckline and a halter neck with an open back. Gabe gave the jumpsuit an appraising eye, then nodded. "Yes. Excellent. Approved."

"I wasn't asking for your approval," Lucy said over her shoulder.

"But you've got it."

"I don't want it."

"But it's yours."

"That." Charlotte pointed at the dress in Lucy's hand. "That one. That's fine." It was a body-con dress, dark blue, with a high neck, no sleeves, and cutouts on both sides.

"This could work," Lucy said, holding it up. "It's always been kind of tight on me, anyway. Try it." She tossed it at Charlotte, then retrieved her jumpsuit from Gabe, who promptly rolled over and buried his face into a pillow while they changed.

"Are you gonna do any additional makeup?" he asked, his voice muffled by the pillow. Charlotte grabbed another pillow and whacked him on the back of the head. "OW. I was just *asking.*"

"No time," she said, dropping the pillow and continuing to wriggle into the dress. Other than being a little wide in the shoulders, it fit pretty well. Charlotte grabbed Gabe's backpack from the floor and stuffed her clothes into it.

Lucy ducked into the bathroom to freshen up her makeup. ("You look fine." "I was just *crying.*")

"Do you want earrings?" she called from the bathroom.

"No, I want to *goooo.*"

"Okay, okay." Lucy walked back out, putting in a second gold hoop earring. Then she paused, looking at the bed. "Um . . . do you . . . it's not that serious, I'd be okay, but—"

"Do you wanna stay at Landon's tonight?" Charlotte asked.

Lucy nodded, looking relieved. "Can I?"

"'Course. Gabe, you can look, we've been dressed for like two minutes."

Gabe rolled onto his back. "Well, no one told *me*. Can I also stay at Landon's tonight?"

"Yes."

He sat up, looking back and forth between the two of them. "Respectfully, you guys look hot."

Charlotte threw his backpack at him, which he caught with a grunt. "Let's go."

"Oh, god," Gabe groaned as they walked down the sidewalk at a pace that was much slower than Charlotte would have liked. Lucy had changed into a pair of chunky pumps with ankle straps, and while she walked faster in them than Charlotte ever would have been able to, speed walking was definitely out of the question.

"What?" Charlotte asked, looking over her shoulder at Gabe. Uninhibited by heels or Gabe's tendency to get distracted by everything, she had to keep slowing down every block or so to let the other two catch up to her.

Gabe pointed at Lucy. "Blossom." He pointed at Charlotte. "Bubbles." Then he pointed at himself. "Buttercup."

"Oh, *no*," Lucy laughed, realizing that the colors they were wearing did, in fact, match those of the Powerpuff Girls.

"And it's not even accurate!" he exclaimed, bumping into Charlotte as she stopped to check the map on her phone. "I'm the Blossom. You're Bubbles. *Charlotte*'s Buttercup. Ah, puppy!" He twisted to watch a fluffy black dog walk by on a leash.

"That's Bubbles behavior," Lucy said pointedly.

"I contain multitudes."

"Solid SAT word," Charlotte said, looking up from her phone and rounding the corner. "The place should be on this . . ." She stopped, and Gabe ran into her again.

"Can you beep or something when you're going to . . ." Gabe trailed off, looking ahead of them. "Shit."

"The line is down the *block*," Lucy said, her shoulders slumping as the three of them looked at the long line of people waiting to get into Roots.

"It's Thursday," Charlotte said, appalled. "What are all these people doing out on a *Thursday*?" She turned to see Gabe and Lucy staring at her. "What?"

"Don't worry about it, Lola." Gabe gave her a pat on the shoulder, then walked past her to get on line. Lucy followed.

"I'm not a grandma," Charlotte grumbled, trailing behind them.

As they joined the line, Gabe craned his neck to try to see the front. "It's not moving very fast," he said. "They're probably only letting more people in once other people come out."

"We don't have time for this," Charlotte said, tapping her foot anxiously. "This might be my only chance to talk to Candice."

"What are you even going to say to her if you do get in?" Gabe asked. " 'Hey, nice to meet you. Have you ever murdered anyone?' "

"Yes, Gabriel, that's exactly what I was planning on asking her. If all goes according to plan, she'll leave to turn herself in and I can catch the last train home."

"What *are* you going to ask her?" Lucy asked.

"I want to find out more about what happened with Jaya." They shuffled forward a few inches as the bouncer let a couple of people inside. "She keeps coming up, but no one seems to know what exactly happened. Even though she's gone, I feel like she's still involved, somehow. Or, at least, still important."

"Are we even sure Candice is still here?" Gabe asked.

"I texted Olivia on the way, and she said that Arielle posted again, like, eight minutes ago. So unless they *just* left . . ." Charlotte groaned, then stamped her feet in a mini tantrum. "But that doesn't matter if we can't get *in.*"

Gabe straightened the front of his jacket and ran his fingers through his hair. "Don't worry, ladies," he said, turning. "I'll handle this." He shot them finger guns over his shoulder before heading to the front of the line.

Lucy watched him leave, then looked over at Charlotte. "Odds he actually handles this?"

"I dunno. The boy *is* charismatic."

"Solid SAT word. Ooh! I did one. I never get to do that."

"That's because you're always the one saying the words." Charlotte leaned out of line to watch Gabe approach the door. "He's walking up to the bouncer," she narrated for Lucy, who had pulled out her phone and begun typing. "He's saying something . . . he's pointing back at us . . . he's doing a chef's kiss . . . oh. I think he's telling the bouncer how hot you are to try to convince him to let us in."

"*What?*" Lucy asked, her eyebrows soaring as she looked up from her phone.

Charlotte glanced at her. "Is that surprising?"

Lucy sighed. "No." She turned back to her phone as Charlotte continued narrating.

"He's pulling out his wallet. Now the bouncer is talking to him. He's putting his wallet away. He's turning. He's walking—yeah, he failed." Charlotte crossed her arms. "Now he's talking to some guys at the front of the line. *Flirting.* He's flirting with some guys at the front of the line."

"Real flirting or your version of flirting?"

"Shut up. Okay, he's walking back. Walking . . . walking . . . walking . . ."

"Didn't work." Gabe slid back into line, shoving his hands into the pockets of his jacket and scowling. "I asked the bouncer if he'd let me cut the line and make me look cool for the two hot women I'm with."

"Aww," Charlotte said flatly. "I thought you were just using Lucy's body to get us in, but you were using mine, too."

"Sure. What're friends for?" Gabe rolled his eyes with a sigh. "But he didn't care. Then I tried to bribe him, and he threatened to ban me, so I left." He brightened. "Then this guy in line invited me to join him and his friend, and I said that was really nice of them, and he complimented my jacket, and I complimented his pants—also, fun fact, apparently the club is having a 2000s theme night—and then I said I was with you guys, and then they said that was too many people to let cut them in line. And now I'm here. And I'm hungry. Did we eat dinner?"

"Yes."

"Weird."

"There are two rice crackers in the pocket of my shorts if you want them," Charlotte offered. "In the bag."

Gabe immediately shrugged his backpack off his shoulder and began digging for the rice crackers as Charlotte scanned the street. "Okay," she said. "There's probably a back entrance farther down the street, or maybe around the corner. I say we find that and try the door. If it's locked, we'll wait for someone to come out, or maybe knock and see if we can talk our way in—"

"Or we can just cut the line," Lucy said, holding up her phone. "With my new VIP pass."

Charlotte's eyes widened. "That's a thing?"

"That's a thing. You owe me a hundred and eighty dollars. Let's go." Lucy stepped out of line and began walking to the front, leaving Gabe (who still had half a rice cracker in his mouth) to steer a spluttering Charlotte out of line to follow her.

"That's *insane.* Why would anyone spend that much money on—" Charlotte stopped as they reached the bouncer.

"Here's my pass," Lucy said, showing her phone and ID to the bouncer as Charlotte and Gabe scrambled to pull their IDs out of Gabe's backpack. "She's my plus one," she said, pointing at Charlotte, "and *he* will be joining that nice boy in the fun pants." She pointed to the guys at the front of the line who had invited Gabe to join them.

Gabe looked up, his driver's license between his teeth as he zipped his backpack closed. "*Whet.*" He removed the card from his mouth. "What."

"I only get a plus one with the pass," Lucy said apologetically as Charlotte handed her license to the bouncer. "Go make friends! We'll see you inside."

Gabe threw his head back, groaning. "*Fine.*" He turned as the bouncer handed Charlotte back her license and gestured for the two women to go inside. "Hey, guys! Still got room for one more?"

The music, which they had been able to hear all the way from their spot at the back of the line, hit Charlotte like a wall of sound as she and Lucy entered the club. She winced.

"IT'S GONNA BE HARD TO QUESTION ANYONE IN HERE," she yelled to Lucy.

"WHAT?" Lucy yelled back.

"EXACTLY."

The club was bathed with purple and blue lights, brighter white lights flashing along to the beat of Cascada's "Evacuate the Dancefloor" (which felt ironic to Charlotte, seeing how the closely packed bodies on said dance floor were doing everything but).

Beyond the dancers were standing tables, round booths, and a three-sided bar. A winding staircase led up to a second level, where more people were packed onto a balcony that overlooked the dance floor.

Charlotte began looking around for Arielle, then realized that if Arielle saw her first, she shouldn't look like she was looking for her. Instead, she turned to Lucy.

"LET'S GO TO THE BAR."

"NOW *THAT* I HEARD." Lucy took her hand and plowed

a path through the crush of dancers, Charlotte following in her wake. Her sneakers squelched across the sticky floor (or, she assumed they did—not that she could hear anything other than the music and her internal monologue of "AhhhhHHHHHHH").

Emerging from the crowd, Lucy deposited Charlotte onto a barstool, and, after a brief struggle to keep the hem of her dress pulled down, successfully got herself up onto one as well.

"YOU OKAY?" Lucy asked.

"YEAH. JUST A LITTLE OVERWHELMED."

"NO BACKING OUT NOW," Lucy said. "YOU SPENT A HUNDRED AND EIGHTY DOLLARS TO GET IN HERE, REMEMBER?"

She smiled sweetly as Charlotte scowled at her. Then she flagged down a bartender and ordered them drinks as Charlotte casually scanned the club.

Surprisingly, she spotted Candice first, recognizing her from the light research she had done on Scoop the day before. Candice Watts: early thirties, White, straight auburn hair in a high ponytail. She was wearing a dark green top and a black miniskirt, and stood around a table with three other women—one of them Arielle, who was wearing a pink jumpsuit that was so bright, Charlotte was embarrassed she hadn't noticed her sooner.

"I found them," she said, leaning in to talk into Lucy's ear. "Three o'clock."

Lucy leaned forward and looked down the bar. "Where?"

"THREE O'CLOCK."

She leaned back to look past Charlotte. "Oh. Yup." She leaned forward again. "More like four-thirty, but I see them. So what's the plan?"

Charlotte chewed on the inside of her cheek. "Try to get Candice alone, I guess. Maybe in the bathroom, if it's quieter in there."

"I'll be super honest with you," Lucy said, smiling at the bartender as they brought over their drinks, "I heard maybe forty percent of what you just said."

"I'M GONNA TRY TO TALK TO HER IN THE BATHROOM," Charlotte said louder, earning her a strange look from the bartender before they walked away.

But Lucy nodded, understanding. "You just have to make . . . YOU JUST HAVE TO MAKE SURE," she said, seeing Charlotte struggling to hear her, "THAT *Arielle*"—she lowered her volume when saying Arielle's name—"ISN'T WITH HER."

Charlotte nodded in agreement, glancing back at the group of women. "WE NEED SOMETHING TO DISTRACT *Arielle* IF THEY TRY TO GO TO THE BATHROOM TOGETHER."

"OR SOME*ONE*." Lucy twisted in her seat to scan the dance floor. "DID GABE COME IN YET?"

Charlotte hadn't been paying attention to the door. She also turned, and joined Lucy in a game of *Where's Gabe?*

"GOT HIM." She pointed towards the far end of the dance floor, where Gabe was dancing to Lil Jon's "Get Low" in very close proximity to one of the men from the line, who was wearing a tight black shirt and bright gold pants.

"GOD, HE'S GOOD," Lucy said. "TRULY IMPRESSIVE."

"ESPECIALLY WHILE WEARING A BACKPACK," Charlotte agreed. She glanced over at Lucy, noticing her face fall. "WHAT'S WRONG?"

Lucy grimaced, leaning in. "I just realized that I'm about to be single for the first time since college. I don't know if I can go back to . . ." She gestured vaguely at the scene before them.

"*Tsk.* You'll be fine." Charlotte leaned back. "I'LL GIVE YOU FLIRTING TIPS."

"OH." Lucy shook her head, smiling. "NO THANK YOU."

Charlotte scowled playfully at her as she called Gabe. They watched as he pulled out his phone, glanced at it, and answered, still dancing with Pants Guy.

"HEY," Gabe's voice came through the phone as they watched him look around.

"WHAT'RE YOU DOING?" Charlotte yelled into the phone.

"TRYING TO FIND YOU GUYS."

"ARE YOU INTERROGATING PANTS GUY?"

They watched Gabe's head whip around, looking for them. "WHERE ARE YOU?"

"BAR."

Gabe looked across the sea of heads towards the bar as Lucy lifted an arm and waved. He pointed at them, then turned back to pat Pants Guy on the chest before leaving him (and his pants) on the dance floor.

"FOR YOUR INFORMATION," Gabe said, squeezing between their stools and leaning against the bar, "HIS NAME IS PIERRE, NOT PANTS GUY. HE'S VISITING FROM *FRANCE*, AND HE'S AN EXCELLENT DANCER."

"HE'S FROM CONNECTICUT," Charlotte replied. "HE WAS HOLDING HIS DRIVER'S LICENSE WHEN WE PASSED HIM IN LINE."

"ALSO, PIERRE IS THE MOST BASIC FRENCH NAME," Lucy added.

Charlotte pointed at her. "YEAH, THAT WAS PROBABLY A LIE, TOO."

Gabe's face fell for a moment. Then he shrugged. "HE WAS STILL AN EXCELLENT DANCER."

"WELL . . ." Charlotte raised her glass to Gabe, "L'CHAIM, THEN." She took a sip, then leaned in. "See the women at the table behind me at three o'clock?"

"Four-thirty," Lucy corrected.

"Blonde in the pink jumpsuit and redhead in the green top?" Charlotte said, ignoring her.

Gabe leaned forward, looking over Charlotte's shoulder. "Oh, yeah." He glanced at Lucy, nodding, and mouthed, *Four-thirty.* Then he looked back at Charlotte. "Redhead's your type."

Charlotte reddened. "I don't—"

"You *do* have a thing for redheads," Lucy said.

"This is NOT the time." Charlotte turned to Gabe, who was grinning. "The redhead is Candice, the blonde is Arielle. I need to talk to Candice without Arielle seeing me."

"So you want me to seduce Arielle," Gabe said, nodding.

"No one was thinking that."

"We *were* kind of thinking that," Lucy pointed out.

Charlotte shook her head. "We just need you to distract her when Candice goes to the bathroom."

"That's what I said. Seduce her."

"Y—" Charlotte rubbed her face. "Sure. Whatever works."

Gabe picked up Charlotte's glass and took a sip. "You got it. But how do you know Candice is going to go to the bathroom?"

"She will," Charlotte said. "She's trying to disguise it as dancing, but I know a potty dance when I see one."

Gabe winced. "Never say 'potty dance' to me again."

"Stop saying you're gonna seduce Arielle."

"Deal." Gabe finished Charlotte's drink, put the glass down, then walked off. A moment later, he was back.

"I don't have anywhere to go yet, I don't know why I left," he said, leaning against the bar again. "It just felt like the thing to do in the moment."

"It looked very cool," Lucy said reassuringly, patting him on the shoulder.

"Can we talk about how I managed to dance with a guy while wearing a backpack?"

Charlotte gave him a congratulatory slap on the arm. "That's what I said!"

They relocated to the far side of the bar to avoid being spotted, and Lucy ordered them another round of drinks as they waited for their opportunity for Charlotte to get Candice alone. "Fergalicious" came on as they were finishing their drinks, and Gabe coerced Lucy to the dance floor, leaving his backpack with Charlotte while she kept an eye on their targets.

Finally, the women left the table and began walking towards the bathroom. Charlotte grabbed the backpack, hopped off her barstool, and hurried over to where Gabe and Lucy were dancing.

"THEY'RE GOING—WHOA." The room spun for a moment as Gabe grabbed her hand and twirled her around. "GABE."

"I'M ON IT." Gabe released her hand and made a beeline for Arielle as Charlotte and Lucy headed for the bathrooms on the other side of the room. They stopped by the door and looked back to see Gabe talking to Arielle. The other three women stopped to watch them, and after a moment, Arielle smiled, waved them off, and let Gabe lead her to the dance floor.

"God, he's *good*," Lucy said for the second time that night. "Probably best that he left the backpack with you, though."

Charlotte shrugged, throwing said backpack over her shoulder. "He could've still pulled it off. Come on." She pushed open the door to the bathroom and walked inside.

As she had hoped, the bathroom was significantly quieter than outside. Granted, outside was so loud, it made Charlotte's bones vibrate, so "significantly quieter" was still fairly loud in most other contexts. Regardless, as the door shut behind them, they found it was quiet enough that the handful of people who were already in there were talking to one another without having to yell.

"Do you have a plan?" Lucy asked as they walked over to the sinks.

Charlotte opened her mouth.

"Don't say 'wing it.' "

Charlotte closed her mouth.

Lucy sighed. "Okay, follow my lead."

"What—"

The door swung open, and "Mr. Brightside" momentarily flooded the quiet oasis of the bathroom.

"I swear to god, I think I follow him on Instagram."

"Is he famous?"

"He has a shit ton of followers."

The two women who were with Candice and Arielle entered the bathroom, with Candice close behind. Charlotte and Lucy watched in the mirror as they walked past them and entered the stalls.

Charlotte was about to test one of the automatic sinks to see if she was still cursed, when Lucy suddenly turned on her.

"It's just inconsiderate!" she burst out.

Charlotte stumbled back a step, startled.

"I understand forgetting to text back now and then," Lucy continued loudly, "but at a certain point it's starting to seem like you don't want to be my friend."

Charlotte's jaw dropped. Lucy raised her eyebrows, then gestured towards her, indicating that it was her turn.

Charlotte didn't fully understand what was going on, but she trusted that Lucy was going somewhere with this (other than publicly berating her in front of one of her suspects). She crossed her arms.

"I don't *not* want to be your friend," she said, raising her voice as she continued talking. "I just have a lot going on!"

"Hey, bathroom!" Lucy called, turning away from Charlotte towards the stalls and the other people standing at the sinks. "Should I keep putting my energy into a friendship when the *other* person doesn't put in the same amount of energy?"

The occupants of the bathroom gave her a resounding, "No!"

Charlotte frowned. She thought for a moment, then said, "Hey, bathroom, what if the *other* person has a lot of responsibilities, and sometimes finds herself having to choose between friendship and those responsibilities?"

The occupants of the bathroom responded with a noncommittal murmuring.

"Okay, sounds like we're a little torn on that one."

"Friendship should come first," said someone standing at the opposite end of the bathroom. The two other people with her (who were either friends or very supportive strangers, both options being equally likely in this situation), voiced their approval of this statement.

"Okay, sure," Charlotte said, hearing a toilet flush and praying her timing was right, "but has anyone ever had to choose their job over friendships?"

The timing was perfect. Candice emerged from her stall, and Charlotte pointed at her. "You. What do you think?"

Candice stopped and looked at her, teetering slightly on her heels, then shrugged, making her way to the sinks. "Yeah, sure."

"See?" Charlotte said loudly to Lucy, gesturing to Candice. "My new best friend gets it. *She* knows how to balance her friendships and responsibilities."

"Not really," Candice said, snorting. She started washing her hands. "You can't make everyone happy."

"But you're able to do what you have to do to do what needs to be done, right?"

Candice looked over at her and blinked slowly, shaking her head. "Girl, I am way too drunk to understand what you just said."

Admittedly, Charlotte was probably a little tipsy, too.

"I *mean*," she said, trying to recover her train of thought, "you seem like a go-getter. Someone who gets the job done, no matter what the cost. That's what I need *my* friend to understand about me."

Candice's friends emerged from their stalls. Charlotte worried that they'd pull Candice's attention away, but they thankfully started their own conversation at the other end of the sinks.

"I guess," Candice said, scrubbing her hands with soap. "I'm just used to everyone being mad at me all the time. I try to do what someone wants, and someone else gets mad. So I do what *they* want instead, and then other people get mad." She waved her hands, sending soap suds flying. "First I'm the boss, then I'm not the boss, then I'm the good guy, then I'm the bad guy. But we still *have* to do Tequila Tuesday tonight, because it's a tradition!"

"It's Thursday," Lucy said gently.

Candice closed her eyes. "What?"

"Today's Thursday."

"Okay?" Candice opened her eyes and gave Lucy a strange look, clearly not processing why this information was suddenly being offered to her. "Thanks for letting me know."

"Well, you said—"

"God, my feet hurt." Candice began rinsing her hands, looking back at Charlotte. "What was the question again?"

"Have you ever chosen work over friendship?"

Candice shook the water off her hands, suddenly looking very tired. "Yeah. I guess. It's complicated."

"How so?" Lucy asked.

"Just don't mix work and friends. Or if you do, make sure you're the only one calling the shots. That's my great advice."

Charlotte and Lucy watched her walk over to the paper towel dispenser and dry her hands.

"You know, you don't have to be the bad guy," Charlotte said. "You can choose to be the good guy."

She didn't really know what she was trying to get out of Candice at this point. At the very least, maybe she could plant the seed in the other woman's booze-soaked mind about possibly working with the union instead of against them.

Candice threw out her paper towel and turned. "Not that easy," she said, looking past Charlotte like she was having trouble focusing on her face. She walked past them towards her friends, who were chatting by the door. "But sometimes I let 'em be the bad guy for me."

Charlotte and Lucy watched as Candice and her friends walked out of the bathroom.

"So are you guys gonna stay friends or not?" asked the person from before.

Charlotte looked over at Lucy, raising an eyebrow.

Lucy threw her arms around her. "Yeah, I guess."

The occupants of the bathroom cheered as Charlotte stiffly received the hug, patting Lucy's arm in return.

"Get anything from that?" Lucy asked, releasing Charlotte as the bathroom chatter resumed.

Charlotte pulled out her phone. "I've gotta write some stuff down. Give me a second."

Lucy fixed her hair in the mirror while Charlotte typed out some notes. When she finished, she cleared her throat.

"So, on a scale of one to ten," she said hesitantly, looking at Lucy in the mirror, "how real was the stuff you were saying?"

Lucy smirked. "I'll admit, some of it was rooted in truth," she said, rubbing a finger under her eye to clean up some mascara residue. She turned to look at Charlotte. "But I know you've also been going through a tough time, even if you don't want to talk about it. And I love you. And I *know* you love me, even though you won't say it out loud."

Charlotte looked at her closely. She wasn't lying. But after almost twenty years of friendship, Charlotte knew when Lucy was withholding something.

"I can say it out loud," Charlotte grumbled, deciding not to dwell on it.

"Say it, right now."

"There's too many people, I'm embarrassed."

Lucy smiled, then reached up to squeeze Charlotte's face between her hands. "It's gonna take more than some ignored texts for you to get rid of me," she said.

"Wuv vu," Charlotte said through squeezed cheeks.

Lucy gasped, pulling her hands away. "Wait, say it again!"

"Nope, I said it, you heard it, let's get out of here."

Laughing, Lucy followed Charlotte out of the bathroom.

It took a bit for them to find Gabe in the crowd of dancers, and even longer to try to catch his eye without Arielle noticing. When he finally saw them, Charlotte shot him a thumbs-up, then pointed upwards. He nodded back.

Charlotte and Lucy made their way up to the balcony on the second floor, leaning against the railing as they waited for Gabe to join them. The speakers that were pointed down at the dance floor were now below them, making it a few decibels quieter where they stood.

Gabe took longer than expected, dancing with Arielle for another full song before they parted ways. Charlotte and Lucy watched Arielle return to her friends at their table, and a minute later, Gabe joined them at the railing.

"How'd it go?" he asked, turning his back on the railing to look at them.

"Charlotte said she loves me," Lucy said before Charlotte could open her mouth.

"No way!" Gabe turned to a scowling Charlotte. "I'm proud of you."

"More importantly," Charlotte said, swinging his backpack off her shoulder and passing it to him, "we found out a little about what happened with Jaya."

"We did?" Lucy looked at her curiously. "It all seemed super vague."

"We did. And credit to you for getting the conversation going. That helped me transition into getting her to talk about the situation with Jaya."

"She started talking about Jaya?" Gabe asked, looking impressed.

"Well, not directly. But I think I've learned a couple things from what she said." Charlotte pulled out her phone to check her notes, and groaned as she realized it had died. She returned it to her pocket as she tried to remember Candice's words.

"She said something like, 'Don't mix work and friends. If you do, make sure you're calling the shots.' I think that could be interpreted two ways. Either Candice is giving advice based on her own experience of being the one calling the shots, or—and I find this interpretation more intriguing—maybe there was a point in time when Candice *wasn't* the only one calling the shots."

Lucy and Gabe stared blankly at her. She sighed, then tried again:

"She might've been saying, 'I've had a bad experience that involved me mixing work and friends, which was made even worse by the fact that I wasn't the only one in charge, so I couldn't just make all the decisions. So if *you're* ever in a situation where you're mixing work and friends, at least make sure that you're the one with the sole power in the situation.' "

Lucy started nodding. "Okay. I see that interpretation now."

"But what does it mean?" Gabe asked. "Isn't Candice the founder and CEO?"

"That brings us to my next point," Charlotte said, pointing at him. "Everything I'd been hearing about Candice gave me this image of her being this resolute, determined, self-assured leader. I mean, Finn said she had even hired someone to work against the union organizing, for a short time, at least." She shook her head. "But then in the bathroom . . ."

"She was whiny," Lucy said. "She was talking like she was trying to please everyone, and complaining that everyone was mad at her."

"Maybe she was just drunk," Gabe said.

"She was," Charlotte conceded. "But I think it's more than that. Arielle told me that she, Candice, and Jaya have all known each other since college. What if Jaya had a bigger role in founding the company?"

"That's kind of a leap," Lucy said doubtfully.

"Maybe. But we keep hearing about how Candice and Jaya were at odds about the union. It sounded like Jaya was just standing up to her as her employee and her friend. But then Candice said that thing about making sure you have the sole power . . ." Charlotte shrugged. "If Jaya was her co-founder and co-CEO, Candice wouldn't have had that sole power. But then Jaya left. Now she has it."

"With no one to keep her in check," Gabe said.

"But why the whole people-pleaser act?" Lucy asked, her

brow furrowing. "For someone who's so vehemently against the union—"

"Solid SAT word," Gabe and Charlotte said in near-perfect unison.

"—she seemed kind of . . . *wishy-washy*."

Charlotte pursed her lips. "Maybe she's cracking under the pressure. If she's used to having a partner in this, even one she disagreed with, she could be struggling to run the whole thing by herself now."

"I mean, that's good news for the union, right?" Gabe asked. "If she's cracking, that means she might give in and work with them."

Charlotte raised her eyebrows. "Or she might feel pressured to take more extreme measures to get what she wants."

"*Or* to get someone else to take those extreme measures," Lucy added. "She also said something about having other people be the bad guy for her."

"So if she's behind any of this—Bernard, Eric, whatever," Gabe said, "she might just be pulling the strings. Jensen's strings?"

Charlotte nodded. "Possibly, yeah."

The three were silent for a moment as they pondered this. The moment didn't last long, as Charlotte realized their current environment wasn't ideal for pondering.

"Should we get out of here?" she suggested. "Not sure if that was worth a hundred and eighty dollars, but I don't really feel like sticking around."

Gabe pushed himself off the railing, pulling out his phone. "Yes. One quick photo, then we'll go."

One quick photo turned into thirty, which turned into Gabe persuading Charlotte into joining them for Beyoncé's "Crazy in Love" at a spot on the dance floor far from where Candice and Arielle were. Charlotte even agreed to stay for another song when she saw the two women leave with their friends, relieving her from the stress of being spotted as the DJ seemingly abandoned the 2000s theme and started playing newer music.

They finally emerged from the club into the warm night air, refreshing after the near-stifling heat of the club. Gabe threw his arms across their shoulders as they passed the line of people shuffling up a few inches as more were allowed inside.

"I could get used to this," he said. "Going to clubs, seducing suspects, getting one step closer to solving a murder. If this is the detective life, I don't know why you quit."

Before Charlotte could come up with a witty retort (or just any retort at all—it was late), she saw something that made her stop in her tracks.

Unfortunately, something saw her, too.

"Charlotte?" Arielle said. She was standing by the curb, alone. Her gaze slid over to Gabe, and her brow furrowed. "How . . ."

Bad, bad, bad, Charlotte thought. They had already accomplished their main objective to get her to talk to Candice—Arielle couldn't get in the way of that anymore. But she still didn't love the idea of Arielle finding out that Charlotte had gone behind her back. Up until this point, Arielle had been one of the most helpful people in this investigation. Alienating her now would only make things more difficult moving forward.

"Hey, Arielle!" Charlotte said quickly, frantically trying to remember how to smile naturally. "Wild seeing you here!" She turned to Gabe, her eyes wide. "This is Arielle, she works with Olivia."

Please catch on, Charlotte mentally willed Gabe. *If you play this off, I'll let you post whatever you want on my Instagram.*

"No way," Gabe said, a smile splitting his face that looked so natural that Charlotte was almost convinced this was actually news to him. "We met inside."

"We did," Arielle said. Charlotte studied her face, trying to determine if she bought it. She was smiling, but there was a guardedness in her eyes.

"So *that's* where you were when you disappeared," Lucy chimed in, elbowing Gabe in a very un-Lucylike manner. Gabe yelped with surprise.

"Yeah," he said, rubbing his side as Lucy winced apologetically. "We danced for a few songs. Arielle's an excellent dance partner."

Charlotte exhaled through her nose as the guardedness in Arielle's eyes melted away. Her brain was whirring so loudly, she didn't even hear what Arielle said in reply to make Gabe laugh.

"Were you there by yourself?" Lucy asked as Charlotte forced herself to listen again. Lucy was historically better at lying after she had a couple of drinks, and right now she was killing it.

"No," Arielle said, glancing down at her phone. "I was here with a few friends, but they left. I'm just waiting for my car to get here." She looked at Charlotte. "Have you had any luck with Eric? Find anything?"

"Still gathering information. Nothing to report." As helpful as Arielle had been so far, Charlotte didn't feel great about sharing any information with her.

"Do you want us to wait with you?" Lucy asked.

Arielle waved a hand. "No, thank you, I'm fine. The car's right around the corner."

"Alright," Charlotte said, desperate to get out of there. "See you tomorrow."

"Tomorrow?" Arielle blinked. "Are you coming back to the office?"

"Yeah. I wanted to talk to some more people . . ." Charlotte paused, seeing a look of stress cross Arielle's face. "Are you okay?"

"I'm just . . ."—Arielle swallowed—"a little nervous for Olivia. Jensen wasn't thrilled about you being in the office today, and I don't want anything to jeopardize her promotion."

Now it was Charlotte's turn to look surprised. "What promotion?"

Arielle grimaced. "I'm not even supposed to know about it." She passed her phone back and forth between her hands. "Candice told me that she's planning on promoting Jensen and making Olivia manager."

"That's fast," Charlotte said. "Olivia just started working there."

"Well, I didn't want it, and Martín's not really leadership material." Arielle cringed. "That sounded harsh, sorry. I just meant . . . he tends to keep to himself. So now Olivia's up for the promotion. But if Jensen gets more pissed, he might say something to Candice . . ."

"Couldn't *you* just say something to Candice?" Lucy asked. "Stick up for Olivia, if necessary?"

Arielle's face fell. "Candice has been kind of upset with me lately," she said. "We've been arguing and . . . I haven't been feeling like the best friend to her lately."

Charlotte winced inwardly. She knew what that felt like.

A car pulled up to the curb, and the driver rolled down the window.

"Arielle?"

"That's me, hi." Arielle pocketed her phone and turned back to Charlotte. "Please don't tell Olivia about the promotion. And maybe just avoid the office if you can. I'm sure there's other stuff to investigate, right?"

"Sure," Charlotte said as Gabe moved to open the back door of the car.

"Oh! Thanks." Arielle smiled at him as she climbed into the back seat. "You guys have a good night."

"You, too."

"Get home safe."

"'Night."

They watched the car pull away from the curb.

"Yikes," Gabe said. "Sounds like Candice and Arielle are having issues."

They resumed walking down the street.

"It makes sense, right?" Lucy asked. "Since she supports the union, she's probably been trying to convince Candice to work with them."

"I don't know," Charlotte said. "She gave me the impression

that she doesn't support the union in front of Candice." She rubbed her face. "Maybe I'm looking at this all wrong."

Lucy looked over at her. "What do you mean?"

Charlotte let out a shaky breath. "I convinced myself that Eric's disappearance had something to do with the union, but . . . ugh, what if I'm wrong? Everything with Bernard, and the union, and Jaya . . ." She shook her head. "What if he just has some unrelated 'secrets,' like Jensen said? Some other reason to suddenly disappear?"

"I'm sorry," Gabe said as they turned the corner, "we're listening to *Jensen* now? The guy's an asshole."

"Well, maybe the asshole is right. Maybe I should be looking somewhere else."

"Your gut's never steered you wrong," Lucy pointed out. "If it's telling you this has something to do with the union—"

"Yeah, well, my gut's been retired for a while now," Charlotte snapped. "It might not be working like it used to."

Lucy pressed her lips together and fell silent. They continued walking down the street.

Gabe finally broke the silence. "You could try taking a probiotic," he suggested.

There was a long pause as Charlotte tried to determine the logic of this seemingly random statement.

"What," she finally said, finding none.

"It's good for gut health." He immediately looked like he regretted the joke. "Sorry."

Lucy let out a choked laugh, then covered her mouth. Charlotte scowled to disguise her smile.

"That was terrible."

"I know, I know . . ."

It wasn't until they were on the train back to Highview that Lucy brought the conversation back to one of her favorite topics.

"So what's the plan for tomorrow?" she asked, looking down

at Charlotte, who was slouched in her seat. Lucy had just finished changing out of her pumps for sneakers, and held up a hand before Charlotte could speak. "No. Your plans are trash. Tell me what you want to accomplish tomorrow, and we'll work out a plan together."

Charlotte stretched her legs out, the seat across from her occupied by Gabe's backpack. Gabe sat next to it, also slouched in his seat, looking at his phone.

"We're still going to the office," Charlotte said. Whether or not Eric actually had some "secrets" like Jensen claimed, she still had people she wanted to talk to, even if it did turn out to be a wild goose chase. "Honestly, it's good that Arielle saw us with Gabe. Now we don't have to leave him behind."

"*Finally*," Gabe said, not looking up from his phone. "That's been happening a *lot* lately."

"It's just because we know you can take care of yourself," Lucy said sweetly.

"Don't bullshit me, Ortega," Gabe said, not unkindly.

"You're our backup," Charlotte offered. "Any good detective knows you need backup in case things go south."

Gabe looked up, pondering this. "Okay. That's badass. I can work with that."

"Who are we talking to at the office?" Lucy asked.

Charlotte began counting on her fingers. "I want to talk to Jane, the HR manager. See if she can tell me anything about the Jaya situation and how Eric was involved."

"That might be hard," Gabe said. "Isn't there, like, HIPAA for HR people? HRPPA?"

Charlotte shrugged. "I guess I'll find out." She raised another finger. "Talk to Sasha, the intern. See if she knows . . . I dunno, *anything*." She raised a third finger. "Maybe try to talk to Martín again. Figure out what that envelope of cash in his drawer is about."

She wasn't sure how she'd get any more information from Martín tomorrow than she had earlier that day (although the bar was set very, very low). A theory had started forming in her brain—one involving Candice letting other people be the "bad guy" for her, and that envelope of cash in Martín's drawer with a "thank you" note attached.

"And have Gabe ask Arielle on a date. For detecting reasons," Gabe finished.

Charlotte lowered her pointer and ring fingers and showed Gabe what remained.

"I'm serious! I think I could get some info out of her."

"Arielle's been the most forthcoming with info out of anyone involved in this. After she stopped lying about not supporting the union." Charlotte crossed her arms. "Now, asking *Martín* on a date, *that* would be helpful."

"Done."

"I was joking."

"Gabe should talk to Sasha," Lucy said. "I'll talk to Martín, you talk to Jane."

Charlotte furrowed her brow. "Reason being . . . ?"

"We don't want to spend too much time in the office. If Arielle's right, the longer we're there, the longer we're jeopardizing Olivia's promotion. So we split up the tasks. You probably freaked out Martín, and I'm used to getting through to people you've already burned bridges with."

"I wouldn't say I *burned*—"

"Sasha probably won't be too difficult to get info out of, so Gabe will talk to her. He can just ask whatever questions you give him and let us know what she says."

Gabe looked up from his phone, eyes narrowed. "I feel like you're saying something about me, but I can't figure out what."

"And you'll talk to Jane," Lucy finished. "She'll probably be evasive to avoid breaking any confidentiality, and you're . . ."

"Persistent?" Charlotte asked. "Tenacious?"

"Annoying."

"I'll take it." Charlotte sat up in her seat as the train began to slow. "Works for me. It's better than my plan."

Lucy narrowed her eyes. "You didn't have a plan."

"I did have a plan, but it doesn't matter now, because yours is better."

Lucy looked at Gabe. "She didn't have a plan."

"Absolutely not," Gabe agreed, not looking up from his phone.

As casual as Charlotte had been about getting attacked the other night, trepidation crept up her spine as they walked down the street, away from the bright lights of the train station. Gabe and Lucy were walking behind her, brainstorming captions for the Instagram post Gabe had been working on. As they passed the spot where she had been grabbed, she held her breath and didn't let it out again until she had rounded the corner.

The relief was short-lived. Charlotte stopped in her tracks.

"What is it?" Lucy asked. A moment later, she and Gabe turned the corner and spotted the lights of the police car outside of Landon's building.

Charlotte didn't hear the question. She was already running.

Chapter 13

Blech

Bzzt bzzt bzzt bzzt bzzt—

Charlotte was rapidly tapping the call button next to her brother's apartment number as Lucy and Gabe quickly caught up. As soon as they stopped, the lock on the door clicked. Charlotte yanked it open, and they dashed inside.

A cop was exiting Landon's apartment as Charlotte skidded into the second-floor hallway. Her brother was standing in the doorway, his shoulders slumping with relief when he saw Charlotte.

"Hey, it's okay, we're okay," he said, holding up his hands as she charged past the cop.

"What happened?" Charlotte asked, screeching to a stop in front of him as she tried to slow her breathing.

"Come inside, I'll tell you." Landon looked past her, spotting Gabe and Lucy, who had given the departing cop a wider berth than Charlotte had. "Hey, Gabe, what's up, man?"

"I'm doing alright." Gabe leaned against the wall, catching his breath. "Haven't had to deal with any cops tonight, so better than you, I'm assuming."

"Are you okay?" Lucy asked. She was the only one of the three who didn't seem at all winded from their sudden sprint.

"Come in," Landon repeated, pushing the door open wider for them to enter.

As they walked into the apartment, Olivia looked over from where she sat on the couch.

"Hey," she said, looking weary. "We're okay."

"I've been told. This is Gabe." Charlotte gestured towards her friend. "Gabe, Olivia."

"Hi, Gabe," Olivia said. "Sorry, we don't usually give visitors a police escort."

"What *happened*?" Charlotte asked again, turning to look at Landon, who had drifted to the other side of the room. He looked over at Olivia, who raised her eyebrows.

"Go ahead," she said, her voice chilly. "You've been taking charge tonight, no reason to stop now."

"Oy . . ." Landon ran a hand through his hair, sighing. He seemed exhausted. "We went out to dinner tonight, and we were walking back home when Olivia got mugged."

"Oh, shit," Gabe said.

Charlotte felt Lucy's gaze on her, but she continued looking at her brother.

"The guy grabbed her and pulled her away from me. She elbowed him in the face." The corner of his mouth quirked up for a moment. "*Hard.* He let go, grabbed her purse, and ran."

Charlotte had already clocked Olivia's purse on the coffee table in front of her. She stayed silent, listening.

"I tried to run after him, but Olivia stopped me. We watched him run down the street and drop the purse before disappearing around the corner. When I went to get the purse, he was gone."

"Did you see his face?" Lucy asked. Charlotte could tell she thought she already knew the answer.

Landon shook his head. "He was wearing a ski mask, and a hood."

"And sunglasses," Olivia added from the couch.

"Did he say anything?" Charlotte asked, breaking her silence.

Another headshake from Landon.

"Take anything?"

"No. Olivia went through her purse, and nothing was missing. But she found . . ." He walked over to the couch, but Olivia was already picking up the slip of paper that sat on the coffee table. She twisted back around and passed it to Charlotte.

" 'Make Charlotte Illes go home. Or else,' " Charlotte read aloud.

"Then," Olivia said, annoyance in her voice, "Landon said he was calling the police. I told him I didn't want that, that it was unnecessary, especially since we *know what this is about,* and that it would only cause problems." She turned around, her back hitting the couch with a dull *thud.* "And he called them anyway."

"I'm sorry, I *said* I was sorry." Landon looked over at her helplessly, his hand having taken permanent residence in his hair. "You'd just been *attacked,* and Charlotte wasn't answering her phone—"

"My phone died," Charlotte said feebly, feeling uncomfortable watching this.

"You grow up with a successful amateur detective for a sister and you still think the *police* can help with something like this?"

"*She wasn't answering her phone.*"

"It died," Charlotte repeated, louder this time. "And you have Lucy's number, you could've called her."

Landon dropped his hand, sighing heavily. "Yeah, I could've . . . I could've . . ." He rubbed his face. "I haven't really been thinking straight this evening."

Olivia snorted derisively.

Charlotte looked over at Lucy and Gabe. Lucy gave her a look that read, *You should tell them.*

"Okay," Charlotte said quietly, almost to herself, before turning back to her brother. "I think it's Jensen. The attacker."

Landon and Olivia both stared at her.

"What?" Olivia asked. She shook her head. "No, that . . ."

"Doesn't make sense?" Charlotte asked drily. "Is it really the most unbelievable thing?"

Olivia blinked, trying to process this.

Landon narrowed his eyes. "How?"

"How what?"

"How do you know it's Jensen? You're good, but you're not that good. You didn't even see the attacker."

Charlotte sighed, then braced herself. "I did. Three nights ago, when he attacked me."

July 18th, 2009

"And you checked the changing rooms when you closed up for the night?" Lottie asked, squinting up at the older teenager who was sitting in the lifeguard's chair. She couldn't have been older than seventeen, but Lottie was eleven, which meant this girl seemed like a full adult to her. However, Lottie had become accustomed to interviewing people of all ages, and was conducting this particular interview as professionally as she could, despite being regularly interrupted by her interviewee blowing her whistle and yelling at kids to stop running by the pool.

"Yeah." The girl kept her eyes on the pool as she responded. "Checked under the doors. No one was in there."

"No . . . one . . . in . . . there . . ." Lottie repeated, scribbling into her notebook. She looked up again. "And when did you find out that the trophies were missing?"

"Next morning. My boss called me, and—*PHWEEEEEE*."

Lottie winced as the whistle cut through the sounds of splashing and yelling.

"BOYS. FOR THE LAST TIME. WALK." The lifeguard rolled her eyes and sat back in her chair. "What was I saying?"

"Your boss called you?"

"Right. She called me and told me the trophies were missing."

Lottie waited, then realized she had finished talking. "Okay. Well, thank you for your time. If you think of anything else that might be helpful . . ." She reached into her pocket and pulled out a card that read *Lottie Illes Detective Service* in bold, handwritten print. She stood on her toes to offer it up. "My phone number's on there."

The lifeguard glanced over, then leaned in a bit to take the card. She gave it a quick look before turning back to the pool. "You're the kid who figured out who started that fire in the woods, right?"

"That was me," Lottie said, closing her notebook and returning it to her pocket. "And my best friend, Lucy. She was the one who found out about the fireworks."

"Wasn't it those boys from Epston High?" the lifeguard asked.

"Yeah. I think they were given community service. Luckily, it had rained recently, so—"

"No, I mean, wasn't it *those* boys?" The lifeguard pointed towards the deep end, where a group of teenage boys were racing each other across the width of the pool.

Lottie's shoulders tensed. It *was* those boys.

"Thank you for your time," she said quickly, walking away from the lifeguard stand and the deep end of the pool. She hurried over to where Lucy sat, so engrossed in *Flowers for Algernon* that she didn't notice Lottie waving frantically at her as she approached.

"Hey," Lottie said, dropping into a crouch behind Lucy's lounge chair, "I think we should get going."

Lucy twisted around to look back at her. "Have you started reading this yet?" She waved her book in the air, a finger stuck between the pages to save her spot. "It's weird, but I like it."

"No, I'm gonna do my summer reading the week before school starts, like a normal person." Lottie peered out from behind the chair, her gaze landing on a woman walking past them. "Do you think Mrs. Harrison is pregnant?"

"Why?"

"She's been wearing these new frilly bathing suits that hide her stomach. And this is her third trip to the bathroom since we've been here." Lottie shook her head. "Never mind. We gotta go. Those boys we got in trouble are here."

"The fireworks boys?" Lucy lowered her sunglasses to look at the pool, where said fireworks boys were climbing out and heading for the changing rooms. "Oh. Uh-oh."

"Yeah. I'll meet you out front. I have to tell Landon we're leaving."

"Are you going to tell him about the boys?"

"No, I don't want him to make a big deal about it. Go, I'll be right out." Lottie headed for the nearby basketball court as Lucy threw *Algernon* into her pool bag.

Landon was playing HORSE with a couple of his friends, which was the most activity Landon and his friends would usually do with a basketball, none of them being particularly athletic.

"Lan!" Lottie called, stopping at the edge of the court.

Landon grabbed the ball from his friend David, then looked over. "What?"

"I gotta go."

"Okay. 'Bye." Landon attempted a left-handed shot, and the ball sailed past the backboard and landed in the grass.

Lottie turned on her heel and returned to the pool area, pausing to let a younger kid run past and cannonball into the pool. The lifeguard's whistle screeched as she passed the changing rooms and headed for the entrance, where she could just make out Lucy waiting around the corner.

"Hey!"

She froze. So close.

Turning, she saw the boys emerging from the changing room,

towels slung over their shoulders and T-shirts thrown over their swim trunks. All four of them had been involved in setting off fireworks that had started the fire. They had been planning on setting off more before Lottie tracked them down and turned them in. She had crossed paths with one of them during her investigation—Rick—who had told her in no uncertain terms that he did not want to see her face again.

Rick: fifteen, White, damp brown hair, significantly bigger and taller than Lottie. He was standing at the front of the group, looking very displeased by the fact that he was seeing her face again.

"Well?" he asked, glaring at her. His friends were giving her similar looks.

"Uh . . ." Lottie glanced over her shoulder. The lifeguard didn't have a clear view of them, and she couldn't see Lucy anymore. "Well, what?"

"Are you going to apologize?" Rick asked. He crossed his arms. "I think you owe us an apology."

"For . . ."

"For getting us in trouble," one of the other boys piped up. "I gotta spend every Saturday this summer working at the senior citizen center. And it's your fault."

"Well . . ." Lottie said, slowly easing backwards, "I'd argue that maybe it was *your* fault for setting off those dangerous fireworks."

Rick took a step closer, his friends close behind. "If you hadn't gotten into our business, we wouldn't have gotten caught. So *yeah,* it's your fault."

Lottie put her hands up. "Okay, let's say it *is* my fault. Aren't you glad that now you have an excuse to spend so much time with the senior citizens?" She took another step back. "I mean, older people have so much wisdom to share. It's a great chance to—"

"Dude, shut *up,*" Rick interrupted. "You're so fucking weird." He looked over his shoulder at his friends. "Come on."

Before she knew what was happening, the boys had surrounded her, grabbing her arms and legs and lifting her off the ground.

"Wh—hey!" She twisted to try to break their grasp as they began carrying her over to the pool, but to no avail. Detective work didn't leave her with much time to build up any muscles that would make her capable of breaking out of the grips of four fifteen-year-old boys.

"Last chance to say sorry," Rick said as they neared the pool's edge.

Lottie remembered her notebook in her pocket and cringed at the thought of it getting wet. Also, she really, *really* didn't want to be thrown into the pool.

"Okay!" she said. "Okay, I'm sorry." She stared at Rick as the lifeguard's whistle pierced the air, and realized, looking at his expression, that an apology (genuine or not) wasn't going to save her from going into the pool.

". . . that . . . your face looks like that," she finished.

The next few seconds felt like they happened in slow motion. Rick sneered, then moved to toss her into the pool, his friends following his lead. Lottie closed her eyes and held her breath. Then she felt an arm wrap around her waist and yank her backwards, her own arms almost getting pulled out of their sockets. She felt the boys let go as her feet hit the concrete, and she stumbled backwards. Her eyes flew open in time to see Landon push her towards Lucy before joining his friends in pummeling the other boys with pool noodles.

David managed to knock two of the boys into the water. Their other friend, Marcus, was yelling so loudly that the boy he was hitting jumped into the pool just to escape. Rick had grabbed Landon's pool noodle, and the two boys played a brief game of tug-of-war before Landon suddenly let go, sending the fourth and final boy tumbling into the pool.

"Hey!" Landon yelled as Rick came up for air. "Stay away from my sister." He grabbed his pool noodle out of the water and threw it at Rick. It bounced off his head as he wiped water out of his eyes.

"Tell your fucking sister to stay away from *us*," Rick yelled, splashing water onto Landon. David and Marcus threw their pool noodles at him, too, amongst a chorus of, "Whatever, man," and, "Enjoy your swim."

"PHWEEEEEEEE." The lifeguard pointed at them from her chair. "All of you, *out*."

Lucy pulled a towel out of her pool bag and silently passed it to Landon as the group walked out. She had a look on her face that indicated the beginning of a solid two-month-long crush (until Labor Day weekend, when she'd watch Landon shove an entire hamburger into his mouth and declare that she was "over it").

Lottie was also looking at Landon, trying to read his face to gauge exactly how mad he was at her.

He didn't say anything as Lucy explained to Lottie that she had gone for help when she saw the boys approaching her.

He didn't say anything when David and Marcus split off to head to their respective homes, excitedly recounting the fight to each other like the other one hadn't also been there.

He didn't say anything when they dropped Lucy off at her house, Lucy insisting that Landon hold onto the towel for as long as he needed.

It wasn't until they reached the front door of their house that Landon said, "Are we telling Mom?"

"No," Lottie said immediately.

"Okay." Finally, he looked at her. "You alright?"

Lottie nodded.

"Okay." He pulled the towel from around his neck and dropped it onto her head. "Give this back to Lucy."

Lottie pulled the towel off and watched him walk into the house.

Later that night, she lay in bed, unable to fall asleep. Climbing out of bed, she walked over to her desk, opened a notebook, and ripped out a piece of paper. Grabbing a pen, she wrote in big letters:

THANK YOU

Then she padded out into the hallway and crouched in front of Landon's door, slipping the paper underneath, before returning to her room and going to sleep.

They didn't talk about that day again for years. Lottie wasn't even sure Landon had seen the note, until a few years later when she was snooping in his room and found it, tucked gently between the pages of a dictionary that sat on his bookshelf.

Present Day

Landon was pissed. Charlotte knew this, not only from the look on his face, but also because he had begun to pace. Landon only paced when he was really, *really* pissed.

"You *knew*," he said, heading for the kitchen before pivoting sharply and walking back across the living room floor, "that my girlfriend's boss was a psycho masked attacker—you knew this because *you got attacked by him*—and you didn't tell me."

"I didn't know the *whole* time," Charlotte argued. She pointed back at Lucy and Gabe, who looked like they had been considering slipping out of the room before they were suddenly thrust into the spotlight. "And I've been telling them that I'm still not positive."

"But you're positive enough to tell us *now*." Landon reached the far wall of the apartment and pivoted again. "Why wouldn't you tell me as soon as it happened?"

"Because I thought it might've been Olivia's weirdo stalker, and I didn't want to worry you until I knew more." Charlotte crossed her arms, feeling defensive, as Landon paced past her. "Her weirdo stalker, might I add, who *you* made up. Just while we're on the topic of keeping secrets."

Landon stopped, then doubled back. "*Your* secret attacked Olivia!" he yelled, stopping in front of her and gesturing behind him to where Olivia still sat silently on the couch.

"I thought I had it under control!" Charlotte yelled back. "I told her to have you pick her up at the train station. I knew if she was with you, she'd be fine!"

"But she *wasn't fine*! She still got attacked! I couldn't . . ." Landon trailed off, rubbing his face.

Olivia spoke up from the couch, reading his thoughts. "I don't need you to *protect* me," she said, not turning around. "I just need you to *listen* to me."

"This wouldn't have happened if she'd told us," Landon said, turning towards her.

"Why not?" She stood up from the couch, turning around to face them, and crossed her arms. "Would we have not gone out to dinner, knowing that Charlotte had a hunch that my boss attacked her the other night?"

Landon was silent. Olivia looked over at Charlotte.

"Obviously I had a sense that something was going on," she said. She cracked the tiniest of smiles. "Especially after your ominous warning this morning."

Charlotte shifted awkwardly. "Sorry about that. And I *am* sorry you got attacked. I wish I could've stopped it from happening."

Landon walked over to the kitchen. He wasn't pacing anymore. Opening the fridge, he pulled out the water dispenser.

"While Landon resets," Olivia said slowly, pulling her gaze away from him, "I have something to show you."

She turned to pick up her purse, fishing out her phone. "I don't usually check my work messages after hours, but Arielle texted me to go look at our team's message thread when we were leaving the restaurant. Right before . . . you know." She pulled up something on her phone, then walked over to pass it to Charlotte.

Gabe and Lucy peered over her shoulders as they all read the new message from Eric.

Eric: Hi all, sorry for being MIA. Had to rush out of town for a family emergency and left my phone and laptop at my apartment. Finally got the chance to log in on a computer. Jensen, I'm not sure when I'll be back, sorry for the inconvenience. Arielle, the new diner graphic options are on my laptop. If you need them, Martin knows my password. I'll send an update when I know more. Thanks guys!

Charlotte finished reading and looked up at Olivia.

"What're you thinking?" she asked.

"I went into the messaging system to try to grab an IP address," Olivia said, "but he's using a VPN. Which isn't weird; a lot of people use VPNs. But I can't figure out where he is."

"Do you think he wrote this message?" Charlotte asked, handing the phone back.

Olivia looked at her phone again. "It sounds like him. It's just weird that he sent one message to all of us. I would've thought he'd just email Jensen, or call him."

"He doesn't really seem worried about whether he'll still have a job when he comes back," Gabe commented. "Scoop doesn't strike me as the kind of workplace where that wouldn't be a concern for him."

"If he's even planning on coming back," Charlotte said.

"Eric has some secrets." Had Jensen been right?

That'd be so annoying, Charlotte thought. *God, I hope that's not true.*

She struggled to fit this piece of information in with what Candice had said at the club, with Olivia being attacked, with all the other information she had gathered. Her brain started to whir uncomfortably, like a laptop with too many tabs open.

"Could someone else have sent the message?" Gabe asked. "Someone with Eric's phone?"

"The Scoop messaging system is also a piece of shit," Olivia told him. "Anyone with access to it could've figured out how to fake a message from him."

"But who would do that?" Lucy asked.

"Gabe," Charlotte said suddenly.

"I would *not*!" Gabe replied, indignant.

"No." Charlotte shook her head, checking back into the conversation. "Not that. You asked if Eric killed Bernard."

"I did?"

Olivia looked appalled. "*What?*"

"After we talked to Finn," Charlotte said as Olivia looked at her, aghast.

"We were talking about the possibility that Bernard was spying on the union committee," Lucy said, remembering. "And how maybe he wasn't killed for being on the committee, but for being a spy."

"And Eric had a reason for keeping the identity of the person helping him from the rest of the committee," Charlotte said. "Maybe because he knew there was a spy there."

"So if he figured out the spy was Bernard," Gabe said, nodding slowly, "maybe he was the one who killed him." He made an impressed face. "I was the one who guessed that? Damn, I *am* good."

"Well, we don't know if it's *true*," Charlotte said, the whirring in her head growing again. "But it could explain why he suddenly left town."

"Hang on." Olivia had been watching them talk in silent disbelief, and was now shaking her head. "Eric would never do something like that. Something must've happened to him. Why else would Jensen or whoever that was be going around attacking us?" Olivia turned to Charlotte. "You saw someone pick up Eric that night, right? Was that Jensen? Did he take Eric?"

"If Jensen sent the message, that could be why it was sent to everyone," Lucy added.

"His roommate said Eric came home that night," Charlotte said softly, not wanting to upset Olivia any more than she already was.

"Then maybe someone told him to leave town. You said that was a possibility, right?" Olivia looked at Charlotte expectantly, like Charlotte could just check an answer key and confirm that this was what happened.

Her chest tightening, all she could do was shrug.

"What about the roommate?" Gabe asked. "If Eric left his phone at home, his roommate could've sent the message from it."

"If the message was fake, his phone probably isn't actually at his apartment," Lucy pointed out.

"Unless the roommate just *wants* us to think that."

"Now you're just saying stuff with no reasoning behind it."

"I'm sure there's *reasoning*, I just don't know what it is."

Their words started to feel farther away as the whirring in her head grew even more. Charlotte wasn't even sure who was saying what.

"So is Jensen behind this or not?"

"Technically, Charlotte's not even sure the attacker was him."

"But if it was, does that mean for sure that he did something to Eric?"

"I don't know, she doesn't know yet—"

"Lottie?"

The room fell silent. The whirring in Charlotte's brain was so loud it took her a moment to process that she was being addressed. She blinked, and saw Landon staring at her, concerned.

"Are you okay?"

You can't do this.

You should have told Landon.

Tell Landon you can't do this.

You put Olivia in danger.
Tell them you can't do this.
Go home. Or else.
You don't know what you're doing.
You're not her.

The last thought startled Charlotte out of her spiral. Now *that* was a road she definitely wasn't ready to go down. She opened her mouth to tell Landon that she was totally fine, and that she was just coming up with a solid theory that would pave the way for continual detection, resulting in a solved mystery.

Strangely enough, none of that came out. To make matters worse, her eyes had inconveniently begun to fill with tears.

"Okay," Lucy said, immediately taking charge of the situation, "it's been a long day. I think it's time for bed." She looked at Charlotte worriedly. "Alright?"

Charlotte once again willed her mouth to assure the others that she was more than alright, and that she just needed to take a minute to process all the clues, put the puzzle pieces together, look at the bigger picture, etcetera, etcetera, etcetera. But her traitorous mouth wouldn't even grant her so much as a single etcetera, so she just nodded and let Lucy steer her to Dale's room.

"Thanks for having us," she heard Gabe say behind them. "Have a good night!"

Landon and Olivia both murmured their good nights as Gabe shut the door.

Lucy deposited Charlotte onto the bed, then crossed her arms.

"What do you need?" she asked.

Charlotte stared at her blankly and shrugged.

"Right," Lucy said, looking at the ceiling. "Forgot I was talking to the Queen of Communication."

"That," Charlotte said, her mouth suddenly working again. "What was that?"

Lucy looked back down at her, brows furrowing. "What was what?"

Charlotte stood, narrowing her eyes and peering into her face. "You're mad at me."

"What?" Lucy took a step back. "No, I'm not. Is that why you're upset? Because you think I'm mad at you?"

"No, that's for another unrelated reason that I'm not ready to confront yet. But, yes you are. You're mad at me." Charlotte crossed her arms, mirroring Lucy. "I saw it when we were talking in the bathroom at the club, and I saw it again, just now. You're still mad about me not replying to your texts."

"I think you're just trying to distract yourself from the mystery," Lucy said, dropping her arms. "After a good night's sleep—"

"Look me in the eyes and tell me you're not mad at me for barely replying to your texts for the past several months," Charlotte said.

Lucy stayed silent, her jaw clenched.

"Tell me—"

"*Yes,* okay?" Lucy burst out, cutting her off. "Yes, I'm *mad* at you. But I wasn't gonna say anything, because I hate *this*"—she gestured between them to indicate their current conflict—"and I really just wanted to move past it."

"Maybe it's better not to move past it," Gabe offered from where he still stood by the door. He looked at both of them cautiously. "If it's bothering you, it might be better to talk about it."

Lucy turned to Charlotte, who nodded.

"Fine," Lucy said. She moved to sit down heavily on the bed. Charlotte sat back down next to her. Gabe dropped his backpack off his shoulder and situated himself on the floor in front of them.

"I . . . really needed you," Lucy started, haltingly, looking down at her hands clasped in her lap. "I've been so miserable, and Gabe's been great to vent to, but I really needed you and you weren't there. And I know you were upset when you found out what I'd been going through, but . . ."

She squeezed her hands together like she was physically

forcing herself to continue talking. "You didn't apologize. Not then, not when we were on the fire escape, not in the bathroom of the club. And you can't even tell me *why* you haven't been talking to me. And that feels . . . shitty. And it makes me mad at you."

A tremor crept into her voice. "But I know you've been having a hard time, so then I feel bad about being mad at you, and then I feel bad that I couldn't be there for you while you were having a hard time, and then I get mad that you won't *let me* be there for you . . ."

She trailed off.

Charlotte took a deep breath. Then let it out.

"Okay," she finally said. She pulled a leg up onto the bed and adjusted her position so she could look at both of her friends. Letting out another shaky breath, she began.

"I've been a bad friend. To both of you." She paused, letting her words sink in for herself, then tilted her head. "Ironically, I think I thought I was being a good friend by . . . distancing myself."

They both gave her questioning looks but said nothing. She continued:

"I know I've been . . . *not great* for a while. Years, I guess. Um, after I decided to stop doing detective work altogether, I was kind of lost. But I figured that was normal. Like, just regular 'young adult finding herself' stuff. But then we graduated college. And we got jobs." She looked at them. "And then *you* started really growing on social media, and *you* moved away, and I was just . . . where I always was. Doing nothing."

She dropped her gaze to her hands, which weren't doing anything of note, but were easier to look at than her friends in that moment. "It wasn't a conscious decision, at first. When Lucy came home for Christmas, and we all hung out at Gabe's, you guys were talking about everything you had going on, and I realized that I had . . . nothing. To talk about. You were moving forward with your lives, and I felt like I . . . um, like maybe I was . . ." She shrugged. "A burden. Like I was holding you guys back."

Charlotte quickly continued before either of them could react.

"I just started replying less and less, thinking that eventually you would realize that you didn't actually need me, so you could finally move on." She glanced at Gabe. "It was harder with you, because I knew if I didn't reply to your messages, you'd eventually just show up at my house."

"True."

"But I started shortening my responses," she continued. "Ending conversations early. Turning down invitations to hang out."

"Charlotte . . ." Lucy said, her expression soft.

"No," Charlotte said quickly, shaking her head. "It's no excuse, though." She glanced over at her before looking back down again. "I *am* sorry. I'm really, really sorry. You deserved better than that. I was just trying to show you that you didn't need me, but I should've been giving you the support you needed."

Lucy grabbed her hand. "Charlotte Illes," she said. "Look at me."

Charlotte forced herself to look up.

"Gabe."

Gabe scrambled to his feet and climbed onto the bed, dropping down to sit next to both of them.

Lucy looked at Charlotte. "Your friendship isn't important to me because of the things you're able to *do* for me," she said. "Do I want you to text me back? Yeah, of course. But I'm not friends with you because I need you to give me amazing life advice—that'd be silly, since your life advice is pretty hit-or-miss."

Charlotte laughed wetly, a tear rolling down her cheek.

"It's important to me because I just . . . need *you*. No matter what you're doing, no matter where you are." Lucy squeezed Charlotte's hand. "I love you. Detective or not a detective, job or no job, whether we're in the same city or on opposite sides of the planet, your friendship could never be a burden."

After a moment, Gabe placed a hand on top of their hands. "Same," he said seriously.

Charlotte let out a huff of laughter through her nose, and Lucy smiled.

"Sorry! She said it really well, I had nothing else to add!"

Charlotte sniffed, rubbing her cheek with the back of her free hand. "I appreciate that. I love you guys, too. *Don't make a big deal out of it*," she added quickly as she saw her friends gearing up to make a big deal out of it.

She sighed heavily. "I just feel like everyone's got everything figured out, y'know? Like . . . when did everyone suddenly become full adults? You guys, and Landon . . ."

"I mean, Landon became an adult at thirteen," Lucy said, her face serious. "We were both at his bar mitzvah."

Charlotte paused, and then laughed weakly. "That's really funny. I didn't expect you to say that."

"That was good," Gabe said, nodding approvingly.

Lucy frowned. "Why are you guys talking like I'm not usually funny? I'm very funny."

"You're hilarious."

"So funny. All the time."

"Anyway," Lucy said, rolling her eyes at them, "*I* definitely don't have everything figured out. I barely have *anything* figured out, I'm realizing now. I thought I could be brave and move with Jake to a new city and work at a fancy private school and make new friends and become this . . . courageous, worldly, city woman." She sighed. "But I'm not, I guess. I'm just a regular old suburban coward."

"I *like* the suburbs," Charlotte offered.

"Plus, you're not a coward," Gabe added. "Are you serious? You're, like, one of the bravest people I know."

Lucy looked over at him. "Why, because I willingly teach middle schoolers?"

"Yes, that. But other stuff, too. Like when the school wouldn't let me and those two other kids have our real names in the yearbook, but you made the changes anyway, even though you knew you could get in trouble."

"Oh," Lucy said softly. "I forgot about that."

"Or when you faced down that dog when we snuck into Dr. West's house," Charlotte said. "Or when you filibustered that town council meeting while I checked people's shoes. Or literally any time we were in a tight spot while working on a case." Charlotte shrugged a shoulder. "You never abandoned me. You complained a lot, but you never ran away."

Lucy looked at her curiously. "That's funny. I always thought you were the brave one between the two of us."

Charlotte shook her head. "No, I'm just an idiot. I don't think things through. You think things through, and then you still do them. That's brave."

Squirming under all the positive attention, Lucy turned to Gabe. "What about you? Do you have everything figured out?"

Gabe sat back on his hands. "Yeah, I mean, my life's pretty great."

"Booooo."

"Come *on*."

"Damn, okay, fine." He sat back up again, scratching his head. After a moment, he said, "I dunno . . . I guess, I feel like it's hard to make friends, as an adult."

Charlotte gave him a look of disbelief. "Seriously? *You* have trouble making friends?"

"Seriously! I don't think I've made a new good friend in years. No one I'm really close with. I mean, I have a few other friends from high school and college who I'll still hang out with, and I'll talk with some of my mutuals online about unimportant stuff, but it's not like . . ." He gestured at the two of them. "You know."

He plowed on before they could react. "And I hate my job, I guess? But I'm also *good* at my job, which kind of sucks in its own way? Because then I feel bad about hating my job, because if I'm so good at it, I should just be happy, right? And I can't quit, because I don't get enough sponsors to make that hashtag influencer life a sustainable career, and I don't know what Susan would do without me, so . . ." He spread his hands. "I guess I don't have much figured out, either. Oh, also, I can't hold down a roommate. But I'm pretty sure that's my great-great-lolo's fault, or something."

"You *guys*," Charlotte said, looking between the two of them. "You're messes like me!"

"Okay, I wouldn't say *that*," Gabe said. "You're, like, A Whole Mess."

Charlotte punched his leg.

"Ow. Yeah. I deserved that."

Relief coursed through Charlotte's body, as if the love from her friends was slowly dissolving the anxiety and guilt she had been carrying around like a necessary sacrifice for the past several months. The negative feelings didn't disappear entirely. She knew there would be nights ahead when the obnoxious voice that lived in her amygdala would try to convince her that Lucy and Gabe were just saying these things because they felt bad for her, and would later regret not leaving her behind when they had the chance.

But that night wasn't one of those nights. That night, as she carefully studied the faces of two of her favorite people in the world, she deduced that her friends actually cared very deeply about her. And the voice stayed silent.

"But actually, though," Lucy said, "while we're riding the Feelings Train . . . do you wanna talk about what was going on out there? You just, like, spaced out, and then almost started crying."

Charlotte let out a long stream of air with her mouth. Then she flopped back onto the bed. "No."

"No, what?"

"No, I don't really wanna talk about it."

"Guys?" Charlotte couldn't see Gabe's face from where she was lying, but he sounded mildly distressed. "Sorry to change the subject, but . . . where are we?"

"What?" Lucy asked.

"Dale's room," Charlotte said, still looking up at the ceiling.

"I genuinely just processed our surroundings," Gabe said slowly, looking around, "and I . . . I really wish I hadn't."

"Are you sure you don't wanna talk about it?" Lucy asked, peering down at Charlotte, her necklace dangling.

"Yeah. Not tonight."

"He has *two* Slave Leia Funko Pops," Gabe said in a strangled voice, looking across the room.

"But I think we should talk about it soon," Lucy pressed.

"Mhm."

"I'm having flashbacks to that time I did shrooms at the aquarium," Gabe said, staring at Dale's tapestry.

"Okay, time for sleep," Lucy said, hoisting herself off the bed. She grabbed Charlotte's hands and pulled her back up into a seated position. "Can you see if Landon has blankets for Gabe?" She went over to the backpack and started digging through it.

"Yeah." Charlotte pointed at Gabe. "How many pillows do you need?"

"Just one, I'm not picky."

"Yes, you are."

"Three, please."

Charlotte swung her feet off the bed. "I'll see what I can do."

Landon was in the kitchen, washing dishes. Olivia was absent, presumably having gone to bed.

Charlotte sidled up to him.

"Hi."

"Hey."

A pause.

"Are you mad at me?"

"No."

Another pause.

"Are you sure?"

"I'm sure," he said, shaking his head as he handed her a wet glass and a dish towel. She began drying the glass as he reached for another in the sink. "I can see, from your weird point of view, why you didn't tell me. I'm not *happy* about it, and I'd *prefer* you tell me the next time you get attacked, but . . . I get it."

"The next time I get attacked," Charlotte said solemnly, "I will tell you immediately." She glanced across the apartment as she finished drying the glass and put it down on the counter. "Is Olivia okay?"

"Yeah, she's tough." Landon handed her another glass. "We talked a little. I apologized. A lot." He started washing a bowl. "I know I worry too much. About Olivia, and Mom, and you. I'm sure it gets annoying."

"It's not annoying."

"You're just all so tough, you know?" Landon turned off the sink, looking at the bowl. "I know none of you need me to, like, protect you or whatever. You've *really* never needed me, even when we were kids."

"That's not true."

"Well, for the most part. I just want to know you're okay. And I want you to know that I'm there for you, if you do ever need me."

Landon turned the sink back on as Charlotte quietly finished drying the glass, thinking about her conversation with Lucy and Gabe. As if summoned by her thoughts, the two emerged from Dale's room and disappeared into the bathroom to brush their teeth.

Accepting the dripping bowl from Landon, she said, "I'm sorry if I've been . . . you know. Distant."

"*If*?"

"Hey, I was trying to do an apology, but if you're gonna—"

"Oh my god, *okay*. Continue." Landon handed her the last plate from the sink in exchange for the bowl and started putting away the dishes.

Charlotte wiped the plate with the towel. "I told Lucy and

Gabe that I was kind of . . . distancing myself from them, because I felt like maybe they were moving on with their lives, and I wanted to give them the chance to . . ." She trailed off, wincing.

Landon glanced over at her as he closed a cabinet. "To what?"

She looked back at him, still making a sour face at what she was about to say. "Leave me behind?"

"*Jesus,* Charlotte."

"I know, I know. It sounds bad." She handed him the now-dry plate. "I don't really know what I was thinking."

"I do," Landon said, putting the plate in a cabinet and closing it. "You have a savior complex."

Charlotte scrunched up her brow. "No, I don't."

"Yeah, you do." Landon took the dish towel that had been hanging limp in her hands and crossed the kitchen to hang it on the handle of the stove. "You like helping people so much that you'll go out of your way to help them, even when they don't need it. And you thought you were helping them by distancing yourself."

"It's more than that, though, I realized." She pulled herself up to sit on the counter. "I mean, I think you're probably right, but—"

"Wait, *wait,* say that again." Landon fumbled for his phone. "Hang on, don't—wait until I start recording, then say that again."

Pointing his phone at her, he started recording. Blank-faced, Charlotte flipped off the camera.

Landon sighed heavily, returning his phone to his pocket. "Lost to history, I guess." He walked over and jumped up to sit on the counter across from her. "Okay, you were saying? I was right, and then what else?"

Charlotte gestured vaguely with her hands. "I guess I was embarrassed. Of where I am in life, of what I've done—or, not done. Especially compared to everything I did as a kid. And I think that's why I wasn't replying to you, either."

"Yeah, I was gonna ask about that. Because you know that *I* can't leave you behind. I'm not saying that to be sappy, I just mean that Mom literally wouldn't let me, even if I wanted to."

The light turned off in the bathroom, and the siblings looked over as Lucy and Gabe walked out.

"I really think if I just posted on Instagram, I could find someone—"

"You're gonna post your address on Instagram?"

"Well, I wouldn't do *that*—"

They closed the door to Dale's room before Charlotte and Landon could hear the rest of Gabe's newest idea for finding a roommate.

"Wait," Landon said, turning his head back, "you're saying you were *embarrassed* to talk to me? Because you . . . what, hated your job? Dude, I have much more embarrassing dirt on you than *that*. Fourth of July, 2006—"

"I don't *know*," Charlotte said, covering her face. Then she uncovered it. "Okay. I'm gonna say something, but I need you not to look at me."

"This apology is taking forever," Landon grumbled, sitting back on his hands and closing his eyes.

Charlotte leaned forward and waved a hand in front of his face.

"I'm not peeking."

"How'd you know I thought you were peeking?" Charlotte accused.

"Because I can feel the breeze of your hand flapping in front of my face, you nut. Just talk."

"*Okay*. I think I was embarrassed to talk to you because I haven't been doing much with my life, and you've been doing so much with yours, and I feel like you've always been weirdly proud of me, but I haven't been doing anything lately to make you proud, so I just felt like talking to you would be a bummer."

Charlotte glanced at him to make sure his eyes were still closed, then continued.

"But I get that that was shitty, because if you wanted to tell me about your life, I should've let you do that, and then . . . I dunno, hung up and just pretended the call dropped if you asked me about my life."

Landon snorted.

"I think maybe overall I was just feeling bad for myself," Charlotte said quietly. "And maybe a little mad at myself? So maybe I was punishing myself by withdrawing from everyone. Or maybe that just felt easier to do than talking about it." She paused. "You can open your eyes, I'm done."

She wasn't sure if she *was* done, but once she started saying "maybe" in every sentence, she knew that she was verging on rambling territory.

Landon was quiet, and Charlotte looked up, wondering if he'd heard her. His eyes were open, so she looked back down at her hands and waited.

"I *have* always been proud of you," he finally said. "I mean, we've talked about this before—some people probably would've hated having a sibling who took up so much spotlight, but I didn't really mind. Especially because I could tell you still looked up to me, even when you were out finding missing rubies or whatever while I was at home building Lego."

"I *did* look up to you," Charlotte said awkwardly. "And I . . . still do, even though you're still building Legos at twenty-seven."

"A lot of adults build Lego; it's actually a really popular adult pastime."

"Mhm."

"I'll always be proud of you, Lottie," he said, just as awkwardly. "It doesn't matter what you're doing. Unless you, like, murder someone, or . . . join a pyramid scheme."

"Valid."

"I'm just saying, answer a phone call every now and then. We don't have to talk about you. You can just sit there while I talk and say, 'Uh-huh,' every once in a while, so I think you're actually listening to me."

"Uh-huh," Charlotte replied automatically.

"Exactly." Landon fell silent for a moment. "You know Olivia and I have been dating for . . . six months now?" His heel hit the cabinet below him with a quiet *thunk* as he shifted positions, dropping his hands into his lap. "Mom wanted me to bring her home for Passover, but I told her Olivia was busy. Truth was, I told Olivia that I sensed you were going through a rough patch, and might not be comfortable with someone new at Seder."

Charlotte looked up at him, alarmed. "So you're saying Olivia *hates* me?"

"No, no," Landon laughed. "She understood. She'd been on enough video calls with Mom by then to know that I wasn't, like, *hiding* her or anything. And, honestly, I think she was a little nervous about going anyway."

"Oh. So you're saying Olivia *owes* me."

"I'm *saying,* I'm not as observant as you, but I'm not a total idiot. (Shut up, that wasn't a question.) I knew you were going through a hard time, but I also knew you wouldn't want to talk about it over the phone. That's why we did that whole fake mystery thing. Even if it didn't end up with you jumping back into mystery-solving, we at least got to see you. You got to meet Olivia." Landon looked across the apartment to the closed door of his bedroom. "I'm really glad you finally got to meet Olivia."

"I'm sure you guys will be fine," Charlotte said, following his gaze.

He looked back at her. "Is that your official theory as a detective, or . . . ?"

Charlotte furrowed her brow. "No, it just sounded like a nice thing to say." She paused. "She didn't make you sleep on the couch, though."

"True." A tired smile crossed his face. "A small victory, but I'll take it."

"And since you won't be needing them . . ." Charlotte said, twisting around to look into the living room, "I will take those couch pillows." She hopped off the counter, then turned. "Um, thanks. And sorry again."

"It's all good."

"*Blech,*" Charlotte said, shaking her arms as if to rid herself of the sentimentality. "Too many feelings tonight." She rounded the counter to retrieve the pillows from the couch. "Do you have extra blankets for Gabe?"

Not only did Landon have extra blankets, but he also had an air mattress—much to Gabe's relief ("I'll be honest, I was *not* looking forward to sleeping on the floor. I was gonna be brave and do it anyway, but this is better").

"'Night, all," Lucy said, hitting the light switch next to the door. Gabe didn't answer.

"How does he fall asleep that fast?" Charlotte asked as Lucy climbed into bed. "I always need at least twenty minutes for my tiredness to overtake my endless stream of thoughts, and that's on a *good* night."

"We could try talking about some of those thoughts. Maybe it'll help you fall asleep faster."

"Nice try."

"But soon, right?" Lucy propped herself up on one elbow. "I think it's important you talk about . . . whatever's going on with you. The other thing, not the 'not replying to texts' thing."

"Yeah, I know." Charlotte rolled onto her back. "I think I was just hoping I could figure it out myself, first."

"How many mysteries have I helped you with?"

Charlotte looked over at her, confused by the sudden change of subject. "I dunno. Most of them?"

"So why do you think you can solve what's going on with you all by yourself?"

"Oooo, slick." Charlotte turned her face back up to the ceiling, shaking her head. "Slick, slick, slick."

"I'm serious!"

"I know. We can talk about it tomorrow."

"Good." Satisfied, Lucy dropped her head to the pillow, pulling the blanket up to her chin.

The room was quiet for a moment. Then Charlotte sighed.

"I need to schedule a session with Helena."

"Yeah."

"I keep forgetting."

"Write it down."

"Okay."

"'Night."

"'Night. Don't be a blanket hog."

"I'm *not.*"

"I know, I'm just preempting."

"*Good night,* Charlotte."

"*Good night,* Lucy."

Chapter 14

Murderer Vibes

Charlotte awoke to a soft melody coming from underneath her pillow. She groggily retrieved her phone and turned off the alarm she had set. Being careful not to wake Lucy, she gently peeled back the sheets and climbed out of bed. Stepping quietly past Gabe (who had rolled halfway off the air mattress and was sleeping with the upper half of his body flopping onto the floor), she slipped out of the room.

Olivia was sitting at the dining table, eating a piece of toast and scrolling on her phone. She looked up when she heard Charlotte exit the bedroom. "Hey."

"Morning." Charlotte leaned against one of the chairs, trying and failing to suppress a yawn. "How're you feeling?"

Olivia shrugged. "Alright. Still a little shaken up, but I'll be fine." She sighed. "Not sure how I'm gonna face Jensen today, knowing it might've been him, but—"

"I was thinking about that." Charlotte pulled out the chair she had been leaning against and sat down. "Landon said you elbowed the guy in the face?"

"Yeah." Olivia took another bite of toast and mimed a sharp

jab with her elbow. "I wanted to kick him in the crotch, but I didn't have a good angle for it."

"Do you think you hit him hard enough to bleed? Or bruise?"

"Hope so."

"If you did," Charlotte said, "the damage would probably show."

Olivia's eyebrows shot up. "So if Jensen shows up to work with a black eye, we'll know it was actually him."

Charlotte nodded.

"Yeah, but . . ." Olivia's shoulders slumped. "*Then* what, right? I don't have any proof. He'd just say he ran into a wall or something."

"Yeah, not sure. Hey, is it cool if I bring Lucy and Gabe to the office today?"

Olivia hesitated. "I . . . don't know," she said slowly. "Honestly, I'm not sure you should come anymore. I know you wanted to talk to Jane and Sasha, but if that *was* Jensen last night, he's going to be in an even worse mood than he was yesterday."

Charlotte nodded. "I get it." She thought for a moment. "I was thinking about checking out Eric's apartment. Maybe I can text you later, and we can figure out a way for me to talk with Jane and Sasha outside of the office?"

Olivia looked relieved. "Yeah, that sounds good." She popped the last piece of toast into her mouth and stood, taking her plate into the kitchen. "Are you going to Eric's apartment to look for his phone? Do you have a theory about the message?"

"Yes to the first thing, maybe to the second. I have a few theories right now, but I don't really like saying those out loud until I'm pretty sure I'm right." Charlotte gave her a half-smile. "It'd make all the detective stuff look a lot less impressive if people knew how many times I'm wrong in my head."

Olivia laughed, putting her plate down into the sink. "Okay, makes sense."

She left to brush her teeth, and Charlotte unlocked her phone to send a text to Ajay, Eric's roommate. She was about to head back to Dale's room when she remembered something and settled back into her chair.

Olivia emerged from the bathroom and went into Landon's room, coming back out a moment later with her purse.

"He's still asleep," she said, pulling her bag over her shoulder as she walked back to Charlotte. "I don't think he slept very well last night."

Charlotte shifted uncomfortably in her seat. She didn't want to get involved, but after talking with her brother last night, she felt a sudden need to defend him.

"Landon's an idiot," she said. *Bad start.* "But . . . he means well. And he really cares about you."

Olivia gave her a small smile. "Thanks," she said. "I know he does. And last night, we had a long talk about the importance of finding ways to deal with situations without involving the police, so . . ."

"Sounds romantic," Charlotte said, nodding solemnly.

Olivia laughed. "Anyway, we'll be fine. But thank you for caring."

Charlotte shrugged awkwardly, then perked up, remembering why she was waiting for Olivia to come back out. "Hey, did Eric ever ask you to help with union stuff?"

Olivia thought for a moment. "Yeah, actually, he did. Last week."

"And you said . . . ?"

"I said yes. But then he messaged me a few hours later and said he didn't need the help after all, and asked me not to bring it up again."

Charlotte leaned forward. "Did he say why he didn't need the help anymore?"

Olivia shook her head, her mouth shrugging.

"Hmm." Charlotte thought for another moment. "Did he text you when he said he didn't need the help anymore?"

"Um . . . no, he did it through the Scoop system."

Interesting.

Charlotte nodded. "Got it."

Olivia looked at her curiously. "I'm very intrigued right now, but I'm also very late."

Charlotte waved her off. "I'll explain later."

"Alright."

Charlotte stood and headed back to Dale's room as Olivia left. Saying all those nice things about Landon was probably the second-hardest thing she'd have to do all morning. The first would be getting Gabe to wake up before nine a.m.

"I take it back, I hate detective work." Gabe yawned, rubbing his eyes. He was slumped in the back seat of Landon's Honda Accord, his feet crossed on the center console.

"What time do you wake up for work?" Lucy asked, glancing back at him in the rearview mirror.

"Like, ten-thirty? I usually 'work from home' for the first half of the day, so . . ." He suddenly pulled his legs back and sat up. "Shit, I forgot I'm technically still working. I have to check my email."

"I feel like you're giving social media managers a bad name," Charlotte said from the passenger seat as Gabe pulled out his phone. Landon had refused to let her drive his car, relinquishing the keys only when Lucy promised she'd be the sole driver. Charlotte had been mildly offended (she was a perfectly fine driver by New Jersey standards) but also pleased (she liked being chauffeured).

"Oh, yeah, no, most social media work is a *lot* more than I do. *I* do the absolute least at my job because they don't expect any more of me. Also, they don't even pay me that well, so I'm not going to waste my untapped talent on them." Gabe glanced up from his phone. "Also *also*, I run social media for a *mattress company*." He stopped there and returned to his phone, as if that statement clearly spoke for itself.

Lucy shook her head, smiling. She had put on her glasses to

drive and readjusted the tortoiseshell frames as she brought the car to a stop at a red light. "So according to Finn, Eric said that Olivia wouldn't help him. But now Olivia's saying that Eric told her he didn't need her help anymore."

"Right," Charlotte said. "Except I don't think it was actually Eric who sent that message. Olivia said it was sent through the Scoop messaging system, which we've learned is super easy to hack."

"Ahh."

"Which probably means that Eric got a similar fake message from 'Olivia' saying that she wasn't interested in helping anymore. Light's green."

Lucy slowly accelerated. "So whoever sent the fake messages is probably trying to prevent Eric from getting help with communications, right?"

"Right, since we're assuming Martín stopped helping for some reason."

"What about Arielle?" Gabe asked. "She said Eric asked her for help a few days ago. She didn't say anything about getting a 'never mind' message from him."

"Maybe the person sending the messages had already decided by that point that they were going to deal with Eric a different way." Charlotte pointed through the windshield, unaware of the silence that had fallen over her friends as a result of that ominous statement. "It's this street coming up on the right."

Ajay had replied to her text soon after Olivia left for work, saying Charlotte could come over any time to look around Eric's room. After rousing Lucy from her sleep and recruiting her to the much more difficult task of waking up Gabe, she had filled them in on the new plan.

"He said you can park here," Charlotte said, looking at her phone to reference the text from Ajay. She glanced back up at the street, then pointed. "There's a spot."

"Eugh." Lucy brought them towards the empty space between two cars. "I hate parallel parking."

"Guess Landon chose the wrong person to drive," Charlotte said smugly.

"I said I hate parallel parking. I didn't say I'm bad at it." To prove her point, Lucy proceeded to smoothly maneuver the car into the spot, though she bumped the curb once, resulting in a victorious "Ha!" from Charlotte.

Glancing at her phone as they climbed out of the car, Charlotte saw she had new texts from Olivia.

Olivia: Jensen's not in today, come whenever
Olivia: text me when you get here

A couple of minutes later, they found themselves inside Ajay and Eric's apartment.

"Thanks again for this," Charlotte said as Ajay shut the door behind them.

Ajay: Mid-to-late twenties; South Asian; curly, dark brown hair that looked mussed from sleep. He was wearing gray sweatpants and a white tank top that read, "LEGALIZE GOOD MUSIC" in big black letters.

"No problem," Ajay said. "Eric was supposed to send me rent money yesterday, so now the situation's personal."

"Very noble of you," Gabe commented, staring at Ajay's shirt.

"You said you heard Eric come in Tuesday night around eleven, right?" Charlotte asked, referencing the notes on her phone.

"Right."

She looked up. "Is it possible you didn't hear him leave again?"

"I guess, but I usually hear him come and go if I'm awake. The door's pretty loud, unless you open and close it real slow."

"Do you remember what time you went to sleep?"

Ajay thought for a moment. "Probably around two a.m. I was working on this sick mash-up of 'Back in Black' and 'Black

Magic.' And he was gone by the time I woke up around nine-thirty, but that was normal for him."

"Why?" Gabe asked.

"'Cuz he goes to work in the mornings."

"I was talking about the mash-up. AC/DC and *Little Mix*?"

"Which one's Eric's?" Charlotte cut in quickly, turning towards the short hallway of doors to their right.

A minute later, Ajay left them to their own devices in Eric's room. It was on the smaller side, with the twin bed in the middle of the room taking up almost half of the floor space. A squat bureau sat against the wall across from the bed, with a small lamp and two plants on top of it.

"I think it was the roommate," Gabe said as soon as Charlotte pulled the door shut.

"You just didn't like his shirt," Lucy said. She turned to Charlotte. "What's the play here?"

"I'm trying to create a timeline of that night," Charlotte said as Gabe began poking around the room. "I saw Eric get picked up by a car around six-thirty. He missed the union committee meeting at ten. Ajay heard him come in a little before eleven."

"And said he would've heard Eric if he left before two a.m.," Lucy finished.

Charlotte's brow furrowed. "So something happened that made Eric miss the union meeting and not tell anyone why. Then he came home."

"Seemingly in a bad mood, according to Ajay," Lucy added.

"Then he left between two a.m. and nine-thirty a.m., and whether it was his own decision or not, he never came back."

"Found a suitcase." Grunting, Gabe pulled a dark blue suitcase down from the top of Eric's closet, stumbling backwards from the weight. Regaining his balance, he dropped it to the floor with a *thud*. "If he *did* plan on leaving, it doesn't seem like he was expecting a long trip."

"Unless he had another bag," Lucy said. She gave Gabe a

pointed look. "*You* were walking around all day yesterday with your clothes in a backpack."

"Yeah, and I regret it," Gabe said, twisting his upper torso and wincing with pain. "Combined with sleeping on the air mattress last night, my back isn't doing so hot right now."

Charlotte had wandered over to Eric's bureau and started pulling drawers open, looking through them. "Doesn't look like he has a lot of clothes missing. Maybe a few shirts, a pair of pants."

She suddenly turned, crossing the room and peeking into the hamper she had spotted inside the closet. "Mostly empty," she observed. "He probably did laundry over the weekend."

"Just to make sure I'm keeping up," Gabe said, sitting down on Eric's bed as Charlotte returned to the bureau. "If his phone and laptop aren't here, that means he was taken, right? The message was from someone else? We go full Liam Neeson?"

"He could've had some reason to lie about them being here," Lucy said.

"Or someone else could've grabbed them after he left," Charlotte added, pulling open the bottom drawer of Eric's bureau.

"Ugh. None of that happens in *Taken*," Gabe grumbled.

Charlotte glanced at him over her shoulder, then looked at Lucy. "He's never seen *Taken*."

"I've never seen *Taken*," Gabe confirmed.

Lucy shook her head, smiling.

Charlotte sifted through the contents of the drawer, then froze. "Oh my god," she said. "Why do I keep finding weird shit in drawers this week?"

"To be fair," Lucy said, "you've been going through a lot of strange drawers this week, so the odds of you finding weird shit are significantly better."

"Is it another envelope full of cash?" Gabe asked eagerly.

"Close," Charlotte replied, pulling out a gun.

"*Jesus*, Charlotte!" Gabe tumbled backwards off of the bed, coming up to peek over the other side. Lucy took a step back, her eyes wide.

Charlotte had picked the gun up with one of Eric's shirts and was cradling it with both hands. She held it out for them to see, eyebrows raised, with a tight smile on her face that read, *This is fine.*

"That's very nice, Charlotte," Lucy said gently, like a parent to a child who brought something weird into the house. "Maybe let's put it down now."

"Back in the drawer?"

"Yes. No." Lucy looked frazzled. "Put it on the bed."

Gabe yelped and dove back down as Charlotte gently deposited the swaddled gun onto the bed.

She straightened, looking down at it. "So."

"So," Lucy echoed.

"Literally, what the fuck," Gabe said, slowly getting to his feet and eyeing the gun like it might go off on its own. "Does this confirm it, then? Eric killed Bernard?"

"Or maybe he had some reason to believe his life was in danger," Lucy suggested. "Finn said Bernard had a gun to protect himself while he did deliveries."

Charlotte thought back. "Eric didn't have anywhere to hide a gun when he delivered to Landon's."

"That wasn't really a normal delivery, though," Lucy said. "Maybe he usually carries a bag or something. Hang on."

She walked over to the door and pulled it open. "Hey, Ajay?" She called down the hall.

"'Sup?"

"Do you know if Eric owned a gun?"

"Nah, I don't wanna know about any of that shit."

"Okay, thanks so much." Lucy closed the door and turned back to the others. "He knows nothing."

"Hmm . . ." Charlotte squinted at the gun. Her thoughts wandered back to seeing the purple pen in Eric's hand.

Gabe looked at her, then at Lucy, then back at Charlotte. He gestured towards the bed. "Are we waiting for it to tell us what it's doing here, or . . . ?"

"Let's keep looking," Charlotte said, turning back to the bureau. "See if we can find anything else. Look for his laptop and phone."

Neither were there. And aside from the drooping plants that Lucy brought to the kitchen to perk up with water, Eric didn't have anything else in his room indicating that something was amiss. After a short discussion, they agreed it was best to put the gun back where Charlotte found it. Gabe once again took cover as Charlotte transferred the weapon back to the bottom drawer of Eric's bureau.

"So we're all clear on the plan?" Lucy asked. "Divide and conquer?"

After driving Landon's car back to his apartment, they had walked to the train station to head into the city. After Charlotte glowered at a couple sitting in a four-seater (a capital offense, in her opinion), she and Lucy settled down in one pair of seats, with Gabe sitting in the row in front of them.

"Yup," Gabe said, resting his arms on the back of his seat as he looked down at them. "I'm flirting with Arielle to distract her."

"*No,* that was last night. You're talking to Sasha." Lucy looked over at Charlotte. "What do you want him to ask her about?"

Charlotte chewed on the inside of her cheek, thinking. "The envelopes," she finally said. "The money in Martín's drawer was in an envelope that matched ones given to all the employees. Olivia said Sasha wrote and handed out those envelopes. I want to know where or who she got those from."

"Great," Gabe said. "I can casually start a conversation about stationery, no problem."

"And then just ask her about Eric, I guess. And Jaya. And Candice, too. She might know . . . I dunno, *something.*"

Gabe nodded, drumming on the back of his seat with his hands. "Very cool. My mission is crystal clear. If crystal was, like, really hard to see through. But I'll make it work. Ow, my knees hurt." He dropped back down into his seat as Charlotte turned to Lucy.

"And I guess just ask Martín—"

"I've got it," Lucy said, holding up a hand. "I have my own plan."

Charlotte raised an eyebrow. "Care to share?"

Lucy settled back into her seat, shrugging. "I'm just going to talk to him."

"*That's* your plan?"

"Yeah."

"That was already *my* plan," Charlotte protested. "And it didn't work."

"Well, y'know . . . you have your ways of getting info out of people, and that's great," Lucy said. "Except when it doesn't work, then it's not so great. But people tend to find me a little more . . . approachable, so I figured I'd just try talking to him and go from there."

"I'm *approachable,*" Charlotte grumbled, sinking into her seat.

"No, no, hey," Lucy said, reaching out to pat Charlotte's head while trying to hold back a smile. "Of course you are. Once people get to know you, you're super approachable."

"That's literally not what approachable means," Charlotte argued. "Approachable means someone would approach me because they can tell that I'm nice right away."

"You're going to correct *me* on a definition?" Lucy raised an eyebrow at her. "I teach language arts for a living."

"I'm not saying you're incorrect, I'm just saying you're wrong."

"That's what incorrect means."

"Well, I figured since we're just *making up* definitions of words—"

"So was that g-u-n in Eric's drawer the one used to kill Bernard?" Gabe asked suddenly, popping back up to look down at them over the back of his seat.

Lucy cocked her head at him. "Why did you spell *gun*?"

"I don't know, I feel like you shouldn't say *gun* on public transportation," Gabe said. "But now we've said it twice, so . . ."

"One time I spent an entire train ride listening to a fully

grown man on the phone talking like a baby," Charlotte said flatly. "I feel like that's worse than saying the word *gun.*"

"Three times," Gabe said. "And no kink-shaming on NJ Transit."

"Do *you* think it was the gun that killed Bernard?" Lucy asked Gabe.

Gabe glanced at Charlotte, who gestured with one hand as if to say, *Go ahead.*

"Well," he said, straightening and folding his hands, "I believe there is indeed a large possibility that the appearance of such a weapon in our missing person's sleeping chambers could perchance be connected—"

"Why're you talking like you're trying to hit a word count?" Charlotte interrupted, making a face.

Gabe paused. "I'm doing, like, the dramatic detective monologue thing."

"When have I ever talked like that?"

"I dunno, I thought maybe you used to do it back in your prime—"

"You think I talked like *that* when I was twelve?"

Lucy put up her hands. "Keep going. With less words."

"Fine." Gabe dropped back down to lean against the back of his seat. "I mean, for one thing, if Eric left his apartment thinking he was in danger, he probably would've taken the gun with him, right?"

"Sure, maybe," Charlotte agreed.

"So . . . that probably means something." Gabe waved a hand at Charlotte. "File that away in your little mental filing cabinet."

Charlotte sat back in her seat. "I've been thinking that it's likely Bernard was killed with his own gun. He told someone he always carried one, but I don't think the police found it at the scene."

"So whoever killed him took his gun with them," Lucy said.

Charlotte shrugged. "Possibly."

"And is that the one in Eric's room?" Gabe asked.

"I don't know."

"But then what?" Lucy asked. "If Eric did kill Bernard, I mean. Did he suddenly get scared and run?"

Charlotte's eyes narrowed thoughtfully. "Weird that he stuck around for a week before getting scared enough to run, if that was the case."

"Maybe he didn't want to seem suspicious by running right away," Gabe said.

"But what about the message?" Lucy asked. "It said his phone and laptop were at the apartment, but they weren't."

Charlotte pondered that for a moment. If someone else wrote the message, what reason could they have for wanting people to go to Eric's room looking for his devices? Maybe they just wanted to paint Eric as a liar.

If the message *was* from Eric, what reason would *he* have for sending someone to his apartment looking for something that wasn't there? Or did someone else take the devices without his knowledge?

"You met him," Gabe said to Charlotte, pulling her out of her thoughts. "Did you get a murderer vibe?"

"I don't know what that means."

"You know, like . . ." Gabe gestured vaguely. "*Murderer vibes.*"

"Oh, thank you, *that* made a lot more sense." Charlotte looked over at Lucy. "I barely spoke to him. Did you talk to him while you guys were planning the fake mystery?"

Lucy shook her head.

Charlotte thought back to when she first bumped into Eric. Despite lying to her face for the sake of the made-up mystery, he seemed nice. Olivia probably wouldn't be friendly with anyone who gave off "murderer vibes," anyway.

She fast-forwarded to seeing Eric again the following night, when he revealed the purple pen. His confusion when she started laughing. Then he left—

Wait. No.

He turned to leave. Then turned back.

"Can I ask you something? As a detective? It's for a friend."

She thought he was going to confess to being a part of the fake mystery. He said . . .

He said . . .

"SHIT!" Charlotte yelled, causing Lucy to jump and Gabe to drop down into his seat as a few of their fellow passengers looked curiously in their direction.

He peeked at them through the space between seats. "What's wrong?"

Charlotte leaned forward, covering her eyes with the bottoms of her palms. "He said something to me," she said, willing herself to remember.

"Who?" Lucy asked. "Eric?"

"When he brought the pizzas, yeah. He said he wanted to ask me something, as a detective. And then he asked . . . he . . . UGHHH."

She uncovered her eyes and slammed her fists into the seat in front of her, causing Gabe to yelp.

"Sorry! Sorry!"

"You're good, I'm okay."

"I can't remember," Charlotte groaned, tilting back her head to look at the ceiling. "I can't remember."

"Okay, time to walk," Lucy said, sliding out of her seat and standing up.

Charlotte looked over at her. "What?"

Lucy gestured for her to join her in the aisle. "You know what my grandma says. 'When your brain is frozen, start moving your feet—' "

" '—and your brain will start moving with them,' " Charlotte finished, sliding across the seats.

"Also, I think you're scaring everyone in this car," Lucy added. "Probably better if we leave anyway."

"Abuela has so many good sayings," Gabe commented, joining them in the aisle as they began walking towards the back of the car. "Mine just tells me I don't eat enough."

He turned to leave. Then turned back.

"Can I ask you something? As a detective? It's for a friend."

Charlotte thought he was going to confess to being a part of the fake mystery. But he didn't seem embarrassed. He seemed . . . troubled? *That's a strong word.* Thoughtful. And hesitant.

"Anything?" Lucy asked from behind her. They had already walked the length of the car.

Charlotte shook her head. "I was so convinced that he was going to admit that he was a part of your scheme that I didn't even process what he started to say." She ascended the stairs that led to the vestibule between cars.

He looked thoughtful. He hesitated.

"Can I ask you something? As a detective? It's for a friend."

And then he said . . .

Okay, on three, I'm gonna remember what he said. One . . . two . . . THREE.

[silence]

Shit.

"I can't," Charlotte whined, coming to a stop in the vestibule. Each side of the area had a row of seats facing one another. Two low walls bordered the entry to the area, with poles connecting them to the ceiling.

Thankfully, the area was empty, so no one else was there to witness Charlotte being a failure of a detective.

She stopped and turned to face them, her shoulders dropping pathetically. "I can't remember."

"You can, and you will," Lucy said as she and Gabe also stopped. "Just relax—"

The train suddenly shuddered, sending the three of them stumbling. Gabe grabbed onto a pole. Lucy grabbed onto Gabe. Charlotte let herself stumble backwards.

"I'm not going to remember," Charlotte said, regaining her balance. Her brain had started to whir again. "I can't remember anything, I can't keep track of anything—"

"That's why you have the notebook," Lucy reminded her. "You've always needed the notebook."

"I never needed the fucking notebook," Charlotte said, frustrated. She swayed with the movement of the train. "I would just use it because I thought it made me look official. I'd always remember all the important stuff. I'd catch all the important clues." She balled up her fists. "I'd actually *listen* when someone was telling me something that would become relevant to a case!"

The train shuddered again, and she stumbled forward this time. Lucy caught her arm.

"You're holding back," Lucy said. "Stop holding yourself back."

"I'm *not*," Charlotte argued, regaining her balance. "I'm not *doing* anything. I just can't do this."

"Stop saying you can't; you *can*."

"You should slap her," Gabe suddenly suggested.

Lucy looked over at him, incredulous. "I'm not gonna—"

"Do it," Charlotte said. She turned to Lucy. "Slap me."

The incredulous look was turned onto Charlotte. "Are you serious?"

"I'll take any help at this point." She squared her shoulders and closed her eyes, bracing herself. "Do it."

"I can't slap you! Both of you need to calm down." Lucy tightened her grip on Charlotte, who still had her eyes shut. "You just need to clear your mind, and—"

Gabe let go of the pole and slapped Charlotte.

"OW-*UH*."

"GABE!" Lucy yelled.

"She asked for it!"

"Not from *you*, maniac!"

"That was good," Charlotte said, rubbing her cheek.

"Really?" Gabe asked, his face brightening as he grabbed the pole again.

"No, it did nothing. But it was an interesting experiment."

"Everyone *shut up*." Lucy took a deep breath. "Take a second.

Close your eyes. Don't think too hard. Just let it come back to you."

Charlotte resisted the urge to roll her eyes, closing them instead. It wasn't Lucy's fault she hadn't realized yet that Charlotte was a washed-up hack.

He looked thoughtful. He hesitated.

"Can I ask you something? As a detective? It's for a friend."

And then he said something. And I thought he was going to tell me that the others had paid him to—

"PAY!" Charlotte suddenly burst out, her eyes flying open. "He said something about paying for something. Or someone getting paid."

"Did he want to pay you for detective work?" Gabe asked.

Charlotte shook her head. "No . . . no, the way he said it, it was like he was talking about something that had happened."

"Like he was posing a hypothetical?" Lucy asked.

Charlotte remembered what Olivia had said to her about Eric before: *"He presented me with a hypothetical that made it very obvious he was talking about himself. He does that a lot."*

"Yes! Exactly." Charlotte thought harder. "He said something like . . . 'What if someone offered to pay you for—' " She looked up. "That's when I cut him off."

" 'What if someone offered to pay you for . . .' " Gabe echoed.

"It definitely wasn't about our fake mystery," Lucy said. "We didn't pay him. I mean, I think Olivia was going to take him out for drinks as a thank-you, but other than that . . ."

"Excuse me, folks."

They all turned to see a conductor staring at them.

"I'm going to have to ask you to sit down." He gestured to the row of empty seats they were standing next to. "And to turn down the volume."

"Yes, sorry about that," Lucy said, pulling Charlotte and Gabe over to the seats. "We'll be quieter."

They all sat down. Charlotte chewed on the inside of her cheek as the conductor walked away. Lucy spoke first.

"Let's say Eric was going to ask about something related to what's been going on," she said. "What payment could he be talking about?"

"A bribe," Charlotte suddenly said, staring across the vestibule out the windows. "The money in Martín's drawer." She looked over at her friends. "What if he was bribed to stop helping Eric?"

"Ohhhh," Gabe said, nodding.

"And if Martín was bribed to stop helping the union," Charlotte continued, "Eric might've been offered a bribe, too. Maybe that's what he was asking about."

She scrunched up her face at Lucy, who was smiling. "What?"

Lucy shrugged. "I just knew you could do it."

"Yeah, well . . ." Admittedly, Charlotte was feeling pretty pleased with herself. But it wasn't *that* big a breakthrough. She still had a lot more mystery left to solve.

But, for now at least, the whirring in her head had stopped.

Chapter 15

Eavesdropping Face

DETENTION NOTICE

Student: Lottie Illes

Date: 9/29/2010

Teacher: P. Duncan

Reason for detention: Lottie was found hiding in a vent (again). She insisted that she didn't mean to end up in the principal's office, but was "aiming for the band room and got turned around." Her screwdriver was confiscated.

"You know, I'm starting to come around to the 'Back in Black Magic' mash-up," Gabe said as they turned onto 43rd Street. "I've gotta find Ajay's SoundCloud."

Olivia met them in the lobby of the office building.

"Jensen sent a message saying he woke up with a cold," she said as she signed them in. "He's working from home today."

"Probably didn't want you to see the damage to his face," Charlotte said.

"Or he got sick crying himself to sleep after you beat him up," Gabe added. He had his backpack on again, significantly lighter than it had been the day before. He'd left most of his stuff at Landon's, the backpack now only holding Lucy's clothes from the day before to bring back to her apartment.

Olivia snorted, putting down the pen. "Doubt it. If anything, he probably stayed up all night trying to figure out new ways to make my job more difficult."

Lucy's brow furrowed as they followed Olivia to the escalator. "Are you worried?" she asked Olivia. "That he might retaliate, somehow?"

Charlotte saw Gabe open and close his mouth, presumably stopping himself from commenting on the solid SAT word.

Olivia stepped onto the escalator. "I don't know. Honestly, I've been thinking about leaving Scoop, anyway."

"Because of the union stuff?" Charlotte asked.

Olivia nodded. "Just seeing how badly the company's been handling it doesn't make me feel great working here. And my boss is an asshole. And Jane isn't very accessible, which isn't ideal, especially since my boss is an asshole." She glanced over her shoulder to check their progress on the escalator, then turned back. "Plus, I've been picking up steam with my app. It'd be nice to have more time for that, instead of just sneakily working on it while I'm at the office." She narrowed her eyes playfully at the others. "Because I'm not ready to be fired just yet, let's call that a joke."

Gabe held his hands up to indicate solidarity. "Hypothetically, I do *so* much personal stuff on company time." He dropped his hands. "Like, this entire visit."

"Do you think I'd be able to get into Jensen's office?" Charlotte asked as they reached the top of the escalator.

"Unlikely," Olivia said. "He always locks it."

"Mm." *I've gotta learn how to pick locks.*

Olivia led them to the hallway of elevators. Charlotte and Lucy both looked over at Gabe, the three of them suddenly slowing.

"What's up?" Olivia asked, turning back to see they had fallen behind.

"Nothing," Gabe said, giving her a shrug so violent it seemed more like a convulsion. "It's all good. All good in the hood. Pretend I didn't say that, I hated that. Anyway, how are you?"

"He's afraid of elevators," Charlotte said plainly.

"I'm not *afraid* of them," Gabe protested, turning on her. "I just don't *trust* them. Like how I don't trust magicians. Or men named Ryan."

Olivia gave him a curious look. "Why—"

"They have too many secrets," Gabe explained.

"Magicians, or men named Ryan?"

"Yes."

"Are there stairs?" Lucy cut in.

"Yeah, but . . ." Olivia grimaced sympathetically. "It's, like, twelve flights."

"Which are you more afraid of?" Charlotte asked Gabe. "Elevators or cardio?"

Gabe thought for a moment. Then he sighed. "I'm going to keep my eyes closed the whole time, and I need one person to hold me and one person to sing 'Ain't No Mountain High Enough' into my ear until we get there."

"And this is for riding the elevator, right?" Lucy asked.

"Can't Lucy do both of those things?" Charlotte added as Olivia hit the button for the elevator.

Gabe gave her a wounded look. "I need the *full support* of my friends right now."

"Fine. Lucy sings."

"I don't know the lyrics," Lucy said innocently as the elevator dinged.

Charlotte groaned as the doors slid open. They walked in, Gabe hesitantly stepping inside and immediately closing his eyes. Lucy wrapped her arms around him, raising her eyebrows at Charlotte as the elevator doors closed.

Charlotte looked over at Olivia, who shrugged.

The elevator began to rise, and Gabe shuddered. "Charlotte."

"Okay, okay." Charlotte stepped in to stand on his other side. "Wait. I don't remember how it starts."

"*Charlotte,*" Lucy said warningly.

"No, I'm not trying to be difficult, I don't remember!"

"Just start anywhere," Gabe said through gritted teeth, his eyes screwed shut.

"Is the chorus good?"

"Yeah."

"Okay." Charlotte paused, thinking.

"Why is no one singing 'Ain't No Mountain High Enough' into my ear right now?" Gabe demanded, his shoulders stiffening.

"Sorry!" Charlotte said, bringing her fists to her forehead, feeling stressed. "I realized the part I thought was the chorus might actually be the beginning."

"*So sing that.*"

"Actually, I might not even be thinking of the right song."

"Lucy, I'm gonna kill her."

"Can I just hug you, too?"

"FINE."

Charlotte threw her arms around Gabe, who yelped and stiffened even more at the sudden contact.

"You're doing great," Charlotte said, her face squished into his shoulder.

"I hate you."

The elevator was silent for a moment.

"Wait, is it, '*Ain't*'—"

The elevator settled to a stop, and the doors slid open.

"Thank *god,*" Gabe and Charlotte said in unison, both of them rushing out into the hallway.

Olivia looked over at Lucy. "So you deal with this a lot?"

Lucy sighed. "I haven't known peace since 2003."

They walked past the door to the balcony and caught up with Charlotte and Gabe outside of the Scoop office.

"Okay, so Gabe's going to talk to Sasha," Charlotte said. "Lucy's talking to Martín, and I'm talking to Jane. Everyone set?"

"I'll try to get you time with Jane," Olivia said, "but she might not be able to talk right now."

"Why?" Charlotte asked.

"Right before I left to get you guys, she said to message her if anyone needed anything and then closed the door to her office."

"Did she say why?"

"Probably a phone call. She usually leaves her door open, even when she's talking on the phone, but sometimes when it's a conversation she doesn't want us hearing, she'll close it."

"How long are her phone calls, usually?"

Olivia winced. "Could be up to an hour."

"Oy. Okay." Charlotte pointed at Gabe. "I'm with you, then."

Gabe raised an eyebrow, tilting his head. "Or . . ."

"You're not talking to Arielle."

"*We'll see,*" Gabe sang, pushing open the door to the office and walking inside.

Arielle was in the kitchen when they entered, filling up her water bottle at the counter next to the fridge.

"Hey, guys!" she said, looking over at them as she returned the water filter to the fridge and closed the door. She smiled at Gabe. "Welcome to Scoop."

"Happy to be here," Gabe said, grinning back.

"I just wanted to chat with a couple people I missed yesterday," Charlotte explained.

Arielle's brow furrowed. "Is this about Eric? Are we still worried about him?"

Charlotte suddenly realized that no one at the office had any reason to believe that something was wrong with Eric after the message they all received the night before.

"Just tying up some loose ends," she said quickly, as Arielle's expression grew more concerned. "Dotting some *I*s, crossing some *T*s. Detective protocol."

The worry slowly faded from Arielle's face. She nodded. "You want to talk to Sasha and Jane, right? I think Jane's on a call right now, but Sasha's at her workstation." She nodded at Olivia. "You go ahead; I can introduce them. Jensen sent a new to-do list while you were downstairs."

Olivia groaned, her head rolling back. "Fantastic. You guys know where to find me." She headed for her workstation. "Or the empty shell of my body working on another useless task."

Arielle screwed the top back onto her water bottle. "Jensen's really been giving her a lot to do," she said, looking sympathetic. "I figure he's testing her for the promotion."

Charlotte remembered Arielle mentioning Olivia being up for promotion the night before, and her asking them not to tell Olivia. She hadn't really planned on keeping that promise, but genuinely just forgot about it after everything else that happened the night before.

"I thought you said it's pretty much a done deal," Charlotte said. "Why would he be testing her?"

Arielle raised an eyebrow. "It's *Jensen.* Of course he doesn't think anyone's worthy of replacing him, but if it's going to be Olivia, he's going to give her a hard time first."

"I hope it's okay we're here," Lucy said. "I know you told Charlotte to avoid the office."

An apologetic look crossed Arielle's face. "Yeah, I'm sorry if I made it seem like I didn't want you here. Like I said, I was just worried about how Jensen would react if you came back, and if it would jeopardize Olivia's promotion."

"Well, it doesn't really matter," Gabe said, looking over at Charlotte and Lucy. "I mean, she doesn't—"

"She doesn't really care what Jensen thinks," Lucy said, quickly jumping in before Gabe could say anything about

Olivia planning on leaving Scoop. Gabe nodded in agreement, catching himself.

Arielle's face brightened a bit. "Well, either way, he's not in today." She cracked a half-smile. "And I know someone who is probably very happy about that."

She passed them and exited the kitchen. Lucy and Charlotte both shot pointed looks at an abashed Gabe before following her out.

Charlotte scanned the office as they rounded the corner. Jensen's office door was closed, with no light coming from underneath. On the opposite side of the office, Jane's door was also closed. But unlike the day before, a light was on inside.

Olivia had settled back into her chair at the center table. Martín sat at the farthest table, earbuds in, focused on his computer. She saw him glance over at them before his eyes quickly flitted back to his screen.

Arielle led them to the young woman sitting at the table that had been empty the day before. Sasha: early twenties; Black; long, black braids that curled at the ends. She wore a light orange buttoned blouse and a dark pencil skirt, an outfit that was slightly more formal than the clothing of anyone else in the office.

"Sasha," Arielle said, walking over to her, "these are Olivia's friends: Charlotte, Lucy, and Gabe. This is Sasha, our rockstar intern."

"Olivia said you were coming. Hi." Sasha smiled and stood, smoothing out her skirt. "She said you were detectives?"

"Yes," Gabe said, a split second before Charlotte and Lucy's, "No."

"She's the detective," Lucy explained, nodding at Charlotte.

"Former detective," Charlotte corrected.

"I'm a detective-in-training," Gabe finished.

Sasha smiled politely, confusion in her eyes. "Oh. Okay."

"I need to get back to work," Arielle said. "Let me know if you guys need anything." She turned and walked back to her workstation. As she did so, Martín got up from his chair and began heading for the kitchen, holding a water bottle.

Charlotte and Lucy exchanged a glance.

"I'll go . . ." Lucy nodded after Martín.

Charlotte nodded back, then returned to Sasha as Lucy followed after Martín. "I'm going to check out Eric's workstation," she said. "Do you mind if Gabe asks you a few questions?"

"Sure."

Charlotte gave Gabe a look that read, *You got this.* In return, Gabe gave her a look that read, *Yeah, I know, but it's very cute that you thought I needed that encouragement.*

Rolling her eyes, Charlotte headed over to the farthest table. She knew she wasn't going to find anything new at Eric's workstation after having already looked through his cabinet the day before. What interested her more about it today was its close proximity to Jane's office.

She crouched down next to Eric's workstation and tilted her head towards the closed door, but could only make out a soft murmuring from the other side.

Crawling across the floor, she kept an eye out to make sure she wasn't in Arielle's or Sasha's sight lines. Olivia's back was to her, finally giving her some well-deserved deniability.

Stopping a couple feet away from the door, Charlotte craned her neck to listen again.

The following is a loose transcription of what she was able to hear (and what she wasn't):

Jane: . . . and then two years here. *[pause]* I would have to say that I don't *[unintelligible]* is definitely my strong suit. *[pause]* *[laughter]* No, of course. I was thinking *[unintelligible]* signing bonus? *[pause]* Perfect. Yes, that's great. *[pause]*

```
Great talking [unintelligible] hearing from
you soon. [pause] You too. Goodbye.
  Arielle: Hey, Jensen wants you to reply to
his message.
  Martín: Okay. [pause] What're you doing?
```

Charlotte looked up at Martín, who was standing a few feet in front of her, holding his water bottle. Lucy stood several feet behind him, a fist over her mouth, her eyes wide.

"Uh . . . dizzy spell," Charlotte said, shaking her head. "Had to sit down for a minute. I'm good now." She scrambled to her feet, then realized that scrambling was probably too fast for someone who allegedly just experienced a dizzy spell. She swayed a bit to try to sell the performance. "I think I'm gonna get some water." *Nailed it.*

Walking past Martín, she shot Lucy a look of alarm. The two quickly escaped to the kitchen.

"I didn't actually have a dizzy spell," Charlotte said quietly, as soon as they were alone.

"Yeah, I know. You had your eavesdropping face on."

"My eaves . . . never mind, I don't want to know. Any luck with Martín?"

Lucy shook her head. "Not really. He—"

"What's my eavesdropping face?" Charlotte interrupted, realizing she did, in fact, want to know.

"It's like this." Lucy raised her right eyebrow and narrowed her left eye, cocking her head to one side.

Charlotte stared at her for a moment. "Interesting. Okay, continue."

"He seemed nervous when I walked in. So I just told him that I was sorry his coworker was missing, and how I knew that was probably rough on him. Then he thanked me, and looked like he was softening up a little."

"Because you're approachable," Charlotte deadpanned.

Lucy gave her A Look, then continued. "I asked him if he had any idea where Eric might've gone, and he said no. I asked if he thought someone would try to harm Eric, and he said he didn't know. Then I asked if he thought *Eric* might've harmed someone, and he said no. Like, really quickly. He left before I could say anything else. Then he caught you eavesdropping, which was pretty sloppy on your part."

"Okay . . ." Charlotte rubbed her face. "So Martín seems to feel pretty strongly that Eric wouldn't hurt anyone."

"That's the impression I got."

Charlotte nodded thoughtfully. "Did it seem like he was hiding anything?"

Lucy sighed. "He kind of just seemed shy. Nervous, maybe, but not necessarily because he had something to hide. How would you react if someone came into your work and started questioning you about your coworker's disappearance?"

"Trick question; I'm unemployed."

Lucy flicked her shoulder. "Okay, smartass. I'm just saying, he could be shy."

"Shy with a chunk of cash in his drawer."

"Shy people can have money, too," Lucy pointed out.

Charlotte shrugged, acquiescing. "Let's see how the boy is doing. I gotta ask him something."

They exited the kitchen and returned to Gabe and Sasha, who were laughing way more than Charlotte had ever laughed while questioning someone.

"I thought his head was going to pop off his neck!" Sasha said.

Gabe's shoulders shook as he laughed. "That's unreal."

"Hi, don't mean to interrupt," Charlotte interrupted. "Could I grab Gabe for a quick sec?"

Sasha nodded as Gabe stood and followed Charlotte several steps away.

Lucy stayed behind, taking Gabe's seat. "So . . . whose head almost popped off?"

"Find out anything?" Charlotte asked Gabe in a low voice as Sasha began repeating her story to Lucy.

Gabe looked appalled. "Are you kidding? I was still warming her up. I haven't even gotten to the real questioning yet."

"What do you mean, *warming her up*?" Charlotte asked, equally appalled. "People start talking to you and they're instantly warm!"

"You're telling me you just come out the gate with . . ." Gabe made his voice gruff and accusatory. "'Where were you on the night of the murder?'"

Charlotte pouted. "I don't sound like that. And you're not supposed to question her about the murder—"

"It was an *example.* Look, it's like conversational foreplay—"

"Okay, never mind, never mind." Charlotte waved her hands to disperse the conversation. "How quickly can you figure out if Jane's currently looking for a new job?"

Gabe raised an eyebrow. "Is she on LinkedIn?"

"Probably."

"Give me three minutes."

"Okay—"

"Wait." Gabe held up a hand, thinking. "Eight minutes."

"Okay—"

"Wait. Five."

"Take as much time as you need," Charlotte said quickly before he could throw out another number. "I'll take over talking to Sasha."

Gabe nodded. "I already warmed her up, so you can just dive in with the questions."

"Sure," Charlotte said, making a face. "Thanks."

She walked back as Gabe pulled out his phone. Now *Lucy* was laughing.

"You *have* to hear this story," she said as Charlotte approached.

"Oh, that's okay," Charlotte said. "I'll save Sasha from having to tell it a third time." She leaned against Lucy's chair and smiled at the intern, determined to show Lucy just how approachable she could be. "So, we're considering the possibility that something might still be wrong with Eric, even after the message that was sent last night. Don't worry," she added, holding up her hands, "you're not a suspect. Unless you had something to do with his disappearance, in which case, it'd make my life a whole lot easier if you just told us now."

Charlotte chuckled, looking over at Lucy to silently gloat about how approachable she was being. Her smile quickly dropped off her face when she was met with the confused/slightly horrified expression on Lucy's face. Looking back at Sasha, she was met with a mix of confusion and nervousness.

"Sorry," she said awkwardly. "That was meant to be a joke." She took a deep breath. "Okay, moving past that: do you remember the congratulations notes you handed out to everyone at the end of the last quarter?"

Sasha nodded, still looking nervous.

"Do you remember the envelopes they were delivered in?"

"Yeah." Sasha nodded again. "Jensen told me to get congratulations cards for everyone and sign them from Candice. I told him an e-card would be more efficient and environmentally friendly, but he doesn't like being told what to do, so . . ." She shrugged, looking like she was resisting the urge to roll her eyes.

"Y'know, I was here yesterday," Charlotte said. "Jensen called me the 'substitute intern' and told me to fill up the water filter, even though it was already full. Can't imagine how that asshole treats the real intern."

Sasha's eyes widened. Then she cracked a small smile. "Yeah, he sucks. I'm just trying to get some coding experience and college credits, but he's always making me do dumb shit."

Charlotte glanced at Lucy, who was smiling approvingly. She was doing it! She was being approachable!

"So," she said, determined to not let this social victory distract her, "did Candice give you the cards and envelopes?"

"Oh, no, Candice doesn't have time for stuff like that. I went and got them from the drugstore a block over."

So Candice never had those envelopes. "And everyone in the office got them? Were there any extras?"

"Yeah, everyone got one. Except Candice, obviously. And no, there weren't any extras. I didn't even give one to myself."

Charlotte nodded, deciding she was finished with the envelope line of questioning. Seeing she was gathering her thoughts, Lucy jumped in.

"Were you here when Jaya was the manager?" she asked Sasha.

Sasha shook her head. "No, Jensen was the manager when I started last month. I never met Jaya."

"Have you heard anything about her?" Charlotte asked. "Anything about why she left, or . . . ?"

"Nothing about that. I think I saw her name in the intern packet that was given to me when I started, but that's all I know about her." Sasha glanced over the top of her computer monitor, then lowered her voice. "No one here really tells me anything good. They're all nice, but I think they think I'm gonna snitch to Jensen or something if they tell me anything juicy."

"So you don't know anything juicy about anyone here?" Charlotte asked, half-jokingly.

Sasha hesitated. "You're friends with Olivia?"

"Yeah. But I won't tell her anything you don't want me to." Charlotte held up her right hand, tucking in her pinkie and thumb. "Detective's Honor."

"That's the Scout salute," Lucy said.

"They stole it from us."

Sasha smiled. "It's fine, I'm not worried about that. Olivia's cool, so if she brought you here . . ."

She leaned in, and Charlotte and Lucy mirrored her. "I was working late, and I heard Jensen in his office arguing on the phone with Candice. I think he thought I had already gone home, and I didn't want him to think I was listening to him when he came out, so I put my headphones on." She tilted her head. "Buuuut I'm nosy, so I didn't turn on the music."

"What were they arguing about?" Charlotte asked.

Sasha fidgeted with one of her braids, trying to remember. "He said something about 'taking things too far'? And how he knew she was his boss, which is how I knew he was talking to Candice."

She paused, thinking. "He said . . . that he knew she was his boss, but he should be allowed to say what he's thinking. Which I thought was ironic, since he's never happy when I tell him what *I'm* thinking." She paused again, then shrugged. "That was basically it. It sounded like Candice was doing most of the talking."

"What do you think he was talking about?" Lucy asked.

Sasha shrugged. "Union stuff? That's where all the tension in this office seems to be coming from these days. I didn't think Jensen supported the union, though, so it was weird to hear him stand up to Candice, if that's what it was about."

"When was this?" Charlotte asked.

"Yesterday."

Charlotte started. "You weren't here yesterday."

"I came in for the afternoon. Jensen asked me to pick up some of Eric's tasks. First time he's actually given me real work to do, and I'm not even in graphic design."

Gabe walked back over, pointing at Charlotte. "I have some info for you, when you're ready for it."

Charlotte nodded, then turned back to Sasha. "You've been really helpful, thank you. Anything else you can think of that might be relevant to Eric's disappearance?"

"No, nothing. I'll let you know if I do, though."

"Thanks." Charlotte straightened. "We'll let you get back to work."

Lucy got up from her chair, and as Charlotte turned to follow her and Gabe out, she noticed that the door to Jane's office now stood open.

A moment later, they were in the hallway outside of the Scoop office.

"What was wrong with the kitchen?" Charlotte asked. Her stomach had started grumbling about halfway through the conversation with Sasha, and she had been hoping to grab a snack.

"For Jane's sake, I didn't want to risk being overheard," Gabe explained. He glanced over at the glass door that led out to the balcony. "Just to be safe . . ."

Charlotte's eyebrows shot up as she and Lucy followed Gabe outside. "So she *is* looking for a new job!"

"Yup." Gabe looked smug, leaning against the railing. "And it only took me five minutes to find out."

"What inspired this investigation?" Lucy asked, looking back and forth between them.

"Jane's phone call," Charlotte explained. "Her tone of voice, plus some of the things I was able to make out her saying—they all sounded like she was on a job interview. Which would also explain why she closed her door for this particular phone call."

"She liked a bunch of companies that have recently posted open HR positions," Gabe said. "Which I thought was very impressive of me to figure out. Then I saw some comments she made on other people's posts where she blatantly said that she's in the middle of a job search right now. Which feels less impressive of me, so let's focus on the first part."

"What does this mean?" Lucy asked.

"It means," Charlotte said, turning back towards the door, "that I might not have to talk to Jane, after all. In person, that is. Be right back."

Back in the office, she made a beeline for Olivia's desk.

"Hey," she said in a quiet voice as Olivia took out one earbud and looked at her, "can I get Jane's number? And more rice crackers, if you have them?"

A minute later, Charlotte returned to the balcony with Jane's number in her phone and a mouthful of rice cracker.

"Gob ib," she said, then swallowed. She passed the package of rice crackers to Gabe. "I'm going to try to call Jane and see if I can get some info out of her."

"Are you offering her a job?" Lucy asked jokingly.

Charlotte smiled sweetly.

Lucy's face dropped. "*Charlotte.*"

"She wasn't gonna tell me anything anyway!" Charlotte said defensively. "I was planning on trying the old 'Pretend I Know More Than I Do So She'll Tell Me Stuff' trick, but this is *way* better!"

"Alright, fine," Lucy said, putting her hands up in defeat. "But have Gabe do it."

Gabe looked up at them, half a rice cracker sticking out of his mouth. "Wub?"

"She's right, you're better on the phone than I am." Charlotte held out her phone to Gabe as he swallowed the rice cracker.

"Okay," he said, accepting the phone, "what's my character? Am I the CEO of a Fortune 500 company? If so, I have a few questions."

"Is one of them, 'What's a Fortune 500 company'?" Lucy asked.

"Yes."

"Her name is Jane Thompson. Just tell her you're a hiring manager calling her back about her application," Charlotte said. "Make up a company name. She's probably sending out so many applications, she'll think she just forgot about this one."

"What if she looks it up while they're talking?" Lucy asked.

"Hmm. True." Charlotte thought for a moment. "Okay, pick a real company, something good enough that she'll want to do the interview, but not so notable that she'll know she wouldn't have forgotten applying for it."

"Got it," Gabe said, putting the phone to his ear.

"Wait!" Charlotte said. "I haven't told you what to—"

"Hello, is this Jane Thompson?" Gabe said in a decent (but nonetheless surprising) London accent.

Charlotte slapped a hand over her eyes as Lucy slapped both of hers over her mouth.

Unfazed by the face slapping, Gabe kept going.

"Yes, hello, my name is Gregory, I'm the hiring manager for . . . McDonald's."

Lucy half-tackled Charlotte to keep her from grabbing the phone.

"I've received your application. Would you be . . . oh?" Gabe paused, turning to look out over the railing of the balcony. Lucy and Charlotte watched him, frozen. "You don't remember applying for our extremely sought-after human resources position? Well, that's fine with me, just one less person to interview. A shame. It's been a long search, and I was really hoping this call would be—"

He listened for a moment. "Well, I don't want to waste either of our time if you're not interested." Another pause. Then he turned back around and grinned. "Excellent! Let's get into the interview."

Chapter 16

Gregory from McDonald's

"This was a bad plan," Charlotte muttered.

"This was *your* plan," Lucy whispered back.

"And I'm big enough to admit that on rare occasions, even I have bad plans."

Lucy shushed her.

". . . and that's T-O-M . . ." Gabe paused. "Oh, T-*H-O-M* . . . is that a French spelling?" He looked at Charlotte and frantically mouthed, *What now?*

Charlotte pulled out her phone and began typing.

"Okay, my first query is," Gabe said, the accent still going strong, ". . . what is your biggest weakness?"

"What're you going to have him ask?" Lucy whispered, peering over Charlotte's shoulder.

"I want to find out if Jaya was actually a secret co-founder," Charlotte whispered back. "And why she left the company. Jane's probably one of the few people who would know."

"What does that mean for the case if Jaya was actually a co-founder?"

Charlotte kept typing. "It'd mean that she might have some

information on Candice that even Arielle doesn't have. Info that could involve Eric." Charlotte looked over at her. "Also, the more she lost when she left, the stronger her motive to take some kind of revenge against Candice."

"Like frame her for murder?"

Charlotte shrugged, turning back to the phone.

"Yes, working too hard is one of my weaknesses, as well," Gabe said loudly, waving his arm to get their attention.

Charlotte quickly finished typing and held her phone out for him to see.

"Right-o then, on to the next query." Gabe squinted at the screen. "Have you ever been faced with two leaders in a company being at odds with each other? How did you handle the status on?"

"*Situation,*" Charlotte whispered.

"*Situation,*" Gabe quickly corrected.

"Autocorrect," Charlotte muttered as Gabe put the phone on speaker.

"Oh, gosh," came Jane's voice through the phone. "I actually had to handle an issue like that a few months ago."

All three of their heads jerked up to look at one another as Lucy grabbed Charlotte's arm.

"Do tell!" Gabe said, his eyes wide.

"There were two people at my current company who had equal roles in high-up leadership positions," Jane said. "We had an issue arise with some of our employees, and the two leaders had very different viewpoints on the matter. It became such a point of contention between them that they called me in to mediate."

"And how was the issue resolved?" Gabe asked.

The line was silent for a moment. "Well," Jane said, haltingly, "we talked it out as best we could, despite there being strong differences of opinion. In the end, we were able to come to a compromise."

"And what compromise was that?" Gabe asked.

"I'm sorry, I'm afraid I can't share that without revealing too much confidential information," Jane said apologetically. "You understand."

"Of course, of course."

There was a pause.

"Did you have any other questions?" Jane asked.

"Uh . . ." Gabe looked over at Charlotte, who was chewing on the inside of her cheek, deep in thought. Lucy gestured for him to vamp.

"Yes," he said quickly. "If you were . . . a bird, what kind of bird would you be?" Gabe winced at his own terrible question.

"Oh! I'd have to say I'd be a pigeon, because I can thrive in difficult environments. Pigeons also have excellent hearing, and I pride myself on being an excellent listener."

"Brilliant!" Gabe made an impressed face at the others. *She had that locked and loaded,* he mouthed, pointing at the phone.

End it, Charlotte mouthed back, slicing her hand in front of her neck.

"Thank you so much for this delightful interview, Ms. Thompson," Gabe said, looking relieved.

"Oh! Uh, of course. I did have a few questions—"

"We'll be in touch. Cheerio!" Gabe quickly hung up the phone and let out a long breath, dropping his chin. "And scene."

Charlotte and Lucy applauded.

"Thank you, thank you." He looked up and flapped his elbows. "God, I'm sweating."

"You did great," Charlotte said. "We need to talk to Jaya."

"You think she's a co-founder?" Lucy asked.

"It makes sense." Charlotte began ticking points off of her fingers. "When we spoke to Candice at the club, she said something that made it seem like she hadn't always held all the power at Scoop. Candice and Jaya have known each other since college. Candice is against the union, and Jaya supported it. Jane said she dealt with two leaders *in equal roles*—not manager versus CEO, but two people in the same leadership role."

Charlotte dropped her hands. "I think the compromise was that Jaya left the company. Maybe she got to keep her stocks or something like that. I don't know how any of that works."

Lucy scrunched up her nose. "From what we've heard about Jaya, do you really think she'd see that as a compromise? Taking the money and just leaving?"

Charlotte shrugged. "There's only one way to find out. I'm going to see if Olivia has her contact info."

The three returned to the office. As she passed the kitchen, Charlotte caught a glimpse of Martín switching off the kettle. She started to hear a sound in the back of her head—muffled, like someone talking in another room.

Shaking it off, she returned to Olivia's desk. "Hey," she said, sitting down, "do you know how I could get in contact with Jaya?"

Olivia frowned. "I'm not sure. I don't have her info. Arielle might."

Charlotte glanced across the office, where Gabe had leapt on the opportunity to talk to Arielle again. Lucy had also gone her own way, talking to Sasha.

"Yeah, I don't know about that," Charlotte said. "I want to talk to Jaya about Candice, and Arielle's been a little jumpy any time I say anything that sounds like I'm considering Candice as a suspect."

Olivia nodded. "Understood. Hang on, let me see if I can find an old staff directory or something."

"Thanks." Charlotte leaned against the table as Olivia tapped on her keyboard. Martín emerged from the kitchen, holding a mug of coffee as he passed Charlotte to return to his desk.

The muffled voice in her head grew louder. *Shh,* Charlotte mentally shushed the voice. *I'm trying to solve a mystery here.*

Lucy finished talking to Sasha and hurried over to them. "I got Jaya's phone number," she said in a low voice.

Olivia stopped typing as Charlotte straightened, her eyebrows shooting up. "Whoa, how?"

"Sasha mentioned seeing Jaya's name in an intern packet

that was given to her," Lucy said. "Thought it might've had some contact info in it, and it did. I guess it wasn't edited after Jaya left."

"You're a genius," Charlotte said. She turned to Olivia. "We're going to head out," she said. "See if we can talk to Jaya."

"I have questions," Olivia said, "but I also have a mile-long to-do list, so you can fill me in later."

"You got it." Charlotte looked across the room at Gabe, trying to catch his eye. She watched Arielle hand him her phone, and he started typing into it.

"Lucyyyy."

"I'm on it."

Charlotte trailed after Lucy as they made their way over to Gabe and Arielle.

"Hey, sorry," Lucy said, walking up. "We gotta bounce."

"Alright." Gabe turned to Arielle. "So I'll see you later?"

"Yup," Arielle said, smiling. "Six o'clock, don't be late."

"I won't," he responded, flashing a grin. Charlotte and Lucy stared at him as he walked away.

"Thank you, guys, for all your help with the Eric situation," Arielle said as they turned back to her. "I'm glad it seems like he's okay." She sighed. "Now I just have to go out to Highview and get his laptop so I can finally update these graphics."

"We can get it," Charlotte said quickly.

Lucy looked at her, confused. "We can?"

Arielle's eyes lit up. "That'd be so helpful, thank you," she said, looking relieved.

"Yeah, no problem." Charlotte ignored Lucy's questioning gaze as they quickly bid Arielle farewell before leaving the office.

"How are we going to get Eric's laptop for Arielle if we don't know where it is?" Lucy asked as soon as the office door closed.

"I don't know," Charlotte admitted. "I just knew it was probably best if Arielle didn't go snooping around Eric's room and stumble across the gun."

"Mmm." Lucy nodded. "Fair point."

"What did I miss?" Gabe asked, leaning against the wall next to the elevator.

"*Dude*," Charlotte said, turning on him. "Are you helping with this case or trying to hook up with Arielle?"

Gabe raised an eyebrow, spreading his hands. "Por qué no los dos?"

"Porque ella es una sospechosa?" Lucy shot back.

Gabe blinked. "I got . . . some of that."

"Because she's a suspect?" Lucy repeated. "And you could get . . . *murdered*?"

"Oh, come *on*," Gabe said as Lucy walked past him to hit the button for the elevator. "Arielle's not a suspect anymore." He shot Charlotte a nervous look. "Right?"

Charlotte hesitated, then sighed. "We can't count anyone out," she finally said. "Even if Arielle isn't directly involved with any of this, she's still loyal to Candice. And that could be dangerous."

Gabe made a whining noise in his throat, shaking his shoulders in a mini tantrum. "But we made *dinner plans*. Plus, she gave me Jaya's phone number!" He elbowed Lucy, grinning. "Then I gave her *my* number."

Lucy crossed her arms, her face stern.

"Eugh. Tough crowd." Gabe hunched his shoulders defensively.

"You asked Arielle for Jaya's number?" Charlotte asked, concerned.

"Yeah." Gabe saw the look on her face and quickly added, "I didn't tell her anything. She seemed curious, but she didn't ask why."

The elevator dinged, and he stiffened. "Oh god."

"C'mon," Lucy said, pulling him into the elevator as the doors opened.

Forty seconds (and a verse and chorus of "Ain't No Mountain High Enough") later, the elevator doors reopened.

As she followed her friends out into the hallway and towards the escalator that would take them to the lobby, Charlotte tried listening for that muffled voice in the back of her head again. What had set that off? And what was it—

She stopped dead in her tracks, her mind suddenly racing.

"Can I ask you something? As a detective? It's for a friend."

"Charlotte?" Lucy called, looking back at her. "You good?" She and Gabe stopped walking and turned to face her.

Charlotte held up a hand, her eyes darting around as thoughts continued ping-ponging around her brain.

"Say someone offered to pay you to—"

An envelope full of cash, tucked away in a drawer that was hard to open.

"Maybe he was already getting help. From Martín."

"He actually did just mention them the other day, though. Sort of."

"He presented me with a hypothetical that made it very obvious he was talking about himself. He does that a lot."

He switched on the electric kettle, then quickly switched it off, as if he'd just remembered he was getting coffee.

Landon filled Olivia's water bottle, his movements molded by habit.

A box of tea in the top drawer.

"Can I ask you something? As a detective? It's for a friend."

It was like the feeling of fitting a piece into a puzzle, and then another piece into that, and then another piece into that—

"I have to go back upstairs," she suddenly said.

Gabe swallowed, glancing at the elevator. "I, um, physically cannot. And not just because your singing sounded like a creepy child in a horror movie."

"I'll be right back," Charlotte said, rushing back to the elevator and pushing the button. The doors immediately opened, and she got on and hit the button for the twelfth floor.

"Hey," Olivia said, looking confused as Charlotte returned. "What's—"

"Forgot something; ignore me," Charlotte said, passing her

and walking over to Martín. He looked up as she approached, taking out an earbud and looking apprehensive.

Charlotte stopped by his file cabinet, jiggling the handle of the top drawer before sliding it open.

"What are you—?" Martín started.

But Charlotte had already caught sight of the envelope, sitting right where she had left it the day before.

"I know you don't know me, or trust me," Charlotte said in a low voice, cutting him off as she closed the drawer. "But I am moderately sure of three things. One, that Eric is in some kind of trouble. Maybe because of the gun I found in his apartment, maybe for his work with the union, or maybe both; I don't know. Two, that you had no idea about the envelope full of cash that's in the top drawer of your file cabinet. And three, that you care about Eric a hell of a lot more than you've been letting on."

Martín stared at her, mild disbelief creeping through his stony exterior.

"If I'm right on any of those counts, we need to talk. I'll be in the lobby." Charlotte straightened, then quickly turned and walked out of the office.

As soon as the door closed behind her, she let out a huge breath. Seriously considering taking the stairs to do something about the adrenaline pumping through her body, she instead hit the button for the elevator.

Lucy and Gabe were waiting in the lobby.

"Hang on," she said, stepping off the escalator as they turned to leave. "We need to wait a bit."

"You have a really intense energy right now," Gabe said. "And I support it. Look, a bench."

The trio settled themselves onto a bench on the far side of the lobby and sat silently for a couple of minutes as Charlotte tried to slow her heartbeat.

"As much as I love intrigue," Lucy finally said, "what exactly are we waiting for?"

"Martín," Charlotte said. "Maybe. Assuming I didn't just alienate him even more."

"Oh, no." Lucy winced. "What did you say to him?"

"Whatever it was, looks like it worked," Gabe cut in, looking up at the escalator where Martín had appeared.

Charlotte watched him, wide-eyed, as he descended the escalator. The three of them stood as he walked over.

"Okay," Martín said, pressing his lips together anxiously as he nodded. "Let's talk."

He led them to a Pret a Manger about a block away, and Lucy went to buy some juices so they wouldn't get kicked out. The three others settled at a table. Well, Charlotte and Gabe settled. Martín seemed decidedly *unsettled.*

"Thanks for talking with us," Charlotte said gently, realizing that maybe she should have gone to get the drinks and left Lucy and her calming presence with Martín.

Nodding, Martín looked down at his folded hands resting on the table, rubbing his thumb on his other thumb in a soothing motion.

"How did you know?" he finally said, looking up at Charlotte. "About me and Eric?"

Gabe's eyes suddenly widened as his knees slammed into the bottom of the table, causing the other two to jump in alarm.

"Sorry, sorry," he apologized as Charlotte glared at him. Martín was nervous enough—he didn't need Gabe making a big deal out of the fact that, *yes,* he had been right.

But Gabe quickly composed himself, mirroring Martín and folding his hands on the table. Lucy returned with the bottled juices, then sat down next to Martín as Charlotte started talking.

"It was just a hunch," she said. "That first day I was in the office, you turned the kettle on and off again, like you had forgotten that you were getting coffee. I thought maybe I was making you nervous."

"You were," Martín said. Lucy dropped her chin to hide a smile.

"Okay, well . . . fine. But then I saw you do the same thing today—switch off the kettle and then leave the kitchen with a mug of coffee. And it didn't hit me until I started thinking about it later that maybe it wasn't a nervous habit. Maybe it was just a *regular* habit."

Charlotte began picking up steam. "Then I thought about why you would be in the habit of turning on the kettle when you use the coffee maker. And, what's changed that now you turn it off as soon as you've realized what you've done? That's when I realized the answer to both of those questions was probably . . ."

Martín nodded. "Eric."

Out of the corner of her eye, Charlotte could see the whites of Gabe's knuckles as he squeezed his folded hands tightly together. She could practically feel the victory exuding from him.

"I found a box of tea in Eric's cabinet when I searched it the first day," Charlotte continued. "My hunch is that you get the hot water for his tea when you go to get your coffee." She shrugged. "Just based on how reserved you seem at the office and with your other coworkers, it seemed sort of . . . intimate."

Martín was silent for a moment. Then he sighed. "We've been together for about four months. We're not . . . we're both out, but I . . . I don't like sharing much of my personal life with people at the office. Eric respected that, so we kept it quiet." He rubbed his jaw. "Getting him his hot water was my way of . . . he's just so outgoing, and I just needed a way to show him . . . I'm sorry." He covered his eyes with one hand, resting his elbow heavily on the table.

Lucy reached out and touched his shoulder. "It's okay. Take your time."

After a moment, Martín uncovered his eyes with a shaky sigh. "I'm sorry," he said again. "I haven't been sleeping well."

"Do you know where Eric is?" Charlotte asked.

"No." Martín shook his head. "We got in a fight the evening before, and when he didn't come to work the next day . . . it sounds stupid now, but I thought he was just blowing off steam somewhere. The way Scoop's been treating the union organizing committee has been taking a toll on him, and he's been talking about quitting the desk job, so I just thought . . ." He trailed off, shaking his head more. "Since Ajay was saying he got home safe that night, I *hoped* that was all it was. And that he wasn't texting me because he was mad."

"Can I ask what the argument was about?" Charlotte asked. Lucy shot her a scolding look, and she shrugged back, *What?*

Martín dug into his pocket. "It actually had to do with this," he said, pulling out the blue envelope from his drawer and setting it down on the table. He looked at Charlotte. "I won't ask how you knew it was in there, but how did you know that *I* didn't know it was in there?"

"It seemed like the money was left for you by someone else," Charlotte said. "But it was strange that you'd just leave it there. Then I realized you probably never go into that drawer. It was hard to open, and only had some paper in it, which I assume you don't use much."

"I never use that drawer," Martín confirmed. "I don't know how much time would've passed before I found that envelope."

"Do you know why it was there?" Lucy asked.

He nodded. "That's what our fight was about." Martín brought his hands into his lap, hunching his shoulders. "I'm able to get access to the contact information of the delivery workers, and I've been helping Eric send out communications about the unionizing efforts."

"Ever since Jaya left, right?" Charlotte asked.

Martín looked at her curiously. "Right. Eric and I had already started seeing each other when she left, so he asked me if I could help. We kept it quiet, since I wasn't technically supposed to be accessing that information.

"Last week, I got a text from an unknown number offering me eight thousand dollars if I stopped helping the union committee. I started to panic, because I didn't know who could've found out that I was helping Eric. But Eric said I should accept the offer, and that he'd ask someone else to help instead."

Martín glanced over at Lucy. "I drive upstate to visit my family about once a month, but I've been having car troubles. The bills are massive. Eric knew that eight thousand dollars would really help me out."

Setting his shoulders, Martín shook his head. "But I couldn't accept the bribe, even if Eric was able to find help otherwise. It just wouldn't sit right with me, and I told Eric I wouldn't do it. He said I was being stubborn, but he left it alone.

"Tuesday evening, we had plans to go out to dinner in Highview. I picked him up from Olivia's boyfriend's—your brother's place." Martín looked at Charlotte.

Realization crossed Charlotte's face. "You were the car I saw picking him up." She suddenly remembered the sputtering sound the car made as it drove away.

"What kind of car do you drive?" Lucy asked Martín.

"It's an old Civic."

Lucy narrowed her eyes at Charlotte. "You said you thought it was a *Jeep*."

"I. Don't. Know. Cars."

"A *Jeep*?"

"It was far away!"

"Ignore them," Gabe said to Martín. "Then what happened?"

Martín pointed at a bottle of lemonade. "Could I have that?"

"Of course," Lucy said quickly, grabbing it and handing it to him.

"Thanks." He unscrewed the cap and took a long drink before putting the bottle down and continuing:

"Later, over dinner, he told me that he'd taken my phone

earlier that day and accepted the offer from the anonymous number. I got angry, and we fought. I felt betrayed, and he still thought I was being too stubborn. Then he said he was going to meet with my replacement and left."

"Arielle?" Charlotte asked. "Eric met with Arielle that night?"

Martín furrowed his brow. "I assumed he was talking about Olivia. Thought it was strange, since he'd just been with her."

"Olivia said he asked her, and then sent her a message later that day calling it off. I think that message was sent by someone manipulating the Scoop messaging system to sound like Eric. Then last night, we saw the message from him, and—"

"What message?" Martín looked confused.

"Olivia showed us the message he sent to the whole Scoop office, apologizing for being MIA. But we couldn't find his phone or laptop at his apartment, so . . ."

Martín pulled out his phone. "I almost never check those messages," he said, tapping at it. "The system barely works, and most of us are in the same office, anyway. I usually just wait for someone to tell me they've messaged me."

He pulled up the message and paused, reading.

"This wasn't Eric," he said.

"How do you know?" Lucy asked.

Martín held out his phone to show the message to them. "He wrote 'Martin.' Not Martín. Even if he was mad at me, he wouldn't do that."

"Maybe he was rushing," Gabe suggested. "Or sometimes the accent shortcuts are hard to figure out. If he was on an unfamiliar computer—"

"He would Google the accented 'i' and copy and paste it into the message," Martín said firmly, cutting him off. "A lot of people skip the accent when they type my name, but not Eric. That's just how he is." Pulling his phone back, he shook his head. "He didn't write this."

"Did you see him again that night?" Charlotte asked.

Martín was staring at his phone, as if it would somehow reveal who had really sent the message. "No. After he left the restaurant, I went home."

"What about the gun?" Gabe asked, a little too loudly for a Pret a Manger.

Martín looked over at him, then back at Charlotte. "You said you found a gun in Eric's apartment."

"Yeah. Is it his?"

"No. No way."

Lucy suddenly pulled out her phone as it began to buzz. She glanced at it, then quickly excused herself and went outside.

Martín watched her go, then continued. "Eric hates guns. I know he's mentioned one or two Scoop workers who carry weapons to protect themselves while making deliveries, but the most dangerous thing Eric would carry is pepper spray. And even that made him nervous." The ghost of a smile crossed his face. "He'd always double-check the lock before putting it in his pocket."

"Where do you think the gun came from, then?" Charlotte asked.

"I don't *know*," Martín said with frustration in his voice. "But it isn't his."

Charlotte nodded, thinking. "What do you know about Jaya leaving?"

Martín took another sip of lemonade. "That was a strange time," he said. "Jaya was helping Eric with communicating to the delivery people about the unionizing effort. Eric told me she was also arguing with Candice a lot. They'd been friends for a while, so I guess she was hoping she could sway Candice in favor of the union."

Charlotte and Gabe exchanged a glance.

"Then one day, Jaya and Eric got pulled into an HR meeting where Jane gave them a lecture about working on other 'projects' during work hours. She told them that they could lose their jobs if the 'problem persisted.' Eric and I had just started seeing each other around that time, and he told me that they never worked on union stuff during work hours. But he really thought he might get fired."

"Why *wasn't* he fired?" Charlotte asked. "With all the other shady stuff we've heard about Scoop, I wouldn't put it past them."

"We still don't really know." Martín screwed the lid back onto the bottle of lemonade. "That meeting was on a Friday. The following Monday, Jaya went up to Candice's office to confront her about sending Jane after them. After a while, Jane got a call to go up there. We didn't know how bad it had gotten until Arielle got a call from Jane asking her to come up and help her mediate." He grimaced. "Jane's nice enough, but she's not great with conflict. And when Jaya gets mad, she gets *mad.* It wasn't surprising that she needed the backup."

"Gregory from McDonald's is going to be very disappointed to hear that," Gabe said.

Charlotte shook her head as Martín looked at him, confused.

"Sorry?" he asked.

"Nothing. I beg you, continue."

"There isn't much more to the story," Martín said, shrugging. "Later that day, Jaya told Eric she was quitting. She was the only one in the office who knew we were seeing each other, and she knew I'd help with communications. He's tried to find out what happened, even after she left, but she just said she couldn't talk about it. But after that, Eric never got into any more trouble about being on the union committee."

Charlotte looked over her shoulder out the big front window, where Lucy was still on the phone. She was fidgeting with her necklace, her face serious, but she shot Charlotte a small thumbs-up when she saw her looking.

"Did you get the sense that Jaya made some sort of agreement with Candice when she left?" Charlotte asked, turning back. "Like, a compromise, something that protected Eric from being fired?"

"We've considered that," Martín said, nodding. "We never really knew how much pull Jaya had with Candice, but . . ."

Gabe looked at Charlotte, raising an eyebrow. Charlotte nodded, then turned back to Martín.

"We have a theory that maybe Jaya had more pull at the company than people thought," she said. "That maybe she was a secret co-CEO with Candice. Would that seem . . . realistic?"

Martín thought for a moment, his brows furrowing. "It's possible, I guess. Jaya's been with Scoop since the beginning. And things did seem to change when she left." Frustration crossed his face. "But what does any of this have to do with Eric?"

"We're thinking his disappearance has something to do with the union," Charlotte said. "It seems like maybe Jaya leaving gave Eric some sort of protection. We're just trying to figure out what happened, and who might have the motive to want Eric out of the picture."

"Or if Eric took himself out of the picture," Gabe added. He glanced at Charlotte. "Right?" he whispered.

"Right," she whispered back.

"Or if Eric took himself out of the picture," Gabe repeated more confidently.

"I don't know why Eric would want to disappear," Martín said, sounding frustrated. "At least not without telling me."

"Did he ever mention Bernard at all?" Charlotte asked.

Martín narrowed his eyes. "The man who was murdered? I'm sure he's mentioned him, why?"

"Careful," Gabe said under his breath.

"It's just, after finding the gun in his room . . ."

"No," Martín said, shaking his head firmly. "Eric didn't have anything to do with Bernard's death. Is that what you think?"

Lucy returned to the table, silently taking in what was happening as she sat down again.

"We're not sure of anything yet," Charlotte said, hoping she sounded reassuring.

"But you think that maybe Eric's on the run because he killed Bernard, right?" Martín asked, his voice growing angry.

"It's just one of a few theories, but—"

"If you don't believe he'd do something like that, then he probably didn't," Lucy cut in, having quickly caught up with the situation. "It's definitely one of the less realistic theories. Right, Charlotte?"

Charlotte nodded, thankful for the interception.

Martín's shoulders relaxed a bit. "I don't know why he'd disappear," he said. "In fact, I don't think he'd willingly disappear for this long without telling anyone where he was. But I know . . . I *know* he wouldn't do *that*."

The others were silent for a moment.

"We wanted to talk to Jaya," Charlotte finally said. "Do you think you could help us get a meeting with her?"

Martín nodded slowly. "I can call her now. I need some air, anyway." He picked up his bottle of lemonade, got up from the table, and walked outside.

Charlotte let out a long breath and sat back in her chair. Then she looked over at Lucy. "Was that Jake on the phone?"

Lucy nodded, shifting in her seat. "He was asking if I was going to be home tonight. And then I . . ." She winced. "I kind of accidentally told him that we needed to talk."

"Ohhhhh boy." Gabe covered his face.

"Yeah. He read into that *right* away."

"Was he mad?" Charlotte asked.

"No." Lucy pushed a bottle of juice back and forth across the table between her hands. "He just sounded nervous. He kept asking what I wanted to talk about, and I kept telling him it wasn't a big deal, but I just wanted to talk in person." A thoughtful look crossed her face. "I think he hasn't been thinking about our relationship for a long time. But once he heard me say *that*, he suddenly realized that it's . . ."

"Expirable?" Gabe asked.

"Broken?" Charlotte added.

"Doomed?"

"A mess?"

"I'm gonna stick with doomed, but you can do another one," Gabe said to Charlotte.

"Never should've happened in the first place because you're way out of his league?"

"My *god*," Lucy said, a small smile on her face. "Yes, F, all of the above. Well, not the last one."

"Are you going to be okay?" Charlotte asked hesitantly.

Lucy paused for a moment, as if taking emotional stock. Looking at her, Charlotte realized she already knew the answer. She felt a small burst of pride in her chest as Lucy let out a long breath, looking like a weight had been lifted from her shoulders.

"Yeah," Lucy said. "I think I'm going to be really, really, good." She paused. "But I'm still probably going to have a solid few weeks with Gabe's breakup playlist on repeat."

"Of course."

"I will literally add some new songs to it right now."

Gabe was about to launch into full playlist curation mode when Martín re-entered the shop.

"Jaya said she'll meet with you," he said, coming to stand by the table as he returned his phone to his pocket. "I did my best to explain things to her. She didn't know Eric was missing."

"Amazing, thank you," Charlotte said as they all stood. "Did she say when, or where . . . ?"

"You can just go to her house; she works from home. She said come any time this afternoon."

"Where does she live?" Lucy asked, collecting the untouched juice bottles and depositing them into Gabe's backpack.

"Jersey. Probably a forty-five-minute drive from Highview."

Charlotte suppressed a groan as Martín gave Gabe the address. They'd have to go back to Highview to get Landon's car. *I should've gotten a monthly train pass.*

"Can I ask something?" Gabe asked as Martín turned to go.

Martín nodded.

Gabe jerked a thumb at Charlotte. "She saw that you and Eric had a meeting with Jane that was canceled. What was that about?"

Martín looked at Charlotte curiously. "How do you find out all this stuff?"

"I do a lot of snooping," Charlotte said, her face serious.

"Right." Martín scratched the back of his neck. "We were meeting with Jane because Scoop just announced a new workplace policy that all full-time workers had to declare any interoffice relationships." He shrugged. "We could've still kept it a secret, but I felt like that was a sign for us to finally tell people we were together. But then I got the message about the bribe, and I . . . got spooked. So I told Eric I still wasn't ready, and canceled the meeting. He was disappointed, but he understood." His shoulders slumped. "I wish I didn't, now."

"We're going to find him," Lucy said. "Don't worry."

Charlotte stiffened but said nothing.

Martín left a moment later, giving them his number in case there were any updates. As soon as the shop door shut, Lucy turned to Charlotte. "I know . . ."

"It just stresses me out," Charlotte said, dropping back down into a chair. "You're promising them on *my* behalf—"

"On *our* behalf," Lucy interrupted. "We're in this together. And I have faith in you."

"No, you have faith in . . ." Charlotte stopped.

"What?" Lucy asked.

"Nothing."

"Didn't sound like nothing," Gabe said, following Lucy's lead as they both sat down across from Charlotte.

"It sounds stupid," Charlotte muttered, resting her arms on the table. She didn't want to talk about it, but she was in too deep now. They weren't going to let this go.

"Maybe," Lucy said. "But wouldn't you rather Gabe make fun of you for whatever it is than keep it bottled up?"

Gabe looked wounded. "I'm not gonna . . ." He paused. "I might make fun of you. Depending on what it is. But that'll be, like, later."

"Okay, fine." Charlotte covered her face. "You don't have faith in me, you have faith in Lottie."

She was met with silence. Then, whispered:

"I thought she was Lottie," said Gabe.

"Yeah."

"But she doesn't want people calling her that anymore."

"Also correct."

"So . . . I'm confused."

"Yeah." Then, louder, Lucy said, "Charlotte? We're confused."

Charlotte dropped her hands. "You have faith in me because of who I was as a kid. But I'm not a kid anymore. I'm not *her* anymore. So I just don't like you promising to people that I'm going to solve their mystery when I'm not the girl who solves mysteries anymore."

"Okay." Lucy folded her hands and rested them on the table. "I hear you. So you think, even at your big age, that Lottie Illes was *smarter* than you?"

Charlotte hesitated. "I mean—"

"Do you think," Gabe cut in, "other than qualifying for a kid's meal, that there's anything Lottie Illes is *better at* than you?"

"At mystery solving, yeah!" Charlotte felt frustrated. "It's just . . . being a detective was *everything* for me, right? It was my whole life. But then I got scared that . . . what if one day I woke up and suddenly couldn't do it anymore? Like, what would I have left?" She looked up at her friends. "So I slowed. And then I stopped. And now I haven't done it for years, and—"

"Bull*shit*, you haven't done it for years," Lucy said. "It's who you *are*. You can't just turn it off. Maybe you weren't running a detective service, but you were still always trying to solve people's problems. And you're always trying to figure people out. You make mysteries for yourself, while trying to convince yourself that you've left it behind."

Charlotte flashed back to all the dates she had been going on. How she'd been telling herself that investigating them was a good way to get to know them better. The pride she felt when she explained to Landon and Olivia how she knew Dale was moving out. And the way she really, really needed to figure out what happened to Eric.

"I think you're getting through to her," Gabe whispered loudly to Lucy.

Charlotte groaned and dropped her head onto her arms.

"I think you're right," Lucy whispered back.

"I hate you guys," Charlotte said, her voice muffled.

"No, you don't."

"No, I don't. Can we go now?"

"Do you promise to have more faith in yourself?" Lucy asked.

Charlotte groaned again.

"I'll wait." Lucy sat back in her chair, crossing her arms.

"Oooo, teacher voice," Gabe said, mirroring her. "Scary. It made me want to shush someone."

"Okay, fine," Charlotte said, lifting her head up and pushing her chair back. "I'll have more faith in myself. Let's go."

Appeased, Lucy smiled.

"Can I just say something, real quick?" Gabe asked as they exited the Pret a Manger.

Charlotte closed her eyes, bracing herself. "I wish you wouldn't."

"*Jensen* told you that Eric had a girlfriend," he continued as they walked, "and nowhere in that big brain of yours did you consider that maybe the walking textbook definition of heteronormativity just *made an assumption*?"

"I have a lot going on, man!" A pained expression crossed Charlotte's face. "That was before I started taking notes, and he was the first person I talked to—"

"And so soon after Pride month." Gabe shook his head sadly. "I thought you were an ally."

Charlotte started hitting him on the arm. "I'm queer, too—"

"Sad, sad, sad . . ." Gabe laughed, trying to block the attacks.

"Oh my *god.*" Lucy looked back at them. "You guys are making a scene."

Gabe linked pinkies with Charlotte and leaned in. "The straights are trying to silence us," he whispered loudly.

"*Gabriel.*"

"Yes, ma'am." Gabe made an amused face at Charlotte, who returned the gesture.

"You haven't even met Jensen," she said as they continued walking. "How'd you know he's the walking textbook definition of heteronormativity?"

"I've heard enough to paint what I believe is an accurate and totally biased mental image of the man. Am I a detective yet?"

Charlotte shrugged, smiling. "You're getting there."

Chapter 17

Charlotte Realizes Something

"I realized something," Charlotte said as they stood in Penn Station, staring at the large screen that would announce their track number. All around them stood fellow travelers, equally enraptured by the screen, ready to run to the track as soon as the number appeared. "Earlier, right before I went back to talk to Martín."

"What's that?" Lucy asked, also staring at the screen.

"When Eric started to ask me something, that night he brought the pizza," Charlotte said, "I remembered he said he was asking 'for a friend.' I thought he was just talking about himself, but I think he was going to tell me about the bribe offered to Martín. Maybe to see if I could help figure out who sent the message."

"That makes sense," Gabe said, getting on his toes as someone walked past so his line of sight to the screen wouldn't be broken.

"Then I remembered Olivia telling me that Eric had *also* recently asked her something posed as a hypothetical, implying that it was about the person he was seeing. Something about them being stubborn about something that would be good for them. That's when I realized Martín might not have even wanted to take the bribe."

"And how you realized they were together," Lucy added.

"Combined with the tea thing, yeah. I just didn't mention it because . . ." Charlotte's shoulders slumped slightly. "I didn't want Martín to know I cut Eric off when he was asking for help."

Lucy reached out to pat her arm, but as she refused to turn her gaze away from the track display, it took her a couple seconds of patting the air before she made contact.

"Thanks," Charlotte said. "TRACK TWELVE."

They all bolted for the train.

After racing to the track, they quickly realized that rush hour hadn't begun yet. Out of breath and slightly embarrassed, they boarded the relatively empty train.

"What about Arielle?" Lucy asked once they were settled into a four-seater. "Martín said Eric was meeting his replacement that night. That has to be her, right?"

"Yeah, that was strange." Charlotte chewed on the inside of her cheek. "Actually, it's more than strange. It's suspicious."

"Okay, wait wait wait, hang on." Gabe looked like a man about to fight for his life. "Is it strange? Yes. Is it even a little suspicious? Sure. But *you*"—he pointed at Charlotte—"said that Eric had to have disappeared *after* he got home that night."

"So?"

"So!" Gabe slammed his fist down onto his knee. "She's innocent!"

"Dude, she *lied*," Charlotte said. "She said she was out with her friends that night."

She paused, suddenly remembering something.

Lucy looked at Gabe. "Defense, your response?"

"Maybe she *was* out with her friends. That wasn't necessarily a lie."

"Tequila Tuesday," Charlotte suddenly said. She turned to Lucy. "Arielle said she was out with her friends for Tequila Tuesday. Then, at the club, Candice said something about that night being Tequila Tuesday."

"Even though it was Thursday," Lucy said. "I figured she was just drunk."

"Or, because it's a 'tradition,'" Charlotte said, "they rescheduled it for Thursday because *someone* was busy on Tuesday."

They both slowly looked over at Gabe.

He shrugged helplessly. "Maybe she had a good reason to lie," he said in a small voice, not sounding convinced.

"Fine. I'll give you that," Charlotte said. "*Maybe* she had a good reason." She turned to look out the window. "Or a bad reason."

"Objection, Your Honor!" Gabe yelped.

"On what grounds?" Lucy asked, looking amused.

"On the grounds of Charlotte is making me think that maybe my date is a bad person."

"Mmm. Overruled." Lucy thought for a moment. "Why would Eric make plans to meet with Arielle if he knew he had a union meeting that night?"

"Maybe the plans with Arielle weren't supposed to take long," Charlotte said. "But then something happened that made him end up missing it."

"Arielle agreed to help the union committee with communications," Gabe said. "Maybe they were meeting about that?"

"Why would she lie about it, then? She *told* me that Eric asked her for help. She even specifically said that they never got the chance to talk about it."

Gabe slumped into his seat and sulked for the remainder of the train ride.

"You know, I'm actually a very good driver," Charlotte commented as Landon once again handed his car keys to Lucy. They had returned to his apartment, where Charlotte requested his car again so they could drive to meet with Jaya.

"Tell that to the dent in your car," Landon said.

"I was rear-ended!"

Gabe narrowed his eyes. "Isn't the dent in the front of your car?"

"Aren't you going on a date with a murder suspect?" Charlotte shot back.

"Hang on, no one said anything about her being a *murder suspect*—"

"Thank you, Landon," Lucy said loudly, cutting them off. "We will be careful with your car."

"Hey," Landon said as Gabe and Lucy got ready to leave, "Mom called a little while ago." He sat down on the arm of the couch. "Wanted to know how you were doing."

"Really?" Charlotte checked her phone. "She didn't call me."

He winced. "She didn't want you to think she was checking up on you."

"Ah." Charlotte nodded. "So she checked up on me . . . with you."

"Well, technically, I wasn't supposed to tell you she called. But I told her you were working on a case. Didn't mention the murder. And I told her you seemed good." He looked at her. "Are you good?"

Charlotte thought for a moment. "Yeah. Yeah, I'm good."

Landon nodded, suppressing a smile. "Good. Also, she said something about mail you haven't opened yet?"

"Oh my *god*." Charlotte shook her head as Gabe reappeared, Lucy right behind him. "Okay, let's go."

"Hurry up and solve the case so you can get home and open your mail!" Landon called as they walked out.

"'Bye, Landon!" Charlotte called back cheerfully. "I'm gonna drive your car!"

"NO. Lucy, do not let her dri—"

They were about halfway to Jaya's when Gabe shared some fun news.

"Here's some fun news," he announced from the back seat. "My company's Instagram account got tagged by an influencer who just bought one of our mattresses, and we're getting a bunch of new followers, and my boss thinks I'm responsible for it, so he just told me to take the rest of the afternoon off."

"Have you done *any* work today?" Lucy asked from the driver's seat.

"Absolutely none." Gabe was silent for a moment, then leaned forward. "Do you guys think I'm under-stimulated by my job, and that's why I hate it so much?"

"Probably, yeah," Lucy said as Charlotte murmured her agreement.

"Wow." Gabe let out a little laugh and fell back into his seat. "What a revelation."

"Is it?" Charlotte frowned. "I felt like that was kind of obvious."

"Okay, we get it, you're a detective."

"That car's been behind us since Highview," Lucy suddenly said, interrupting Charlotte's impending protest as she looked at the rearview mirror.

The other two immediately twisted around in their seats to look out the back window.

"Which one?" Charlotte asked.

"The Buick."

"Mmm . . ."

Lucy sighed. "The big, black one."

"Ah."

"I mean, we're on the highway," Gabe said, turning back around. "It's not the strangest thing to be around the same cars for a while."

"I guess," Lucy said, not sounding convinced.

They exited the highway several minutes later, the Buick quickly disappearing from sight. Soon after, Lucy parked the car in front of a brick ranch house. A small white mailbox stood along the curb, and a silver Corolla sat in the driveway.

"Huh," Gabe said, peering through the car window. "Not really the house of someone who got a lot of money in return for stepping down from her co-CEO position."

"Some people like to *save* their money," Lucy said pointedly, turning off the ignition and taking off her glasses.

They climbed out of the car.

"Besides, I never said she got 'a lot of money,'" Charlotte said. "I said maybe she got stocks or something."

"Or maybe the compromise Jane was talking about was just that Eric's job would be protected if Jaya stepped down," Lucy added.

"I actually have a really good idea about how to figure this out," Gabe said, walking around the front of the car.

"Is it to go in and ask Jaya?" Charlotte asked, staring hungrily at the mailbox.

"We could go in—" Gabe stopped. "Yes."

"Charlotte, no." Lucy snapped her fingers at Charlotte, who had begun opening Jaya's mailbox. "That's illegal."

"I was just gonna bring it to her!"

"No, you weren't."

"Like you've never watched me do anything illegal before," Charlotte grumbled. But she closed the mailbox and followed the others up the driveway and to the front door.

Gabe knocked, and immediately a dog started barking.

"Cricket!" yelled a voice from inside. "It's okay, c'mere."

A moment later, the door swung open. Jaya: early thirties, South Asian, black hair piled into a messy bun. She wore a green tank top and shorts, and was holding a squirming miniature pinscher in one arm.

"Hey," she said. "Martín's friends, right? I'm Jaya." She held the door open wider for them to enter. "Anyone afraid of dogs?"

"On the contrary," Gabe said as they stepped inside, "I would like to give them scratches, please."

"Her name's Cricket," Jaya said, closing the door behind them and bending down to release the squirming dog. "And she loves scratches."

Gabe dropped to his knees as Cricket ran over to him. "Okay, I like detective work again," he said, joyfully scratching behind the dog's ears.

Jaya stood back up as they introduced themselves. "So Martín said Eric's . . . missing? For how long?"

"Since Wednesday morning," Charlotte said as she and Lucy followed Jaya through a doorway into the living room. Gabe trailed behind them, urging Cricket to follow.

"Do you have any idea what might've happened?" Jaya asked, sitting down in an armchair. The others sat on the couch, Gabe holding Cricket in his lap.

"We think it might be related to his work with the union committee," Charlotte said. "Did you hear about the Scoop delivery person who was found dead?"

"God, yeah, terrible." Jaya tucked a stray hair behind her ear. Then her eyebrows raised. "You don't think Eric could also be . . . ?"

"We're hoping for the best, since we haven't heard anything yet," Lucy said quickly.

Charlotte nodded. "We just thought maybe you could give us some insight into Candice, since you've known her for so long."

Jaya's brows raised even higher. "Candice is a *suspect*?"

"We have to consider anyone who'd have anything to gain from the union committee losing one of their key organizers," Charlotte explained.

Jaya sat back in her chair. "Yeah, but . . . Candice wouldn't do that." Jaya looked like she was considering her next words, then added, "She wants to work with the union."

Charlotte paused, surprised. She had expected Jaya to anger at the mere mention of Candice's name, not immediately jump to defend her. Especially not by claiming that Candice wanted to work with the union, which contradicted everything they'd been told about the CEO.

"We had an issue arise with some of our employees, and the two leaders had very different viewpoints on the matter."

"In the end, we were able to come to a compromise."

If Candice supported the union, then . . .

"You don't hold any resentment towards her for what happened?" Charlotte asked.

Jaya pursed her lips, thinking. "I'm not sure exactly what you're referring to," she finally said.

"We were told that you might've left the company not under the best conditions," Lucy said gently. "That you and Candice had a . . . a falling out."

A muscle twitched in Jaya's jaw. "I left because I was unhappy with the leadership at the company. I can't really talk about any more than that."

"Really?" Charlotte asked. "Even if Eric's life could depend on it?"

Jaya stayed silent, looking down.

"Okay," Charlotte said, leaning forward, resting her forearms on her thighs. "Let me tell you what I think, then. I think that you and Candice were co-CEOs of Scoop. When the delivery workers started talking about unionizing, you wanted Scoop to support them. But Candice didn't want that, so you had to go behind her back to support the union. Candice found out and was going to fire Eric. But you had her agree that if you stepped down, and gave her full control of the company, that Eric's job would be safe. *And* she'd also pull back on the more severe union-busting practices, like the union avoidance consultant she had just hired. So you left. But you were still determined to take Candice down. So *you* killed Bernard—"

Lucy tensed up, her head snapping over to look at her. Gabe looked up from the dog, alarmed.

Charlotte plowed on. "—because you knew it'd put suspicion on Candice. Then Eric agreed to disappear to put even *more* heat on Candice. You knew that with just enough pressure, she'd finally crack and give in to the union's demands to protect her and the company's image. By the time Eric reappeared, it'd be too late for her to go back on her word."

Jaya's jaw was hanging open. "That's . . . that's not true at all."

"Really?" Charlotte straightened, cocking her head. Lucy and Gabe were still staring at her, aghast. "Prove it, then."

"I . . . I . . ." Jaya stammered. "I can't talk about it; I signed an NDA—"

"Fine, just tell me this: were you the co-CEO of Scoop?"

"No," Jaya insisted. She hesitated, then added, speaking deliberately, "*I* wasn't the co-CEO of Scoop."

"We had an issue arise with some of our employees, and the two leaders had very different viewpoints on the matter."

Charlotte nodded. "Thank you. Sorry for accusing you of murder. Come on, guys."

"Wait, *what*?" Gabe scrambled to his feet as Charlotte herded him and Lucy out of the living room.

Jaya scooped up Cricket and silently followed them to the front door, looking troubled. Charlotte turned and gave her one last nod before pulling the door shut behind her.

"What is *happening*?" Gabe asked as they hurried down the driveway.

"Where did *that* theory come from?" Lucy pulled out Landon's keys and unlocked the car.

"It was just an old half-baked theory, that maybe Jaya was trying to frame Candice." Charlotte pulled open the passenger door. "I only said it to try to get Jaya to say something helpful to defend herself."

"That was *helpful*?" Gabe asked as they all got into the car. "She just disagreed with what you said."

"No, she said *she* wasn't the co-CEO of Scoop," Charlotte explained.

"So who . . ." Lucy suddenly went very still, her confused expression melting into realization. "Shit."

"What? WHAT?" Gabe looked frantically back and forth between them.

"Let's get going," Charlotte said, twisting around in her seat to cheerfully pat Gabe on the knee. "We gotta get this guy to his date!"

"Why—" Gabe froze. "Oh. Oh *no*."

Chapter 18

Oh, *Yes*

"Okay, but consider this—what if Jaya's lying?"

They had barely made it to the highway, and Gabe was already deep in denial.

"She's not," Charlotte said. "It makes sense. Arielle went to school with Candice, same as Jaya. She was with the company from the beginning. When I asked why she was never made manager, she said she preferred working out of the spotlight. When Jane was talking about two people in high-up leadership positions fighting, she wasn't talking about Candice and Jaya. She was talking about Candice and *Arielle*." She slapped the dashboard, images suddenly racing through her brain. "Arielle had a card in her filing cabinet drawer. That was probably the card that came in the blue envelope. God, I was looking through her stuff so fast, I barely noticed it."

"She was the one who bribed Martín," Lucy said.

"And she was encouraging me to investigate in other places. I thought she was just trying to protect Candice by keeping me away from the office, but I think she wanted me to find that gun at Eric's."

"How did she know about the gun?" Lucy asked.

Charlotte gasped. "She *planted the gun*."

"Okay, *that's* wild," Gabe said. "How could she have done that? And when? And why?"

Charlotte turned in her seat to face both of them. Her mind was racing, her body almost vibrating with adrenaline. "Ajay said that Eric sounded like he was in a bad mood when he got home that night. Because he just grunted, instead of saying hi. What if that wasn't Eric?"

"Oh my god." Lucy shivered.

"Something happened when Eric and Arielle met that night," Charlotte said. "Then she took his keys, went to his apartment, grunted at Ajay when he said hi from the other room, planted the gun, and left quietly, so Ajay wouldn't hear her leave."

"You said some of his clothes might've been missing," Lucy said. "Maybe she took some for him."

"Which is a good sign for Eric," Charlotte said, nodding. "Might mean he's still alive."

"But why would Arielle plant a gun in Eric's room?" Gabe asked. "What's the point?"

"To make us think that Eric killed Bernard," Charlotte said. "Because *she* killed Bernard."

"WHAT?"

"Gabe, you're *screaming*," Lucy said, her shoulders tensing at his yell.

"Yeah, well, I'm the one who has a date with a *murderer*."

"And whose fault is that?"

"Charlotte's! You can't just introduce two hot people and expect them to *not* go on a date!" Gabe pulled out his phone. "I'm going to cancel."

"No!" Charlotte reached back and slapped his phone out of his hands.

Gabe stared at her, his hands still hanging in midair. "Okay, that was a lot."

"Sorry, I have a lot of adrenaline right now." Charlotte waited for him to retrieve his phone from the floor, then said, "You have to go on the date."

"You didn't want me to go when she was just a suspect," Gabe said, straightening. "But now you want me to go knowing she's a *murderer*?"

"We need to check her apartment," Charlotte said. "You can get us her keys during the date, and we'll go check it out while you keep her occupied."

Gabe groaned, covering his face. "That's a lot of pressure."

"You'll be fine," Lucy said, glancing at him in the rearview. "You're a great actor."

"Yeah, and a *terrible* liar."

"Okay, so just pretend you're playing a part!" Charlotte said. Seeing the pained look on his face, she added, "If you do this, you can graduate from detective-in-training to junior detective."

Gabe narrowed his eyes. "And I get shotgun next time."

"You don't even like riding shotgun!"

"I know, I was just trying to think of something else to add to the agreement." He held out his pinkie. "Deal?"

Charlotte rolled her eyes, linking her pinkie with his. "Fine, deal."

"Gabe, you didn't give her your real number, right?" Lucy asked nervously, as if Arielle were about to leap out of his phone and appear in the car with them.

"No, I gave her the dummy number that bounces texts to my phone. Usually I give that out in case a date turns out to be a creep or a transphobe or, like, a little *too* into their sister, but now I guess it's also for *wanted murderers and union-busters.*" He paused. "I should've switched those. Ending on 'union-busters' isn't as dramatic."

Charlotte chewed on the inside of her cheek as she turned back around. She didn't love the idea of leaving Gabe alone with someone who was seemingly capable of murder, but if they were going to try to get into Arielle's apartment, having her keys would be the easiest way to do so. Besides, they'd be in public. What could Arielle do to Gabe in a restaurant?

Not realizing that was a hypothetical question, her brain started automatically listing all the terrible things Arielle could do to Gabe in a restaurant:

Terrible Things Arielle Could Do to Gabe in a Restaurant:
An Involuntary List by Charlotte's Brain

1. Poison his meal
2. Poison his drink
3. Poison the free bread
4. Poison the candle on the table that somehow only affects him
    a. Note to self: look up if poison candles are real
5. Tell the waiter it's his birthday, and then, when everyone's singing—

"Um, change of topic," Lucy said, interrupting Charlotte's list. "The Buick's back."

Charlotte and Gabe looked out the back window, and sure enough, the big, black car was a little ways behind them on the highway.

"Odds it's a different person?" Gabe asked, not sounding convinced.

"It's the same person," Charlotte said. "The driver keeps edging towards the right side of the lane, then moving back to the center. They were doing that earlier, too."

"Should I . . . do something?" Lucy asked, her jaw tightening.

"I dunno. You can't really go anywhere."

They were on a long stretch of highway, surrounded by trees and farmland. Besides, they needed to get back to the city in time for Gabe's date. Trying to lose the person following them would waste time.

The car fell silent as they continued watching the Buick. For several minutes, it remained at a distance, always leaving two or three cars between them.

Then, it merged into the left lane and began accelerating.

"Here they come," Gabe said, his voice tense.

Lucy glanced at her side-view mirror. "Can you get a license plate number?"

As the space between the two cars shrank, Gabe got out his phone to take a photo of the license plate.

"I don't think that'll be necessary," Charlotte said, finally getting a good look at the Buick's ski-masked driver. "Pretty sure that's Jensen. Also, no plates."

"*God,* I should've known," Gabe groaned. "That car fits my mental image of him *perfectly.*"

"It also makes sense why he keeps drifting to the right," Charlotte said. "Olivia hit him in the face. His left eye is probably swollen."

The Buick suddenly tore across two lanes, clipping the back of Landon's car as he pulled up behind them.

Charlotte and Gabe both cursed loudly as Lucy wrestled with the wheel to keep the car driving straight.

"Is he trying to KILL US?" Gabe yelled.

"Seems like it," Lucy replied, gripping the wheel.

Charlotte peered out her window as she reached for the grab handle. The ground along the side of the highway had begun to slope downward, leaving a significant drop-off. Not necessarily enough to kill them, but definitely enough to warrant a bystander calling an ambulance. And Charlotte did *not* want to have to pay for an ambulance.

Lucy tried merging left to get away from the edge of the road, but the Buick's engine roared as it swerved, pulling up next to them and blocking their escape. Accelerating, Lucy tried to pull ahead, but Jensen kept pace with her.

"I can't get around him," she said, gritting her teeth.

"INCOMING!" Charlotte yelled as the Buick jerked to the

left, then came crashing back towards them, slamming into the side of the car.

They swerved dangerously close to the edge of the road. Knuckles white, Lucy glanced at the rearview. "There's no one behind me, right?" she asked.

Charlotte looked back. "No, all clear."

"Okay. Everyone buckled?"

From the back seat, they heard a seat belt click.

"GABRIEL REYES, WERE YOU SERIOUSLY NOT WEARING A SEAT BELT?"

"STOP YELLING AT ME WHEN WE'RE ABOUT TO DIE!"

The Buick veered to the left again.

"HANG ON!" Lucy yelled, and slammed on the brakes.

Landon's car screeched as they quickly slowed, Jensen shooting ahead of them as he swerved to the right. With nothing remaining between him and the side of the road, the Buick flew across the right lane. The car jerked as he tried to stay on the road, but it was too late. They watched as it spun and slid backwards off the side of the road and into the trees.

Lucy quickly accelerated, and they sped past, leaving Jensen behind them.

"Holy SHIT!" Charlotte yelled, still gripping the grab handle. "That was INCREDIBLE." She twisted around in her seat to check on Gabe, who looked dazed but unharmed.

"Where did you learn to drive like that?" he asked in awe.

"Defensive driving class," Lucy said. Her glasses had slid down her nose, and she pushed them back up, slowing down a bit. "Remember how I tried to make you guys take it with me? It got me a discount on my car insurance."

"Well, you didn't tell me *that* when you pitched it to me," Charlotte said, turning back around.

"I definitely did. Do you think he's okay?"

"He should be. He was just sliding down instead of flying over the edge. And that car is built like a tank." A sharp laugh suddenly bubbled out from Charlotte's chest.

Lucy glanced over at her. "What?"

Charlotte tried to reply, but the laughter wouldn't stop. Her head dropped limply as her shoulders continued to shake.

"You're freaking me out, what? What is it?"

"I think she's in shock," Gabe commented. "Do we have one of those shiny blankets?"

"No . . . I just remembered." Charlotte lifted her head, trying to catch her breath. "I'm getting kicked off my mom's health insurance next year." She covered her face with her hands and started laughing again.

"Oh my *god*." Lucy pursed her lips to hide a smile as Gabe started to laugh, too. She flicked the turn signal to take the exit.

Returning to Highview, they dropped off Landon's keys and explained to him why his car now had a bunch of new dents and a bent side-view mirror. Lucy apologized approximately seventeen times, despite Landon repeatedly assuring her that it was okay, and that it sounded like his car (and the three of them) would have been in a whole lot worse shape without her behind the wheel.

Gabe went to take a quick shower ("Doesn't matter who it's with, I refuse to go on a date smelling like this.") as Charlotte and Lucy filled Landon in on everything they'd learned.

"So," Landon said when they finished, "you're saying my girlfriend's currently sitting in the same office as a murderer?"

"We're not *sure* she's a murderer," Lucy said quickly.

"Your girlfriend's currently sitting in the same room as a very likely murder suspect," Charlotte corrected.

"I'm calling her," Landon said, patting his pockets. "Where's my phone?"

"Wait, hang on," Charlotte said, spotting his phone on the kitchen counter and going to grab it. "You can't tell her too much. She might start acting weird, and Arielle could suspect something's up."

"Well, I can't just *sit here*," Landon said, waving his arms helplessly.

Charlotte handed him his phone. "Call Olivia and tell her you're taking her out to dinner in the city."

Landon accepted the phone, narrowing his eyes. "Okay . . . ?"

Charlotte glanced at Lucy. "We're gonna go to Arielle's apartment while Gabe's on the date." She looked back at her brother. "Can you and Olivia keep an eye on him while we're gone?"

Landon nodded slowly. "Yeah. Yeah, we can do that."

"What if Arielle sees them?" Lucy asked.

"We can try to keep out of sight," Landon suggested.

"Worse comes to worst, it'll just be a hilarious coincidence that you guys ended up at the same restaurant. Nothing wrong with that." Charlotte glanced over her shoulder as Gabe emerged from the bathroom in fresh clothes, scrubbing his hair with a towel. "Landon and Olivia are going to babysit you on the date."

"Can we call them my bodyguards? I'm twenty-five."

"Wait, should I put on a suit?" Landon asked, patting his shirt self-consciously. "I feel like bodyguards wear suits."

Gabe made a thoughtful face. "What did Kevin Costner wear in *The Bodyguard*?"

"Have you seen *The Bodyguard*?" Lucy asked.

Gabe huffed. "Do I have to see a movie to ask what a person wore in it?"

Charlotte raised her hand. "Can we go?"

"Yeah, let me put on some socks real quick." Gabe disappeared into the bedroom, humming "I Will Always Love You."

Since it was a Friday night, the train was already packed with New Jerseyans going into the city for the evening. Unable to find any seats, they stood by one of the doors.

"Here's a question," Lucy said, leaning against the wall as the train picked up speed. "What motive does Arielle have for killing Bernard?"

"I've been thinking about that," Charlotte said, nodding. "I think Bernard might've been *her* spy. She sent him to keep an eye on the union and report back to her."

"Then why would she kill him?" Landon asked.

Charlotte shook her head. "I don't know for sure. Maybe she realized he knew too much about her. Or he threatened to expose her if she didn't pay him more. Or she just had all the information she needed, and didn't want any loose ends."

She looked over at Gabe. "Just so you know, it's likely she asked you out because she's trying to get information about the case. Or maybe even to feed you false information to help cover her tracks."

Gabe shrugged. "I could care less."

"You mean you *couldn't* care less," Lucy corrected.

"No, I actually kind of really care about it." Gabe's shoulders drooped.

"Okay, *but*," Lucy quickly added, "she probably would have come up with some other strategy if she didn't think you were hot." She elbowed Charlotte sharply.

"Ow! I was gonna agree!" Charlotte rubbed her arm, scowling. "Yeah, of course she likes you. Otherwise she wouldn't have danced with you last night before she knew who you were."

"That's true. Interesting." Gabe rubbed his chin thoughtfully. "Two people, playing for competing teams, yet hopelessly attracted to one another. It's sort of a *Mr. and Mrs. Smith* situation." He fanned himself. "Making me kilig."

He held up a hand as Charlotte opened her mouth. "I've never seen it."

"Actually, I was just going to say you should tell her that we suspect Eric ran off to hide something big," she said. "Let her think everything's going according to plan."

"'We think Eric ran off to hide something big,'" Gabe recited. "'Everything's going according to plan.'"

"No—"

"Kidding." Gabe grinned, then shot them two thumbs-ups. "I've got this."

Lucy raised an eyebrow. "You're a lot more confident than you were before."

He shrugged. "I realized if I can impersonate a McDonald's hiring manager, I can impersonate someone who doesn't know that their date is a murderer."

The others stared at him.

He sighed. "And I took a CBD gummy."

The group arrived outside the restaurant thirty minutes before Gabe and Arielle planned to meet. Landon had told Olivia to call him when she left the office, and updated her on everything that was going on. She showed up a couple of minutes after them with fire in her eyes.

"—So when she was all like, 'Gee, I really hope the union wins!' I guess she was just fucking *lying* to me?" Olivia was five minutes into her diatribe against Arielle, with so much ammunition that Charlotte wondered how much Olivia ever really liked her coworker in the first place.

Lucy glanced at the time on her phone, looking over at Charlotte, who nodded. She knew they should get into places soon, but didn't want to rush Gabe, who was in the middle of what he called his "predate warm-up."

Gabe shook out his hands, shifting his weight back and forth.

"Y'know," he said when Olivia finally ran out of steam, "this is kind of fun, because usually my first-date jitters have to do with stressing about when I'm going to mention to them that I'm trans." He rolled his head to stretch his neck. "With this date, all I have to worry about is making sure she doesn't leave early and catch you guys breaking into her apartment. Easy."

Charlotte chewed on the inside of her cheek, her mood starting to dampen with worry as Gabe's continued to brighten with excitement.

"I know this is shitty to say last-minute," she started, "but we can figure out another way to do this if—"

"No. Shut up. I'm doing this." Gabe leaned over to touch his toes. "Besides, I've got Olivia as my bodyguard."

"I'll fuck her up if she tries anything," Olivia said, cracking her knuckles.

"And I am also here," Landon chimed in cheerfully.

"Appreciate the moral support, bud," Gabe said, slowly rolling his spine to stand up straight again. "Okay. I'm ready."

The group split: Gabe, Olivia, and Landon going into the restaurant, and Lucy and Charlotte retreating to a coffee shop across the street and a few doors down the block.

"There she is," Lucy said as Arielle came into view, walking down the sidewalk. They were sitting at a table by the shop's front window, peering out from behind magazines they had bought in Penn Station.

They watched Arielle walk into the restaurant, then lowered the magazines.

"Let's give it a couple minutes, and then I'll tell Olivia to call." Charlotte began drumming nervously with her fingers on the tabletop.

"I like Olivia," Lucy said, nodding thoughtfully. "As Landon's ex, I approve."

"Having a two-month unrequited crush on someone doesn't count as being their ex. But, yeah, I like her, too."

"Maybe they'll come visit more often so we can all hang out."

Charlotte narrowed her eyes. "What do you mean, 'Come visit'?"

Lucy gave her a puzzled smile. "Like, come home. To Frencham."

"Yeah, but why are you saying that like you'll be there?"

"Because . . . I'm moving back to Frencham?"

Charlotte went still. "What."

"What's keeping me here? Not my job. It might be tough finding a new teaching position in Jersey so close to the new school year, but I'll figure something out." A mixture of disbelief and amusement painted Lucy's face. "Did you really think I was going to stay here after I break up with Jake?"

"I don't . . . I didn't really think about it . . ." Charlotte fell silent, pressing her lips together as she played with the corner of her magazine.

Lucy peered into her face. "Are you crying?"

"No!" Charlotte quickly opened the magazine and held it up between them. "That's nice that you're moving back." Her voice wavered. "I'm sure Gabe will be really happy to hear that."

"You're a clown," Lucy said affectionately, gently bopping her on the head with her rolled-up magazine.

Charlotte spent the next minute pretending to be engrossed in her magazine before shooting off a text to Olivia.

Charlotte: go for it
Olivia: our text message history is WILD
Charlotte: one day I will send you a normal text
Charlotte: today is not that day

About thirty seconds later, Lucy glanced outside. "Arielle's out!"

Charlotte joined her in looking out the window. Arielle was standing outside of the restaurant, talking on the phone.

A moment later, they got a text from Gabe.

Gabe: I got her keys
Gabe: we didn't really discuss what happens with the keys after you guys break into her apartment
Charlotte: it's not breaking in if we use her key

"That's definitely not true," Lucy said out loud.

Charlotte ignored her and kept typing.

Charlotte: we'll just leave them outside her door when we leave

Charlotte: it'll look like she dropped them on her way out

Gabe: okaaaaaay

Gabe: I'll bring them out soon

Gabe: I already anxiety-ate all the free bread

Charlotte texted Olivia, telling her she was good to end the call. A minute later, Arielle returned inside.

"Let's go," Lucy said.

They left the coffee shop and crossed the street, walking down the sidewalk to the restaurant. Stopping a few yards away from the entrance, they waited.

"What're you doing?" Lucy asked Charlotte, who had pulled out her phone and begun typing.

"Looking up poison candles," Charlotte replied, scrolling through Google's search results. "I need to see if they're real."

"*What?*"

A few minutes later, Gabe came running out, looking around. Catching sight of them, he ran over.

"Does anyone have a cigarette?" he asked, handing Arielle's keys over to Charlotte.

"You don't smoke," she said, pocketing them.

"Yeah, but my *character* does. At least, he started smoking as soon as I said, 'Gotta go out for a quick smoke.' "

Lucy pointed at the door. "Go back in there and tell her you forgot you quit smoking."

"On it. Good luck!" Gabe saluted and ran back inside.

Charlotte and Lucy jogged a couple of blocks to the subway, only to be met by a delay announcement that sent them running back to the surface.

"Citi Bike," Lucy said, starting to jog down the street.

They ran to the nearest Citi Bike station, before Lucy realized she needed to re-download the app.

"I really thought I'd use this more often," she said, frantically tapping on her phone. "Shoot, what was my password . . . ?"

Two failed password attempts and several minutes later, they were both on bikes and heading for Arielle's apartment.

"We should've ordered a car," Charlotte grumbled as they returned their bikes to a station a couple of blocks from Arielle's apartment. "Or just ran."

"For twenty-three blocks? Absolutely not."

They found Arielle's apartment building and used the fob on her keychain to get in. After climbing the stairs to the third floor, they found themselves outside the door of her apartment.

Charlotte unlocked the door.

She didn't know what she expected to find. In fact, Charlotte had snuck into so many rooms and apartments and houses that she had long ago abandoned the notion that she could know exactly what she was about to see before even opening a door. No matter how confident she was, there was always something unexpected. It was always better to just go in with an open mind, and see what she saw.

The apartment itself was very nice. To the right of the front door sat a vintage chest of drawers, juxtaposed by the very modern kitchen. In the living room, the aesthetically pleasing art on the wall matched the couch and throw rug. A vase of wilting flowers sat on the coffee table in front of the couch.

"You checked with Olivia to make sure there are no roommates, right?" Lucy whispered as Charlotte closed the door behind them.

"'Course. No roommates. Figure a co-CEO's salary is enough to afford to live on your own."

"I love these counters," Lucy said, walking over to the kitchen and running her hand over the marble countertop. Then she turned around, wincing. "Did that sound like my mom?"

Charlotte shrugged. "I prefer it to how you used to talk when we'd sneak into places." She walked into the living room and looked around.

"How would I talk?" Lucy asked.

"Y'know, like . . ." Charlotte brought her fists to her chest and widened her eyes. "'Okay, I'm leaving in five minutes, with or without you.' And then five minutes would go by, and you'd say, 'I'm serious. Two more minutes, and I'm out of here!' "

Lucy made an appalled face, laughing a little. "What is that *voice*?"

Charlotte poked at some magazines on the coffee table. "That's exactly what you sounded like. It was an incredible impression."

"I didn't sound like a mid-1900s Disney princess sucking helium."

Charlotte crossed the room and opened a door, revealing a linen closet. "And then you'd say, 'Lottie Illes, if we get caught, this is gonna go on my permanent record. And I'll *never* speak to you again.' "

Lucy followed her into the living room. "Yeah, and you'd be like, 'I have to get to the bottom of this case, and this is the only way, because I'd rather sneak into places to find clues than talk to *any* more people today.' "

"Oh my god," Charlotte said, turning around. "I wasn't *angry*. You made me sound like a mini-Batman."

"Yeah. A mini-Batman who needed to get home to feed her rabbit."

"Rusty had a very strict diet," Charlotte said, turning a corner that led down a short hall with two doors. She stopped in her tracks.

"Luce."

"What?"

"C'mere."

Lucy walked over and joined her at the end of the hall.

Charlotte pointed towards the door farthest from them, at the end of the hallway. "See that?"

Propped up against the door was a long silver rod. One end

had a claw that fit around the bottom of the doorknob. The other end had a square black base that sat firmly on the floor.

"That's a security bar," Lucy said. "My dad got me one when I lived off-campus at school. You stick it under the doorknob, and no one can get in from the other side."

Or out, Charlotte was about to say, before a loud banging behind the door caused both of them to yell and leap back.

"Hello?" called a voice as the banging stopped. "Help! I'm in here!"

"Oh my god," Lucy said as they rushed forward.

Charlotte kicked the bar out of the way, and Lucy yanked open the door as it clattered to the ground. They both stepped back and stared, wide-eyed, at—

"Holy shit, thank you," Eric said, pushing past them. "She only gave me a sandwich for dinner, and I'm starving."

Lucy and Charlotte watched, stunned, as he disappeared around the corner. They looked at each other, then quickly followed him.

"Has . . . has Arielle been keeping you here this whole time?" Charlotte asked as Eric threw open the refrigerator door.

"Yeah," he said, bending down to look inside. "She kept me locked in that room. Made me go into the attached bathroom and talk when she brought me food, so she knew I wasn't standing by the door when she opened it."

"Are you . . . I mean, this sounds silly to say, but . . ." Lucy's voice was soft with concern. "Are you okay?"

Eric emerged from the fridge, holding a plastic container of what looked like sesame noodles. "Probably not," he said, kicking the door closed and turning towards the kitchen drawers. "Right now, I'm more relieved than anything. And hungry. Which one of these has forks, you think?" He pulled open a drawer. "Aha!"

"Why was Arielle keeping you here?" Charlotte asked as Eric grabbed a fork from the drawer and popped open the top of the container. "I assume you found out that she's been working against the union committee this whole time."

"Yeah, a little too late," Eric said, shoveling a forkful of noodles into his mouth. He chewed for a moment, then swallowed. "I came over to talk to her about helping us get in contact with the last bunch of delivery workers we needed to be able to hold an election. Then out of nowhere, she started talking about how she could talk to the CEO and try to get us some of the stuff we were asking for without actually moving forward with the union." He put more noodles into his mouth. "The energy got really weird out of nowhere. I finally realized that she wasn't actually planning on helping with union stuff."

He swallowed. "I started to leave, and then she offered me ten thousand dollars if I helped her . . . well, she said a lot of stuff, but basically she was asking me to help her union bust."

"And you said no," Charlotte said.

"Of course. And *then*, because I'm an idiot, I told her I was going to report her." He pointed the fork at them. "My coworker was anonymously offered a bribe to stop helping me with union stuff, and I realized that must've been her, too."

Charlotte nodded. "We talked to Martín. He's really worried about you."

"Oh." Eric's expression softened, reading Charlotte's face. "*Oh.*"

"What happened then?" Lucy asked.

Eric put the container down on the counter. "She freaked out. Said I couldn't tell anyone. Told me no one would believe me. Then she left the room, and I headed for the door."

He rubbed the back of his head. "Next thing I remember is waking up in that room with a headache. She must've hit me in the back of the head while I was leaving. I tried to leave, but the door was locked. And I've been here ever since."

"Did she say anything about what she was planning on doing with you?" Charlotte asked. "She couldn't have kept you there forever."

"I'd ask her that, but she never answered. Only yelled at me to go stand in the bathroom when she brought food." The excitement from escaping the room seemed to be taking its toll on him. Eric suddenly looked very tired. "I'd like to leave now. I need to see Martín, tell him I'm okay."

"Of course," Lucy said. "Let's go."

Charlotte nodded in agreement, pulling her phone out of her pocket to text Gabe an update. A chill ran through her as she was met with a notification for thirty-two new texts from Gabe and five missed calls.

"Did you see these texts?" she asked Lucy, quickly unlocking her phone.

Lucy shook her head as Eric walked over to stand next to her. "I put it on silent. That's on *my* breaking-and-entering checklist."

Charlotte quickly skimmed the first several messages.

Gabe: HELLO she just left

Gabe: she was looking in her purse for something, realized her keys were gone, and just left

Gabe: so maybe leave???

Gabe: actually definitely leave. LEAVE!!!

Gabe: pls reply

Gabe: if you guys get arrested I'll be so sad

Charlotte shoved her phone into her pocket. "Yeah, we really have to go."

They all froze as the stairwell door slammed at the end of the hall, followed by the sound of running footsteps.

Lucy bolted for the door, Charlotte close behind her, hoping to lock it before—

The doorknob jerked, and the door swung open.

They both stumbled backwards to avoid being hit by the door as Arielle burst into the apartment.

The room fell silent.

Arielle took a slow step inside, letting the door close behind her as she surveyed the group in front of her. Her lips were pressed tightly together, her eyes darting to Eric, then to Charlotte, then to Lucy, then back to Eric. For lack of a more recognizable metaphor, she looked like a deer in the headlights.

It's okay, Charlotte thought. *First, Lucy will try to talk to her. That probably won't go over well. But it's three against one, and the gun's at Eric's.*

The deer suddenly bolted out of the headlights, lunging at the cabinet by the door, yanking open a drawer, and pulling out a gun. Gripping it with both hands, Arielle aimed it at Eric.

Update: there's a second gun.

"Easy," Lucy said, holding her hands in front of her in a calming gesture. "There's no need for that."

"Did she turn off the safety?" Charlotte muttered to Lucy out of the corner of her mouth. "I know that's, like, a thing."

Arielle glanced at the weapon in her hand, then moved her thumb to flip a switch along the side of it.

"She didn't, but nice job reminding her," Lucy muttered back.

"Okay, well, now at least we know."

"Can you please *shut up*?" Arielle gestured at them with the gun. She was breathing heavily, and her hands shook.

"Sorry," Charlotte said. "I talk a lot when I'm nervous." She glanced behind them at Eric, who was glaring at Arielle, his shoulders tensed.

"She also talks a lot when she's *not* nervous," Lucy added, taking a small step towards Charlotte to put herself between Eric and the gun. "She really just likes hearing herself talk."

"Stop moving," Arielle demanded.

"Quick question: you wanted to fire Eric, right?" Charlotte glanced sideways at Lucy. Not that she had been particularly happy about the gun being pointed at Eric, but she *really* didn't love it now being pointed at her best friend.

She stepped to the side, hoping to draw Arielle's attention

away from the other two. "You're the co-CEO of Scoop. And when you found out that Eric and Jaya were helping the union committee, you wanted to fire both of them."

"Stop *moving*," Arielle repeated, turning the gun onto Charlotte.

Charlotte obeyed. "So what was the compromise with Candice? That they could keep their jobs, and in return, she'd stop fighting you about the union? Because Candice actually supports the union, right?"

Arielle scowled. "She doesn't *support* them. I know she doesn't. She just acts like I'm forcing her hand while I'm doing all the work to protect our company. I have to play bad cop while she gets to sulk about people being angry with her."

"But sometimes I let 'em be the bad guy for me."

"She seemed kind of . . . wishy-washy."

"Mmm." Charlotte slowly blew air through her mouth as she looked around the apartment.

Stall, stall, stall.

"What was the plan?" she quickly asked as Arielle opened her mouth to speak.

"What do you mean?" Arielle asked tightly.

"I *mean*, you had Eric locked up. If you let him out, he'd report you for union-busting. Not to mention the whole, y'know, kidnapping thing."

When Arielle didn't answer, Charlotte cocked her head. "I don't think you had a plan when you knocked him out. You just knew you had to stop him before he left the apartment. Once he was safely locked away, that's when you started planning."

Arielle stared at her silently, her face cold. Charlotte took that as permission to continue.

"You killed Bernard, right?" She lowered her chin, looking at Arielle. "I'm not just drawing assumptions because you're currently pointing a gun at me. He was your spy. He'd spy on the union committee and report back to you. He was how you found out that Jaya was helping Eric."

Silence.

"So what? Were you just finished with him? You didn't need the loose end, so you murdered him?"

"I didn't mean to kill him!" Arielle burst out.

Lucy inhaled sharply as Charlotte fell silent.

"He said he wanted more money," Arielle continued, almost whining, "and he said he was going to tell people I hired him if I didn't pay him more. He was *blackmailing* me." She paused as her lip trembled. "He had a gun. I grabbed it, and pushed it away, and it went off. And then he was dead." Her face screwed up as she tried not to cry.

"You took the gun," Charlotte said slowly. "You didn't know if your fingerprints were on it, and you didn't want to leave it for the police."

A small nod.

Charlotte furrowed her brow. "Were you working with Jensen?"

Arielle snorted derisively, the pitiful look on her face replaced with contempt. "Jensen's an idiot."

"Okay, so Jensen was working for you." Charlotte looked away, thinking. "So you found out that Olivia's boyfriend's former detective sister was visiting." She gestured to herself, then continued. "Maybe you overheard Olivia and Eric talking about me working on a mystery. You thought I was here to investigate Bernard's death. So you told Jensen . . . um . . . oh!"

Charlotte snapped her fingers, then held her hands up defensively as Arielle stiffened. "Sorry, got excited. Jensen's obsession with Candice: true?"

"Yes." Arielle seemed impatient. She also seemed like she wasn't sure what to do next. All she could do was stand there and let Charlotte continue.

"Jensen's obsessed with Candice," Charlotte said, nodding. "So you . . . told him she killed Bernard?"

Arielle's eyebrow twitched.

"Okay, maybe you *heavily implied* that Candice was involved in

Bernard's death. Either way, you told Jensen to try to scare me into leaving." Charlotte grimaced dramatically. "Uh-oh! Didn't work. And now I'm *actually* poking my nose into your crimes."

She paused, then looked over at Lucy. "Did I say the thing yet about how she left the gun in Eric's room to frame him?"

"No," Lucy said, her eyes flicking back and forth between Charlotte and Arielle, "I don't think you did."

"Right." Charlotte turned back to Arielle. "So, you did that. Maybe not specifically for me, but once you realized I was on the case, you tried to steer me in the direction of finding the gun. OHHHH!"

Again, Arielle tensed, her eyes going wide.

"Sorry," Charlotte said, wincing. Then in a quieter voice, she said, "Ohhhh. *You* sent Jensen to talk to me about Eric's 'secrets.' Gotcha. That was weird, but it makes sense now. I assume Olivia's 'promotion' was also a lie. It was all just a ruse to drive me away from the office and towards Eric's apartment, where the gun was."

Arielle didn't confirm or deny. The only response she gave was the tightening of her jaw.

Charlotte took a deep breath. "Okay, so *then* you started getting worried that I was never going to go to Eric's apartment and find the gun. So you told Jensen to attack Olivia, knowing that since I didn't leave after the first attack, something like that was only going to spur me on."

She looked over at Lucy, who looked back, her lips pressed tight. She knew Charlotte couldn't keep this up forever. Thankfully, there was still more to talk about.

"But Jensen was starting to get nervous," Charlotte said, turning back to Arielle. "He told you he was worried you were taking things too far."

Arielle's eyes narrowed. "How did you know about that?"

Charlotte had realized that the phone call Sasha had overheard hadn't been between Jensen and Candice, but between Jensen and Arielle. However, on the off chance that they didn't make it out of this encounter alive, she didn't want to put a target on Sasha's back.

"I'm a detective," she said plainly, shrugging. "So," she continued, quickly plowing on before Arielle could ask again, "you talked Jensen into going through with the attack on Olivia. Then you went into the Scoop messaging system and sent the 'message' from Eric, mentioning that his phone and laptop were at his apartment, trying to get me to go there to find the gun." Charlotte paused, remembering their last conversation with Arielle at the office. "That's also why you mentioned that you needed the laptop. You *wanted* me to offer to go get it."

Charlotte's eyes suddenly flicked down as she noticed a shadow move under the door to the apartment.

"Everyone freeze!" she said loudly, throwing her arms out dramatically.

Thankfully, Arielle seemed to have grown used to Charlotte's outbursts, and didn't startle this time.

"What," she snapped.

The shadow under the door paused.

"God, sorry," Charlotte said, still talking loudly, "I need to stop yelling while you're pointing a GUN at me. My bad. Where was I?" She dropped her arms, peering at the weapon. "Right. So I *finally* found the gun at Eric's. Though, I guess you didn't know that until just now, right? Because I didn't actually do anything about it. Is that why you sent Jensen to drive us off the road? More 'motivation'?"

"You were supposed to take the gun to the police." Arielle sounded annoyed.

"Yeah, well," Charlotte said, "I spent a good chunk of my childhood solving mysteries that full adults couldn't. I might have a little trouble trusting 'authority.' "

"Okay," Arielle said, scoffing a little. "Save it for your therapist."

"Oh, she's heard it," Charlotte said, nodding. "Many times. Lucy?"

"Yeah."

"I forgot to schedule a session with Helena."

"Told you to write it down," Lucy said, keeping her voice even.

"So, let's say I took the gun to the police," Charlotte continued. "That would make Eric a suspect for Bernard's murder." She narrowed her eyes at Arielle. "What then? You tell him he needs to go on the run to avoid getting arrested? Say that no one will believe if a murder suspect says his sweet coworker kidnapped him? Maybe you'd even pay for him to leave the country, if you were feeling generous."

Arielle tilted her head slightly. "I thought I'd just tell him he was wanted for murder and go from there. But, yes, that was basically the plan."

Charlotte steeled herself. "And if Eric didn't take you up on your offer?"

Arielle was silent.

"Would you have killed him?"

Silence.

"I don't think you would've," Charlotte said, taking a slow step forward.

Arielle's arms stiffened. "Stop."

"Charlotte," Lucy said warningly.

"You didn't mean to kill Bernard," Charlotte said, taking another slow step. "And you had Eric here for three days and couldn't kill him." She shook her head. "I don't think you can do it."

Another step. Then another.

"Stop," Arielle suddenly said, backing towards the door to put more space between her and Charlotte. She looked panicked. Then she swallowed hard.

"When I . . . killed Bernard," she said, her voice strangled, "I didn't even see it happen. When I grabbed the gun, my eyes were closed." Her face screwed up with anguish and fury as she looked at Charlotte, the gun still pointed at her chest.

Then Arielle closed her eyes.

"GABE!" Charlotte shouted.

Arielle's eyes flew open as the front door slammed into her. She fell forward, the gun still gripped in one hand. Charlotte dove towards her as she hit the ground, grabbing the wrist of the hand holding the gun and slamming it to the floor, trying to get her to let go.

Howling with anger, Arielle clawed at Charlotte with her free hand. Suddenly, Gabe and Olivia were on her other side, grabbing Arielle's arm and pulling it away. Landon dropped down and grabbed Arielle's shoulders, keeping her pinned to the floor. Lucy appeared next to Charlotte and helped her pry the gun out of Arielle's hand, putting the safety back on and sliding it out of reach.

"Don't touch it," Lucy ordered as Eric bent down to pick it up.

He hesitated, then straightened and kicked it under the couch.

"Fine, that works."

Charlotte looked over at Gabe, her heart racing. "Thanks," she said breathlessly.

Gabe gave her a weak smile, pointing at himself. "Backup."

"Please," Arielle pleaded, her face turned towards Charlotte as they kept her arms pressed to the floor. "This company is my life. It's everything to me. I was just trying to keep them from messing it all up. I didn't mean to hurt anyone." She started to cry. "Really, I didn't mean to hurt anyone."

Charlotte looked at the others, then back at Arielle. She could've said something snarky or profound. She could've said something that would put a neat little bow on this whole ordeal—the perfect line to, say, end a chapter on.

Lottie would've had something to say.

But Charlotte didn't. So they all sat, silent, as Arielle continued to cry.

Chapter 19

Chekhov's Letter

"Remember when we got our drivers' licenses and were all like, 'We can go anywhere now! The world is our oyster!' " Gabe paused to lick a melted drop of ice cream off of his hand, his feet propped up on the dashboard of Lucy's new used car.

The sun had just set, the streetlamps casting shadows on their faces as they sat in the empty parking lot of the Frencham Public Library. The picnic tables at their local ice cream parlor were often populated by an undesirable mix of screaming children and people they went to high school with, so the quiet library parking lot was their go-to for enjoying their ice creams in peace.

"Are you insinuating that we should be somewhere else right now?" Lucy asked, licking her spoon.

"Solid SAT word. And no, I like this. I just think it's funny."

"I've never said, 'The world is our oyster,' in my entire life," Charlotte chimed in from the back seat, taking a premature bite out of her cone.

A month had passed since they found Eric, who was, according to Olivia's most recent update, doing well. He didn't return to Scoop, instead dedicating all his time to helping the union committee. Candice was more than happy to distance herself from Arielle by publicly coming out in support of the union.

Martín, who put in his two-week notice at Scoop as soon as he was able to line up a new job, continued helping however he could. With that support combined with the tireless efforts of Eric, Finn, and the rest of the union committee, they ended up receiving signatures from an impressive 73 percent of Scoop workers.

"They're still going to hold an election, even though they technically don't need to with Scoop's support," Olivia told Charlotte over the phone. "But the committee's been getting a lot of support. Eric's confident they'll win."

Arielle didn't end up needing much encouragement to confess to everything. Jensen, on the other hand, refused to admit to his involvement, presenting alibis for all three attacks. Despite his swollen eye ("Slipped in the shower," he had said), there was no sign of the Buick, and it seemed like there was no way to prove the ski-masked attacker was him.

Until a week later, when Charlotte got a phone call from Gabe.

"Hey."

"LOOK AT THE VIDEO LUCY TOOK OF YOU AT THE BAR THAT TIME."

Charlotte moved the phone away from her ear. "What?"

She heard Gabe take a deep breath.

"That night you were attacked," he said, calmer, "Lucy sent me a video of you guys doing shots. Please go watch that video."

Charlotte scrolled through her camera roll. "I don't think I have it."

"Jusko . . . hang on, I'm texting it now."

A moment later, the video came through. Charlotte pressed play.

"To Gabe," said Charlotte in the video. "Wish you were here to convince us to make even worse decisions than this. Cheers."

"Cheers!" came Lucy's voice from behind the camera.

Charlotte looked at the background of the video as past-Charlotte took the shot, trying to see what Gabe was freaking out about.

And then she saw Jensen.

He was sitting at the bar, almost out of frame, a baseball cap pulled low over his brow. But it was undeniably him.

"Hoooooly shit," she said.

"That's him, right?" Gabe asked excitedly. "At first, I was like, 'That older dude in the back is kind of good-looking,' and then I was like, 'WAIT.'"

"He told the police he went straight home after work that night," Charlotte said. "But he was following me the entire time. Holy shit. Gabe! Holy *shit*!"

"This *has* to be enough to promote me to senior detective."

"Promotion granted," Charlotte agreed, saving the video to her camera roll. *Gotcha, asshole.*

Once Jensen's first fake alibi was uncovered, his other two alibis were quickly disproved, and he confessed.

Feeling bad about the pretend interview, Gabe connected with Jane on LinkedIn and endorsed her highly for multiple skills. That's how they eventually found out she had accepted a new job—at a Fortune 500 company (not McDonald's).

However, she still had a good amount of work to do before leaving Scoop. Not only did Jensen, Arielle, and Eric all need replacements, but so did Olivia, as she was hot on Eric and Martín's heels leaving the company.

True to her word, Olivia had begun dedicating more time to her own app, a social platform for app-based delivery workers to communicate with each other about traffic accidents, assaults, and, of course, any unionizing efforts. She also talked to some friends until she found a new internship for Sasha to work at for the rest of the summer—one that would not only give her actual coding experience, but was also paid.

Dale moved out, to no one's surprise. Landon leaped on the opportunity to ask Olivia to move in with him, and she happily accepted. She then pointed out that with her work and Landon's basically remote job, it didn't make much sense for them to pay so much to live so close to a city neither of them worked in. So they began looking for a new place together, somewhere closer to both of their families.

"But not too close," Landon had said to Charlotte. "I don't want Mom coming over every time she gets some junk mail addressed to me."

Lucy broke up with Jake, to Jake's surprise. As a breakup gift, she gave him her VIP Roots pass.

Gabe and Charlotte were at her apartment the next day, helping to pack up her stuff.

"*A History of American Law*," Gabe read, holding up the thick book so Lucy could see it. "This isn't you, right?"

Lucy gave him A Look.

"Okay, just checking." He returned it to the bookshelf and grabbed two other books instead. He passed them off to Charlotte, who deposited them into one of the boxes she had taken from Landon's apartment.

"Dale can get his own boxes," she had declared as she and Gabe walked out with the pile of flattened cardboard.

"So I'm going to move in with my parents for a bit," Lucy said, taping a box shut. "Which is their dream come true. But hopefully, I can find a new place soon."

Charlotte froze, her hand stopping on the way to take another book from Gabe.

"Need a little more reach than that," Gabe said, waving the book at her. "I can't stretch that far."

"You should move in with Gabe," Charlotte said. "He needs a roommate."

Gabe's jaw dropped (as did the book he was holding).

"YES," he said loudly as the book hit the floor with a loud *THUNK*. "Yes, yes, a thousand times yes." He stood and leaped over a bunch of boxes, cursing as he tripped over one, and crossed the room to Lucy, dropping to one knee.

"Lucy Ortega," he said, rummaging through his pocket and pulling out his key ring. "Will . . . you . . . hang on, I'm trying to get my apartment key off the ring . . . god, this is hard . . ."

Lucy glanced over at Charlotte, raising an eyebrow.

"Better than your mom waking you up at seven a.m. every Sunday," Charlotte said. "And you lived *here* for a year, so the laundry room cockroaches won't be anything new."

Gabe finally wrangled the key off of his key ring and held it aloft with a hopeful smile.

Lucy thought for a moment, a smile growing on her face. "Okay. I'm in. Or, I do, or, whatever."

She took the key from Gabe as he whooped, jumping to his feet and lifting her up into a bear hug.

Charlotte grinned, turning back to the books.

"I do need that key back, though," Gabe said, finally releasing Lucy. "That one's mine."

"Oh, right. Here."

And Charlotte went home. Visited Maggie at the diner. Ate dinner with her mom. And finally, *finally* scheduled a session with her therapist.

Charlotte also emailed back the woman from the magazine, declining to interview for the piece.

"I'm still trying to figure out where I am now," she wrote. "So when I do, I'll let you know."

She paused, then added, "If you're still interested by then. No worries if not."

A month later, she found herself in Lucy's new used car, eating ice cream with her friends.

"What does 'the world is our oyster' even mean?" Gabe asked. "Like, how did that become a thing?"

"Speaking as the child of a Shakespeare professor," Charlotte said, "I can almost guarantee you it came from him. Does anyone have a napkin?"

Lucy twisted around in her seat. "Did you drip ice cream in my new used car?"

"No, I swear, it's just on my hand."

Gabe also turned around. "Just lick it."

"I don't wanna lick it."

"I'll lick it, hold out your hand."

"DO NOT LICK MY HAND."

Lucy laughed, putting down her ice cream and digging into her purse for napkins. Then she sighed. "I can't believe summer's almost over."

"Why are you talking like you're at the end of a coming-of-age movie?"

Lucy chucked a balled-up napkin at Charlotte.

"Have you seen your new classroom yet?" Gabe asked, helping himself to a napkin.

"Yup. Already started decorating."

Lucy had reached out to one of their old language arts teachers from middle school to see if she knew of any job openings in the area. As it turned out, the teacher had just retired, and the school was still scrambling to find a replacement before September. Lucy's "interview" consisted mostly of the principal thanking her repeatedly for saving them.

Charlotte had also begun hitting the job boards again, until Lucy offered to help her get certified as a substitute teacher.

"You don't have to do it forever," she said to Charlotte one day over lunch at the diner. "But it's steady money, since teachers are always calling out."

"I do like money," Charlotte said.

"Plus," Lucy continued, "if you sub at the middle school, we can eat lunch together!"

"I do like money," Charlotte repeated. She dodged the French fry that was flung at her, smiling.

Gabe had begun looking for other social media work, realizing that if he had to run someone else's social media accounts to make money, he wanted it to be a company he actually cared about (at least until he started getting bigger brand deals and could quit altogether).

Plus, he was still trying to get Charlotte to be more active on Instagram.

"It'll be great," he said, bringing it up a few minutes later. "You can brand yourself as 'The Internet's Detective.' People can hire you to solve their mysteries—"

"I don't want strangers on the Internet messaging me about their mysteries," Charlotte said. "It's just gonna be a bunch of people asking me if their boyfriend is cheating on them. And I will tell every single one the same thing: if they're asking me, it probably means they should break up."

"Facts," Lucy agreed, pointing her spoon at Charlotte. A drop of ice cream fell onto her seat. "Oops."

"DID YOU DRIP ICE CREAM IN YOUR NEW USED CAR?" Charlotte and Gabe both yelled.

Lucy covered her face as they laughed. "Leave me alone," she groaned, her voice muffled.

"I *have* been thinking about detective stuff," Charlotte said once they calmed down. "Y'know, I didn't want it to take over my life forever, so I quit. But nothing I've tried doing since then has felt . . . as *right*, I guess." She thought for a moment, chewing on the inside of her cheek.

"Stop that," Lucy said.

"What?"

"You're tearing up the inside of your cheek. I'm gonna get you a stress ball to give you something else to do."

Charlotte snorted, but stopped. After a moment, she said, "Do you guys ever think about what your younger selves would think if they could see you now?"

"Literally all the time," Gabe said immediately. "That little trans boy would lose his goddamn mind." He paused. "And then probably judge me for not being rich and famous yet. Luce?"

"She'd be happy," Lucy mused. "Probably confused why I'm not married with two kids by now, but she'd like that I'm a teacher." She looked at Charlotte. "And that we're still friends."

Charlotte's throat tightened a bit, and she tried to play it off by acting like she had some ice cream stuck in it, which is not how ice cream works.

"I don't know," she finally said. "Like, I genuinely don't know what Lottie Illes would think if she saw me now."

"Wait," Lucy said, "you're asking this because of the letter, right?"

Charlotte furrowed her brow. "What letter?"

"The time capsule letter."

"*What* time capsule letter?"

"OH MY GOD." Lucy's jaw dropped. "My mom gave me mine a few weeks ago. I meant to talk to you about it, but I guess I forgot with all the moving stress."

Charlotte let out an impatient breath. "Forgot about *what*?"

"In fourth grade, when we were, like, ten, Ms. Goodman had us write letters to ourselves in fifteen years." Lucy looked at her pointedly. "They were delivered two months ago."

Gabe gasped dramatically as Charlotte put a fist to her forehead and groaned.

"That stupid pile of junk mail," she said as Lucy started the car. "I keep meaning to go through it in case there's anything important."

"That's so cool your teacher did that," Gabe said, dropping his legs down from the dashboard as Lucy pulled out of the parking lot. "The most memorable thing my fifth grade teacher gave me was abandonment issues when she left in the middle of the year to have a baby."

"Oh, buddy," Lucy said sympathetically, laughing a little.

"I thought she died."

"What?"

Several minutes later, Lucy pulled up in front of Charlotte's house.

"Mom!" Charlotte called, pushing open the front door. "Your favorite daughter is here! And Gabe and I are also here."

"Hi, guys!" Evelyn called from the living room.

Lucy and Gabe stuck their heads into the room to say hi to Charlotte's mom as Charlotte dashed upstairs to her room.

"Quick question for you," she heard Gabe say. "The phrase, 'The world is your oyster—' "

Charlotte ran into her room and dove for the pile of mail sitting on her dresser, half-hidden under a couple of shirts she had thrown on top of it.

"Junk . . . junk . . . junk . . ." she muttered as she sorted through the pile. Then she stopped.

Lottie Illes (Age 25) was written on the front of the envelope in faded blue ink. Ms. Goodman's name was printed in the top left corner, along with her elementary school's address. But she knew who it was really from.

Charlotte sank to the floor as she carefully opened the envelope and pulled out the letter inside. Unfolding it, she was met with familiar handwriting, an earlier iteration of her own.

Reverently, she began to read:

June 11, 2008

Dear Older Me,

I feel dumb writing this because you are me. What can I tell you that you don't already know? Ms. Goodman said we're supposed to ask you questions, and that is also dumb. By the time you answer the questions you will be me, and then we'll already know the answer.

From, Lottie Illes, Age 9 (almost 10)

Dear Older Me,

Ms. Goodman said I need to write more. I told her that she invaded my privacie by reading my letter. I just looked at Lucy's letter, and she already asked FIVE QUESTIONS!!! I asked her what she would ask future me, and she wants to know if we're still friends. I told her you said yes of course. Now she's ignoreing me.

Ms. Goodman always says my paragrafs are too long so I'm making a new one. I'm going to tell you about me, because I still think asking you things is dumb, and maybe you don't remember stuff as good because your old. I'm 9 years old. I'm good at math and reading and I HATE gym. I'm a detective. I'm good at solving mysteries. I like solving mysteries a lot. I like helping people find stuff espeshully.

Lucy just reminded me to use commas, because I always forget them. I just went back and wrote a bunch of them. I hope there right. I also started a new paragraf. I wonder what I'm like when I'm 25. You're probably married. I hope you can still solve mysteries sometimes but you're probably too busy. That's okay though. I think you're probably doing whatever you want to do. Unlike me who is being FORCED to write this letter!! Anyway I need to ask Joey D. what he had for lunch yesterday because I am trying to solve The Case of the Ugly Chalkboard Drawing of Mr. Spenser. This better be enuf writing for Ms. Goodman. See you in 15 years!

From, Lottie Illes, Age 9 (almost 10)

A minute later, Lucy and Gabe came upstairs to find Charlotte still sitting on the floor, re-reading the letter and giggling to herself.

"I'm scared," Gabe whispered as they paused in the doorway, surveying the scene in front of them.

Lucy walked in and sat down next to Charlotte. "What's funny?"

Gabe joined them on the floor as Charlotte took a deep breath, trying to calm down.

"I just thought this letter was going to, like, *magically* show me what I need to do now." She waved the piece of paper. "And this little idiot gave me *nothing*. She's too busy to give a shit about *me*."

"So why should you give a shit about *her*?" Lucy asked, without missing a beat.

"Oooo." Gabe pointed at Lucy. "Excellent point."

Charlotte thought about that for a moment, looking at the letter again. "Yeah. Yeah, you're right."

She carefully folded the letter back up and returned it to the envelope. Then she sat back, leaning her head against the dresser. After a long moment, she said, "I can't make mystery-solving my whole life again. But I guess I'm always going to be a detective. So . . ." She shrugged. "I'm going to have to find an in-between."

Charlotte looked at her friends to see what they thought of that.

Lucy smiled. "That's the first good plan you've had in a while."

"The world is our oyster," Gabe said seriously, nodding in agreement.

Chapter 20

A Demotion

"Oh," Gabe suddenly said, breaking the comfortable silence that had fallen over them. "Change of subject: I remembered yesterday that I was supposed to remind you to ask Olivia how quickly she got hired at Scoop."

Lucy started laughing as Charlotte shook her head. "You're back to junior detective."

"Noooooo!"

Acknowledgments

I read a lot as a kid, and especially loved mysteries—Cam Jansen, Encyclopedia Brown, The Boxcar Children, The Hardy Boys, and, of course, Nancy Drew. That's definitely a big reason why, when I was pitching "pilots" for my next TikTok web series to my followers, my favorite video was the one about a twentysomething former child detective who was trying to put mystery-solving behind her.

It can't be emphasized enough how this book would simply not exist if it wasn't for my editor, Shannon Plackis, who saw that video and its book potential. Writing books has been a dream for most of my life. I'm so grateful to Shannon for giving me the opportunity to work to achieve that dream, and for her help and kindness as I navigated such unfamiliar terrain as a person who gets (unnecessarily) anxious about asking too many questions.

My agent, Melissa Jeglinski, is another person I have to thank for helping me with the aforementioned unfamiliar terrain navigation. It's been a constant comfort throughout this whole process to have Melissa in my corner, and to know from my first interactions with her that she is a person who genuinely cares about the stories and authors she represents.

A big thank-you to all the folks at Kensington: Lynn Cully, Jackie Dinas, Adam Zacharius, and Steve Zacharius. Thank you to Alex Nicolajsen, Lauren Jernigan, Vida Engstrand, Kristen Vega, Kristine Noble, and Susanna Gruninger. And thank you to my publicist, Larissa Ackerman! Thanks also to copy editor, Scott Heim.

Thank you to my amazing sensitivity readers: Nico, Stephanie Cohen-Perez, and Nathaniel Glanzman. Their thoughtfulness and insight helped me create stronger and better characters, and I am so grateful for the time and care they took with their notes (and my follow-up questions).

Some more thanks:

Thanks to Nicole for the accountability FaceTimes, the osenbei (fictional and real), and for being the first human person to read this book. Thank you for the assurances that yes, I actually wrote a real story that exists for other people outside of my own brain.

Thanks to Jamie, the Lucy to my Charlotte (or the Charlotte to my Lucy—we contain multitudes), who replied to many texts from me over the span of months for help on everything from alcoholic beverage orders to zodiac signs. Thank you for being another early human person to read this book and assure me that yes, I actually wrote a real story that exists for other people outside of my own brain.

Thanks to Tara for naming Gabe, and for conducting train research so I could confirm that my mental image of an NJ Transit train was accurate (it was—but I appreciated the visual confirmation).

Thanks to Milena for the feedback on my no-context Spanish texts.

Thanks to Jerry and Divya for the ruthless but fair critique of my middle school–era writings that we found while I was working on these acknowledgments (and Rosh for the silent support). Can't wait for you guys to tear into this one!

Thanks to Elise and Stanks just for some good ol' general Support™ and for listening to my progress updates with love and excitement.

Thanks to Blob and all the other friends and family who shared their excitement and support for me throughout this process.

While this book came to be because of the pilot of the Charlotte Illes web series, I used the story from the series as a jumping-off point for this book, so thank you to the friends who helped make the web series happen: Jazmynn, Frankie, Milena, Jack, Ariadne, and Jamie.

Speaking of, thank you to all the people on TikTok who liked, shared, and commented their excitement for the Charlotte Illes pilot. Support artists you admire whenever you can, however you can—you never know what might come of it!

Thanks to all my old fanfic readers from back in the day. Most of you were, like, ten, but I was, like, fourteen, which is probably why you thought my writing was so good. I assume as twenty-two-year-olds you will now hold me to a higher standard, but I hope I still delivered.

Thanks to Ally Carter for my love of lists and other inserts in books. I have yet to do a mission report, but there's always book two.

Thanks to Rick Riordan for my love of funny chapter titles. I hope to one day write one that's even half as iconic as, "I Become Supreme Lord of the Bathroom."

Thanks to whoever invented sticky notes. It seems like there's some controversy around who you are, so I'm just gonna throw out a general "thank you" and hope it . . . sticks.

Thank you to all the readers, especially the queer readers. There are so many amazing queer stories out there, and a lot of forces at work trying to keep them from you. Don't wait for an algorithm to deliver, or for the one month of the year folks make more of an effort to recommend them. Seek 'em out!

Thanks to those of you still reading this after the terrible "sticks" joke.

Finally, thank you to my parents. (I thought that making a joke before writing this would keep me from tearing up. Plot twist: didn't work!) Without their support of my video creation, I might've never made that first Charlotte Illes video. In a perfect world, everyone would have the ability and time to pursue their passions, and I am so grateful to my parents for giving me the chance to pursue mine.

Mom and Dad: thank you for not only supporting me, but for always sharing your excitement and interest in the things that I do, whether it be listening to me talk about my flop era, or throwing half-baked ideas at me and saying, "I dunno, you can probably do something with that!"

Mom, thank you for my love of mysteries, and Dad, thank you for my love of telling stories. I'm so proud to be your kid.